CAPE COD
LIGHT

Maryann McFadden

This is a work of fiction. All of the characters, events and organizations portrayed in this novel are either products of the author's imagination or are used fictitiously.

ISBN: 978-0-9848671-8-9 paperback
ISBN: 978-0-9848671-7-2 e-book

Library of Congress Control Number: 2018910040

Book Design by Booknook.biz

SECOND PAPERBACK EDITION
Originally published as *So Happy Together*
by Hyperion Books

Three Women Press
www.threewomenpress.com

ALSO BY MARYANN MCFADDEN

The Richest Season

The Book Lover

The Cemetery Keeper's Wife

With all my love

To my parents

Jack and Angie Abromitis

Who were always my safe harbor

ONE YEAR AGO

PROLOGUE

ⅠT WAS THE LIGHT THAT FIRST CAPTURED HER.

It was said the quality of light on Cape Cod could be seen only in a few other places in the world. Venice, perhaps; the Greek Islands. Some called it a magical radiance, others a pure, mystical glow that emanated from sea and sand. One thing was certain, the light on Cape Cod had been luring artists for more than a hundred years.

More than anything, Claire Noble wanted to see the famous Cape Cod light. Sitting in her eighth-period Honors History class, she stared at the brochure and application for the Cape Cod Arts Center while her students completed their final exams. She reread the workshop description, glancing up every few moments to check for straying eyes, carefully hidden cheat sheets. Only ten would be chosen to participate in the photography workshop. They would study with one of the best photographers in the country. In a place that could transform an idea; where one's vision might transcend the ordinary.

She was disappointed there were no photos on the brochure. She wondered if it was a lack of funds, or if they chose to leave the light to the reader's imagination.

Nearly every quote on the brochure was about the light: "legendary," "alive," a "supernal glow." Claire grabbed her dictionary, wondering if supernal was a typo. No, it had to do with the heavens, she read, therefore a "heavenly glow." What more could she ask for?

And then, a few paragraphs down she read: "This curling finger of sand jutting into the sea at the tip of Cape Cod has beckoned artists and writers for over a century." Followed by a quote from Thoreau: *A man may stand there and put all America behind him.* And she felt like everything she'd once wanted was finally there before her. She simply had to reach out and grab for it.

She stared out the classroom windows. Sloped green fields surrounded the high school, and a ring of blazing pink azaleas lined the parking lot. With all the windows open, the drone of honeybees seemed to fill the warm air. Already she saw students slipping out to their cars, intent on enjoying the glorious day.

Claire felt it, too, as she did each June. The end of the term. The seductive weather. Maybe it was being surrounded by teenagers each day, the contagion of raging hormones. Or perhaps it was the thought of not being touched in more years than she could count. A longing she hadn't felt in months suddenly ignited again like sap runing through her body after a hard winter. As always, her thoughts turned to Liam.

She heard the scrape of a chair and looked up. Daniel Stout brought his test up and laid it on her desk. She gave him a smile and turned the brochure over to the blank application page.

She'd first read about the Cape Cod light in an Art History class she'd taken at the local college, just after Amy left home. Devastated, she knew she had to keep busy or she'd lose her mind with worry. Then when her daughter still hadn't come back, Claire had moved on to a photography course. Suddenly, it was as if she'd found herself again, after all these years.

She was tired of teaching. Twenty years of trying to coax lazy or apathetic students into a love of learning had exhausted her. But every once in a while there was a student or two who felt the excitement of history, the relevance of the past. Those were the students she couldn't cheat. The last thing she wanted was to be deadwood in the classroom. Those students deserved better. And the apathetic ones deserved someone who was still willing to give them a fighting chance.

Sometimes she felt alone in this belief. Her teaching friends were hardly secretive about riding out their last five or ten years to catch the brass ring of their profession: an early pension at fifty or fifty-five. It was what had lured them into teaching fresh out of college. That and the safety net of tenure. A life of security.

Not Claire. Maybe security had lured her in the beginning, when she didn't really have a choice. But she wasn't going to coast through her last years, no matter how crazy people might think she was to walk away from a pension that was just a little over ten years off. Besides, although she loved history, teaching hadn't been her original goal. She'd had bigger ideas in college, bolder dreams. But then again, little in her life had turned out as she'd thought it would back then.

Looking at the application, anticipation hummed within her like an electric current she could barely contain. She was wired, a term her students used when they were so excited they felt like they were jumping out of their skin.

She picked up her pen and began filling out the application as one student after another laid a completed test on her desk. She would have most of the summer to compile a portfolio of photographs. The chances she'd be chosen were slim, she knew, but she would give it her best shot. Because after a twenty-five-year detour, Claire Noble was ready to go after one of her dreams again.

I

Secrets & Dreams

1

~~

I T WAS BARELY DAWN WHEN RICK LEFT HER BED, THE
sky still dark gray. He tiptoed into the bathroom, so quietly, trying not to waken her. As the water ran, Claire stretched her hand
across the bed. The sheet was still warm where he'd slept. She wondered how long his warmth would continue to hold there. She was
missing him already. In just a few days, he would be leaving for
Colorado to meet his brothers for an early bachelor celebration.
Although their wedding wasn't until September, finding two weeks
that would suit all the men had been a feat. June was the best they
could manage. But to Claire, it was perfect. She would be leaving
for Cape Cod a few days after Rick, so they'd both be away at the
same time, although her trip would be longer.

Altogether they would be apart for two months. An entire
summer. She wondered again about the Cape Cod light, if it could
possibly live up to her expectations now. A year ago, it had been
nothing but a dream. Now it was about to happen. Her entire life
had changed, it seemed, in the past year. But the best change of all
was Rick, no doubt about it.

At first, he'd offered to come up to Cape Cod in the middle of
her stay, after he returned from Colorado. No, she decided. She'd
be consumed; they had warned her about the intensity of the work.
Besides, it would be so much more exciting when they finally saw
each other again. There was a thrill in longing like that, anticipat-
ing that first moment again in each other's arms. And then Rick

had smiled and agreed. "You're right," he joked, "abstinence makes the heart grow fonder."

As she lay there, her mind thick with sleep and scattered thoughts of their reunion, and then their wedding in September, the bathroom door opened. He came out quietly, a towel wrapped around his waist. In the softening light, she could see beads of water clinging to the dark hair across his wide chest. With her eyes half-closed, she watched him slip on his shirt, the first rosy rays of dawn beginning to come through her sheer curtains. It could have been a dream. Or a lovely photograph. She imagined, then, capturing him at that moment, in the soft shaft of light, part of him in shadow. His face perhaps. Yes, she thought, his face half in shadow, the other half illuminated.

"Hey, I know that look."

She smiled. "Oh, really?" she asked, suggestively.

He turned and slipped off his shirt, dropped the towel. A moment later, he was lifting the sheet, and then her white muslin nightgown. His skin was damp and warm as he lay on top of her.

She didn't tell him he was wrong about the look. He pressed into her and she wrapped her arms around his neck, pulling him inside, wondering again about the beauty of the light; and how she'd go a summer without Rick.

Marveling at how lucky she was. She, Claire Noble, who'd resigned herself long ago that luck was something that came to other people.

THIS WAS ANOTHER ONE of Claire's bright ideas. Fanny stood near the ladies' room door of the senior center, trying to decide what to do. If she could drive, she'd just leave. But after a few terrifying attempts years ago, she'd given up trying to learn. Besides, Joe had argued, more nervous at the thought of her behind the wheel than even she was, he took her everywhere, anyway.

Joe was parked in front of the big-screen TV. He didn't seem to mind coming—she deduced that from his lack of complaining. Joe had never been a talker, but as the years of their marriage grew, his conversational skills seemed to wane further. Unless he was unhappy about something. Then he made it perfectly clear what he thought.

Fanny actually didn't mind so much that Joe was in front of the TV. At least he'd rest for a while. He tired so easily lately with the effort of trying to do everyday things that used to keep him busy. Just this morning he'd tried to change the oil in their car, something he'd been doing their entire marriage. He loved to tinker with cars. But after a while, he'd come inside, exhausted and shaking. Defeated. Here at least he was forced to relax.

Fanny had tried to approach this ordeal with a positive attitude, as Claire had instructed her that first day a week ago. It was true, as her daughter pointed out, that all of their friends were either dead or in Florida. Or, worst of all, in a nursing home. Yes, she'd agreed with Claire, they really didn't have much of a social life anymore, except for Claire's comings and goings, church once a week, and yearly visits from Eugene and his family. But this was Claire's way of assuaging her guilt at being gone for the summer, shuttling them off to this senior center five days a week. How could a mother not see that?

Fanny had kept an open mind anyway. She walked into this place with her head and her hopes high last week. Just in time for lunch to be served. Joe, who never ate lunch, went right for the TV, where a few other old men sat mute and mesmerized by Judge Judy.

She'd walked over to the only chair at a table full of ladies waiting to be served. However, the closer she got, the more her heart seemed to go a little crazy in her chest, sputtering like a faulty motor. All the old women looked up at her. Her mouth went dry.

"Hello. I'm Fan—"

And before she could even finish her name, a white-haired pageboy cut in: "I'm sorry, this seat is taken."

"Oh." Fanny turned. The next table was completely empty, not a soul there. She turned back to the wrinkled pageboy to suggest she could just pull one of those chairs over and squeeze in. But the woman had already turned her back on Fanny and began chattering to a blue-haired prune who nodded vigorously at her every word.

Now, standing at the ladies' room door a week later, Fanny knew the lay of the land as surely as she knew the age spots on her hands. Gladys, the white-haired pageboy, was the queen bee; Helen and the rest of the blue-gray brigade were the drones. Fanny put a hand to her own short curls, still more black than gray. A gift from Mama, who'd died without ever coloring her hair.

Fanny shook her head as she surveyed the scene. This was just how her granddaughter Amy had once described high school: bitchy girls who'd terrified her that first day as a freshman. Fanny now realized that bitchy girls apparently became witchy old women. *People don't change*, Mama had often warned her.

She could go sit with the men at the TV. There were even a few of them playing Texas hold 'em. Maybe she could lure someone into a game of canasta; that would kill a few hours. She scanned the room and found not a single prospect.

She walked over, sat in a chair in the corner, and pulled a book out of her purse. In the middle of the book, she found the bookmark, a blank recipe sheet. She stared out the window. If she was going to make a meal for these old witches, what would it be?

She would start with a lovely bowl full of creamy white ricotta. Tender leaves of baby spinach. Smooth cloves of garlic, as slippery as pearls. Fresh plum tomatoes, red and firm. She would roll out the dough, cut the squares, fill them, and crimp the edges. Then she would spread the little raviolis like tiny pillows from heaven across her bed to dry on a clean white sheet.

That would impress them, she thought.

But it was years since she had made ravioli like that. Her energy was disappearing along with Mama's old recipes. Not that anyone seemed to notice or care. Claire, it was obvious, had no interest in cooking. But Amy, she'd always thought Amy did. Amy, who'd loved to stand on a chair and watch her cook, whose smile when she tasted something seemed to light up the world. Who thought the sun rose and set in Meema's kitchen. Meema. She hadn't been called that in years. And Amy…It was what now? A year and a half? Maybe more.

Fanny clutched her book to her chest, staring out the window, wondering where her granddaughter could be. And what had really happened with Amy and Claire to make her disappear for so long.

EACH YEAR IT SEEMED as if the whole town turned out for gradu-ation at Lincoln High School. The bleachers were full, and those who couldn't find seats spilled around the fence lining the football field. Marching in with the procession of ninety-eight graduates, faculty, and administration, Claire gazed at the ring of mountains encircling Lincoln, holding all of them in this small green valley like protective arms. This was her twentieth graduation ceremony. Even though she was ready to leave teaching, she never failed to feel a tug of emotions at this moment.

She looked up into the stands for her friend Abbie and her daughter, Missy, who had Down's syndrome. Tom wasn't with them, and Claire knew that meant one thing: he'd been drinking again. Sitting with Abbie, instead, was Claire's other good friend, Esther, the school nurse here, who knew everyone's secrets and scandals. It was Esther who'd ripped the ad for the Cape Cod Arts Center out of one of the magazines in her office last year and given it to Claire.

The speeches began. First the superintendent of schools, who talked about the advantages of a small town high school like Lincoln's in this day and age. Then the principal, highlighting the achievements of this class. No matter how she tried, Claire's mind wandered. She and Rick had everything set for the wedding in September, just four weeks after she returned from Cape Cod. Fifty of their closest friends and family in her yard, surrounded by her beautiful pine trees. A modest affair because it made more sense to put that money toward their new town house in Arizona, where they would move next June. She thought about her dress, hanging in the spare bedroom closet, simple but elegant.

A sudden round of applause snapped her back to the football field. She looked up to see the Baker's Dozen, the school's elite all-girl choir, begin the first notes of "Climb Every Mountain." Claire watched them now, looking so wholesome in their starched white blouses and long black skirts. And her thoughts turned to Amy.

Amy had tried out for the Baker's Dozen when she was a freshman, and she'd been picked. Amy not only had a lovely second soprano's voice, she could sing beautiful harmony, thanks to Fanny. But Amy had quit after a month, ranting to Claire that they were nothing but "militant *Sound of Music* wannabes." Claire was heartbroken, and wondered after a while where Amy might end up in the difficult pecking order of high school. Amy had joined and quit a lot of things over the next two years. And like a lot of kids, she hadn't quite fit in anywhere. Claire regretted, as she often did when thinking back over her mothering skills, not forcing Amy to stick to something like the Baker's Dozen or the debate club. Yet she was unsure if it would have made any difference in the pattern that seemed to establish Amy's future: bouncing around from school to school, without graduating college, and then from job to job.

She looked over at some of her Honors History students; bright, attentive overachievers with clear plans for their futures mapped out at just eighteen. Even she felt daunted by them, at times. But she knew, too, that kind of drive was sometimes unhealthy in someone who wasn't quite an adult yet. Last year, she'd had to fail Sarah Keating for cheating on her final exam. Sarah had not only plummeted in class rank, she'd lost a basketball scholarship because of the F. Her father, an intimidating man who ran the butcher shop on Main Street, had come in to talk with Claire. But she stuck to her convictions. What kind of message would she send her students if a cheater was allowed to pass?

As her mind wandered, she remembered, ironically, that she'd been filling in the application for the Cape Cod Arts Center when she happened to look up and catch Sarah with a cheat sheet peeking out of her blouse sleeve. She'd felt sick, even hesitated, wondering if she'd be better off ignoring what she saw. But she couldn't. And it seemed that everything went wrong after that. Her mother had fallen and broken her hip. Claire had spent last summer racing from the hospital and then the rehab out into the countryside to photograph for her portfolio. And then her father had been diagnosed with Parkinson's disease. Eugene, her brother, had offered to send enough money for her to put a first-floor bedroom on her house to take her parents in. She'd felt her life slipping away.

And then, suddenly, everything changed. Her mother recovered. Claire met Rick and they fell in love. Her father began a regimen of medications that seemed to halt the progress of the disease. Then, a month after sending in her portfolio, she'd been accepted to the Arts Center for this summer.

Claire looked up at the bleachers, filled with people she'd known for years. Friends and neighbors here to see their children graduate. She'd come to Lincoln by default all those years ago and built a good life all by herself. For her and Amy. But now it was her turn. In just a few days, she'd be leaving for the summer in Cape Cod. She was forty-five years old, and as Esther so aptly put it, it was about time she stopped living her life for everyone else and started putting herself first.

2

Early Saturday, Fanny heard the car outside and quickly wiped her tears on the hem of her apron. She pulled it off and threw it in a kitchen drawer. Scattered across her counter were the ingredients for her mother's braciole. She hadn't made this dish in…actually she couldn't remember the last time she'd really cooked. These days it seemed she fantasized more about cooking than she actually did it. Only lately Joe wasn't eating enough and the braciole had always been one of his favorites.

But as she'd begun mixing the ingredients, she knew something was missing. What? She couldn't remember. And that had set her heart firing away. Not remembering something terrified her. She'd read somewhere that Alzheimer's might be genetic. Mama had had it. That made Fanny's chances even greater. And Mama had never written down a recipe.

"Mom?" She heard Claire call out as the front door closed, and then, to Joe, who was in front of the TV, "Hi, Dad."

A moment later, Claire was in the kitchen doorway and Fanny's eyes filled with tears.

"Mom, what's wrong?"

Fanny shook her head. "Nothing, nothing. Now, are you all packed? Do you have that spray I got you?"

"Mom, I think that stuff you got is illegal."

"Slip it in your bra. That's what Annie and I did years ago, when we worked in Greenwich Village. Hid our money in our brassieres."

"Mom, Cape Cod is like Lincoln. People go to the beach and leave their doors unlocked. It's nothing but artsy people and rich families."

Then Claire took a deep breath. Guilt. Fanny recognized the sound.

"I don't have a lot of time. I still have to finish putting a portfolio together."

"Your pictures are beautiful. They'll love them." Fanny knew Claire didn't believe that. That it was just a mother talking. But Claire's photographs were special, even Fanny could see that. "Oh, before you go, I almost forgot. I have something for you," she said. "Sit, have a cup of coffee."

"What are you making?" she heard Claire ask, as she rooted through the hall closet.

"Oh, nothing," she said, searching for the gift bag. "Joe? *Joe?*"

"What is it?"

"Where's Claire's gift? I put it in the hall closet."

"I put it in the spare room."

She wanted to go and smack him; it couldn't have been in his way. Instead she trudged slowly up the flight of stairs without complaint because Claire would just launch into her favorite new subject: how they needed to move into a one-floor house. In Claire's old bedroom, now filled with Fanny's old sewing machine, an ironing board, and other odds and ends, she found the gift bag, sitting on the treadmill like an accusation. She hadn't used the treadmill in what? Five, maybe six months? Eugene had sent it after she broke her hip, to make sure she strengthened it. Now Joe was after her to get rid of it. He would get rid of everything if she let him.

Slowly she went down the stairs, the ache in her left hip now a little knife slicing through her groin. In the kitchen she found her daughter sitting at the table, staring out the window with that look.

"What?"

"Nothing," Claire said, with a shake.

She knew Claire didn't like to bother her with her problems. Didn't want her to worry. But Fanny knew that look. Claire was thinking of Amy.

"Wait until you see what I found!" she said, putting the gift bag on the table in front of Claire. "You won't believe it!"

Claire opened the bag and Fanny had the pleasure of seeing first confusion and then astonishment cross her face.

"Where did you...I thought this was gone."

"No, no. After you moved out that first time years ago, I shoved a few boxes of your things in the crawl space. Your father doesn't go in there, the clutter would give him a stroke, so I knew it wouldn't get thrown out. It's been buried in there all these years."

Claire held up the camera, an antique now perhaps, nearly thirty years old. She looked through the viewfinder, turned, focused on her mother, and clicked.

"There's no film in it," Fanny said.

"I know. I just wanted to feel it. I remember the last roll I shot with this camera, just before I left college and came home to live again."

Fanny said nothing, hoping this wasn't more sadness being dredged up.

"Well, now you can use it in Cape Cod."

Claire smiled. "Thanks, Mom, this means a lot, it really does." Then she stood. "Let's do this quick. I don't want to get all emotional."

"No, we don't want that." Fanny stood there, took a step forward, put her hands on Claire's shoulders. "Two months will be gone before you know it."

"If you need anything, don't forget my friend Esther, she's a nurse and only fifteen minutes away. And there's always Eugene, maybe he—"

"Eugene is too far, and too busy. We'll see him in August; they're coming for a long weekend. So don't worry about us."

Claire gave her a quick hug and then was gone. She heard her call out, "Bye, Dad," and the front door closed. She sat looking at all the ingredients on the counter, her desire to cook, to fill a few empty hours, gone. She swallowed hard. Claire would be gone for ten weeks in total. If something happened to Joe, she could take care of him. But what if something happened to her? Fanny knew that Joe would be helpless.

But that wasn't going to happen. Tomorrow she was going to start using that treadmill again and get her hip stronger. *Use it or lose it,* that's what Mama used to say.

She began putting the items scattered across the counter back in the refrigerator. When she was putting the frying pan away, it hit her. Fennel. Just a pinch. That's what she'd forgotten.

DRIVING AWAY FROM her parents' house, Claire turned onto Route 75, which followed the Pohatcong River back to Lincoln, just a half hour north. She worried about being so far away from her parents, but they seemed to be doing okay. Thank God her father was still driving, so they could get to the store or the senior center on their own. One day she knew the Parkinson's would progress and he would not be able to. She dreaded it. Because she and Rick would be living in Arizona by then.

But now she had to think about getting ready. The last weeks of school were so hectic, and she still had last minute packing to do. It was hard to plan for an entire summer when you could only take three bags. And one was filled with her camera and equipment.

The old Kalimar camera lay on the floor of her car, in its worn leather bag. She kept glancing at it, unable to believe it was there. She'd bought it in her freshman year of college, when taking an Intro to Photography course. Everyone else had had expensive

Nikons or Minoltas. Claire had never heard of Kalimar, a Russian brand, but it was a single-lens reflex. And it was all she could afford then.

Now it was as if she were back in that second-floor apartment at college, a rat trap of a place where five girls pinched pennies and dreamed about their futures. It was a weekday afternoon in her junior year and the others were at class. Liam sat at the kitchen table, barely able to look up. She'd leaned against the chipped sink, quietly shooting pictures of a still life for her class. Secretly taking shots of him. Waiting for him to say something.

She was pregnant. She assumed they would get married.

It was what they planned when she graduated anyway. Not that her parents knew. They'd hated Liam since she'd first met him on a dance floor, her freshman year of high school. It was the old cliché: he wasn't good enough. Especially when he began getting into trouble. But Liam had problems at home. His father had been killed in a car accident, leaving his mother with three boys to raise alone, and little insurance. She'd begun waitressing to make ends meet. Coming home later and later, drunker and drunker. Not exactly a role model for a grieving teenager.

Liam had been sent to live with his aunt Bonnie, his father's sister, in Mechanicsburg. She'd enrolled him in Claire's Catholic high school. He was tall, with long black hair that touched his shoulders, ivory skin, dark blue eyes. No one knew a thing about him as he shot brooding looks at the girls changing classes in the halls. When he walked over and asked Claire to dance in the sweltering, airless gym that last dance of their freshman year, she thought she would die. Everyone stared as he held her so close her breasts pressed against his beating heart. It wasn't even like they were dancing. He was just holding her, their feet not leaving the floor, swaying to the music.

"Hey you've got nice eyes," he said, looking down at her, his breath sweet and heavy.

"Really?" She was stunned. Her eyes were like her mother's, everyone said so; dark brown, almond shaped.

"Yeah," he said, his crooked smile growing. "Sexy eyes."

As they danced, her head fit perfectly in the crook of his shoulder. He kept running his fingers through the long strands of her hair.

Later, sleeping over at her best friend Robin's, they'd relived the night again and again. Robin told her that she'd overhead some guys saying Liam had been drunk. She didn't care. Liam's gaze was like the prince's kiss in a fairy tale. She felt as if she'd finally woken up that night. As if someone had really seen her for the first time.

She looked over at the camera again, thinking about the girl she'd been. And wondering what had ever happened to that last roll of film, the pictures of Liam. That was the last time she'd ever used the Kalimar.

AT TEN O'CLOCK, just like every other night at that same time, Fanny slowly trudged up the long flight of stairs to go to bed, the throb in her hip like a toothache now. Joe was still watching TV, and, according to this ritual set into place when he'd had to quit his part-time job last year, he would stay there until nearly midnight. The diagnosis, she knew, had scared him. And he'd worried about making mistakes. It was just a few hours a week in the hardware store on Main Street, but still. It had given him some purpose.

Fanny had locked the doors, slid the deadbolts, and even turned the lock on the basement door, a new one she'd had installed a year ago when she read about a robbery in their neighborhood. In her nightstand, next to her book, lay a little can of hot pepper spray. Her husband, she knew, couldn't protect her anymore. For years, the warm, solid shape of him beside her in bed was security enough that she slept like a baby. Not anymore. He was slower now, leaning forward, the Parkinson's taking over his body bit by bit. He should have a cane, Fanny thought. Anyway, the pepper spray was just a little insurance.

She'd bought one for Claire, too, and made her put it into her purse. Not long ago a woman was carjacked in the Morris County Mall, a half hour east of Lincoln. The world was changing; she didn't have to watch the news twice a day, like her husband, to see that.

Their own block was testament, too. Edie Dixon and maybe one or two others were the only old-timers left on Irwin Street. The neighborhood had become a mix of nationalities, like a little UN. Fanny tried to be friendly when they walked by as she swept her stoop, but they rarely looked at her. She still paid taxes, still shopped and contributed to the local economy. But she knew what it was. She was old. People's eyes didn't linger on you anymore. It was like you had one foot in the grave already. You barely counted.

She thought of Claire, so busy with her own life that she hardly had time for her anymore. Fanny washed her face, took out her teeth and set them into the plastic cup, and watched the liquid fizz. Claire had looked happy. But she also looked tired, as if there was worry in her eyes. Oh, Claire would tell her it was all the stress of this trip, but Fanny wasn't a fool. It was Amy. How could Claire not worry about her? Not an hour went by that Fanny didn't wonder where her granddaughter had gone.

She walked down the hall and into her bedroom, propped her three pillows, and sat down in bed with a moan, as her hip settled into place. She opened her nightstand drawer and reached for her book, *Wild Montana Nights*. Claire laughed at these books. "Bodice rippers," she called them. Fanny looked at the cover, a chiseled cowboy holding a buxom blonde with, yes, a low-cut gown and long, flowing hair. In the background, the Montana mountains encircled them, jagged white peaks like she'd never seen in her life. Fanny hadn't traveled much. Not like people today. She'd been to Florida a few times, a drive so long and torturous, she swore never again. Once, they'd gone to a cousin's in Kentucky. No, she could probably count on two hands the number of times she'd left New Jersey since moving here from Brooklyn when Claire and Eugene were little.

But in her books, she lived in a way she never had. She traveled the world, without even leaving her house. And she lived and relived the romance that had eluded her all her life. As a girl in Brooklyn, she had waited breathlessly for romance to walk through her door. How, where, she wasn't sure. But she was certain it would come. Everyone had one great love in their lives, even if it wasn't the one that lasted. Now Fanny knew better. Look at her. She was seventy-seven years old and still waiting.

Once, long ago, when she wondered if she'd made a mistake marrying Joe, she'd asked Mama if Daddy had ever told her he loved her. She knew Daddy had, but they weren't outwardly demonstrative. *Pretty words mean nothing*, Mama had told her. *It's what a man does for you that shows you how he really feels.* Then Mama had said, *Real love*, and she'd emphasized the words, *comes after marriage.*

And then there was Claire. When Claire had gotten pregnant in college, when Fanny had voiced her doubts, Claire had told her that Liam was the love of her life. Fanny had said nothing after that. What could she say?

Fanny reached over to shut the nightstand drawer and spied her vial of pills. The doctor had given them to her at her last checkup when she admitted she didn't sleep well, or much, anymore. It was common in seniors, he told her (she knew he meant elderly, but was being diplomatic). But why suffer? he'd coaxed. She'd never taken a single one. Because she knew how easy it was to get hooked on things like that.

What she hadn't told him was the real reason she couldn't sleep. Mama had died in her sleep, a few years younger than Fanny was now. A blessing, so many had said. That's the way to go, she now heard people her age say. It made the nights a thing to dread, and getting into bed terrifying. She put off turning out the lights until she was dizzy with exhaustion. Fanny didn't want to die in her sleep. She didn't want to die at all. She was in good shape; better than most people a decade younger, her doctor had said, despite her broken hip last year. And Fanny didn't feel her age, most times. Except now, at night, when all the terrors the dark held made her feel like a child. And she wished Mama could hold her hand, as she used to when she was sick. Or that Annie was still alive. They'd always talked about growing old together. Annie wasn't just her sister, she was her best friend.

They would talk on the phone for hours. Fanny would tell her now that even though she was old, she still felt like she had living to do. Not that she knew what or how. But just that she wasn't finished. Not yet.

Fanny opened the book finally. She had forty pages to go, the best part really. These books were all the same. Two people who wanted each other, who sometimes did or didn't know it. And then there were a few hundred pages of keeping them apart. Predictable. In fact, Fanny sometimes thought she could write one herself. But they helped the hours go by. By the time she finished it, Joe would be making his way upstairs. She would turn on her side and curl an arm around his chest. Then she would pray, for everyone in her family, the dead and then the living, ending with a special prayer to Mama to watch over Amy.

Fanny prayed out of habit. She wasn't sure she still believed in all those saints. After all, half of them had been...what was the word? She couldn't remember, except that now many of the saints she'd learned about as a girl were no longer considered saints. And now you could eat meat on Fridays and go to church without a hat on, too. The rules had been changing for years. Fanny began to wonder what else the men in Rome were going to decide wasn't valid anymore about it all. But still she prayed. It was hard to undo years of habit. Habit, she'd learned long ago, kept a rhythm to your life, and there was comfort in that. So she kept praying, just in case. Somehow, during these long prayers, she would fall asleep.

It was late when Claire left Rick's and drove across town to her own house. His flight to Colorado for the bachelor celebration with his brothers was first thing in the morning, so he needed some sleep. If she stayed, he'd teased, he'd have a hard time getting any sleep at all, knowing they would be apart for two months. He was in high spirits after coming in second at his golf tournament. When she walked in, he'd picked her up and swung her around, hooting that he'd been invited to play a tournament at an exclusive country club near the city. The tournament was in September, just a week before their wedding, when they'd be knee-deep in last minute details. In his excitement, he didn't seem to remember, and she didn't want to burst his bubble. He'd already made reservations for them at a nearby Hilton. "You've got to think like a winner to be a winner," he kept saying. "It's all about positive thinking." He planned to win.

They ate Chinese takeout while he finished packing, his bags neat and orderly, his backpack like something out of an L.L. Bean catalog. Claire thought of her own bags, and her haphazard packing, throwing this in, tossing that out. Rick was neater and more organized than any man she knew. Well, except for her father. But his was a different kind of tidy.

She cleaned up while Rick made his last minute real estate calls. He both loved and hated his job. It was a 24/7 commitment, and they were often interrupted on dates or during dinner by sellers or buyers who were frantic about a deal. But when he made a big sale, like the 150-acre farm that was now being developed for town houses and a country club on a mountain overlooking Lincoln, he thought there was no better way to make a living.

That sale had changed everything. With the land commission, and the hope of getting the listings on each home sold, he'd landed the wind-fall he'd always dreamed of. And golf became his new job. The dream of moving to Arizona became a reality. As she was scraping plates into the garbage, she heard Rick's voice rise on the phone. "They're nothing but tree huggers. Forget about them."

Claire didn't like it when he talked like that. In truth, she could probably be labeled a tree hugger herself, and would no doubt argue with him if he weren't her fiancé. But she usually steered clear of topics that might cause them to argue, telling herself it was a small difference of opinion when you considered all the things she loved about Rick.

A moment later, as she was cleaning off the counter and loading the dishwasher, Rick came up behind her, wrapping his arms around her, then slowly unbuttoning her blouse. Even now, turning onto Linwood Street, she felt a blush of heat rise up from her middle, remembering. He'd turned her around, lifted her up onto the counter above the dishwasher. They'd done it right there, like two high school kids, crazy with desire. She missed him already.

As Claire turned into her driveway, she slammed on the brakes. She felt her entire body go still as her heart jumped into her throat. Sitting in her driveway was an old green Volkswagen Beetle. She hadn't seen that car in nearly two years. Not since the day she told her daughter to get out and grow up. Words she regretted five minutes after Amy had driven off in that car.

She pulled in behind the Beetle and turned off her car. What was she walking into? The last time Amy had called, it had to be several months ago, her few words were a repeat of all the other times. She was fine; she wasn't coming home anytime soon.

For the thousandth time, Claire wondered: how had things spiraled so out of control? Since Amy had graduated high school, it seemed one minute she was frantic with worry over her, how she was going to survive without a degree, what kind of future she would have. The next moment, Amy's lack of responsibility and maturity would make her furious, and they'd fall into the same patterns of fighting all over again.

If Amy had struggled in high school, she seemed to blossom at first in college. Or that's how it had seemed to Claire, who thought that getting out of Lincoln might be the answer for her daughter, after all. But then the grades came in. And Amy returned for weekend visits looking more tired each time. By the end of her freshman year, she'd gained the obligatory freshman fifteen. And she'd flunked a class and gotten Ds in two others. Claire put her foot down. She wasn't paying for tuition when Amy was obviously at college to party. Amy came home, and the next few years were a roller coaster of community colleges, part-time jobs, more weight gain, more partying.

The day she threw Amy out, she'd just discovered that her daughter had stopped going to classes mid-semester. Arriving home to confront her, Claire walked in to find her daughter smoking pot with a new friend, Tish something or other. She'd lost it. Thousands of dollars in tuition thrown down the drain. Her daughter throwing her life away. Claire exhausted from taking on after-school tutoring jobs to make more money.

That day Amy drove away, Claire assumed she'd be back by nightfall. She'd waited up until eleven, but when the knock came and the door opened, it wasn't Amy. It was Abbie, who'd been driving around, mad at Tom. Could she sleep on Claire's couch again? she'd asked. This happened every three or four months. They sat at the kitchen table drinking tea, as Abbie told her how she came back from showing houses that evening to find Tom unconscious on the couch. For once, Claire couldn't concentrate on Abbie's saga with her alcoholic husband. When she interrupted and told Abbie that she'd thrown her daughter out, Abbie covered her face with her hands.

"Oh, my God, I should have told you," she said. "I knew I should have told you."

"What? Told me what?" Claire asked frantically.

The week before she left, Amy had gone to Abbie's house to see Missy. "She's the only normal friend Missy has, you know," Abbie reminded her. Missy, who was working the carts at the local ShopRite since graduating high school, told Amy she hated her job. Abbie was in the kitchen with them, fixing dinner, and heard Amy say that she hated college. A minute later, Amy was sobbing, and when Abbie sat down with them, she confessed to her that she couldn't go to her classes. Now that she finally really wanted to finish school, she couldn't. It started one day a month ago, she told Abbie, as she'd sat in her car in the school parking lot, frozen with panic, her heart hammering in her chest. She felt like she would die if she had to step into that classroom. She made Abbie swear she wouldn't tell Claire. And Abbie agreed, on the condition that Amy would tell her mother herself and get some help.

"She kept saying, I gotta get out of here. I hate Lincoln," Abbie told Claire as Claire sat at her kitchen table, sobbing. "I think she wanted to leave, but she didn't really know how to do it. Or was too scared. So she made you do it for her." All of which made Claire feel even worse. Her daughter had serious problems, and she hadn't even realized it. She was a failure as both a mother and a teacher.

"I'm sure she'll be back in a day or two," Claire had told Abbie that night, with more certainty than she felt. "I'm sure she just wants to punish me."

But it was a month before the first phone call came. Claire begged Amy to come home. How could she be surviving? Claire's imagination ran wild, picturing her daughter preyed upon, a victim of white slavery, or even homeless, living on the streets somewhere, begging for quarters.

Walking from the driveway now into the back kitchen door, she saw no lights on except the one in the kitchen. She called out as she walked through the downstairs rooms, but there was no answer. She found Amy upstairs in her bedroom, asleep under a mountain of covers, despite the warm night. Her bags and things were strewn across the floor. Already Amy was taking over. And not for the first time since she'd pulled in did Claire think about the uncanny timing of her daughter's arrival just before her own big trip.

She flipped on the overhead light and Amy sat up as if a rifle had been shot.

"Mom?" She looked startled, as if she forgot where she was, looking so much like the little girl she'd once been.

Claire went over and sat on the bed, staring at her daughter, unable to believe she was really here. She put her arms around her and pulled her close. Amy looked awful; puffy-faced, black circles under her eyes. And as Claire held her, she realized she'd gained even more weight.

"Oh, Amy, how I've missed you," she whispered, hearing her voice crack with emotion. Seeing her, all the anger, animosity, everything slid away.

"I missed you, too, Mom."

Claire was surprised to feel her cheeks grow wet against her daughter's. Amy rarely ever cried.

Pulling away, she looked at her. "Are you okay? You're not sick, are you?" She put a hand to Amy's forehead, which felt cool, but clammy.

Amy shook her head. "I'm fine, just exhausted. Can we save all the questions for tomorrow? I just want to sleep. I've been on the road all day."

"Where did you come from?"

Amy gave her that look, the one that said, *Didn't I just ask for no questions until tomorrow?* Then she shrugged. "Okay, just one. I came from North Carolina."

Claire got up and walked to the door. As she reached for the light, Amy spoke again.

"I saw suitcases and things all over the place. You going some-where?"

Claire nodded. "I'm going to Cape Cod in a few days. To study photography."

Amy's eyebrows went up. "Photography? Since when?"

Claire switched off the light. Before closing the door, she said, "Since I was losing my mind worrying about you and had to fill it with something."

"Thanks a lot," she heard, as she shut the door.

She shouldn't have done that. She should have kept her mouth shut.

Already the old patterns were surfacing.

3

AMY SLEPT LATE. CLAIRE WASHED CLOTHES AND packed, worrying already that she wasn't taking enough cool weather clothes. Cape Cod was seven to eight hours north, jutting far out into the Atlantic. She threw in a hooded sweatshirt and a fleece jacket for good measure. The house looked messy even though she'd just cleaned it. She'd have to give it a thorough going over before leaving, especially with Amy here. But she couldn't think about that now; she had to prioritize. Rick always told her that was her downfall, flitting from one project to another and not staying focused. Now she would tackle the bills and finish them before starting something else. The final packing, the last clean sweep, could be done Monday morning.

She was paying everything ahead for the ten weeks she'd be gone, because she didn't want to think about mail or bills or checkbooks while she was on the Cape. She was so looking forward to those two months of freedom.

As she sat down at her desk in a corner of the kitchen, Amy walked in.

"Good morning," she said, smiling, hardly able to believe Amy was here.

"Morning," Amy mumbled.

"Did you sleep in your clothes?"

Amy was wearing a baggy purple muslin hippie dress, long and flowing, with an unzipped sweatshirt. Her long, black hair was pulled back in a sloppy ponytail. Claire hadn't realized how much weight Amy had gained until she saw how bloated her face was now in the daylight.

"There's coffee on the counter," she said.

To her surprise, Amy took the teakettle and filled it.

"Listen," she said, as Amy rooted in the refrigerator, "you need to go see Grandma and Grandpa today, they—"

"What!" Amy turned and glared at her. "Don't tell me you already told them I'm here. Oh my God, I—"

"Stop it," Claire interrupted, getting up from the desk. "Grandma called this morning to talk and I told her you were here, yes. She's been frantic about you. We all have been."

"I'll bet," Amy muttered. "Where's the toaster?"

"In the cabinet under the cutting board. I hardly use it, and it was cluttering up the counter." Rick had surprised her one day while she was in the shower, clearing her counters and reorganizing what remained on them. He'd teased her, calling her a "borderline slob." Next to him, she sometimes felt like one.

She sat back down at the desk, finishing the bills, then opened her bank statement.

"You have to come with me," she heard Amy say.

"Come with you?"

"To Grandma's. Come on, you know how Grandpa's gonna give me the look. Like I'm such a letdown. A loser."

"That is not true," Claire said, but she knew the look. Hadn't she felt it herself often enough over the years? "Anyway, I'm swamped with everything I have to do before leaving."

"Oh, right, Cape Cod. And when are you leaving again?"

She stood up and walked over to the table. Amy was nibbling on a piece of toast, crumbs settling like snow on the table. "The day after tomorrow. Listen, we have to talk about a lot of things. So much has changed—"

"Not now, okay?" Amy interrupted. "Come with me to Grandma's, please? I promise, we'll talk after that. I just want to get it over with. This'll be like going to the dentist."

IT WAS WORSE THAN THE DENTIST, Claire thought, as they were driving back three hours later. Amy sat beside her, sniffling, looking out the passenger window as she tried so hard not to cry.

"He looks so old, he doesn't even stand up straight anymore," she said. "I can remember him carrying me on his shoulders around the yard while he cut the grass. He was so strong."

"That's the Parkinson's," Claire said.

"And when did he get it?"

Claire sighed. "He's had it for a while, probably, but they finally diagnosed it last fall. Sometimes it goes undetected for a long time. But his handwriting was getting smaller and smaller. Their bills were getting sent back and a few checks were returned. Turns out, that's one of the early signs."

"Why didn't you tell me when I called?"

"I didn't want to worry you, honey. What could you do? And he's been doing okay. They put him right on medications that can halt the progress for a long time, hopefully."

"At least he doesn't shake so bad, although his head wobbled, did you notice? I remember that priest we had, his hand just shook so hard, like his whole arm was gonna fall off."

"The doctor said it's different for different people."

"That's why you didn't want them to drive to Lincoln? I can't believe he still drives."

"Not far. And probably not for much longer."

"God, that'll suck," Amy said. "They'll be trapped then."

Claire turned onto Route 75. "I know. That's going to be the worst. I can't even imagine it. He's always been so strong." She felt her own throat clog with sadness. "I told your uncle Eugene a few months ago, we have to start thinking about the future."

"Oh my God, not one of those homes!"

"They're not like that anymore. Some of them are pretty nice, actually, like little country clubs."

"Yeah, right, like Grandma would fit in with that."

Claire couldn't take much more, and decided to change the subject. "All right, enough. So, how about we talk now."

"You first," Amy said, flashing her a challenging smile. She'd beat her to the punch, as usual.

"Okay," Claire said, and took a deep breath. "Do you remember I told you I was seeing someone? Rick Saunders? Well, we're getting married in September."

Amy looked at her like she'd turned into an alien. "You're getting married?"

She nodded, unable to help the big grin that made her feel like a fool sometimes. Just saying it made her feel so happy.

"You like him?"

She laughed. "I love him, honey, or I wouldn't be marrying him. He's a great guy."

"Wow, that's fantastic, Mom. See, me leaving was probably the best thing that could have happened to you. You're a photographer now, you're getting married…"

Claire heard the hitch in Amy's voice.

"Honey, do you think I could be happy with any of that without you? My heart was torn in half, I was trying to survive, and things just happened—"

"Right, everything in your life happened to get better after you threw me out."

Claire bit her lip. She didn't want to do this. Their time was too short, too precious.

"I think you wanted me to throw you out, Amy. Looking back, I think you sat in this house smoking pot with that friend of yours just so I'd come home and go ballistic."

"I wasn't smoking pot," Amy said. "Tish was. I told her not to. I told her to stop, but she just kept going with it."

Claire pulled the car over onto the shoulder of the road and turned to her daughter. "Why didn't you tell me all of this then?"

Amy shrugged, looking out the window at the river. Refusing to look at her. "It doesn't matter, Mom. It's water over the bridge, or under the dam, or whatever the fuck that saying is."

Claire leaned over and cupped Amy's face, making her look at her. "Amy, I love you, why can't you see that? I've only ever wanted the best for you."

Amy said nothing for a moment, staring at her with a stony face. "Let's just go home, Mom. You have to get ready for your big trip and I've gotta hit the road."

They drove the rest of the way home in silence.

WHEN THEY GOT HOME, Claire went back to finishing the checkbook finally, canceling the paper and the mail, pointedly wiping the crumbs from the kitchen table. Amy disappeared into her room again.

A few hours later, Claire went upstairs, hoping Amy was in a better mood. It was time to get some answers about where she'd been, where she was going.

Amy sat on the radiator, twisting a strand of her long hair around her finger again and again.

"I'm going back to North Carolina, okay?"

"To do what? To stay where?"

"Doesn't matter, I'll be out of your hair in plenty of time."

"Look, I'd like to explain about this trip and why you can't stay here, because—"

"Mom, stop," Amy cut in. "I just told you it doesn't matter."

"It matters to me. I want you to understand that there's some-one—"

"Mom! I told you, I was just passing through. I'm leaving first thing Monday morning, so your big plans won't be ruined."

"Don't say that!" Claire shouted. "You know that's not how I feel."

Neither of them spoke for a long moment.

"Look, you don't have to leave. Go and stay at Grandma's. They'd love it, you know that. You saw how much they missed you."

Amy shot her a look, the one that said, *Don't you ever get it?*

"If you're trying to punish me for what I did, you're too late," Claire said, walking to the bedroom door and then turning one last time. "I've been punished for a year and a half with worry and lost sleep. I regretted doing what I did five minutes after you left. But I don't suppose you'll ever understand."

She slammed Amy's door shut.

As angry as she was, she couldn't help lying awake that night, tears streaming down her face onto her pillow. She'd spent nearly twenty-four years trying to make up for a father who for all intents and purposes had abandoned Amy. But to Amy, it seemed even that was Claire's fault.

FANNY TURNED OFF THE FAUCET and began taking off her clothes. It was still light out, barely seven o'clock, but every bone in her body was aching. Maybe it was a summer storm rolling in later that night, but something was brewing in her joints.

All afternoon Fanny wanted to call Claire. To tell her there was something about Amy—not that she could put her finger on it, but...it didn't matter. Claire wouldn't listen to her, she knew. Claire was preoccupied, Fanny could tell, with getting ready for her trip and her fiancé being so far away. Lowering her body into the old claw-foot tub, she moaned with pleasure. And pain. Her hip was killing her. Claire didn't believe in her intuitions anyway. But sometimes—not every time—Fanny had a way of knowing such things.

The whole time Fanny had kept company with Joe, she had an odd feeling, similar to this; something she couldn't quite identify. Not that she'd voiced those feelings to either Annie or Mama, both of whom couldn't stop raving at how handsome Joe was, what a catch—especially for someone who was practically an old maid. So she kept her feelings to herself, only to find out her suspicions were right.

It was at her own wedding party when Charlie Hoffman, an old friend of Joe's who'd been in the service with him, had too much to drink and began teasing Joe about the one who got away. Standing there in Mama's lace wedding dress, that Mama's own mother, Nana, had brought from Italy, Fanny had felt her stomach pitch and her face flame and go numb with embarrassment. And stupidity. She thanked God it was just her, Joe, and Charlie in the little hallway of the restaurant; no one else had heard.

What made her think of Charlie Hoffman now? He'd died more than five years ago, so his phone calls each New Year's, the ones that were a reminder to her that her husband loved someone else, had disappeared with him. In the beginning those yearly calls were torture, and ruined more than one New Year's celebration. Then, about ten years or so after they'd married, when the children were still little, Charlie had actually shown up on their doorstep early on a Saturday morning, weeks before the holidays even started. When Fanny answered the door, he saluted, asking for PFC Joseph M. Noble. He'd lost his hair and gained some weight; Fanny didn't recognize him at first. He explained that he was driving through on his way to Buffalo.

Claire and Eugene were stretched out on the living room floor watching *Lassie*. Fanny had been doing laundry. At first Joe looked startled when he came up from the basement, where he'd been tinkering with the boiler, almost alarmed when he saw Charlie standing in the kitchen.

"Hey, Joey Boy," Charlie laughed, and then gave Joe a hearty handshake.

"Charlie Hoffman, I'll be damned," Joe said.

They sat at the kitchen table, and though it wasn't noon yet, Joe got the old bottle of Four Roses whiskey from the cabinet high over the refrigerator. They drank several shots, Charlie smoking one Chesterfield after another. She'd sent the kids out to play without doing their Saturday chores and she quietly polished the dining room furniture, where she couldn't be seen, but could overhear their conversation.

Joe had never talked much of his time in the service, before he'd met her. Most of Charlie's loud babbling was about a "mean old son-of-a-bitch sergeant" they all hated.

"Yeah, but looking back, he doesn't seem so bad anymore," Joe said. "We turned out all right, didn't we?"

"That's for sure," Charlie said. "We were nothing but kids, far from home and lonely as hell." Fanny heard another match strike. "Hey, remember that pretty little thing you spent all your time with? What was her name, Anna? No, Ava, that's it."

And there it was, what she'd been waiting to hear about all these years. There was a long silence.

"You couldn't have forgotten, Joey Boy. Christ, you spent every moment of leave with her."

"I remember," she heard her husband say quietly.

"She was some looker, with that long, wavy dark hair. We used to call her Ava Gardner, remember?"

In the dining room mirror, from the corner of her eye, Fanny could see Joe nod his head.

"Yeah, we all thought you were a goner, pal, you had it bad."

"Nah," Joe said.

"And then when we thought you went AWOL, there was talk you'd eloped."

"No, I wasn't AWOL, I was sick in the infirmary with that nasty flu we all got."

"Whatever happened to her, you remember?"

"She married that Portuguese guy her family had picked for her," Joe said. "So what about you, why aren't you settled down yet?" Conveniently changing the subject, Fanny thought.

She sat quietly then in one of the dining room chairs. Knowing in that moment what she'd long suspected, that something had been missing from her marriage all along: her husband's heart. It wasn't that he was cold, or undemonstrative, as Mama said most men were. It was that his heart had been captured by another woman. The love of his life, from the way it sounded. Her intuition all those years ago had been right.

That night Charlie left before they went to the Prudential awards dinner. Joe received a citation for sales in his territory in town and Fanny applauded with everyone else, watching this handsome man in the new navy suit that she'd picked out for him just the week before at Sears and Roebuck, to highlight his blue eyes. This man who was a stranger to her at times.

Charlie had never visited again. And Fanny had never once brought up the name of Ava. Not once in all the years they'd been married. Lying in the tub now, she wondered what had made her think of Charlie. Because of Amy? Because the uneasiness she felt about Amy was the same unsettled feeling she'd once felt with Joe?

No, it was his balance. Joe's wide shoulders now drooped, his back was curling forward. He probably could use a cane now. But he refused. Maybe that was it; Amy had asked if they couldn't do something to help him stand straighter. And after they left, Fanny envisioned his perfect posture when she first met him. Her brother Anthony telling her it was from being in the service. And that must have brought the thoughts of Charlie.

Slowly she stretched out and leaned her head against the sloped back of the tub. Everything she did in this tub was slow, after the horror of falling in it last year and breaking her hip. But she wasn't going to think about that now. Or Charlie Hoffman. Her mind seemed to ramble lately, skittering across thoughts and memories that were a lifetime ago, but seemed like just yesterday.

It was Amy who needed her thoughts and prayers now. Amy, sitting in the living room with Joe, trying to make conversation, looking lost. When Amy went to the bathroom and Fanny voiced her fears, Claire said Amy was just doing what a lot of kids her age did: party too much, sleep too little, eat fast food. But it wouldn't be the first time they'd had a difference of opinion over Amy. No, that struggle for control swayed many times in the early years, as Fanny cared for Amy while Claire finished college and began taking teaching jobs, hoping to land one with tenure to secure her future. For a time, Amy had seemed like her own child, and after a while, the poor girl cried that she didn't want to go home when Claire would come to pick her up. Then Claire took the teaching job in Lincoln, when she could just as easily have gotten one here in Mechanicsburg. It was obvious she was trying to break Amy away from her.

The first week she didn't have Amy, Fanny felt as if someone had jabbed a hot poker in her heart. It hurt so badly she almost couldn't take a breath. She imagined her little sweet pea with a sitter, a stranger really. Someone who wouldn't love and care for her the way Fanny did. After that, she'd stopped being Meema, which sometimes, when she was excited and talking fast, came out of Amy's little mouth as Mama. After their move to Lincoln, Fanny became Grandma.

She could worry all she wanted, torture Claire all she wanted. Just like back then, it would do no good. Amy was her child, Claire would say. And she would decide what was best.

4

By one o'clock, Claire was ready, her red bags lined up in the living room, her spare key for Abbie under the doormat, all the planning of the past months finally down to this moment. Her flight to Boston was at four, with a switch to a tiny prop plane for Provincetown which would get her there at five-thirty. She was told it was just five minutes from there to the Arts Center, where she could unload her bags in a dorm room and change for the welcome reception. She didn't know what made her more nervous, the split-second timing of the trip or the thought of a tiny plane crossing Cape Cod Bay. Claire was a reluctant flyer.

The butterflies that had swooped through her stomach each time she woke during the night—which was frequently—were back now, nibbling at her gut. It reminded her of class trips back in her grade school days, waking at dawn, waiting for the yellow buses, so excited you thought you might throw up. Once, her best friend Robin did, and no one had ever let her forget it.

She paced in front of the window, waiting for her cab, wondering if Amy had really gone back to North Carolina. She was gone before Claire got up this morning, her room cleaned out, the bed unmade, a dirty towel on the floor. There was nothing she could do for her daughter, if Amy refused to let her in. She had to focus on the trip, on her work; otherwise she'd make herself crazy. It was ironic, because that had been her mind-set a year and a half ago when she'd rediscovered photography.

She wondered what Rick was doing at that moment in Colorado. Were they riding rapids or having a campfire on the banks of the river? Two months was a long time to be away from the man you were about to marry, her mother had said when she first told her about this trip. It was also a long time to be away from a bored mother who called you three times a day, and that was closer to the truth. Her friend Abbie, who was a part-time Realtor with Rick's office, had teased her that every single woman within fifty miles would be swarming around him, decked out in thongs and Wonderbras.

But Claire trusted Rick. He might not be mysterious or full of twists and turns, but Claire had had her fill of that with Liam. Rick was good, honest, and dependable. Claire loved the life they were building.

Her parents still didn't know that she and Rick were moving to Arizona next year. Every time she thought about telling them, her stomach clenched. Rick suggested waiting until she returned, which seemed like the wise thing to do.

The phone rang and Claire went to get it.

"I just wanted to remind you to bring your phone charger," her mother said.

She knew her mother was terrified she wouldn't be able to reach her in an emergency.

"I have it, Mom."

Then she heard the front door.

"I gotta run, Mom, the cab is here."

She hung up and walked quickly toward the front door, startled when it opened before she got there.

Amy stood before her, seeming just as stunned as she was to see her.

"I thought you left," her daughter said. "Where's your car?"

"I put it in the garage while I'll be away," she said. "I thought you left for North Carolina."

"I…forgot something," Amy said.

Just then they heard the cab pull up and beep.

"It's okay, Mom, I'll be out of here in a minute. Go ahead."

Claire watched Amy walk across the living room and start up the stairs. And then she turned.

"What? Don't you trust me?" And then her daughter made a face, like a grimace. "I promise, I'm gonna get my stuff and hit the road. I'll lock the door on my way out."

Claire looked out the window again. As the driver got out of the car, she heard the bathroom door slam. A moment later the driver was at her door. It was Ray Kohler, who lived down the street, apparently moonlighting again.

"Can I get your bags for you, Claire?"

Claire turned and looked at the red suitcases, a gift from her parents. She'd been arranging and rearranging things all morning, afraid of missing something. And afraid of having so much she wouldn't be able to put it all on the plane.

She took a deep breath. "Yes, you can take them. I'll be right out."

As he wheeled the bags out the door, she heard a noise upstairs.

"Amy?" she called.

She looked at the brass clock on the mantel. She needed to leave now. There would be traffic. Security, she'd heard, was awful at Newark Airport.

She heard the noise again. It sounded like a moan.

"Amy, are you okay?"

A moment later the bathroom door opened. Amy came down slowly. Her face was white and Claire could see a sheen of sweat on her cheeks. Claire wondered for a moment if her daughter had been taking drugs upstairs.

"Go ahead, don't miss your flight," Amy said, nodding at the front door.

"Honey, there's someone—"

But before she could finish the sentence, her daughter doubled over with a moan. Claire froze as Amy sank to her knees on the wood floor. A strange, guttural scream tore through the house as Amy rolled onto her back. Claire's hand flew to her mouth when she saw the blood trickling down her daughter's leg.

"I think...I'm having...a baby," Amy whimpered between gasps.

Her legs fell apart and her baggy dress rode up, enough for Claire to see her daughter's thighs streaked with pink mucous.

Claire sank to the floor as if in a daze beside her daughter. She was dreaming, this couldn't be...With a mighty grunt, Amy's face screwed up, as every nerve in her body began to push, her legs spreading, and Claire saw the slick black head crowning at the same moment she heard the cab beeping for her to leave.

CLAIRE TRIED TO DRIVE FASTER, but her legs were trembling so badly she had a hard time keeping her foot on the gas pedal. The ambulance had sped away as she stood on her porch, Ray Kohler looking at her questioningly. It seemed just a moment later that she was backing out of her driveway, pulling away, watching him carry her bags onto the porch in her rearview mirror.

Turning onto Route 75, all she could think of was how tiny the baby was. When the medic had wiped her quickly and whisked her away, Claire saw that her hair wasn't dark, like Amy's, but long strands of reddish gold. Her tiny fists had pumped at the air, as if she were fighting someone. This new world, perhaps. Just like Amy, Claire thought.

Amy had been silent and still afterward, staring at the ceiling as if she were hypnotized. Claire knelt at her side as the medic attended to her, a small white blanket now covering her lower half. Claire took her daughter's hand and squeezed it reassuringly.

"Amy, honey?"

A tear slid down the side of Amy's face.

Claire reached with her other hand and gently brushed the tear.

"She's…" Claire tried to say something. What could she say? How could this be real? She? Who was she, this baby? "Amy, she's so beautiful."

Her daughter just stared at the ceiling, and a moment later, she and the baby were taken away. The baby had barely made a sound, Claire just realized. That couldn't be good.

She began to pray, for the baby, and for her daughter. As she drove, her prayers were interrupted by images of Amy screaming, the baby with the blue, pulsing cord still attached, and then Ray Kohler's horrified face as he came in for the last suitcase. Twenty minutes later, those images were pierced by the acrid smell of the foundry, an odor she'd hated for more years than she cared to remember. She was almost back to Mechanicsburg. The rolling fields soon gave way to a gas station, an old strip mall, and houses that had seen better days. On the outskirts of Mechanicsburg, just before the road merged with Route 32, on the edge of the dreary industrial city, she turned into the entrance for Jefferson County Hospital, just two miles from her parents' house.

Her parents. What would she, could she, possibly tell them to explain this? They would no doubt see it as another failure on Claire's part as a mother. As she searched for a parking spot, Claire realized that she wasn't just a mother anymore. She was now a grandmother.

5

THE MOON WAS A SLIVER OF WHITE LIGHT JUST ABOVE the mountains as Claire drove home at nearly midnight. She wanted to stay at the hospital, to sleep in the chair in Amy's room, but the nurse wouldn't let her. The nurse did ask Claire if she'd like to give the baby her first bottle. Sitting in a rocker in the nursery, Claire looked down at those dark blue eyes as the baby sucked, first tentatively and then with a fierce hunger, her crying reduced to little whimpers as she got used to the nipple. A little dimple appeared and reappeared in her cheek as it puffed in and out. In those long minutes, Claire finally began to think about what would happen next. She would bet money that Amy did not have a job or a place to go back to. Where would they live? How would they survive? The one surprise was that Amy did have health insurance. So she had been working a real job somewhere.

The pattern of Claire's own life had been set into motion years ago. Duty and responsibility first, herself always last. She could see the writing on the wall as clearly as if a graffiti artist had painted it in neon orange on the nursery walls. But that was the old Claire. She had waited too many years for love to come back into her life, and for a chance to be free. As she and the baby stared at each other, Claire told herself not to fall in love. Because it would be so easy to do, as that little face looked up at her, drinking her bottle, her tiny hands curled into fists at her chin. She was just five and a half pounds. The baby stared at her with innocence, and a bit of suspicion in that little frown, as if wondering just who, in fact, this woman was who was feeding her.

Turning off Route 75 now, a sign greeted her: "Welcome to Victorian Lincoln, Preserve Our Past, Protect Our Future." When she'd gone back to Amy's room after feeding the baby, it was empty. Amy wasn't in the bathroom. And then Claire noticed that all of her daughter's things were gone. Her heart in her throat, she'd turned and run down the hall, searching for Amy. The hall looped around the nurse's station and when she rounded the corner to the nursery once again, there was Amy, leaning against the glass, a plastic bag dangling from her hand. The exit door was not ten feet away.

"What are you doing?" she asked, walking slowly toward her.

Amy turned and looked at her. Her face was like stone. "Just looking," she said.

Claire put her arm around Amy and turned her toward her room. Together they walked back, Amy's steps short and tentative. There had been tearing during the birth, and Claire knew the stitches must hurt.

"Did you know you were pregnant?" she asked Amy as she settled into the hospital bed.

Amy shrugged. "No. Sort of."

"What...I don't understand. How could you sort of—"

"Because I didn't want it to be real!" Amy cried. "When I came home I...I thought I had more time to figure it out."

"Where's the father?"

Amy shrugged again.

"You don't know? Or you're not telling?"

Just then a nurse came in and gave Amy a stern look.

"Well there you are," she said as she wound a blood pressure cuff around Amy's arm and began pumping. "We thought you'd run off."

Claire felt her heart sink.

"Your baby's Apgar scores are fine, although she's probably

three or four weeks early," the nurse went on, sticking a thermometer in Amy's ear. "But under the circumstances here, the doctor felt it would be best to have a social worker assigned to your case."

Claire was stunned at that, although she realized now, pulling into her driveway, that she shouldn't have been. Her friend Esther, who was the nurse at the high school, had told her countless times of girls who had no idea they were pregnant, then panicked at the end and left their babies in Dumpsters or on doorsteps. She knew Amy wasn't like that, but Amy had looked as if she might be abandoning the baby, after all.

It was after eleven when Claire turned off the car, and she sat for a moment in the dark, looking up at the old Victorian she'd bought for them all those years ago. A struggle on a single teacher's salary, even though it had been beat up. How hard she'd worked to make it a nice home. Here she'd learned to strip fifty-year-old wallpaper that had been painted over. And how to work a drill to get screws into plaster walls so she could hang pictures. She'd learned about perennials, so she didn't have to buy so many flowers that she really couldn't afford each year. She learned how to kill slugs with a dish of beer, lifting the bottle in a toast to them on humid July nights as she polished off the last sips herself. Here she put together a life, all on her own, for herself and her little girl. Always with an eye on someday. Someday when her burden was lessened. When responsibilities eased. When she could do whatever she wanted as Claire, and not worry about anyone else.

Walking up the porch steps, she thought she heard music. She hesitated a moment. She was certain she hadn't left the radio on. And lights? They were blazing through every room. A flicker of unease ran through her and her pulse began to beat as if a little drummer were tapping away at her heart. She put her hand on the doorknob and turned slowly, pushing the front door open.

There must have been a storm here. A power surge that jolted everything on. Of course, that would explain it. She dropped her purse on the table in the foyer and walked through the living room and dining room to the kitchen in the back, to pour a glass of wine. As she pushed on the swinging door into the kitchen, it suddenly came back at her and hit her smack in the nose. Then she was face-to-face with a strange man.

"Oh my God!" she screamed.

"Wait!" he cried, grabbing her arms. "Hold on! It's okay. Are you Claire?"

She nodded, a hand to her nose, her fingers wet with blood.

"I thought you left on your trip today. It was today, right? I found the key under the mat, just where Abbie said it would be."

Claire sank to a chair at the kitchen table and stared at the man. Jesus, after the baby came, she'd forgotten all about him. When she knew she was going to be gone for two months, it seemed like a perfect idea. Her house would be cared for, and she'd get paid. She'd been trying to tell Amy that someone would be renting the house, but then Amy had collapsed on the living room floor.

Across the kitchen, the man stared at her, eyebrows raised, waiting for an explanation. This was her new tenant, John Poole.

CLAIRE POURED TWO GLASSES of wine and then sat at the kitchen table with John Poole. Her nose, which ached, had stopped bleeding. She took a long sip, but he just sat there watching her, barely veiled annoyance in his eyes.

"Yes, I was supposed to leave today. You were right. Obviously, that didn't happen. Things…things in my life are in a bit of turmoil. I'd rather not go into it. But I won't be leaving right away. I'm sorry, maybe in a few days or a week. Look, there's a small motel on the outskirts of Lincoln. I'd be happy to cover a few nights for you until you can find something else."

He took a sip of wine, and she could see him considering her words. Then he smiled kindly, shaking his head, and relief flooded through her.

"Sounds like you've had a day," he said sympathetically. "I know how that feels. You see, I've had a day, too." And then his look hardened as he continued. "Actually, I've had a few hundred of them, and they didn't exactly go as I'd planned either. But here I am, trying to do something about it. I'm not going to a motel. I'm not leaving. We had a deal, and like it or not, you're going to have to honor it."

She couldn't believe this. He spoke slowly, with the soft r's and the long, drawn-out consonants of a city boy. Or perhaps someone from New England.

"I'm sorry, Mr. Poole, but this is my house. And right now I'm not going anywhere."

He got up and walked to the counter, draining his glass of wine. Then he opened a backpack and pulled out papers. After a moment, he turned, holding up a few stapled pages. "And this is my lease. Signed by you. And me. And your pal, Abbie, the Realtor, who obviously drew it up. Notarized even. I'd say I'm the one who's not going anywhere."

She sat there staring at him, so exhausted his face was beginning to blur. This was Rick's idea, really, another way to save every dime for the new town house and a small RV for their big future. Abbie had handled it all. Now what? She could call Esther, who lived alone, and crash on her couch. Or drive back to Mechanicsburg and stay at her parents'. But it was nearly midnight; calling anyone would cause a panic. She couldn't drop this bomb on them in the middle of the night.

But what was she thinking? Amy would be released from the hospital in a day or two. And the baby. Where would they go? She had to stay, at least until they figured this out.

John Poole put the papers back into his pack and zipped it up as if everything was final. She finished her wine, got up, and went to the sink. She rinsed her glass and set it on the drain. Then she picked up his dirty glass and turned to him.

"My granddaughter was born today on my living room floor, just a few minutes before I was supposed to leave. Right now, she's in the hospital, with my daughter, who I haven't seen in a year and a half." She took a deep breath. "I have no idea what happens next, except I need to get some sleep and then tomorrow I need to get a crib and diapers and formula and the million other things a newborn needs that I don't have. So," she went on, holding out his dirty wineglass, "you'll have to wash your own glass and somehow stay out of my way until we figure this out. Because I'm not going anywhere, except up to bed right now."

She was halfway across the dining room, weaving from fatigue when she heard him call out, "I feel for you, Claire, I really do. But I need a place for the summer and a little motel room isn't going to work. So I'm not going anywhere either."

In the foyer, just as she walked toward the stairs, she stopped and looked at the photograph hanging over a small table where she tossed the mail each afternoon. An old gnarly tree, with a dozen twisted branches growing in all directions. *The Family Tree*, she'd called it, the centerpiece of the portfolio she'd sent into the Arts Center with her application. How proud she'd been when she printed it in her darkroom all those months ago. And excited, because for the first time she felt like she might have a chance at being accepted into the course.

She didn't bother hanging her clothes up. She left them in a pile on the floor, like Amy used to do. Then she crawled into bed in just her panties, since her nightgowns were packed in the suitcase downstairs.

It wasn't until she closed her eyes, drifting to sleep, that she remembered. She needed to call Rick and tell him what had happened. He would be shocked, no doubt. How could he not be? And he'd probably have a dozen questions, none of which she really had answers for just yet. But it was nice to know she didn't have to face this alone. Finally she had someone she could turn to, to lean on, to help her figure this out.

Or could she? Rick was a bit self-centered, which was to be expected in a forty-five-year-old man who'd never been married or had children. He liked to have fun, and his free time revolved around golf. Weren't they moving to Arizona next year so that he'd be able to golf twelve months a year?

Maybe it was better for her to wait to tell him this. There was no cell service where he was, so she'd have to use the rafting company's phone number, which was for emergencies. Yes, she'd wait. And hopefully, by the time he returned, she would be able to figure things out for herself.

6

On Sunday morning, Fanny went downstairs and started the coffee. Claire would be there soon, to take her to the first mass at seven-thirty. And then Claire would go home and sleep, before getting up to grade papers the rest of the day.

Fanny wondered when life had gotten so complicated. Once, Sunday was her favorite day of the week. It was all about family. Now it was the loneliest day. No one came. Eugene would call, later on, because he was three hours behind. But somehow, his calls just made her more lonesome. There were no more Sunday dinners. Everyone was rushing around trying to fit in errands or extra work before they actually went back to work the next day.

On Sunday mornings in Brooklyn, she would come home from mass with Annie and her brothers, and Mama would have the meatballs already simmering. They would sit down to a small dish, the meatballs small and tender, not like those hard rocks as big as baseballs you got in restaurants now. She would dunk a piece of soft bread in Mama's tomato gravy, and chunks of onion and garlic and sweet basil would explode in her mouth.

After that, they would sit in the yard until dinnertime, reading the Sunday papers, talking, playing cards, her brothers tossing a ball. Daddy would check his plants in the garden, the fig tree, the grapes, his precious basil and oregano plants. It was a tiny yard, but Daddy called it his "little piece of heaven."

Mama had once told her that when her own grandmother,

Nana's mother, came over from Italy in the 1890s, she'd really been told that the streets of America were paved with gold. She had no reason not to believe it, and was heartbroken when she'd gotten off the boat and had her first look at the teeming city that would become her home. What else, Fanny asked as she braided her long dark hair, laced with silver, had she been told that would turn out to be untrue? She found out soon enough. Life in America was just as hard as in Italy. At just sixteen, she'd married an American man, against her parents' wishes. They were so afraid of losing their traditions. But she'd clung to her cooking, the old ways. Fanny tried to hang on, too, to that little bit of her heritage, but Mama had been gone for so long now, and Annie, too. The old traditions were fading each year; the fish supper on Christmas Eve, the little cups of demitasse on holidays. The meatballs and gravy on a Sunday morning. Just like the mass.

She went over to the desk in the corner of the kitchen to get her envelope for the collection. It wasn't there. She began rooting through the papers across the desktop, thinking to herself that for a man who couldn't stand clutter, or a thing out of place, Joe kept his desk, where he paid the bills and took care of paperwork, like a pigsty.

She opened the top desk drawer. No envelopes. But on top of the pile of papers was the brochure of the Cape Cod Arts Center that Claire had given them. She'd circled the phone number, since cell service was sketchy up there. She'd also clipped some pictures of the town and beaches she'd gotten from the computer. It was all to keep them interested, maybe get them excited, too. Fanny looked at the brochure now, confused. There were words written on the sides of the pages in Joe's barely legible handwriting. It looked like *trueo* or *truro*, maybe *true*. Another that could have been…*and*? *ana*? *any*? None of it made sense. She heard a car out front and turned to check the time. Claire was terribly late, the mass would be starting in just ten minutes.

Oh no…

Fanny turned back to the brochure. How could she have forgotten? Claire was gone. She wouldn't be coming to take her to church. Or going home to grade papers, because school was over. That was two things. How could she have forgotten two things?

Because she didn't want to believe it? And then her stomach dropped, like she was roaring down a roller coaster. Was she getting like Mama?

She threw the collection envelope in the garbage. She wouldn't go today. Joe needed an hour or more to simply get up, go to the bathroom, and make his way downstairs. Although he was managing, she had to admit to herself what was staring her in the face each day. The Parkinson's was finally becoming a presence in their lives. Those first little symptoms that had been so easy to ignore were turning into bigger things. Last night, when she'd come downstairs after her bath, she found him standing in the kitchen. It was a moment before she realized he couldn't move. Not that he'd admitted it.

"Can't you walk?" she'd asked in alarm.

Then his feet began to move. "I can walk. I was just trying to decide what I wanted."

She wasn't the only one dancing around the truth.

"I can fix you a snack," she'd offered. "How about some cheese and crackers, or a sandwich?"

He shook his head. "No, never mind." And he'd gone back into the living room to watch more television.

Who could blame him? Once they started talking about it, there was no going back. Their ordinary life would become something else. And right now, their quiet, ordinary life didn't seem so bad.

CLAIRE WAS UP EARLY and called her friend Abbie, who had arranged for John Poole to rent her house. Abbie, of course, was stunned to hear her voice. Claire was surprised Abbie didn't already know what had happened. In Lincoln, when the rescue squad showed up, news of it was usually all over town within minutes. Especially since Ray Kohler, her driver, was there to witness it all.

Briefly, without going into the details, she told Abbie that Amy was home and things were complicated. But then she begged her to find John Poole another place to live. Abbie wasn't too optimistic.

Claire left for the hospital at eight o'clock, to avoid running into the tenant. Pulling out of the driveway, her head foggy, her body like lead, she felt like she'd been up partying all night. One glass of wine and little sleep was not an option anymore at forty-five if you had to function the next day.

She avoided Main Street and took side roads, in case anyone she knew, who knew she should be gone, might be out already. Maybe she was being a bit paranoid. But she wanted to come up with a way to make this the least devastating as possible. Especially for Amy, who'd always felt her life was under a microscope in Lincoln anyway.

She turned onto Route 75 north and followed the Pohatcong River toward Mechanicsburg. Twisting and tumbling through the northwest Jersey foothills, the Pohatcong formed the eastern border of Jefferson County. As she drove, her eyes were drawn to the water, shimmering to her right not twenty feet from the highway, where sunlight filtered through the trees. This river that seemed to define her life.

Over the years, she'd made this drive to Mechanicsburg, twenty minutes ahead, at the western edge of the county, where the Pohatcong emptied into the Delaware, more times than she could count. She could probably navigate with her eyes closed. Just behind her, on the eastern border of the county, lay Lincoln, a quaint Victorian town that the modern world seemed to pass by.

In the nineteenth century, Lincoln was the bustling hub of the horse-drawn carriage industry in the northeast. But by the turn of the century, with the advent of the automobile, Lincoln had already passed its heyday. Even the Pohatcong Canal, once a thriving artery of shipping that brought goods and customers to local stores, had also dried up, thanks to the railroad. But by the fifties, the rail service, which had been operating at a loss for years, ceased as well.

Locals didn't seem to mind, especially these days. While most of northern New Jersey had exploded in the last real estate boom, Lincoln had been blessed—or cursed, according to a few local progressives—by being situated in an inconvenient location: too far from the interstates to attract commuters heading east, where most of the big jobs were. In the last hundred years, the population of Lincoln had remained pretty much the same: thirty-four hundred and eighty something people.

Claire could understand how Amy felt about Lincoln. Confined. Shut off from the world. Amy had struggled from the beginning, when they'd first moved there, trying to fit in with kids who'd been in the same tiny classes since kindergarten. By third grade, when Amy walked in as a new student, there were already cliques and power plays in place. By fifth grade, when Amy began to develop, another girl in her class, Jen Palmer, decided to make Amy's life hell for an entire year.

It was awful; her daughter had been a child with the breasts of a well-endowed woman. It was then that a distance began to develop between them. Esther had told her it was normal adolescent angst, just a little early, but Claire wasn't so sure. She'd tried talking to Amy, hoping to convince her that things would get better, that the other girls would catch up, anything that might help. But a self-consciousness Amy had never had before had overtaken her. She even began walking differently, to keep her breasts from bouncing. And she never played sports again.

As she neared Mechanicsburg, Claire thought about going to

her parents' house. It wasn't eight o'clock yet, but her mother, she knew, would be up. She'd have to tell them sooner or later. She turned toward the hospital, though, not sure she could deal with her mother's thousand questions yet. All of which would make Claire feel that this was somehow her fault.

CLAIRE WAS STARTLED when she walked past the nursery. She stopped and stared. The baby had an oxygen tube clipped to her nose. She was sleeping in just a diaper, a heat lamp perched above her to keep her warm. Claire watched her tiny pink chest rise and fall with each breath. She felt her own breath catch.

She stopped at the nurse's station.

"My…granddaughter," she said, uttering the surreal word for the second time. "Is she all right?"

The nurse, whom she hadn't seen yesterday, looked at her blankly. "Which one is your granddaughter?"

"Noble. Baby girl Noble."

The nurse shuffled through charts. "Oh, yes. It says here the pediatrician on staff felt her breathing was becoming a bit thready. We'll need to get her lungs stronger before we let her go."

"Is that normal?"

"Well, it's not that unusual. All her other vitals seem fine."

"Does it say when she'll be able to go home?"

"No, you'll have to wait and ask the doctor."

"What time will he be in again?"

"It varies."

Buzzers rang and the nurse excused herself, but not before telling Claire that the baby couldn't go home without a name. Or a father's name. Claire walked slowly down the hall.

One blessing in this ordeal was that Amy was alone in her room; the bed in the opposite corner empty. As Claire sat in the chair, she watched her daughter sleeping. Amy's long black hair was spread across the pillow and her face looked so peaceful. To Claire, Amy could almost have been fifteen again. She felt her heart squeeze with love for Amy. She'd seen it again and again, as a teacher. Some kids sailed through life so easily. And for others, every step was a problem. She'd only ever wanted what was best for Amy. An education, a job, a secure future.

Amy's eyes fluttered, then slowly opened. She stared at the ceiling for a long moment, the peaceful mask gradually stiffening. Claire assumed that the reality of where she was, what had happened, must have dawned on her. Amy had always been a heavy sleeper. Claire had had to resort to extreme measures at times to wake her for school. A few times, she'd thought that sleep was a place for Amy to escape.

She reached over now and took Amy's hand. With the other hand, Amy found the remote and pressed a button, and the bed slowly rose her into a sitting position.

"We need to give your little girl a name," Claire said in a light tone, hoping to ease into things.

"No, we don't," Amy said softly. And then she turned and looked at Claire. "I'm putting her up for adoption."

Claire blinked hard, convinced she couldn't have heard correctly.

"Honey, what are you saying? That's a huge dec—"

"Oh, right. And I'm not capable of making huge decisions, am I? You, of course, know what's best, as usual?"

She took a deep breath, refusing to be baited into an argument. "Honey, I'm not saying any of that. I'm just saying that you must be exhausted. You shouldn't make a decision like this when you're so tired."

With that her daughter lowered the bed and closed her eyes. "Please pull the curtains closed when you leave."

She felt anger bubbling from her stomach up her chest and into her throat, until she wanted to explode with it. Maybe she shouldn't be agonizing like she'd been, assuming this was going to be her problem. Maybe she should simply just leave, let Amy figure it out for once. After all, her daughter had managed somehow for eighteen months and all of the sleepless nights when Claire wondered where she could be, how she might possibly be surviving when she'd left with just eighty-five dollars and a twenty-seven-year-old car that was on its last legs.

On her way out, she stopped at the nursery window and stared at the baby for a long moment. She'd given Amy twenty-two years of her life. Given up everything, done everything to put her first. Now she was ready to live her own life, finally. She was ready to get married, to start a new career, perhaps. This baby was a stranger to her. She was Amy's, not hers. And maybe Claire should keep it that way. Because if Amy truly intended to put the baby up for adoption, maybe it would be the best thing for the child, after all. Amy certainly wasn't mother material. And Claire had no room in her life now for a baby.

Driving back to Lincoln, Claire realized one thing. Even if she wanted to raise the baby herself, there was Rick. He'd made it clear that he'd never wanted children. He'd been one of six, and laughingly said he had enough family to last him a lifetime. He'd mapped out their future to the tiniest detail. He and Claire were going to have a beautiful life in Arizona, filled with golf, photography, and travel.

IT WAS NEARLY NOON when Claire hung up the phone after calling the Cape Cod Arts Center. The woman she'd talked to, Zoe, was sweet and sympathetic when Claire said that a family matter was going to delay her. Zoe assured her she'd relay the message to Charles Meyer, who was giving the workshop. When Claire said that maybe she should just reapply for later in the summer, Zoe told her not to bother. They were already booked a year ahead. "Just get here as soon as you can," she'd advised.

Now she sat staring out the kitchen window, fighting tears. How many months had she dreamed of this chance? She could still go, she knew that. She could leave Amy and her baby and their problems and be up there in Cape Cod in a few days. But Claire knew that wasn't really an option, no matter how frustrated she was with Amy. Not yet, anyway.

She heard a noise and turned. John Poole stood in the kitchen doorway, arms folded across his chest. Quickly she turned from him and blotted her eyes.

"Rough night?" he asked.

"Rougher morning," she said.

"Where were you supposed to be going, anyway?"

"Cape Cod."

"Really? What part of the Cape?"

"The end of it. Provincetown. Why? Do you know the Cape?"

"I just came from there myself, actually."

She frowned. "That's quite a coincidence."

He shook his head. "I don't really believe in coincidences. Anyway, I'd like to apologize."

She raised her eyebrows.

"You don't have to look so surprised. I'm really not a bad guy, although some people might not agree with that. I've had a rough *year*, myself." He took a deep breath and she waited. "Anyway, I'd like to offer you a deal."

"A deal?"

He smiled for the first time. Claire was startled to see that he was handsome, in a rugged sort of way. "Yeah, a deal. Your friend Abbie called me a little while ago. Seems there's an old house outside of town I might be able to move into. An old lady died a few months ago and they need to settle the estate. So the house won't be sold for a while. She thinks they'll let me take it for the summer. I figure if I take it and move out of here, you owe me."

"Look, I'll gladly refund what you've already given me." Even though she'd already spent it.

"Uh uh," he said, shaking his head. "It's not money I'm looking for." And then he turned around and picked up something and held it up. "You did this, right?"

It was the calendar she'd done for the PTA fundraiser, *The Trees of Jefferson County*, which had been hanging in the attic. The feedback from that calendar had inspired her to go back and do a series on *The Family Tree* for her portfolio application. More than anything, Claire loved photographing nature.

"Yes, those are my photos."

"They're very good."

"Thank you."

"Okay, then here's the deal. I'd like for you to take some pictures for me. If you agree, I'll move out."

"Pictures of what?" she asked.

"I'm a freelance writer, I'm not sure if you know that."

Surprised, she shook her head. He didn't look like a writer. Or what she thought a writer would look like. He looked more like a football player. She remembered now that Abbie had told her he was here for the summer working on a special project, something to do with the environment. She'd assumed he was an engineer of some sort. He'd had good credit and he'd paid up front; that was all that mattered to her at the time. And she wouldn't have to pay someone to cut the grass or water her flowers.

"I specialize in environmental topics. I'm doing a piece on the canal that ran through here years ago. You can be my photographer."

"You want me to photograph the old canal?"

"Yes. My payment will be the refund of my rent. You can keep it."

She hesitated. "Why me?"

He smiled, as if she were missing the big picture. "It's simple. You live here, you know the area and you take good pictures, which I don't. It saves me from having to find a freelance photographer."

"How long do you anticipate this taking?" she asked.

"Oh, six weeks tops, give or take."

"And where will your article, and my photos, appear?"

He shrugged. "Not sure yet."

She paused a moment. "What if you don't sell the piece?"

He shrugged again. "Doesn't matter, you still keep your money."

There wasn't much to think about. His two thousand dollars was gone, spent on air fare and tuition for the program. Both non-refundable.

"I'm actually doing this to help a friend. He's a canal buff and it's going up for historic preservation later this year."

"And what was it you were doing up in Provincetown?"

"A piece on the fishing industry. I have to go back and finish it when I'm done here." He paused and then laughed. "Why do I feel like I'm getting the third degree?"

"I just want to be careful, that's all."

She looked out the window again. The bird feeders were quiet, the morning rush for food over. She thought about what would happen next with Amy. Was she really serious about the adoption? Even if she was, how could Claire just leave her? It would be devastating. And if not, Amy and the baby would need a place to live. As resentful as she felt, she knew she couldn't just turn her back on them. She'd give Amy the summer, but that was it. Because in September she was getting married. And Rick would be living with her here until they moved to Arizona next June.

She realized that she'd have to call the Arts Center and cancel completely.

She stood up and held out a hand to John Poole, who'd been

standing at the sink, waiting for her answer. "Okay, you have a deal," she said.

He held out his own hand and shook hers hard.

"I guess I should say thank you," she said.

He gave her a crooked smile. "I guess you should."

7

Fanny hung up the phone and sat at the kitchen table. The longest day of the year was approaching and it was hard to get ready for bed while it was still light outside. But she was tired. Although she'd done nothing, really, all day.

After trying to convince Joe to take a ride, anywhere, just to get out since it was such a gorgeous day, she'd given up and spent the afternoon in the yard, in a chair in the sun. First, she'd crocheted for a while, but then her crooked fingers began to ache and she put the yarn away. She didn't really like to crochet. It was busywork, but you had to do something to fill the long, empty hours of a Sunday.

At six o'clock, after she'd fixed a bowl of soup for herself and made Joe a sandwich, arranging his pills next to his plate so he wouldn't forget to take them, she'd finally called Eugene. Her son usually called her by noon on Sundays to talk a few minutes. Always she could hear his children in the background, laughing or shouting, Barbara's voice scolding them and reminding Eugene they had to leave soon for wherever it was they were off to. Eugene had a big job and traveled a lot, and Fanny thought he should take it easy on Sundays. Her daughter-in-law, who always had him hopping, should give him a break once in a while. But it was different for fathers today. Not like when she'd raised her kids. Eugene not only worked, he cooked on weekends and coached a few nights a week.

When they were young, Joe would come home from work

hours after the kids got in from school. She would have a meal on the table, the wash and ironing done. She'd already be thinking about tomorrow night's dinner. After supper, Joe watched the news and dozed as she did the dishes, the kids at the table with their homework spread out. Then he'd go out on an appointment, hoping to sell life insurance to a newly married couple or convince one of his older clients it was time to invest in a whole life policy.

She could understand Eugene being spread so thin if Barbara worked. But Barbara had packed in her career when they had kids. At forty-three, she was ready to embrace motherhood full-time. She expected Eugene to do the same. Only Eugene worked long hours. There was no answer on the phone and Fanny worried that maybe something had happened. And then she remembered that they were going to the beach for the weekend with another family. Eugene and his kids were so far away that they spent many of their holidays and vacations with friends. Friends who were more like their family now than their real family. But Fanny didn't complain. At least he was married, finally, and had children. For years he had worried Fanny to no end.

She sat at the kitchen table now, looking through the archway into the front hall, remembering as if it were yesterday the day Eugene left home. She'd been right there when it started, sitting at the same formica table with a cup of coffee, waiting for the kids to leave for school, when she heard shouts. She'd raced to the hallway in time to see Eugene's lips tremble as Joe ordered him to leave. He was seventeen. His hair, curling past the collar of his Catholic school uniform, was enough of an affront at Mechanicsburg Catholic to have spurred one of the nuns to call their house early that morning. Eugene was violating a dress code and couldn't return to school until he got a decent haircut. Now he was refusing.

The next thing she knew, Claire, who never talked back, was yelling at Joe, telling him that he was lucky to have such a kid, that

Eugene was quiet and didn't drink or lie, and they could have had it a lot worse. Besides, Claire had gone on, everyone had long hair.

"Cut it or get out," Joe barked.

Fanny was in the hall by then, her heart in her throat. Eugene shook his head and the movement sent a tear spilling down his cheek. Without a word he turned, opened the door, and a moment later was gone.

Six months later, ironically, he'd had his head shaved when he enlisted in the army. And he'd never come home to live again. Although for months, Fanny had watched that door, waiting. Hoping.

As Fanny sat there now, staring into the darkening hall, the door slowly opened, as if answering her thoughts. Her breath caught in her chest. She wondered if she were going crazy and blinked hard, but the door was still opening. But that wasn't possible; Eugene was long gone, and Claire was off on her trip...and...but as Fanny tried to assemble her confused thoughts, she saw Claire walk into the hall, through a shaft of light from the sun, which set on the side of the house. Claire, whose face was a composed mask, but whose eyes, Fanny could see even from where she sat, because her distance vision was still sharp as a tack, those eyes had been crying. What was Claire doing here and not in...

"What?" she asked, standing up, her voice a wail of fear. "What's wrong?"

"Mom, it's okay, everyone's all right, nobody died," Claire said, coming into the kitchen and taking her hands. "Let's sit down a minute. I have to tell you something."

As Claire told her about Amy and the new baby, Fanny's pulse settled down. "I knew it. I knew there was something, Claire, I just couldn't put my finger on it."

Claire sat there shaking her head, fighting back tears, Fanny could tell, by the way she nibbled on her bottom lip and her nostrils quivered from time to time. She knew there was more, something else Claire wasn't telling her. Trying to protect her. But Claire looked so miserable she didn't push it.

"What about your trip?" she asked. And then Claire's eyes did swell with tears and she got up, and went to make a cup of tea.

"What do you think?" she asked, filling the pot. "How could I possibly go now?"

She put the pot on and went to use the bathroom. Fanny knew she didn't have to, that she just wanted to be alone, to let the tears out without her mother seeing them. The last time she'd seen Claire so upset, my God, it was years ago, Amy just three or four.

Claire had suddenly wised up and left Liam, that bastard, and she'd moved back home. It was supposed to be only for a few weeks, so she'd put all of their things into storage. Claire took her old room, and Amy slept in Eugene's. But a few weeks became six months, and when Claire finally got her first teaching job and found a tiny apartment, she'd gone with Joe's pickup truck to get their things. She'd returned with the same look on her face that she wore this morning. All of her things, and Amy's, were gone. She'd stood there, so calm, telling Fanny in such a soft monotone that the storage facility had sold everything because she'd forgotten to pay the last few months.

When Amy woke from her nap, Claire had asked her in that same controlled tone if there was one thing she could have, what would it be. "Daddy's monkey," Amy said, "I want my monkey." Amy, of course, didn't understand. When Claire tracked down the woman who'd bought all her things, the woman wouldn't sell the stuffed monkey back to her. Her own son now slept with it, she said. Claire explained that the monkey was a gift from her child's father, who was gone. The woman didn't care. When Claire returned empty-handed, Amy threw herself on the floor, screaming for Daddy's monkey. And then Daddy. Fanny thought her heart would explode with sorrow for Claire, who carried the whimpering child upstairs.

"I can't believe I let that happen," Claire kept saying. "How could I have been so careless?"

Now Claire came back into the kitchen, her cheeks pink, eyes shiny, but composed.

"The baby," Fanny asked, "what does she look like?"

"She's beautiful," Claire said with a sad smile. Then she sat down again. "Listen, I can't deal with telling Daddy. I just—"

"Don't worry," Fanny said, putting a hand up to stop her. "I'll tell him later on. It'll be better that way."

SHOPPING WITH HER MOTHER was an ordeal, one for which Claire had to dig into her dwindling reserve of patience. Today, though, she had little left. They browsed through Orr's, the old-fashioned department store a few miles from the hospital, her mother humming with purpose as she picked out tiny undershirts, booties, receiving blankets; murmuring how Amy would love the choices—as if Amy had any idea what a layette even was, Claire thought. Claire knew her mother was just trying to cheer her up, but she just wasn't in the mood.

When her mother's questions had begun as they sat in the kitchen drinking tea the previous day, Claire had said nothing about Amy mentioning adoption. She convinced herself that Amy was just lashing out. She told her mother that she and Amy hadn't really discussed the baby's father yet; a white lie, but almost the truth. As for where Amy had been, Claire told her, "North Carolina," in a tone of certainty that seemed to end further questions on that matter. But then all the questions about the baby came again, and by the end of the conversation, her mother's face had lit up with something Claire hadn't seen in years.

When they were done shopping, Claire's trunk was loaded with all the items they could think of that they would need to bring the baby home. Her mother had paid for it all with the birthday money Eugene had sent her a month ago. A big check, more than she needed, her mother told her. Guilt money, Claire knew.

She watched Amy's eyes widen as she saw Fanny walk through the door into her room, a stuffed pink bear in one arm, a gift bag hanging from her other with a "decent nightgown and robe" for Amy. Claire didn't bother to tell her that Amy hated pink, especially when it was dotted with thousands of little roses. When Claire had told her mother that that was how the baby looked, her face like a little pink rosebud, her mother had launched with gusto into finding anything to suit the theme.

"Hello there, my sweet pea," Fanny said softly and then stooped awkwardly and wrapped her arms around Amy. Amy's arms barely came up to touch her grandmother, as she glared at Claire over Fanny's stooped shoulder.

"Don't you worry about a thing, this will all work out, you'll see," Fanny went on, and then sat with a big sigh in a chair next to the bed. Claire knew the shopping trip, and then the long walk through the hospital corridors, had been hard on her mother. She had a sneaking suspicion her mother probably needed a new hip, not that she ever complained about that. After she'd fallen and broken her hip last year, her mother had stopped complaining about anything physical.

"Now, what are you going to name that precious little doll?" her mother went on. "I was thinking Rose would be nice, since she looks like a little rosebud." When Amy didn't say anything, Fanny just kept talking through the long silences, something she had lots of practice with at home. "But that may be a little too old-fashioned…"

One thing her mother often did complain about was that her father barely talked. But as her mother rattled on, Claire thought once again that she knew why: because he could never get a word in edgewise. Now her mother went through the tales of her own births, Mama helping her, living with them for a few weeks, etc., until she came full circle back to the original topic.

"...so naming the baby is very important..."

As if on cue, a nurse walked in with a clipboard in her hand. "All right, Ms. Noble, we really do need to get this birth certificate filled out before you're allowed to leave."

Claire waited, her heart in her throat, as the nurse sat on the windowsill, pen poised above the clipboard.

"I can't," Amy said, in a voice they could barely hear. "I can't name her."

The nurse looked at Claire in exasperation. "She can't go home without a name."

"I'm not taking her home," Amy said. "I want to put her up for adoption."

Claire felt her mouth fall open. And then her mother turned to her, her eyes wide with alarm.

CLAIRE TOOK HER MOTHER HOME and then returned to the hospital for the meeting with the social worker. The interview was brief. The social worker asked a series of questions, which Amy answered in one or two words. The most upsetting was that she had no idea who the baby's father was. Claire could just imagine it: Amy drunk, or at a party, caught up in a moment of stupidity. At least she'd been in love with Liam.

Afterward, Claire went with the social worker to her office, on the hospital's main floor.

"You don't remember me, do you?" the social worker, whose badge read Donna Laverty, asked, as soon as she shut the door and Claire sat down. "Donna Bellis? Now Laverty, of course. Mechanicsburg Catholic High School?"

Claire stared at her a moment, the gray blond hair, the gaunt face. This woman couldn't possibly be the chubby, dark-haired girl who was a year or two ahead of Claire. When they both didn't make the squad, Robin had hissed that Donna had been picked as a cheerleader because her football player brother's girlfriend was cheering captain. And a judge.

"Oh, of course…"

"No, come on, don't lie. I know I look different," Donna laughed, with a wave of her hand. "Fifty pounds disappear, you decide blondes do have more fun, and suddenly no one who knew you before recognizes you anymore."

Claire didn't have the heart to say she'd been prettier before. Maybe a little weight back on would soften the lines in her face, puff out the hollows under her eyes. She looked almost anorexic. And then Claire wondered if Donna was sick.

"Didn't you marry that hottie? Liam Walker?" Donna asked, as she opened a drawer and pulled out a file.

She hesitated. "Briefly." Claire didn't want to go there. Hadn't wanted to, ever.

"Is he her dad?" she nodded toward the ceiling. She meant Amy, of course.

"Yes, he is."

"But her name's Noble?" Donna had her papers settled and now looked at her, waiting.

"It's a long story," Claire said, hoping that would end the conversation.

"Didn't you go to Florida with him on spring break, what was it…your junior year? You and that other girl…Robin?" She didn't wait for a response, as she looked out the window, thinking back. "No one went on spring break back then, not like today. Wait! Now I remember, you hitchhiked with Robin…"

Claire felt a burn of embarrassment crawl up her cheeks. After thirty-something years, the shame of running away from home with Robin, hitchhiking to Florida, trying to find Liam in that ocean of kids, was enough to make her want to run out of that room. But things had been strained between them since her parents had forbidden her to see him. When he left for Florida, she'd been so afraid of losing him to someone else.

When he'd walked into her life at fifteen, Liam had opened a door into another world she desperately wanted to enter. And didn't she see it again and again each year as a teacher? There was a bad boy in every class, it seemed, mysterious, good-looking, with an ability to make girls, even smart ones, do stupid things.

"Hardly earth-shaking when you think about what kids do today," she joked, to cover her discomfort.

Donna chuckled. "You got that right. Especially with what I see." Then she opened the file and they got down to business.

As she sat there talking to Donna about her unnamed granddaughter's future, Claire couldn't help drifting back in her thoughts to the girl she'd been herself. Desperate to grow up and get far away from home. Crazy about Liam, certain he was her one and only love, her future. Afraid of losing him. Was she so different than Amy? Lonely, searching, trying to find her anchor in life. Trusting her heart to a boy who could never really be there for her. Then getting pregnant.

She had to tell Donna now that she had no idea who the father could be. Or what Amy had been up to the last year and a half. Again, not so different from herself. Her parents had had no idea she'd kept on seeing Liam long after they'd forbidden it during her sophomore year. She'd had a whole secret life of her own.

Donna wrote in the file for a long time, then closed it and looked up at Claire.

"This may be for the best. I know it's hard, but we have to think about the baby. Under the circumstances, the way she was born, your daughter's obvious reluctance…well," she smiled, as if running out of comforting words, "anyway, it was really nice seeing you again after all these years. You look great."

Claire stood up, a lump of sadness was rising in her throat. "Thanks, Donna."

She hurried out of the room.

8

STANDING IN THE MIDDLE OF A FIELD UNDER THE blazing morning sun, Claire looked across the Rockport Road Valley at the long, grassy furrow winding into the distance. Sweat trickled down her cheek and insects buzzed all around her. It was hard to believe that the empty gully she was trying to photograph here in the middle of nothing was once the hub of commerce. In other parts of the state, huge remnants of the canal had been obliterated by development. But in Jefferson County, large stretches of it remained untouched since its demise at the end of the last century. Empty of water, it now snaked through fields and woodlands, overgrown and lost in many places.

From where Claire stood beside the towpath, it was easy to see the remains of it, winding across the fields as far as she could see. She focused the camera again for a long distance shot. The rolls she'd taken the day before were disappointing. No matter how she shot it, trying to get an overview photo of the canal stretching into the distance, it still looked like nothing but an old ditch. In black-and-white there was no sense of the scope of the canal. So much for her talent with perspective.

She kept telling herself it didn't matter. She was just fulfilling her end of a bargain. Besides, maybe John Poole would never get his piece accepted, and these photos would end up, with his article, in a drawer. Somehow, that reasoning didn't work. Because she did care. As soon as she'd stepped out of her car and walked across the quiet field, she could sense the past and felt a tremor of excitement. It was the chance to bring history alive for people today.

Well over a hundred years ago, people in Lincoln and the surrounding parts of Jefferson County had relied on the canal for the essentials of daily life. Mules pulled barges loaded with flour, sugar, cotton, and tobacco along the towpath where she now stood. The Pohatcong Canal, once fed by the Pohatcong River, just a half mile to its east, ran from Pennsylvania to New York and bisected Jefferson County.

She finished shooting and zipped the camera back into her bag. It was time to go see Amy. As she got into her car on the shoulder of Rockport Road, Claire heard a distant rumble of thunder and looked up. It was the worst summer she could remember, thanks to El Niño wreaking havoc with the jet stream.

Driving toward Mechanicsburg, the thing she'd tried to keep off her mind since yesterday kept flashing before her on her windshield, like the quick images of a movie trailer. Her tiny granddaughter. Her mother, holding the baby, silent tears streaming down her cheeks. And then in Claire's own arms, her mouth rooting for the nipple of the bottle and then latching onto it ferociously, as if it might be taken from her at any moment. But mostly, those dark blue eyes staring up at her, the tiny dimple as she sucked. At that moment, Claire had realized it might be the last time she held the baby. Because if Amy went through with the adoption process, Claire would have to keep her distance. Already, despite her own internal warnings to herself, she was bonding with her.

Claire knew she had two choices: to let the baby go and let Amy move on with her life, as she seemed determined to do. Which would enable her to move on with her own life. Or to put all of her energy into stopping this, even if it meant raising the baby herself and putting her own life on hold for another twenty years, possibly losing Rick. At that point, when she'd finally be free, she'd be sixty-five, ready for Medicare.

Of course, her mother had offered to do it all. Fanny's desperation was a pitiful thing; the panic in her eyes, the harsh grief in her voice, as they sat in her kitchen yesterday after that hospital visit.

"You can't let her do this, Claire."

Claire had said nothing, staring out her mother's kitchen window at the cemetery in the distance.

"I can help. I could watch the baby. I could come and move in for a few weeks. Or Amy could live here, with me."

Claire knew Amy would never move in with them.

"Mom, you've got enough to do taking care of Dad. He doesn't seem to be doing well the past few days. He's moving much slower. And shaking more."

"He's upset about the baby. The doctor said stress really aggravates the Parkinson's dyskinesia."

Claire didn't ask how she'd told him, or what he'd said. She didn't want to know.

"Mom, maybe it's for the best, did that even occur to you? Think of the baby."

"That baby is our flesh and blood. There's a part of you and me in her, and Mama and Annie. Who knows who might get her? What if they abuse her? What if we never see her again, even if we try to find her!"

Claire had put her head in her hands and closed her eyes. She didn't need a guilt trip. She was consumed with enough guilt to power a small city.

"Amy's just scared," her mother went on. "She doesn't want this. Can't you see that? She's terrified. It'll make her grow up, don't you see, Claire? It did for you."

Claire had gotten up and walked out. She'd driven from her mother's house with her camera and began scouting locations to begin shooting for this morning. She had to ignore her mother's frantic pleas, escape the memory of the baby's searching eyes as she'd held her. She had to keep busy, or she'd lose her mind. Now, turning into the hospital parking lot, she again forced her mind away from her mother and the baby.

She conjured up images of Rick, rafting down the Colorado as he and his brothers plowed through rapids, roared over rocks. Rick loved to have fun. That was one of the things Claire loved about being with him. He was spontaneous, where she was serious. Everyone adored Rick; he was the center of every party they went to. With him, she felt like a kid again. For her entire life, it seemed, she'd been the grown-up, the care-giver. And though sometimes he seemed a bit selfish about indulging his whims, like his obsession with golf, she knew he'd worked hard all his life and earned the right to play.

As she walked past the nursery now, she stopped and stared at the baby's Isolette. It was empty. Could she really be gone already? Claire pressed her lips together, warning herself not to fall apart. This was for the best, no matter how difficult it seemed right now. She needed to be strong for Amy. As she walked away from the nursery, her throat began to ache with a growing lump of grief and unshed tears. She tasted something warm and metallic, and realized she'd bitten her lip. She reminded herself that Amy could barely take care of herself, much less this baby. And she wasn't ready to be a grandmother, much less a mother again. The baby would be adopted by a loving couple, well off, with everything a child could dream of. Donna, the social worker, had assured her of that yesterday.

Walking into Amy's room, she stopped suddenly, stunned. Her parents were sitting in the two chairs by the window. Her father was holding the baby across his lap, his arms trembling slightly, his head wobbling like one of those bobble-head dolls Eugene once had in the back of his car. Her mother looked up with a triumphant smile. They hadn't spoken since Claire had walked out of her kitchen.

Amy was sitting on the edge of the bed. "Her name is Rose," she said, her lips quivering as her eyes filled with tears.

In that instant, Claire turned and hurried back down the corridor. She found the ladies' room, shut the door, and locked it. In the mirror, she saw her face crumple, as tears of relief spilled down her cheeks. They were keeping the baby. Oh, how on earth had she imagined otherwise?

9

Tʜᴇʏ ᴡᴇʀᴇ ᴄᴏᴍɪɴɢ ʜᴏᴍᴇ ᴛᴏᴅᴀʏ, ᴀɴᴅ Fᴀɴɴʏ wished with all her heart she could be there to help. But she could sense Claire's tension, and when Claire was like that, Fanny knew it was best to keep a little distance. She'd go tomorrow. Joe would drive her to Lincoln; hopefully he'd be up to it. And she'd spend the afternoon helping Amy learn to care for her baby. If there was one thing she was good at, despite her age, the pain in her hip, and her diminishing energy, it was taking care of infants. Some people knew their true calling at an early age, and for Fanny it was babies.

When she was twenty-five, and almost ready to give up on marriage, Fanny worked at the dress factory in Greenwich Village. But she also helped Mama care for the house and her two older brothers, Anthony and Michael, who were also unmarried, but under no pressure like she was. Annie, who was five years older, had been married for seven years already, and had two babies. Each time she'd given birth, Fanny had gone with Mama. It had been like a long pajama party, cooking, eating, holding the babies, feeding them, talking and laughing in the middle of the night in hushed tones.

Annie was living on Long Island then, and Fanny missed her desperately. Fanny would take the middle-of-the-night feedings that no one wanted. And in the darkened room, with the hall light coming through a crack in the door, she would hold Annie's baby, a tiny hand clutching her finger, innocent eyes locked on her face, and she would feel a rush of love so fierce it hurt her heart. After two weeks, Fanny didn't want to leave. But Annie's husband, Phil, wanted his house and his wife back, even if it meant helping with the children himself. Fanny's vacation time was up anyway. Her heart broke as they pulled away, wondering if she'd ever have a husband, much less a baby, of her own. She lamented that without marriage there couldn't be babies. And as much as she was still waiting for love to enter her life, she'd wanted a baby even more.

She went upstairs now to get the laundry, ignoring the little electric prong jabbing her hip, tuning out Judge Judy's harsh voice lambasting another trashy defendant. Today, she would get everything done that she could; cleaning, laundry, ironing. Tonight she would cook a big pot of minestrone soup, because they would need nourishing food, especially Amy, who needed the iron. She would even make a few bottles of Mama's fennel tea, which all their babies drank to prevent colic.

What was that song Mama used to sing to their babies when she came to stay? She began to hum, trying to find the melody. Mama's own father had sung it to Mama and his other children. Something about birds. My God, she hadn't heard the song in over forty years. Pigeons, yes. And then it came to her, the melody as certain as her breathing:

My pigeon house, I'll open wide and set the pigeons free/They'll fly o'er fields on every side and light on the tallest tree/And when they return from their merry flight, I'll shut the door and say good night/ Coo a roo, coo a roo, coo a roo, coo a roo, coo a roo, coo a roo, a roo...

The steps blurred and Fanny stopped, holding the railing. She could hear Mama's voice singing that song, as clearly as if she were in the room. *Oh, Mama. How I miss you. And Annie. If only you were here to see our little Rose.*

It happened like that sometimes. She could go for years thinking about them, missing them, and her emotions would stay in check. And then suddenly, at an odd moment like this, the ache of longing for her family would take her knees out from under her. She sat on the steps. Because Mama and Daddy, Annie and Anthony and Michael were all gone. She was the youngest, and the only one left.

Stop it. Now there's Rose. And not just Rose. Claire and Amy both needed her, whether they'd admit it or not. Tomorrow morning, after their first night home with the baby, would be here before they knew it. They would be exhausted. So she'd better get her own work out of the way.

Babies brought lots of work: dirty diapers, boiling bottles, endless laundry, and exhaustion. But babies also brought songs, and smiles, and coos, and soft cheeks that were a miracle to kiss. Fanny intended to savor every moment of it. She would make sure Joe didn't stay up too late tonight, so they could leave first thing in the morning. Especially since he'd been acting upset since she told him about the baby. Maybe agitated, that would be the word.

Yes, it was embarrassing, for them at least, a granddaughter having a baby out of wedlock. No husband, not even a boyfriend in sight. But it was something more; Fanny couldn't quite put her finger on it. She'd started off by saying in general how different things were today, and wasn't it wonderful that even if a baby was illegitimate, people didn't hold it against the child anymore? Because after all, it was hardly the child's fault. The usual faint tremor of his hand began to accelerate. She kept going, though, talking next about poor Amy; her father had walked out when she was just a little thing and had nothing to do with her life, the bastard. No wonder she always seemed to be searching for something, having a hard time in life.

At one point, Joe held his fork midair, and it seemed he couldn't quite get it back to his plate. As it began to wave, she was afraid he'd hit himself in the face or poke his eye. She was just ready to reach over and steady his hand—which she never did, because he'd snap at her and tell her he could manage on his own—when he did get it back to the plate, where it fell with a clatter.

He sat there looking stunned then, when she finally got to the point of her story: that Amy had a baby. Quickly, she rushed on about how beautiful she was, and how they had to be supportive because Amy needed them.

He'd asked one thing only. "Where's the father?"

"She won't say. Probably another bum like Liam, who doesn't want to be part of his child's life."

And then Fanny got up and brought a coconut custard pie to the table, Joe's favorite. "But we're not going to bring that up. Because the most important thing is to make her realize she can't give that baby away. She's our great-grandchild, Joe. Our great-granddaughter!"

AT MIDNIGHT, Claire sat on the living room couch with her feet up, holding the baby, who'd just finished her bottle. It had taken her an hour to drink two ounces. She began heartily, her mouth rooting all over Claire's robe, her tiny fingers grabbing at the fabric, in a frantic search for food as Claire heated the formula in a pot of hot water, holding the baby in one arm, bouncing and shushing to calm her. Now, the baby was sated and fast asleep. Claire, though, was wide awake.

She stared at the baby's face. Rose. Her mouth was as pink and curved as a tiny rosebud, pursing every so often as if she were still drinking. She was doing well. Luckily she'd only had to be on the oxygen for part of that one day. For a newborn, and one who was early, she was exceptionally beautiful, without the puffy nose and distorted head that usually stayed after birth for a few weeks. Perhaps because her passage had been so quick. Swaddled like a papoose, she almost looked like a doll in Claire's arms, tiny and perfect.

How many parents thought that about their babies, only to be disappointed later on in life as they grew up? One thing Claire knew now, especially after all of her years teaching: when they placed that baby in your arms, you had no idea what hand you were being dealt. She'd seen it time and again with the parents of her students coming in to talk about a problem in school. Often they sat there, lost and perplexed, explaining that their son or daughter had been an easy, loving child. That there had been no indication of problems early on. And suddenly, as they became adolescents, blooming into their own adulthood, things had changed.

Some, like Amy, struggling to find themselves in the confusing landscape of high school, found themselves on treacherous paths, drifting far away from the children they once were. Like Jason, Abbie's oldest, a star athlete who'd gotten caught up in drugs. And yet Claire watched other kids navigate that same landscape, bypassing those treacherous paths and doing well. High school seemed to be the playing field where the seeds of so many futures were sown, but did it have to be that way? She knew she'd worried too much about Amy, but who wouldn't with what she'd seen? Some flew the nest and soared; some tumbled time and again.

Staring down at Rose, her mouth parted, her eyelids fluttering as her sleep deepened, Claire felt her innocence almost painful to behold. Claire wondered what Rose would be like when she reached those difficult teenage years. And if there really was anything to be done to change any of it.

Claire knew she hadn't been a perfect mother. She never claimed to be. If she was guilty of anything, it was trying too hard. Because an only child who asked for brothers and sisters, who longed for a father, who just wanted to be like most of the other families in this small town, was a child you caved in too much to. Even Claire could see that now.

Walking past Amy's room with Rose in her arms, Claire saw that Amy was fast asleep. Amy had begun to bleed heavily again yesterday, and the doctor had released her under one condition: she had to keep her feet up for a few days, and no exertion. Even in the light from the hall, Claire could see the dark circles under her eyes, her pale face slack with exhaustion. Tears filled her eyes as a surge of love for her daughter rushed through her. Why couldn't Amy forgive her, let her back into her heart?

Laying the baby in the bassinet in her own room, she thought of what she'd done early that morning, before leaving to pick them up at the hospital. She wasn't proud of her actions. But she'd felt she had no choice. Amy's tie-dyed bag had been left behind in the rush that afternoon she had the baby. For two days Claire circled it when she was home, trying to decide. Her friend Abbie, she knew, would call her crazy for even thinking twice. Esther, who was the high school nurse, kept secrets for half the students and part of the faculty. She'd understand her agony. No matter what, there were some boundaries you didn't cross. Maybe, though, that's what had gotten them to this estrangement in the first place, trying too hard to be fair. She should have been more of a hard-ass. Only that's how her own father had been, impossible to reach, or even talk to. Years ago, while still a teenager, Claire swore she would never treat her children that way.

But back then everything was so different; all her friends' parents were strict. Claire wondered if everyone felt this way as they got older, looking back on their own youth. Back then, just twenty-five years ago, living with someone was still a sin. And having a baby out of wedlock was an embarrassment that touched the whole family. Wasn't she proof of that? She could almost feel her parents' shame when she was pregnant with Amy, as her stomach grew and the neighbors looked at her questioningly. Now the nurses in the hospital hadn't blinked twice when Amy said she didn't know who the baby's father was. The baby came home as Rose Anne Noble. Her mother had gotten "Anne" thrown in at the last minute for her sister who died years ago. It was a nice name, Claire agreed, although she thought it a bit old-fashioned. Not really a choice she could ever have imagined Amy agreeing to.

But really, what did she know of her daughter anymore? Digging through Amy's purse, she'd found her driver's license and saw an Ashville, North Carolina, address. How or why Amy had ended up there, Claire had no idea. She'd also found a second license, for driving a bus. That was odd.

There was little money, but there was a health insurance card in the wallet, which relieved Claire because she knew the hospital stay would run into the thousands, and she'd wondered if Amy had been lying about being insured.

It wasn't until she opened the door to Amy's ancient VW Beetle that the reason for Asheville was answered. The car, like Amy's room, was a dump. Papers and food wrappers all over the floor, the seats piled with discarded clothing, shoes, loose change. It almost looked as if Amy might have lived out of the car for a while.

Scavenging through the debris, Claire had found a few lined sheets of paper, with Amy's blue slanted scrawl covering them. After the first few lines, Claire realized what she was holding—journal pages—and nearly stopped. This was sacred ground. As a high school teacher, if not a mother, she knew that. But it was too late. The first line hooked her:

> I've only met my Aunt Bonnie a few times in
> my life, the last about four years ago, when she
> showed up unexpectedly on a Harley with some
> old hippie who turned out to be a minister. When
> my mother opened the door and saw who it was,
> I thought she would shit a brick. But Bonnie had
> been pretty cool. When no one was listening, she
> whispered in my ear, "Listen, honey, you come see
> me anytime. I know I'm not your dad's favorite
> person in the world, but…well, that's just a lot

of bad history. I never had kids of my own and I'd love for us to get to know each other better."

Luckily, after driving hundreds of miles after my mother threw me out, she hadn't changed her mind.

Her house smelled like dogs, damp and stinky. I shuddered to think what the yard must be like, landmines everywhere.

Here, Claire had paused, almost laughing. Imagine Amy criticizing anyone else's cleanliness. She kept reading.

At first I thought, maybe this wasn't such a good idea, after all. But Bonnie sat me at the kitchen table and made some kind of tea. We talked for hours, even though my arms ached from all that driving, and I felt like I might fall asleep. I could see the resemblance to my father and me. Bonnie has the white skin and dark blue eyes, but her black hair is mostly silver now, in a long braid that falls halfway down her back. She wore dangly silver earrings and a purple tent of a dress. She looked like an old hippie. Under the baggy dress, I could see the soft mounds of her big boobs and I realized then the mystery of my own massive ones. It's not like my mother or grandmother have much in that department.

If Bonnie was surprised I showed up out of the blue, she didn't show it. She seemed to totally buy my story that I was taking a semester off and traveling. She joked about her nephew, my father that is, being this stuffy guy now and who would have guessed when he was "such a little wild boy." I didn't say anything to that.

Finally, she put me in a little room with a pull-out couch that seemed to be for the dogs. But I'm so wired from the tea and the drive, I can't sleep. A big, black dog named Barney keeps laying on my feet, so I can't move. Tomorrow, Bonnie says she's taking me to work with her.

What am I doing here? It seemed exciting when I first came down the mountains into Asheville. A whole new place to be someone else. But now, in bed, it's still just me. I wish she'd let me sleep for a week. Or maybe the whole summer. Maybe I'd wake up different somehow. I asked her if she knew where my father was. She said we'd talk about it tomorrow.

The baby whimpered and Claire put the binkie in her mouth. She began sucking immediately and calmed right down. Claire turned the night-light on and lay back down in her own bed. She was exhausted, too. Closing her eyes, she thought about the agreement she'd made with the social worker. Six months. They would let Amy take the baby home if Claire would allow them to live with her for six months, so that she could oversee the baby's care. Otherwise, they were calling in the Division of Youth and Family Services for a full evaluation before releasing Rose with Amy.

"Claire, you don't want DYFS involved," Donna had told her, as they sat in her little office again. "I had a long chat with your daughter. She could really use some counseling, and I'm going to make that part of our bargain here. I think she's a good kid. But," and here Donna shuffled papers and put down her pen before leveling her gaze at Claire again, "she's like a lot of kids who never had a father."

"I tried to…"

"No, no. I'm not saying this is your fault in any way. I see the dead-beat dad situation day in and day out. But we're just starting to realize that these kids have effects that carry on into adulthood. Abandonment issues. Depression. Inability to commit."

She knew Donna was doing her a favor, and that she was right about everything. So Claire had agreed to the six months, even feeling guilty about harboring any high school resentments against her. Staring at the ceiling now, she knew this promise changed everything. Rick would be moving in with her in September, after the wedding. Would he be willing to share his home with Amy and the baby? She had to believe he would. Rick was a good man, a kind man. They would work through this somehow. Besides, there was still her mother, who was dying to help out.

Her mother was in fact coming tomorrow. Claire decided now that that might also be a good opportunity to go out and shoot more pictures of the canal. Between being at the hospital and staying home so much, she was already feeling trapped. She had to hang onto her new life, even if it was just by her fingernails.

10

They'd been late because Joe insisted on picking up a crib for the baby. Fanny told him emphatically that the bassinet would be fine for at least two months, maybe three. But he pulled into the department store anyway. Fanny knew it was really more that he needed something to do. They would be at Claire's for hours helping with the baby, and Joe needed to kill time.

Claire was unloading bottles and nipples from the dishwasher when she'd walked in, urging her to hurry outside to help him carry the big box inside.

"He's so damn stubborn," she said to Claire. "We should have been here an hour ago."

"It's okay, Mom, I'm sure he meant well," Claire said, drying her hands and hurrying out the door.

Together they'd carried the box up the front porch and into the hall. It was flat and wide, and heavy. Claire's father was gray and huffing as they stood in the hallway.

"Dad, let's leave it here for now," Claire said, as he pulled a handkerchief out of his pocket and wiped his face. "I have to make room for it upstairs."

Now, as Fanny fed Rose, she could hear him banging away, putting it together in the spare bedroom upstairs. He was so obstinate, he was going to give himself a heart attack one of these days.

Sitting on the couch, she looked down at Rose, lying across her lap. Was there anything more innocent, Fanny wondered, than an infant falling asleep? Nearly finished with her bottle, Rose's eyes began to roam from side to side as her lids lowered. Her mouth became still, like an O, and Fanny pulled the bottle away. A drop of milk clung to her lower lip. Looking up now at Fanny, she began making little noises, like tiny purrs. Her eyes began to roll back, flutter, then come back to Fanny again. She remembered the first time Eugene had done this, she'd almost screamed, thinking he was having a seizure or something. Not knowing yet that babies had many ways of falling asleep. Oh, Eugene had scared her so much, with his asthma and rashes; allergic and constantly sick, it seemed. Yes, she had spoiled him, she knew that. And poor Claire, just a toddler, left to play alone, or propped in her high chair while Fanny tried to soothe Eugene or take him into the bathroom and run the shower to ease his breathing. Claire had been such a good, easy baby. Like little Rose.

"Hey, Grandma."

Fanny looked up. Amy stood in the doorway wearing pajamas, her long black hair wild, her face as white as a sheet.

"What are you doing up? The doctor said to keep your feet up."

Amy came in and sat beside her, staring at the baby. She put her feet up on the coffee table.

"There. My feet are up. What's all the banging about?"

"Your grandfather is putting together a crib for Rose. It's white, with roses carved on the sides."

Amy's eyes filled with sudden tears that spilled quickly down her cheeks.

"What, sweet pea?"

Amy said nothing. Fanny took one of Amy's hands. "It's going to be all right. You'll see. And don't forget, your body is readjusting its hormones."

"I..." But Amy couldn't continue; her mouth twisted trying not to sob. After a few moments, which Fanny let her cry out, she breathed a shaky sigh. "She's so beautiful, Grandma. I don't deserve her."

Fanny squeezed her hand. It seemed just yesterday that Amy was a tiny baby lying across her lap, filling her heart with such love, such joy. And her life with purpose.

"You did the right thing, Amy. She's our flesh and blood."

"I don't know. I feel like I'm being selfish. Maybe the right thing is to give her a real home. A mother and a father, people with real jobs and money. What do I have to give her? I don't have a career. Christ, I don't even know what I want to do with my life. What kind of life can I give her?"

"We'll help you. Don't worry about that. It would be different if you didn't have a family."

Amy closed her eyes. "I don't know. I'm just so tired. I feel like I'm going to be tired the rest of my life."

"Close your eyes, honey. Rest. I'm going to put Rose in her bassinet and I'll heat up the minestrone I brought. It's full of iron."

Fanny was glad Claire had brought the bassinet downstairs to a corner of the living room when Joe insisted on taking the crib up, because now she didn't have to climb the steps.

"Gram, no!" Amy shouted, as she lay Rose in it.

"What?"

Amy got up and came over, turning Rose onto her back.

"But babies love to sleep on their stomachs."

Amy shook her head. "No, the doctor said not until she's older. To prevent SIDS."

"SIDS?"

Amy looked uncomfortable. "Crib death," she said softly.

"Oh."

She'd never heard that. She didn't want to tell Amy that the stomach was better because if they spit up they wouldn't choke. Suddenly she felt uncertain, and went into the kitchen. As she put the big soup pot on the stove, Claire walked in the back door.

"How did it go?" Fanny asked.

"Oh, I'm not sure yet," Claire said, putting her camera bag down on the desk. "I'm just experimenting with shots right now. I didn't really want to do this project at first, to be honest, but it's actually a good challenge for me. And a distraction. Especially since I'm not going to Cape Cod."

Fanny turned to her daughter. She, too, looked pale and tired. A baby could take a lot of energy. "I know how much that meant to you."

Claire shrugged and gave her a little smile. "What could I do?"

Suddenly, something crashed upstairs.

"Oh, Jesus," Claire muttered and ran out of the room.

Fanny sat at the kitchen table, feeling as if the life were suddenly draining out of her. Was today the day? Because it was coming, she knew that as certain as the beating of her heart. One day it was all going to change. It was only a matter of time.

"TELL ME YOU DIDN'T let him drive home," Amy demanded.

"Honey, he insisted; you know how he can be. I think he's fine."

"Are you crazy? What if he...I don't know, can't move his foot or something."

"He just lost his balance; he was trying to keep the crib together while he put the screws in. He should have waited; it's a two-person job. Besides, Grandma thinks he forgot to take his pills this morning. We made sure he took them with his lunch."

Amy shook her head and gave her the look. Claire knew there was truth to what Amy was saying. But her father was...her father. No one argued with him, or talked back. How did you tell a man like that he couldn't do something? You didn't tell a man like him anything. He was the one who did the ordering.

"How are you feeling?" she asked to change the subject.

"Tired."

"Are you still bleeding?"

"Yes."

"Maybe you should call the doctor, he said—"

"I know what he said."

"What were you doing in Asheville?"

Amy gave her an angry look. "Snooping through my things?"

Claire slammed the bottle on the counter. "Amy, this is ridiculous. You won't tell me a thing, we've got the social service people monitoring us—"

"Oh, right, because I'm unfit. And you are."

"Jesus, why does everything have to come down to what a lousy mother I am?"

Amy shook her head and then, to Claire's surprise, began to sob. She turned and ran out of the room and up the stairs.

Hormones, she thought, as she went in the cellar to start a wash. Hopefully this would get easier. Rick would be back in just a few days. It had to.

AT TEN O'CLOCK that night the phone rang.

"Can I sleep on your couch?" Abbie asked.

"What do you think?" Claire answered, as she did every six months or so.

Ten minutes later Abbie walked in with a bottle of wine.

The first time Claire had dinner at Abbie and Tom's, just a few months after Abbie sold her the house in Lincoln years ago, she'd noticed that although both of them talked a lot, they didn't actually talk to each other. She and Abbie had become fast friends right away, and so did their little girls, who were the same age. In those early years, Amy played with Missy and they were young enough not to notice the big differences at first. But, as Amy matured, Missy remained trapped in the world of a child.

Claire let Abbie vent for the first half hour as they polished off their first glasses of wine.

"I hate him," she said. "I don't know why he doesn't get it."

Tom was a functioning alcoholic who held a job, got through life, and provided for his family. In the beginning, Abbie wondered why he couldn't just stop drinking if he really loved her and Missy and Jason. Now, after years of it, they shared only a house, the responsibilities of Missy, and the occasional dinner with friends. Abbie went through a predictable cycle every few months or so that Claire could now almost chart on her calendar. Anger, then distance from her husband, followed by a dismal malaise, then depression. Then came the worst period of all, the "what a waste" cycle, where she lamented that she was on the far side of forty and living without sex or love, wanting more, trapped in this situation that she didn't seem able to extricate herself from. Claire didn't even know anymore whether if Tom did quit drinking, Abbie could love him again. But Tom didn't seem to be affected by Abbie's actions. If anything, he seemed to be drinking more and more. Claire had run into him at Nykun's deli one morning, and his breath had reeked. Did he drink in the morning, she wondered, or was it from the night before? She knew one thing, though; if Abbie didn't do something soon, she might end up taking care of both Missy and Tom.

"Anyway, enough about me," Abbie said, pouring them each another glass of wine. "You've heard this all before, ad nauseum. What about you? How's it going? Have you told lover boy yet?"

Claire took a big sip and shook her head. She always felt guilty complaining to Abbie. Over the years her worries and complaints about Amy had always seemed silly compared to what Abbie faced with Missy having Down's syndrome. And then Jason on drugs. Next to them, Amy just seemed like the typical rebellious teenager. And then the typical floundering young adult.

"Come on, out with it," Abbie urged.

Claire took another sip, so tired, the wine buzzing through her already. "I'm not ready for this." It came out half laugh, half cry. "I don't want to be tied down. I was about to spread my wings for the first time, really, in my adult life."

"Oh, sweetie," Abbie whispered.

"I love that baby already. She's just beautiful. When I held her before, she had hiccups and her gold hair stuck up straight; she looked so helpless, so innocent. Amy was sleeping, oblivious. She's had a hard time, with the bleeding and everything. I don't know, Abbie." She sat there, as if blindsided suddenly by it all. As if it had all finally sunk in. "This was supposed to be my chance. I'm supposed to get married. I was going to have a dream summer on Cape Cod, become a real photographer, studying with this world-renowned teacher. Rick has everything planned out, everything I've been waiting my whole life for."

"You have every right to feel this way, Claire. Who wouldn't? Because you haven't had it so easy. Oh, as much as I complain, at least I had Tom, he's been there all along, I didn't do it alone. You did. I always admired that, you know. How you raised Amy all by yourself. And I didn't have the guts to leave him and do the same thing."

"Don't say that." She grabbed Abbie's hand and shook it. "Do not say that. If anyone deserves a medal, it's you. I don't know if I could have done what you have with Missy. She's your whole life, she'll always need you. At least with Amy, hopefully after these six months..."

"That's what scares me the most," Abbie said, tears filling her eyes. "What happens when I'm gone someday? Who will take care of her?"

"Maybe Jason..."

Abbie shrugged. "Maybe. I pray to God. I light a candle for him every day. I don't know what's worse, a child who can never get better, or one who could but chooses not to."

They finished off the wine and Claire covered Abbie with a blanket on the couch.

She went upstairs and checked on Rose, who slept soundly in her new crib. Amy was snoring softly, spread out on her stomach on her bed. Claire felt a flood of emotion for them, her two girls, with the promise of their whole lives ahead of them. But she wasn't young anymore. She was at an age where you were suddenly aware that you only had a certain amount of time left. And it was supposed to be for her.

11

WAITING FOR THE SUN TO RISE, CLAIRE COULD ALMOST imagine that it was a hundred years ago. She stood at a secluded stretch of the old Pohatcong Canal, nothing more than a grassy ravine winding through a leafy patch of woods. From her vantage point on the old towpath, there were no houses, no electrical wires visible, and even the traffic on Rockport Road just a quarter mile away seemed nonexistent this early in the morning.

Her vision was to capture the first golden rays of sunlight filtering through the canopy of trees and illuminating the old canal. She checked her watch again. Still five minutes to go. She scanned the mountains to the east, watching the brightening pink band of sun lift the gray light of dawn that hung over the mountaintops. She pulled her camera to her eye, adjusted the viewfinder, and waited. And her mind began to wander.

Rick was coming home tomorrow, and once again the little drummer began tapping at her stomach. When he'd called her cell the night before, she didn't tell him that she was home, in Lincoln, and not in Cape Cod. She said nothing of Amy and the baby. She planned to be waiting for him at his house when he returned. And then she would tell him everything.

The first fiery tip of the sun peeked over the mountain, and she pulled the camera to her eye again, quickly focusing the viewfinder and clicking the first shot. Her new plan was to frame the series with a dawn and dusk shot of the canal. Again and again over the next five minutes she snapped the shutter, moving constantly as she changed angles, searching for the perfect image: the quiet canal wakened by the first light of day. Three rolls later, she zipped her camera into the bag, excited. The lighting was perfect, rose-colored beams of sun splashing through the branches, lighting the canal like a vision from the past. In black-and-white, they'd look like crepuscular rays from heaven.

As she walked along Rockport Road back to her car, a sleek racing bike whisked by. A moment later, the rider stopped and then turned and pedaled toward her.

When he removed his helmet, she was stunned to see it was John Poole.

"Well hi," she said.

"You're out here early," he said, as he caught his breath.

She held up her camera bag. "Just catching some sunrise shots of the canal. Fulfilling our little bargain."

"I'm glad you brought that up," he said, wiping his face on his shirt-sleeve. "You really don't have to, you know. It wasn't fair of me—"

"Too late," she said, "I'm already into it. I love history. In fact, I'm a history teacher." And she didn't want to owe this man anything.

"I didn't know that." He paused. "I should have called you so we can talk a little more about it. I realize I haven't given you much direction."

"That's all right. I've been experimenting with some ideas."

"Well, this is perfect timing. Can you follow me back to the house? I have something I've been wanting to show you."

"What about your ride?"

"This is the end of the ride for me, I was heading back anyway," he said, strapping his helmet back on. "Come on. You'll be amazed at what I've found."

He gave her directions and rode off. She stood there for a

moment in the early morning sunlight. It was tempting, but she really needed to get back. She'd planned to at least get these rolls developed before Amy and Rose woke. She'd fed the baby just before she left. And then her parents were coming to stay with Rose, while she drove Amy to her first counseling session. Her bleeding had stopped, but she still wasn't allowed to drive. Amy had wanted to put it off until she was feeling a bit better, but Claire didn't want to cancel the appointment, which Donna Laverty had arranged before releasing Amy.

Still, it wasn't even seven o'clock. She could develop the rolls tonight. She threw her things into the car and headed up Rockport Road. A half hour wouldn't hurt.

FANNY COULDN'T REMEMBER the last time Joe had gotten up so early. She made him breakfast, then went upstairs to shower and dress. Dutifully, she did five minutes on her treadmill first. She was thrilled. They could be at Claire's by nine and spend the entire day, hopefully. True, she was exhausted yesterday by the time they got home. And Joe had groaned a few times when he'd moved in bed last night. She wondered if he was sore from falling. Not that he said a word about it. Luckily he'd landed partly on the mattress. Last night, as she couldn't stop talking about Rose, how adorable she was, how Fanny could swear she'd made a cooing sound already, Joe had listened quietly.

"She must look like the father," he'd said then. "The gold hair."

"I suppose," Fanny had said. "But don't forget, Claire had blond hair until she was about five, and then it changed."

"She doesn't look like Claire," he said.

"No, she doesn't." She really didn't look like any of them, Fanny thought.

Taking off her nightgown, Fanny realized with a start that it was July. No wonder it was so hot. It was so easy to lose track of the days and months when you didn't have a routine anymore. After Joe had stopped working the part-time job after he'd been diagnosed last year, one day seemed pretty much like the next. He didn't need to get up early anymore. Meals could be whatever time they wanted them to be. But she'd clung to the routine of their former life, needing the regularity to her days. Otherwise, she knew she'd feel like someone just floating through life. Mama, even in her last years with them, when everything was such an effort, began each day by having a cup of coffee and planning the day's meals. And that had become the sun around which her days revolved.

Forty minutes later, Fanny put on a light shift. It was already humid and sticky, so she turned on the window air conditioner as she dressed. She'd have rather had the windows open, felt the soft summer breeze, heard the birds. But it was becoming unbearable.

When she went downstairs, she was surprised to see Joe standing in the middle of the kitchen.

"Didn't you hear me? I've been calling you," he cried.

And then she realized that he was stuck there. He couldn't move. His legs trembled with the effort of trying to take a step. His plate was on the linoleum floor, cracked in half, toast crumbs scattered.

"Oh my God, Joe," she said, going to him, taking his arm. "How long have you been standing there?"

He glanced at the clock on the stove. "Thirty minutes."

"You haven't been able to move for thirty minutes? Did you remember to take your pills?"

"Yes! I took the damn pills."

She took his arm and began pulling gently. His feet didn't move, planted like a stubborn child who wanted his way. She tugged harder.

"No, don't…"

He began to sway. She stepped next to him, leaning her weight against him to steady him, wrapping an arm around his back. But he was too off balance, wobbling now harder and harder. For a moment she thought about just stepping away. He was going to fall. And if she stayed beside him, she was going down with him. She pushed harder, trying to keep him upright, but his weight was coming down on her, her own knees buckling. She glanced at the phone on the wall, realizing too late that she should have called someone first.

PULLING INTO THE LONG gravel driveway, Claire was surprised to see a charming old two-story house in the middle of a grassy clearing surrounded by woods. The white clapboard was peeling and there were slates missing on the roof, but as Abbie would say, "it had good bones." Rick would probably call it a "tear-down." Old shrubs hid the foundation and wild orange lilies bloomed everywhere.

John Poole was just getting off his bike beside the house as she walked toward him. "Take a look around, I'll just be a minute," he said, unzipping his jersey as he walked to the side of the house.

She realized she was looking at the back of the house from the driveway, and walked around to the front. She nearly did a double-take. Not twenty feet from the house she saw a piece of the old canal, the same grassy swale, with the worn towpath beside it. But there were also the remains of an old lock still evident, where barges had been lifted and lowered to a different level of water, depending on which direction the boat was heading. The canal appeared to parallel Rockport Road. No wonder his crankiness had disappeared.

This would be a great place to wander with a metal detector, she thought, imagining what might have been dropped and buried over the years. At the sound of water, she turned and saw John standing under an outside shower on the side of the house. He was wearing nothing but the black spandex biking shorts. Quickly she turned back to the lock.

A few minutes later he was beside her again, in cutoff jeans and a T-shirt. She followed him into the house. It was like a time warp; she'd stepped into the 1950s. The first floor consisted of just two rooms, a living room and kitchen. The living room was brimming with a floral sofa and chintz curtains, vases of plastic flowers, books and doilies, and all the other evidence of an old woman. Here and there were the odd items that must be John's. A small stereo, a pair of work boots, a baseball cap. Then she noticed the old bookcase filled with recent titles and two shelves of books on CD. She stopped to scan a few titles.

"My secret vice," he said.

"I guess as a writer, you must get tired of reading so much."

He shook his head. "Nah, I'm actually dyslexic."

She looked at him. He was broad-shouldered and rugged-looking, his black hair cut short, his angular face deeply tanned, and she thought again that he seemed more an outdoorsman.

"I spent my first ten years in school thinking I just wasn't as smart as anyone else. Then I had a teacher who wasn't going to pass me until I could write a term paper for real. Until then, I just got pushed along with the crowd. I was a decent ball player, you see."

"But didn't you get any special help?"

"No. I come from a pretty poor neighborhood in Boston. No special ed for us back then. Just the school of hard knocks. Anyway, Mrs. Tickner, she was a tough old broad, but man could she dissect a novel. So I became an expert on Dickens and finally managed to work through my problem. Let's just say 'it was the best of times, it was the worst of times.'"

She found herself laughing. He was a pretty interesting guy, and not as intimidating as she'd first thought.

"Anyway, come into the kitchen, that's where the big surprise is."

The kitchen was a big, sunny room with a woodstove, an old metal table, and chairs like those she remembered from her childhood. The counter was filled with painted canisters, an old toaster and coffeepot, and again it was like stepping back in time. She sat at the table and looked out the wide window, overlooking the canal. As he pulled a plastic storage bin from the pantry, John explained that he'd found an old trunk tucked in a dark corner under the rafters.

"It was falling apart," he said, setting the container on the big metal table. "But inside was all this."

He pulled the lid off the bin and the deep, musty smell of aged paper rose up. She looked at the jumbled pile of postcards, newspapers, a few notebooks, and some old papers.

Still kneeling beside her, he looked up and smiled. They were inches apart, and she could see that he was still overheated from riding, with little beads of sweat trickling down his neck. Their eyes held for a brief second and then he looked down into the bin.

"Some of the things were damaged or just fell apart when I tried to take them out," he said.

She lifted an old sepia-toned photo carefully out of the box, its brittle edges cracking at her touch. She looked at it closely. A boy of about sixteen was leading a mule along the towpath. A rope tied around the animal's neck pulled a barge through the waters of the canal. The boy had long, scraggly hair and wore no shoes. In the distance she saw an old building that looked familiar.

"I want to get all of it organized," John Poole said in the silent room. "And make sure the estate won't mind us using some of it for a while. I doubt they even knew it was up there."

She looked up at him. "This building looks like Raynor's feed store," she said. "I know where this was taken, just on the west side of Lincoln. I didn't realize the canal ran through there."

John stood and looked over her shoulder. "The store probably got its supplies brought in by canal barge back then. Just like people get their stuff delivered by truck today."

"That store's still there," she said, amazed by the thought. "I get my birdseed there."

John handed her another photo. "What do you think of this one?"

A stern-faced man stood beside a woman with a baby on her hip. They were dressed formally and stood rigidly, as if she might have over-starched their clothes. They stared into the camera like deer caught in headlights.

"That's the one thing I always hate about these old photos, you never see anyone's true expression. Do you know what I mean? The look in their eyes at that moment. Were they happy? Depressed? They couldn't move or blink for almost a minute or the picture would blur," she explained.

"It must have been a hard life."

Claire nodded. She looked at the details in the background, her favorite thing in old photos, all the little trappings of a life gone by. A line of wash in the yard, a broom propped by the fence, lace curtains in the windows. She noticed the trim around the windows and the odd little front door.

"Oh my God, John, it's—"

"This house," he said, nodding his head with a smile. "They must have lived here. He was obviously the lock tender at one time."

"You know, it would be interesting to take pictures at these exact same locations today." She looked up at him. "And then print them next to the old photos, to show how they've changed, or not changed, in the last hundred years."

"That's exactly what I was thinking."

"You're kidding. You were thinking the same thing? That's quite a coincidence."

He was already shaking his head.

"Oh, right, I forgot, you don't believe in coincidences."

"Maybe I'm crazy, but I don't. I think some things are meant to happen." His eyes held hers.

It was an odd thing to say.

"Anyway, I was going to suggest that once I get the okay, you take all this with you," he went on, "and sort through it. See what you might want to use, and then…"

She looked back at the photo. It felt so good to be distracted for a little while. Because for the last thirty minutes or so, she hadn't thought about Amy or the baby or how she was going to tell Rick tomorrow night when he came home. And these pictures were incredible; visual proof of a past that existed right here where they now stood. She thought of all the dramas in life that might have taken place in this very house. The woman in the picture, her own life unfolding within these walls. The thought thrilled her.

"…so if it's all right, we could meet again next week and see if that works," John concluded, and she realized she'd daydreamed through half of what he'd said.

She looked up. He was watching her, waiting for her answer. "Sure, next week is fine." She looked into the box, at the jumbled heap of things. Pieces of people's lives, remnants of history. Like treasures from the past. "And if you get permission, I'll take just a little at a time home with me," she said. "I wouldn't feel comfortable taking the whole thing."

Twenty minutes later, when Claire finally arrived home, she could hear the baby crying from the driveway. Amy was on the couch, holding her and rocking back and forth, when she walked in. The baby's face was red as she flailed, arching her back against Amy's shoulder. Amy was shushing her, patting her back. Claire's heart stirred at the scene.

"Where have you been?" Amy cried out. "Grandma called. They're at the hospital!"

FANNY SAT in the hospital room looking at her husband, the IV in his hand feeding him painkillers, a monitor strapped to his chest. It was here, she thought. Everything would now change, just as she'd been fearing. She was a fool. She should have been ready.

She'd been blaming him, for not taking his pills, for not using a cane. And for getting worked up about stupid things. But the doctor said it was just the way the disease progressed. There would be good days and bad days. Some days he might seem almost normal. Others he would have a hard time moving at all. At some point, the Parkinson's would advance to the next stage and the good days would be gone. But he assured them that they weren't there. Not yet. Luckily, neither one of them had been hurt too badly.

They'd both been examined on arrival, but Fanny knew she was fine. She'd be sore tomorrow, no doubt. But Joe had a slight fracture of his pelvis. Still they would keep him only a day or so, evaluate the Parkinson's more fully, structure a new course of medication.

Claire walked in now. She'd been outside using her cell phone.

"Eugene is in Europe on business," she said. "Barbara's trying to reach him."

She'd asked Claire not to call him. She hated for Eugene to hear this while he was in a business meeting or driving to an appointment. He would be so upset. And what could he do, really, from thousands of miles away?

"The nurse came in a few minutes ago," she said, as Claire leaned on the windowsill. "They want to keep him for a few days."

Behind Claire, she could see through the window that it was a beautiful summer day. Even though it was so hot, the sun shone cheerfully, tiny white clouds sailing across the blue sky. The kind of day she would have sat under a shady tree in the yard with the baby in her arms, feeling like she was in heaven for a little while.

"How is Baby Rose doing?"

"She's fine."

"Did she get up a lot last night?"

"Three times."

"You look exhausted."

Her pretty daughter, who'd never looked her age, suddenly did. Her hair was pulled back in a clip, brown wisps all over the place. There were gray crescents under her eyes. And she was biting her lip the way she used to when she was little, when she'd sometimes make it bleed.

"I could come and stay tonight and help," Fanny offered.

"Mom, how could you do that?" Claire shook her head. "It would be too much. Daddy needs you now. Let's just see what the doctor says, okay?"

"Mmmmn nt shhhing," Joe mumbled.

I'm not staying. Already Fanny knew what he was saying, drugged and half-asleep. But she knew he could talk all he wanted, no one would be listening to his orders now. The doctor thought a little time in rehab with some physical therapy might improve things a bit, once they got his medicine right.

But that meant he wouldn't be coming home for a little while. And Fanny had never spent a night alone. Ever.

She knew she was being selfish. If she went home with Claire, then Claire would have to bring her back and forth from Lincoln tomorrow, besides taking care of Amy and the baby. Fanny knew she needed to be here in the hospital as much as she could, because she knew nurses everywhere were overworked, and she'd just read in her AARP magazine that the most important thing when a loved one was hospitalized was for someone to be there. Mistakes were made all the time.

But if she had to be here for Joe, she wouldn't be able to help with the baby.

EUGENE CALLED HER, waking Claire up just a half hour after she'd finally fallen asleep. Before she could get a word out, he broke into a string of excuses as to why he couldn't possibly come just now.

Was she supposed to applaud?

Over the years, more than anything, Claire had wanted to feel the closeness to her brother that they'd once shared when they lived together in their parents' house. Back then when they were kids they'd shared the same secret dream: to escape the prison of their home. They would joke that they were the inmates, their father the warden. Their mother, of course, was the cook. Late at night, after their parents were asleep, they would talk out loud about the places they would live, exciting, adventurous, far away from Jefferson County. When Eugene enlisted in the army at just eighteen, she'd cried. He promised he would always stay in touch. But time and distance were a cruel enemy.

Now he sounded rushed and distracted.

"Look, we need to start thinking ahead. We're lucky Mom didn't get hurt, too," she told him. "If Dad can't come home for a while, or if Mom can't take care of him, we need to have a plan." The way she figured it, she'd held down the fort without his help all these years. It was his turn now. Maybe he could add a wing onto his McMansion.

"Well, what about looking into one of those assisted living places? It's not like a nursing home, which Mom would dread," he said. "A friend of mine moved his parents into one out here and they just love it. He says it looks like a country club, but the medical help is there if you need it. And it sounds like they should get Dad stabilized and functioning pretty well after some therapy, so it could be perfect."

"That's a great idea," she said. "Maybe you could check that one out. California is always a step ahead. I'm sure it would be nicer than anything here."

"Come on, sis, you know they'd never live here. Christ, they've never even come out for a visit. They'll want to stay near you. Near home."

She took a deep breath. "Look, I can't take care of them, I just can't. You need to step in here. My life has just gotten a whole lot more complicated than I—"

"I know, I know. Mom told me about the baby. Congratulations."

Congratulations? She was too tired to argue with that one.

"The point is, I've got my hands full, Eugene. My fiancé is going to be home tomorrow night. I'm supposed to get married at the end of the summer, remember? Rick has already sold his place and is supposed to move in here. I'm not sure how he's going to handle Amy and the baby, but I can guarantee you one thing: throw in Mom and Dad and it'll all be over."

She realized she'd just voiced the thing she'd been dancing around in her own mind since Amy had the baby. She'd been dreading being away from Rick for the summer. Now she was almost dreading him coming home. He'd be surprised, and happy to see her. But how would he react to the reasons why?

"Listen, I have to run," Eugene said. "We're just finishing a business dinner and dessert's about to be served. That's when we nail them. If anything changes, just call Barbara, she'll have my contact info."

Sure, Claire thought, as if Barbara would care. When Eugene married her, Claire knew any hope of getting close to her brother again was long gone. Barbara, who'd grown up with a nanny and a maid, made no secret of her desire to stay as far away from Fanny and Joe and their blue-collar life as possible.

She hung up and turned the light off. Now that the baby was sleeping, she knew she had to get back to sleep quickly. And that was the kiss of death. As she lay there, she thought about Amy. She'd come out of her room earlier and offered to do the eleven o'clock feeding. Claire had been surprised, but glad. She stayed in the kitchen to watch, while quietly doing the day's dishes, readying the bottles and pacifiers for the next twenty-four hours. When the baby didn't burp, just fussed and whimpered against Amy's chest, Claire had taken her and sat her on her lap, a hand on her stomach while patting her back. A loud burp came instantly. Amy left the room in a huff, as if Claire had committed a crime.

Rolling onto her back, Claire knew she wouldn't fall asleep now. She'd felt like this in college, the night before a final; or when she was being observed teaching. She tried to picture Rick, probably back at the hotel by now, having a final dinner with his brothers. He had such a good relationship with his family. He often joked that it was because they lived so far apart and couldn't get in each other's hair. How was he going to react tomorrow night when she told him about their surprise additions?

The next six months weren't going to be easy. Amy had to find a job. Arrange day care. Get her act together. Claire had done it all, and she'd been even younger than Amy. But it was hard, she'd certainly admit that.

FANNY MADE TWO DECISIONS that night. She was going to learn to drive. And she would no longer let herself be afraid to sleep in her own house alone.

She locked everything up and turned on the television, even though she was too tired to watch it. The noise, the voices, even the blaring commercials were comforting. It was normal, she realized, and more than anything, she wanted to feel normal.

Because a slow panic was beginning to rise in her chest. Aside from Alzheimer's, her other biggest fear was going into one of those homes. Not that she needed one. No, she was just fine; she'd manage here as long as she could. But Joe wasn't just fine.

The doctor had told them that falls were common with Parkinson's patients. With some physical therapy Joe might get by with a cane, which he'd been avoiding, but a walker one day soon was more likely. He said they were lucky; the fall could have been worse. And then he said the words she'd been dreading: he didn't think Fanny was going to be able to take care of Joe by herself. And he mentioned the words "assisted living." Fanny was no fool. It was like the statement that junior high school got you ready for high school. In a year or two they'd be graduating, and going into a full-fledged nursing home.

She brewed a pot of decaf, figuring she'd save the extra in the fridge for tomorrow night. Then she opened the yellow pages. There were lots of driving schools. How hard could it really be? she thought. Kids learned how to drive every day, and she was certainly a lot smarter than a sixteen-year-old. Then she could drive to the store, or church, or if she really got brave, even to Lincoln to see the baby, without bothering Claire or having to waste so much money on a taxi.

As she grabbed for the phone, it rang suddenly, and she dropped the phone book, startled. She was even more nervous than she'd realized.

"Hey, Ma. How's Dad doing?"

"Oh, Eugene." And damn, she tried so hard, but she started crying. "He just looks so pathetic. Like he aged twenty years."

"Yeah, but the doctor said he'll be okay. They'll get him up and walking tomorrow and start the therapy."

"You talked to the doctor?"

"Of course. Look, I know I'm far away, and sometimes it seems I don't..."

"Now, Eugene, don't even start. You send us so much money, it's crazy. You have a hard job, little kids, I don't want—"

"Ma! *Ma!* Stop." She could hear him take a deep breath. "I know I can't be there, but I'm going to make sure Dad gets the best treatment, the best doctors, possible."

"But did the doctor tell you that maybe it would be better if Daddy didn't come home?"

A big pause. "Yeah, Ma, he did say something like that. But you know what?"

"What?"

"Maybe that wouldn't be such a bad thing. I was telling Claire, some of those places out here, they're like country clubs. You can play cards, get dressed up for dinner, you'll have friends your own age, people to talk to. You two are alone too much."

Fanny thought about the five days at the senior center. "It's not my home, though. I like my own house. And once he has the physical therapy, I can take care of him. We could get one of those home health aides in to help if we need it. And he's determined to be as independent as he can. You know your father."

"I know, Ma, I know. But just keep an open mind, okay?" And then he said the words he knew she wouldn't be able to argue with. "We have to do what's best for Dad, though, don't we? This can't be easy for him; he's always been, you know, so strong."

How could she argue with that? Instead she changed the subject.

"You're right, I guess some things will have to change. So I'm going to take driving lessons."

"What? Are you serious, Ma?"

"Well...Of course I'm..."

"Ma, do you remember that time I tried to teach you? We nearly got killed on Route 75. Those roads are even busier now and..."

His words faded as she remembered. She, Fanny, behind the wheel on Route 75, where it became three lanes on each side, facing the oncoming tractor trailers as she tried to turn left. Her legs had turned to jelly and her hands, damp with sweat, slid all over the steering wheel as each car and truck careened just inches past her. As she watched, they seemed to be coming right at her head-on. She'd lurched, and Eugene had grabbed the wheel. After-ward, when she'd finally somehow made that left turn, he had her pull into a diner parking lot. She started to shake uncontrollably. She never wanted to drive again. She didn't know how people faced traffic like that day after day.

She closed the phone book. "All right. You're right."

"I just want you safe, Ma, that's all."

"I know."

"And I'll be out there as soon as I can. I just found out Evan is having some surgery, tubes in his ears, and I want to get home…"

"No, no, don't even think of it. Your boys and Barbara need you right now. Your dad's going to be fine, don't worry."

She heard a scraping noise in the yard and turned on the back light, still holding the phone, losing track of what Eugene was say-ing. She looked, but saw nothing.

"What was that, Eugene?"

"I said I'll check in tomorrow."

"Is tomorrow little Evan's surgery?"

"Yeah, but don't even think about it, it's very routine. You've got enough to think about with Dad."

She hung up and looked again, her eyes scanning the yard. She'd just leave the back light on all night, just in case. And maybe she should think about getting a dog.

THE FOLLOWING NIGHT, Claire sat in Rick's living room with the lights off. It was dusk, and he'd be arriving any moment. Outside, bottle rockets broke the quiet night, although the Fourth of July had been weeks ago.

Claire closed her eyes and remembered that morning, eighteen days ago, when Rick left. When her life had stretched before her like a long-awaited dream. The sweet feel of his skin on hers. The excitement of leaving for Cape Cod. And butterflies in her stomach at the thought of their upcoming wedding. Good butterflies. After he'd gone, she'd lain there a long time, thinking how lucky she was.

Even now, in the darkness of his living room, she felt the tug of longing at the thought of him. How could everything have changed in less than three weeks? She was so tired, having spent the past two days helping with the baby and driving back and forth to the hospital. Her father seemed to be shrinking. When had he lost weight, and how had she not noticed? Her mother looked worn out, too. Claire imagined her mother was frightened sleeping alone in the house, but what could Claire do? How thin could she spread herself? And why couldn't Eugene, for once, be here when he was really needed?

She'd brought Amy and the baby to the hospital with her today, hoping to cheer her parents up. But Rose was really fussy and her crying only agitated Claire's father. And her mother's hands seemed to be crocheting the air, she seemed so nervous. When Claire pulled her out into the hall and mentioned that it was time they talked about other options, her mother had yelled at her for the first time in years.

"I don't want to talk about it," she'd cried, and gone back into the room.

This line was becoming like an annoying song refrain Claire couldn't seem to get rid of, between her mother and daughter both throwing it at her now.

She heard a car door and looked out the window. A trunk opening, the driver's door closing. Rick's feet on the front steps.

The door opened and a light flipped on.

"Hey there, handsome."

He dropped a bag and turned and she could see his frightened look.

"Jesus, Claire, you scared the shit out of me." He put the big suitcase down. "What on earth are you doing here? Why aren't you in Cape Cod?"

She smiled, as the carefully rehearsed words stalled in her throat.

"I...didn't go." She'd barely gotten the first two words out before he pulled her into his arms and began kissing her, her words buried in his neck.

"Talk later," he whispered, his lips traveling up her neck, in her hair, his hands slipping up her blouse. "You're here, that's all I care about."

They didn't even make it into the bedroom. As he pulled her down on the couch, Claire let herself go, her body taking over, her mind shutting down, the problems flying out the window. Oh yes, she had Rick. She still had this.

"Wow," he laughed ten minutes later, pulling a leg out from under her. "And I thought I was coming home to a long, lonely night all by myself."

"Surprise," she giggled. "Although I guess I should have said that ten minutes ago."

He pulled her close and kissed her cheek. "I don't care, it's still a nice surprise."

Then he sat up and began pulling his shirt on. "So...did you come home for the weekend to surprise me?"

She shook her head, pulling her shorts back on. "No. I didn't go. I actually had a little surprise myself a few days after you left."

"This must be good, because I couldn't imagine wild horses keeping you from that trip." He stood, then held out a hand and pulled her up.

When she told him about Amy showing up out of the blue, and about delivering the baby herself, his jaw nearly hit the floor.

"Holy shit," he said softly.

"Yeah, holy shit is right."

"Doesn't that make you...a grandma?"

She shrugged and gave a little laugh. "Yeah, it does."

"You look too sexy to be a grandma."

"I don't feel so sexy right now," she laughed. "I feel exhausted."

And then she told him about the terms laid down by the social worker, Amy and Rose living with her for six months. A frown began to darken his face.

"Claire, aren't you the one who told me how your daughter knows how to play you?"

"Yes, but this doesn't—"

"Honey, it does. She knows you'll pick up the pieces like you always do."

"But if I don't, the baby might not—"

"What about her father? Why can't he help out with the situation?"

"She says she doesn't know who the father is."

"I meant Amy's father. I mean, face it, you've done everything for her. The guy was basically a sperm donor."

She shook her head. "It would be the fair thing, wouldn't it? But that's not going to happen. Remember, he owes me a bundle in back child support."

"Bastards like that give men a bad name."

"Right. If he steps up to the plate, he gets himself into a ton of trouble and has to pay up." Claire hesitated. "I think Amy tried to find him while she was gone. But I don't think she had any luck."

"You need to think with your head, Claire. Not your heart."

"I know, you're right." She hesitated, and he waited. "I have to help her, Rick. I couldn't live with myself if I didn't."

He gave her a quick peck on the lips.

"Don't worry, it'll work out. I'm beat now, though. And you look like you could use a good night's sleep. Let's hit the hay."

"I can't. I need to go home."

He stood there with his hands on his hips. "Okay, fine."

"I'm sorry."

He walked her to the door. "Cheer up, babe. Just think, by next year you and I'll be living in Arizona. Our days'll revolve around my golf clubs and your camera. Hang onto that. So what if we push the wedding back a few months? It won't matter in the long run."

He lifted her chin and looked into her eyes. "You don't get what you deserve, Claire. You get what you *think* you deserve."

Getting into her car, she kept thinking about his words. Pushing the wedding back. Why was she surprised? She'd blindsided him with this, and it certainly made sense. It gave her a chance to get Amy on her feet. And a little more time to somehow get her parents settled before telling them she would be moving away to Scottsdale.

But as she drove home, she thought about what else he'd said. *You don't get what you deserve, you get what you think you deserve.*

What did she *really* think she deserved?

12

F ANNY SAW HER HUSBAND SITTING IN A WHEELCHAIR in the hallway outside the physical therapy room. For a moment she couldn't move. He was staring at the wall before him in deep thought, oblivious it seemed, of the noises and groans from the physical therapy room. As she got closer, he looked up at her, and for a moment, his face registered nothing. She waited for him to recognize her. A frightening moment, one she remembered all too well with Mama. It had seemed that overnight the Alzheimer's had taken her memory. She didn't know who Fanny was for years before she died. Worse, she'd stare at herself in the mirror and ask Fanny who that other woman was looking at her.

Now Fanny watched her husband's face, as his eyebrows pressed together into a frown or grimace.

"I've been sitting here for almost thirty minutes," he complained.

Before Fanny could answer, a young man with a ponytail and a little silver hoop in each ear came through the open doorway.

"Now, Mr. Noble, you've been waiting for ten minutes, that's all. And I'm sorry, but now we're going to get started." Then he turned to her. "I'm Seth. We're off to have some fun in PT."

He seemed nice enough, but he was the type of guy who could set Joe off. Even after all these years, after all the problems with Eugene, Joe had a thing about long hair on men.

Fanny went back down the hall and got a cup of tea while

Joe was in physical therapy. She sat in the lounge, sipping her tea, looking out at the cheerful garden planted by a local women's club. Everything was upbeat, but Fanny knew this was all part of the scheme. This could go one of two ways: Joe might come home and they would somehow manage. Or they wouldn't be able to, and life as she'd known it would be over. She knew what she wanted. She was going to fight for staying at home, because she was just fine. There was no way she was going into assisted living. She'd overheard Claire on the phone the other day talking to someone about it. Fanny was frustrated and she wanted to blame Joe. Because there was nothing she could do.

When the hour was up, Fanny walked slowly up the hall and saw Seth already pushing Joe's wheelchair into his room. As he helped Joe into bed, Fanny came into the room and heard the awful moan of pain.

Fanny sank to the chair in the corner and began to cry. A moment later, Seth was pulling her out into the hall.

"Listen, the first days of therapy are always the worst. It's hard on them, but don't cry. There's nothing you can do." He gave her a little hug, his words buried in her shoulder. "It's all just *dukkha*."

"It's doodoo?" she mumbled into his shoulder, still crying.

"No, *dukkha*. It's a Buddhist term."

When he was gone, Fanny sat in the room with Joe, a bag of crocheting on her lap. She kept thinking about what she'd heard. *Dukkha.* What did it mean? And how on earth would she know anything about Buddhism?

THE BABY, who'd been sleeping, began to cry as Claire undressed her. Amy stood beside her, hands on hips, her annoyed sighs a clear message as to what she thought about all this. The problem, though, was that Rose was sleeping all day. And once again, she'd most likely be up all night. Baby Rose, like so many infants, had her days and nights mixed up already. It was ten o'clock at night, and Claire was dizzy with exhaustion. But the stub of the cord had finally fallen off and Rose was able to have a regular bath now.

By the time she'd unfastened the wet diaper, the baby was screaming, her face red and angry, her little fists and legs pumping the air. As she carried Rose across the kitchen, Claire could see Amy's hands shaking as she followed with the baby soap and shampoo, towel and washcloth. She put them on the counter, as Claire had instructed a few moments ago.

Amy's lips were pressed tightly. Claire could see that she was nervous, because she kept wrapping a strand of her hair around her finger, over and over.

"This is cruel," she blurted out suddenly. "Look, she's shivering."

"Lots of babies shiver when they cry," Claire said. "Babies love water. Don't forget that she was in water for nine months. And giving them a bath before bed at night gets them into a routine. We need to get her into a routine."

As if proving the point for her, little Rose stopped crying as soon as Claire laid her in the warm bath. She stopped, in fact, in mid-cry. A surprised frown knit her barely visible brow, and her dark blue eyes stared up at Claire. Slowly the frown softened and she seemed to calm down. Amy handed Claire the soap, and as she did, the baby's head slowly turned and she looked at Amy, standing beside Claire.

"Look at that. She's young to do that," Claire said.

"I thought babies didn't really see at first?"

Claire realized that Amy must have been reading somewhere.

"I never believed that," she said. "When you were just a week old, I swear you were already trying to tell me something. You would stare into my eyes and move your mouth like you were about to speak." She turned to Amy. "Hopefully, after all this stimulation, she'll stay up for a while. Then you can feed her and she'll maybe sleep for a good part of the night."

Amy said nothing; she just stared at the baby. There were dark circles beneath her eyes and her hair was pulled back in a sloppy clip. At that moment, Amy looked like she might be about fourteen years old instead of almost twenty-four. When she'd left home, she was still twenty-two. She'd had a birthday that Claire had no part of. A life Claire still knew nothing about, really. Every time Claire tried to question her, Amy clammed up, walked out of the room, or began sparring defensively with her favorite line: *I don't want to talk about it right now.*

"Would you like to hold her and try washing her?"

Amy shook her head. "She looks too slippery. I'm afraid I'd drop her."

Claire wondered how many nights, how many baths, it would take before Amy would take over. Or if she would. Because she'd been at this point before. Where she tried so hard to get Amy not to fail at something; where she wanted Amy to succeed at something more than Amy herself seemed to want to.

Like the one credit term paper that would have saved her college career. Amy had turned into a party girl in college. By the end of her sophomore year, the writing was on the wall: she'd lose more credits because of Ds. After two years and thousands of dollars, which Claire was still paying for, Amy's transcript was a parent's worst nightmare. But Amy had a chance to salvage her GPA. An English professor offered her a chance to raise her grade point average by letting her write an extra term paper. Amy was already home for the summer, but the final grades could be submitted up to two weeks later. The day the paper was due, Amy finished writing it in longhand. And Claire typed like crazy because she typed faster than Amy. As she sat down at the keyboard, Claire knew she was doing the wrong thing, that Amy should have finished the paper sooner so she could type it herself. But her fingers flew, because she couldn't bear the thought of Amy failing.

Because then what would happen to her daughter? What kind of future was there without a degree? If she could get Amy to finish college, there would be a light at the end of the tunnel.

Amy always complained that Claire wanted things for her more than she did. *It's my life. So what if I don't finish college?* she'd said the day she left. Claire imagined she was bad-mouthing her to pieces with the psychologist. The two sessions she'd gone to already, she'd obviously spent a lot of time crying. She'd come out to the car with red, swollen eyes, her mouth pressed tight, refusing to say a word. Claire wished she could go in there and tell her side of the story, but that would probably be a bad thing, because the psychologist needed to be convinced that Amy could be a real mother to Rose. And Claire's complaints certainly wouldn't help that cause.

Lifting the baby out of the water and wrapping her in the warm blanket now, she held Rose to her chest. And then, as if by reflex, Claire buried her lips in the baby's soft neck.

13

SITTING IN THE KITCHEN OF JOHN POOLE'S HOUSE, Claire found her gaze drifting out the window once again. In the clearing on the side of the house, John was splitting wood. She watched the powerful muscles of his arms rise and swell with the rhythm of an ocean wave each time he swung the ax over his shoulder. A little while ago she'd sat mesmerized as he peeled off his shirt suddenly and dumped his water bottle over his head. Drops of water had clung to his chest hairs like shimmering jewels in the sunlight. He wasn't a handsome man the way Rick was. Where Rick's features were fine-boned, John Poole's were sharp and angled, his hazel eyes startling under heavy brows. But he was strong and quick, like a bird of prey with its own fierce beauty. He was chopping wood for the outdoor hearth. He spent his evenings outside, he told her, watching the stars.

She'd come here to go over an old map he'd found in the trunk, but when she arrived, he handed her the book that was now open on the table. She'd been sitting at his kitchen table for a half hour, her thoughts racing between her daughter and her parents. And Rick.

"Find anything interesting?"

She looked up to see John at the kitchen door. He'd pulled his shirt back on and there were dark blotches where it clung to wet skin. He had called last night suggesting they finally catch up. She was glad to escape her house. She loved the baby, and Amy was making tiny bits of progress. But Claire needed her alone time. She was starting to feel trapped. And she was starting to feel comfortable around John Poole. She'd never worked this closely on her photography with anyone before. She suspected that he might be overseeing her work so carefully because of her lack of professional experience.

She held up the notebook in her hand. "You're right, it's more a ledger than a journal. It details the boats that passed through here and some of the people on board. Lots of recipes exchanged, which is making me start to wonder if your lock tender wasn't a woman."

He came over to the table and glanced down at the book in her hands. She could smell him, fresh air, sweat, and musk, a pleasant, masculine scent that reminded her of the river.

"I didn't really notice before, but it does look like a woman's handwriting," he said.

She nodded. "Small and delicate. Although it's possible the lock tender couldn't write. Lots of people were illiterate back then, so maybe his wife did the books."

"Or maybe he was dyslexic?" he said, his eyebrows raised.

He walked over to the sink and ran the faucet, washing his hands. "I try to imagine them here sometimes, in these same rooms, cooking or sleeping, waiting for the next barge to show up. If only these walls could talk," he said with a little laugh.

"I always say that about trees."

He gave her a quick smile, then turned and dried his hands. She went back to her book. She heard the kitchen door close and looked up. He'd left her alone. She laid her head on the table, her cheek pressing the pages of the journal as she took a long, shaky breath. She wasn't sleeping much. And when she had the opportunity, she couldn't seem to shut her mind down. Closing her eyes, she inhaled the mildewed parchment of the journal's pages, the dust of years, the timeless odor of age. She thought about the canal and the river that fed it. Drowsiness overtook her and she started to drift, then realized John might come in and find her dozing at his kitchen table. Hardly a ringing endorsement of enthusiasm for their project.

When he did return a few minutes later, she was gazing at an old photograph that had been tucked in between several pages. A woman in a long calico dress and bonnet, a baby on one hip, walking beside a mule as it towed a barge. The same woman as in the other photo she'd studied a few weeks ago. She was thin, sturdy, and smiling despite her labors.

"Look at her, she seems so happy," she thought out loud. "And soon it would all just vanish, that whole way of life."

He came over and placed a hand on her shoulder. "Once the trains came through, it was just a matter of time. Except for the old towpaths and a few of these houses, no one would ever guess the canal had been here. Who would have known?"

Claire stared at the woman's eyes. "She knew."

He walked around the table. "What's wrong? You look so sad."

She shrugged, but didn't look up. "Nothing." And then she gave a little laugh that held no humor. "Everything."

"It couldn't have been easy," he said. "Not going to Cape Cod."

"Actually, it was easy. I couldn't have done otherwise."

"But…"

"Yes, there's a but. But it does eat away at me sometimes. I'm missing the chance of a lifetime. What could have been."

"You were supposed to study with Charles Meyer, right?"

She nodded.

He opened the pantry and took out a bag. "I told you before that I know his work, didn't I? I've seen it in the galleries up there."

He handed her the bag and she could see that his hands trembled slightly. This was weird, she thought, as she opened the bag. She pulled out a large book with a white cover. *Cape Cod Light* by Charles Meyer. The white cover simply served as the matting to dramatize the photo. It was a sunset shot of water, boats bobbing on the dark surface. But the white boats almost seemed illumi-nated, as if the light was coming from within.

"It's gorgeous," she said softly.

"Just because you couldn't go doesn't mean you can't still be inspired by his work. I hope you enjoy it."

"Oh, I couldn't—"

"Claire!" he interrupted. "I'm sorry," he said more softly. "Please take it."

"Thank you."

She held the book, staring at the beautiful picture. She could have been there right that moment if everything hadn't changed.

14

CLAIRE THOUGHT THINGS WOULD GET EASIER ONCE her father went home, but she was wrong. They'd already tried two different health aides in the house, but he wouldn't let either one touch him, refusing to give in to the little indignities that had suddenly descended on him.

His pelvis would take weeks to heal, and walking up the stairs was painful. Once up there, he wouldn't be able to come down again. So he insisted on sleeping in his recliner in the living room. Claire tried to rent a hospital bed, even just for a week, but he wouldn't hear of it. And though it would have been easier to pee in the plastic bottle the rehab had sent home, along with a handful of other gadgets to make his life easier, and her mother's less complicated, he insisted on hobbling to the bathroom while leaning on one of their shoulders.

Claire was exhausted from driving back and forth, doing double duty in tending to Rose and helping her mother. And her mother looked worn out. Yesterday she'd brought Amy and the baby along, not just to bring a little joy into the house for her mother, but to ease her own burden driving back and forth. She thought the time in the car would be a good chance to engage Amy in a conversation about the future. But Rose fussed most of the ride, and when they got to Mechanicsburg, her cries once again agitated her father, and her mother became more nervous than before. Yesterday, Claire had tried once again to broach the subject of other options, but this time her mother had actually yelled at her.

"I don't want to talk about it," she'd cried. She couldn't seem to stop cleaning and she barely gave Rose a second glance.

When Rick mentioned having a party, Claire had thought: *That's just what we all need.* And that's what she loved about him. He always found the best in any situation. She hadn't seen him much since the night he'd arrived home. At first, she worried that he was freaking out over her situation. And then she reminded herself that she was supposed to have been in Cape Cod. Of course he had other plans, and he was working to catch up with his real estate business after being away. So the fact that he didn't have time for her right now meant nothing, really.

She was having the party in the yard this afternoon. She had to stop hiding, which she knew Amy preferred. Rick could meet the baby, and Eugene, who had finally arrived last night. He'd called to say he'd bring their parents, for which she was grateful. She'd also invited Esther and Abbie. Esther couldn't make it, but said she'd stop by later in the week with a gift for the baby.

Claire had asked Amy if she'd like to invite anyone. There had been several phone calls for her since she'd come home, from old high school classmates and a few kids she'd hung around with once in a while. But Amy hadn't taken one call. "What will we talk about?" she'd asked. "Diaper rash?"

"Maybe they'd be excited to see Rose. She's so beautiful."

Amy's face softened. "I know. Sorry, but I don't think so. I'm not ready for that."

Standing in the yard now, wiping down the grill, Claire felt a sense of well-being for the first time in weeks. It was a beautiful July day and her perennials were at their peak. A sea of Shasta daisies lined the back porch. Purple coneflowers and black-eyed Susans surrounded her tiny pond. She looked up. Her glorious pines, a wall of green, made her yard like an urban sanctuary. When she and Rick moved into their new town house in Arizona next year, she would miss the trees most of all, but everything would be new. She'd have none of the frustrations of a hundred-year-old house: pipes that refused to stop dripping, outrageous oil bills, doing laundry on a dirt-floor cellar. By pooling their monies, and buying out west, where prices and taxes were cheaper, not to mention the beautiful weather, they'd be free to travel and golf and enjoy life. But for her, the most exciting part would be having the time to invest in a photography career. The other night she'd also finally confessed to Rick her secret dream: one carefully chosen photo of each of the fifty states as they traveled, to compose a coffee table book.

Rick was the first to arrive, around five. Amy, who was on her way to the shower, answered the door in a towel. Not exactly a great introduction for her fiancé and her daughter.

"Hey, you're my new dad?" Amy asked.

Rick blushed.

"Ignore her," Claire told him as Amy ran upstairs. "She's into shock intros. Then she's over it."

Fifteen minutes later, Amy was still in the shower. Claire sat Rick at the patio table and went in to get the baby. Rose was in a little stretchy one-piece sleeper with a spit-up stain. Claire quickly changed her into the new pink dress her mother had bought at Orr's. As Claire pulled the dress over her head, Rose fought her, kicking her legs as Claire pulled on the tiny tights. Then she slipped on the matching pink hair band through Rose's reddish gold hair, and Claire felt her heart expand. Rose looked beautiful, although she was screaming by now. So Claire held her close, shushing and bouncing her as they headed out the back door. She grabbed Rose's binkie off the counter, and the baby's mouth latched onto it, her cries slowing to little whimpers by the time they went out into the yard.

"This is little Rose," she said to Rick with a smile. "Would you like to hold her?"

Rick shook his head, and Claire could see he was nervous. "Uh uh, you hold her. She's so tiny I'd be afraid I'd drop her or something."

"You just hold the back of the head like this," she said, showing him how to brace her neck.

"She's beautiful, Claire. In fact, she looks like a doll. But no, I don't want to hold her. Babies aren't really my thing."

"That's okay."

She went and got Rose's bouncy seat and put her in it on the table. Rose's eyes went up, looking at the trees as she sucked on the binkie, her little frown softening. Claire realized that the green branches and flitting birds were probably better entertainment than a mobile could ever be.

"Hello there!"

She turned to see Abbie and Missy coming into the yard. Tom was bringing up the rear, holding a giant watermelon. Things seemed to be better, Abbie had told her last night on the phone. He was really trying. And he was such a different person when he didn't drink. Today Abbie's voice sang with happiness, and Claire, too, felt a sense of hope, although they'd been down this road before.

"I'm gonna dance at your wedding," Missy sang to Rick in her guttural voice, her wide, soft face breaking into a sudden smile.

Rick got up and gave Abbie and then Missy a kiss on the cheek. Missy blushed and turned and buried her face in her mother's shoulder.

"Well, I'll hope you'll save at least one dance for me, Missy," Rick said.

She peeked up at him and gave him another shy smile. Just then a horn honked out front, and Claire realized her parents must have arrived.

"Will you keep an eye on the baby for me?" she asked Abbie. "I'm going to help Eugene. I'll be right back."

As she rounded the yard, Claire turned and once again felt a feeling of contentment. The white tablecloth, the blue plates, and her own flowers in an old-fashioned glass jar as a centerpiece—it all looked like something out of cottage living.

And then she caught Rick's eyes, traveling up and down her pink sundress. He winked, and she couldn't wait to be alone with him later.

FANNY HAD A HARD TIME getting out of the backseat. Her hip had ached the entire ride because her legs were cramped and her knees were up too high. But she wouldn't complain; Joe was too tall to sit in the back. And Eugene was driving. During the ride, Eugene told them stories about the boys and their life in California. Every so often he'd comment on how things had changed in Jefferson County as they passed a new strip mall or housing development.

"Jesus, I remember the ride from Mechanicsburg to Lincoln on the school bus, when we played them in football. There was nothing on this road for miles."

"Some of the farms have been preserved," Joe said. "But they need to do more or suburban sprawl is going to take over the entire county."

Fanny looked out the window. Since Eugene had come home, Joe seemed to have perked up. Eugene was the picture of success. His hair was cut short now, and Fanny couldn't believe he had a sprinkle of gray across his sideburns and temples. But it looked very distinguished. His clothes, even his jeans, looked expensive and were pressed with creases.

He'd brought presents for both of them. For Fanny he had a gorgeous embroidered shawl with jet beads that reminded her of a dress Annie owned once. When she laughed and said, "Where would I wear something like this?" he told her she'd wear it to Claire's party.

Joe was dressed nicely, too, in a light blue dress shirt and black pants. Although it was hot, he'd felt cold, and Eugene had given him a beautiful cashmere cardigan, which he now wore. Even at his age, Joe was a good-looking man, Fanny had to admit. Years ago, when he'd first come home with her brother Anthony for dinner that Sunday afternoon, Mama had whispered in the kitchen, "He looks like that actor, Montgomery Clift." Fanny had agreed.

When they pulled into Claire's driveway, Eugene honked the horn and Claire was there a moment later. Fanny felt her eyes fill with tears—why couldn't she seem to stop these tears? But she was so happy to see her two children together. They would have this day, just the four of them, like the family they used to be years ago. No Barbara to put an air of tension into the afternoon. And Eugene wouldn't be distracted by his wife and sons. Plus there would be Amy and Rose. Fanny felt so blessed. Until they went into the yard and she saw Claire's fiancé and her friend Abbie and her family. Then she felt disappointed. Just for a little while, she wanted it to be only her own family. Like it used to be.

Joe and Eugene sat down with Rick and Abbie, and Fanny gave baby Rose a kiss. She was fast asleep in her bouncy seat, looking like a little angel in the pink dress Fanny had bought her. Her hair looked like spun gold in the late afternoon sun. Who did she look like? Fanny wondered. Certainly not Amy or Claire, or even that bastard Liam.

She decided to use the bathroom before sitting down. The thing she hated about Claire's house, she thought as she went inside, was that there was just one bathroom, upstairs. Slowly she made her way up, but halfway up the flight, she paused to catch her breath. She could hear Amy, obviously talking on the phone. And then she heard a word that made her freeze.

"But Dad, isn't there some way…" and then a long pause. "It

doesn't matter, she won't. Don't you want to see Rose? She looks like you."

A lie, Fanny thought, standing there quietly, waiting for the call to end. But somehow Amy had tracked down Liam.

CLAIRE WAS TRYING TO STAY CALM, but things were spiraling out of control. On one side of the table, Eugene and Rick were deep in a heated political debate. Her liberal brother was beginning to insult her conservative fiancé. Tom, who was still on his first drink, must have had a few before coming, because he was talking nonstop to her father about the new train service in town, an example of what Abbie frequently labeled his "diarrhea of the mouth." And her father sat there, mute, staring at the baby, who'd been woken up, no doubt by their rising voices. Claire could feel his silent disapproval over Amy's shame, just as she had with her own pregnancy so many years ago.

"I don't care what you say," Eugene went on, "if we don't do something about our reliance on oil, then by the time this baby is grown up, it's going to be a pretty sad world."

"Look, global warming is part of nature. It's cyclical," Rick said. "History proves it. Ice ages and warming trends have always—"

"So what?" Eugene interrupted. "It doesn't matter. There's still more carbon in the atmosphere..."

Suddenly Rose began to wail. Claire was setting a platter of cheese and crackers on the table as Abbie and Missy followed with plates and napkins. Missy loved to help. Her dream was to work as a waitress. Amy still hadn't appeared, and Claire wondered where her mother had gotten to. She could have used some help.

"Come on, you two," Claire teased her brother and Rick, "you're scaring the baby."

Her father was beginning to sway in his chair, a sign he was agitated, and his hand tapped rhythmically on the table, as the baby's crying escalated. She turned toward the house, but there was still no sign of her mother or daughter. Eugene and Rick were oblivious to everyone else. Missy began to rock back and forth, humming as she stared at Rose, not a good sign. Then her father put his hands on the arms of his chair and went to stand up.

"Eugene, help Dad," Claire said loudly, as she picked up Rose. "Okay, sweetie. Oh, you're soaked."

Halfway up in his chair, Joe began to wobble. Claire went to reach for him, but the baby was in her arms. "Eugene," she shouted, but it was too late.

Her father fell hard, back into his chair, just as a wet stain spread across the lap of his gray pants. He let out a loud moan and it was a moment before she realized he was trying not to cry.

As Eugene jumped up and went to help him, her father began pushing him away in anger and then began to sob, humiliated. Rose was now screaming in her arms. Missy kept rocking and humming, and began to cry, as well.

Claire turned to Rick, to hand him the baby for a moment. But Rick was standing there with a horrified look on his face.

15

Fanny woke with a start. The book had slipped onto the floor. She must have fallen asleep as she was reading in bed. As she came fully awake, she realized someone was talking. She could hear a low, urgent voice. She wondered if Joe and Eugene were still awake downstairs. The party at Claire's had been a disaster. After the accident, Joe had insisted they leave.

She should have thought to bring a change of clothes. She hadn't told Claire or Eugene that since coming home, he'd had a few accidents already trying to make it to the toilet. She'd told no one and called the doctor, who said the stress of the fall and his hospital visit were obviously still affecting him. He said to give it a few weeks, and if things didn't improve, they'd up his medication again. But Fanny thought it was his balance. He still refused the cane. She thought about his perfect posture when she first met him, how those strong, wide shoulders made something flutter in her heart.

She got up now and went out into the hall. She could hear Eugene talking in his old bedroom and realized he was on his cell phone, probably talking to his wife, even though it was late. California was, after all, three hours earlier. But it wasn't Barbara, she learned, as soon as he spoke again.

"Yeah, Claire, yeah, I get it. I'm not stupid."

Silence.

"No, I—"

Silence again.

"I know your hands are full. I know you've been waiting a long…Listen, it's time we—"

His voice was tense and Claire interrupted him again and again. Her only two children, who she was so happy to have together again, were fighting. About her and Joe.

"Look, my life's not so easy, either. Barbara and I are going for counseling. The boys have been sick all year…"

He hadn't told Fanny he was having problems with Barbara. Not that she was surprised. But she knew he didn't want to worry her with his problems. Oh, her kids, their lives weren't easy.

Another long silence.

"Yeah, sure, you deserve it, I know I've got no room to talk. And I know this is a lot to dump on Rick. I don't blame him for backing away…"

Fanny felt her blood turn to ice. Was Rick breaking up with Claire, because of her family?

Downstairs, Joe was still sleeping on the recliner. Fanny could hear his raspy snoring from the top of the stairs. If she went down to check on him, Eugene would hear her. And her hip would ache for a half hour.

"Okay, okay, we'll talk tomorrow," she heard Eugene say now, and she realized they were getting ready to hang up.

Fanny turned around and quietly went back to bed. She sat there, in the dark, with just the glow of the streetlight casting shadows in her room. Eugene would be going back to California soon. Claire would be stuck with them, and perhaps lose her fiancé, and the future she'd always dreamed of. Amy would no doubt be leaving at some point, as well. That's what children did these days.

Fanny knew what was happening wasn't what Claire deserved. And she had to do something to change that.

16

THREE WEEKS LATER, THE SUN WAS JUST SETTING when Claire walked in through the back kitchen door of her house. The psychologist had squeezed her in after normal hours, insisting that she had to see Claire today.

"Why didn't you tell me?" Claire now blurted out to Amy, who was at the sink, washing out bottles.

Amy turned to her with a defiant look. "Oh, and why didn't *you* tell *me*?"

Claire sank into a kitchen chair. She was hoping to hear from the psychologist that Amy was making progress with her problems and that the psychologist was optimistic about the end of this six-month commitment. But the conversation revolved around one thing only, Liam. What Claire found out as soon as she sat down was that the resentment and pent-up anger her daughter could barely control was directed at *her*. It wasn't misplaced anger at her father. Oh, no. In spite of everything he'd done, and not done, over the years to make things difficult, Amy was choosing to blame her.

"What did he say to you?" she asked Amy. "And where did you find him?"

"He lives in Florida now. He hates the cold. He wasn't at my high school graduation or Christmases or anything else because he was afraid you'd have him arrested as soon as he showed up in New Jersey."

"That's ridiculous," Claire said.

"Is it?" Amy asked, her hands on her hips, circling closer like a TV prosecutor. "Didn't you in fact try to have him arrested in Delaware when he was living there?"

"Amy, he owed that money to *you*. You needed things, special shoes, a bicycle like all the other kids, and I was barely making enough for us to survive back then."

"I didn't give a shit about that money!" Amy began to cry. "Every school play, every holiday, every fucking event in my life I watched kids whose parents were divorced and hated each other at least have the guts to put things aside and be there for their kid. Not me, though. I never had my dad, while everybody else had both parents, no matter how much they might have hated each other. For one hour, or one day, they put that kid first."

"This is so unfair, Amy." Claire's heart was breaking at her daughter's pain, while at the same time the anger was flaring up inside her, nearly burning her throat with words she wanted to scream out loud. But didn't. She took a deep breath, and in a calm voice said, "I would never have kept him from you. Never. I knew how much it meant."

"Well, that's not how he puts it."

"And when did you find all of this out?"

"He'd like to come and see me. And Rose. Then he finally told me last week, the day of your little party, why he couldn't."

"And you said nothing to me. I had to find out from your psychologist."

"Isn't that what we're paying her for? To listen to all our little secrets and lies?"

Claire slammed her fist on the kitchen table and got up. She walked to the sink and looked out the window. The gray net of dusk was falling, but in a corner of the yard, the last rays of sun lit her flowers with a golden light. Butterflies were circling her purple coneflowers, a sure sign of August. Bees hummed as they buzzed from bloom to crimson bloom on her monarda plants. She took another deep breath. God, she didn't want to fight with Amy. She turned to her.

"Did you ever hear me bad-mouth him? Ever? No. I've tried over the years to keep my feelings, my impatience, my frustrations, even my anger at your father to myself. Because I knew anything I said against him would only hurt you more. Do you think I wanted to hurt you? To say, *Oh by the way, sweetie, now he owes us thirty thousand, now he owes us forty thousand*, and on and on. Because he chose not to pay child support, then chose to disappear."

"He had to disappear. He would have gotten in trouble otherwise."

"He could have sent fifty bucks. Anything. It was for you, not me."

The monitor on the counter began to crackle. They heard Rose whimper and then begin to cry.

"If I wasn't trapped here, I'd leave today with Rose," Amy said and walked out of the room in a huff.

Claire sat there, furious with Liam. God, how she hated him at that moment. To think how she'd loved him. How she'd trusted him with her heart. And Amy's.

A moment later, Claire heard Amy's voice over the monitor.

"Shhh, don't cry, my sweet pea." Sweet pea. What Claire's mother had called Amy as a little girl, and still called her in tender moments. "Oh, I know, I know, you're all wet. And you're hungry. Mommy will fix all that. Mommy loves you so much. Somehow, I'm going to protect you from everything, my sweet girl."

Claire picked up her purse and went back out through the kitchen door.

Pulling out of the driveway, she realized that it was too late to shoot photos. She should really stay and work in the darkroom on her new idea for double exposures of the old and new prints. But the last thing she wanted to do on this sultry night was be trapped in her darkroom. So she just drove for a while, out of town, then down Rockport Road, through the wide open valley, watching the last crimson flare of the sunset as it sank behind the mountains ahead of her.

Rick was at some sort of golf junket with Seymour the developer, or she'd have gone there. But that wouldn't be good anyway, even if he were there. The last thing she needed to do was to dump this, and the rest of her frustrations, on him. The clock was ticking; it was less than four weeks until his house closed and he moved in with her.

As a sharp little finger of fear jabbed at her gut, Claire told herself that Rick would take it all in stride. He and his brothers had fought over the years; he'd told her last week after the party. Especially he and Randy, who were less than a year apart and shared a room. He knew the ups and downs of a family. She had to give him credit; he would be able to handle this. Maybe he'd even bring a new perspective that could help the situation.

As she drove the meandering curves of Rockport Road, she caught the silky flash of river in the distance. She found herself riding past John Poole's driveway. A moment later, Claire turned the car around, went back, and pulled in. Maybe she could look through more of the papers in the old trunk. Suddenly, it was dark, the driveway tunneled by tall old trees, and she flipped on her headlights. She probably shouldn't surprise him like this. He might not even be there. But it was too late; there was no place to turn around, and the narrow driveway was impossible to navigate in reverse. As she wound along the gravel drive, the gleam of her headlights soon reflected off the bumper of his Jeep. So he was home. And then she saw the fire, in the midst of the clear, unwooded patch of land beside the house.

It was an outside hearth. As she turned off the car, she saw flames licking toward the sky, and the errant whoosh of sparks as a piece of wood settled. On the edge of the fire's glow, she saw a seated figure and the unmistakable flicker of candlelight. She opened her door.

THE NIGHT AIR was cooler here as she crossed the grassy field. The fire's roar must have drowned out the crunch of her tires, because he still hadn't looked up. As she got closer, she could see he was bent over something, intent, a candle in his hand.

"Hello, John."

He turned, startled, and his eyes widened in surprise. Then he stood and smiled a crooked smile. "Claire!"

"I hope I'm not disturbing you. I was driving by and I thought I'd…"

But her words ran out before she could make something up.

"No, it's great," he said quickly, rescuing her. "I'm just waiting for the Perseids. It starts tonight."

"The Perseids?"

"A meteor shower. The same two nights each year in August. A guaranteed fireworks show."

"I've heard of it, but I don't think I've ever actually seen it."

"Well, you're in for a treat, then. It's not nearly as good as the Leonids in November, but it's a lot warmer."

He got another chair and brought her a glass of wine from the house. He was drinking his from a plastic cup. She took a sip. It was a flavorful red, slightly sweet and fruity. She looked up at the sky.

"You won't really be able to see anything for a few hours. Besides, the light pollution from the fire will make it tough. When it's time, we'll move to a darker corner of the yard."

"It's lovely. What were you reading?"

He picked up a piece of cardboard and handed it to her. It was a star chart. Notes were scribbled all over it.

"You've got quite an interest in astronomy, I take it."

He laughed a little. "Yeah, it is a passion of mine."

"And yet you became a writer?"

"Well, I just didn't have the confidence back then. Astronomy, majoring in a science, is tough enough. Throw dyslexia in, and it just seemed more than I thought I could handle at the time."

"And now?"

"I have no regrets, really. Reading will always be a challenge for me, but writing isn't so hard, except for my spelling, but that's what spell-check is for." He shrugged. "I believe some things are meant to happen. Writing's an opportunity to give voice to the things I really care about. I can still sit here and look at the stars."

"That's true."

There was a pause and he looked at her, taking a sip of his wine. His eyes in the firelight looked almost golden under the heavy, straight brows.

"I have lots of regrets," she said, instantly wishing she could take the words back. "I'm sorry, I shouldn't have…"

"It's okay, Claire. You look like something is eating away at you."

She looked at him questioningly.

"The way you nibble on your bottom lip."

She smiled, staring into the fire. "It's just, I don't know, I feel like whatever I do it's never the right thing. Or never enough. No matter what my intentions."

He sighed and smiled. "I can sympathize with that."

"Oh?"

He hesitated, took another sip of wine. He got up and threw another log onto the hearth. Sparks shot out, glowing orange embers in the darkness. He turned to her, the fire behind him, so that he was in silhouette.

"I thought I did everything right, too. And in the end I lost my son."

He spoke softly, without anger, although as the story went on, she imagined there had to have been some deeply bitter moments. He fell in love with Patty a few years out of college. She, too, was from a rough neighborhood, and they had a lot in common, hoping to break away from that life, to make a difference. They married and after a few years had a son, Ryan. "He was everything to me. It was like a lightbulb went on in my head when he was born; suddenly everything in this world seemed so much clearer to me." He smiled. "He became my world. But Patty, I don't know, something went wrong. She got postpartum depression. Her mom came and stayed for a while, but when she left, my wife couldn't seem to handle it. The doctor put her on something after a while."

He paused, sat down, and didn't talk for a few moments.

"She started going out at night, after I'd get home from work. I'd gotten my foot in the door with a local magazine that covered Boston entertainment, not really what I wanted, but it kept me close by and I started making a name for myself. Patty liked that, all the going out, the excitement. But it wasn't really what I was looking for."

Claire imagined him covering clubs and bands and plays, and it seemed a stretch. He was so quiet, so into nature.

"Anyway, long story short, she met someone else. A fun guy. He took her to parties, got her into drugs, it was a mess. She wound up with a substance abuse problem, which I should have seen coming, but I didn't. We were fighting like crazy by then, if you can imagine."

"My God, of course I can."

"I couldn't get her to stop, even when I threatened to take Ryan away. Which I eventually did. We got divorced and I got full custody and started freelancing for different magazines, doing environmental pieces, which let me work mostly from home. Patty had visitation only with me there."

"But...I thought you said you lost him?"

He chuckled, but there was no humor in the laugh. "Her boyfriend wound up in trouble, finally. Patty found herself alone, and I wouldn't let her come back. I just thought it was too much for Ryan; he was in school by then. Eventually, over the next few years, she met another guy, Gerry, and suddenly she began to change again. For him. I couldn't fucking believe it, because they got married and suddenly she wanted Ryan back. We went back to court and she proved herself and got to have weekends. Next thing I know, Ryan is telling me he wants to live with her for a while. So we tried this summer."

"Oh, John."

He shook his head. "Nah, don't feel bad for me. It's actually good for him. He sees her as he should see his mother. She's there for him now and he needs that. He never really had a mother, you know. And now he does."

"But you must miss him so much, it must hurt."

He shrugged. "That's how I wound up here in Jersey. When my buddy asked me to do him a favor on this piece about the canal, it gave me more of a chance to see Ryan. Patty lives just a few hours from here."

"But soon you'll be leaving to go back to the Cape?"

He nodded. "No kid should see what he did with her. He tells me he doesn't touch drugs or alcohol, and I believe him. So maybe there's a silver lining in that. But he's a freshman in high school now and that can make him a bit of an oddball, what with the peer pressure. I worry about him. I guess as a parent you never stop."

"I think that's true." She thought about her own mother, who still seemed to worry about her as if she were a child.

"I can't believe I just told you all of that," he said, shaking his head. Then he got up. "How about another glass of wine and we'll move over there, where it's darker."

"Sure." He seemed uncomfortable suddenly, as she followed him back to the house. "You know, my story is a lot like yours. Liam, Amy's father just hasn't been there for her, ever. So for all these years, I've done it all. And now, suddenly, I've become the villain."

He opened the door and turned to her. "Sometimes I think when you're a parent, you can never win."

She smiled. "I think I remember my mother saying that years ago."

They sat in beach chairs away from the fire, which was dying down now. John reclined his chair all the way back, and she did the same. The sky above was soft black and filled with thousands of stars.

"Oh, there's one," Claire cried, as a streak of light shot across the sky. "My first shooting star all summer." She should make a wish.

"Most people call them shooting stars, but they're actually meteorites, just tiny bits of rock and space dust. This is actually a great place to see the Perseid meteor shower, because we're so far from the lights in town. And there's no moonlight, either."

"Oh, there's a big one," she cried excitedly, as a bright golden ball arced across the sky like a firework.

"That's a fireball."

"This is amazing."

"Just wait, when it peaks, just before sunrise, you might see up to sixty an hour."

"Oh, I don't think I'll be able to stay for that. Will you stay up?"

He nodded. "I'll probably grab a blanket and doze now and then, but I'll be outside for the peak. Just like I am every year."

"And it comes just like that, every year?"

"You bet. It's the most popular meteor shower because it's so predictable. And it gets its name from the constellation Perseus because the meteors appear to originate there."

She stood up. "I should probably get going. I left in kind of a huff. Amy has no idea where I am, and I didn't take my cell."

"She's doing okay with the baby?"

She nodded. "Getting a little better. Well, this was truly lovely, John. Thanks for taking in a stray for the evening."

"It was my pleasure, Claire. I enjoyed the company."

He walked her to her car. As she was opening the door, he called her name.

"Claire."

She turned. He was just inches from her, looking at her so intently. She stood there, unable to move. He leaned toward her, and her breath caught. Suddenly, he folded his arms across his chest.

"Thanks for stopping by."

"Sure," she said.

Quickly she turned, got into her car, and pulled it around. In her rearview mirror, she could see his shape in the darkness, standing there, watching her leave.

17

THE NOISE IN A SCHOOL IS NOT SOMETHING YOU realize until you're there for eight or nine hours a day, week after month after year. The noise never ends, and there is no place to catch a moment to yourself, except in the bathroom. Then she would come home and Amy would have music blasting, the kitchen would be torn apart, and the trail of her things would lead up to her bedroom, which was a disaster. But the teenage sloppiness of girls was something she heard about way too much from her students' parents. She decided that in the complicated choice of which battles to wage, this was simply one that was not worth it. Apparently, it was something they outgrew once they got a place of their own. Or so some of the older parents said.

Claire hadn't been alone in her house since Amy returned in June. After she'd thrown Amy out long ago, it had been difficult. In all her life, Claire had never lived alone. But once she knew that Amy was still alive and they'd settled into that long siege of occasional brief phone calls, she'd actually begun to enjoy being by herself.

She began to feel a sense of peace once she got home from school each day. She'd have a cup of tea, sort through the mail, then indulge in an hour of *Oprah*, read a novel, or sit in the yard with a new photography book before thinking about dinner, grading papers, and the night ahead. The countertop would still be clean, the living room tidy. She began to love her old house.

When she began doing photography, she realized it was the peacefulness of being alone out in nature, studying a tree, a flower, or a bird, that was so soothing to her. It was a solitary pursuit; just the wind, the sun, and her thoughts.

It wasn't that she didn't love Amy. Or Rose. My God, the baby was so beautiful. Claire went to her now the moment she walked in the door, to see what was new. Rose was changing by the day, becoming more alert, with more facial expressions. Her reddish gold hair was long for an infant, covering the tops of her little ears, falling into her eyes. Amy caught the top in an elastic and pulled it off her face. The brief little curve of one side of Rose's mouth was now turning into real smiles. Her eyes, bluer each day, lit with joy as Claire would coo and coo, waiting for the tiniest of responses. And when Claire gave her a bottle, her fingers would latch tightly around one of Claire's, and she'd hold on as she drank, looking up at Claire the whole time.

Claire went up the stairs now and into Rose's room, which had been her spare bedroom. She opened the closet door and took out the hanger, laid the garment on the bed, and unzipped the heavy plastic cover. She pulled out the white dress, held it up, and looked at it. It was a straight white silk dress, knee-length and sleeveless. It was the jacket that made the outfit. Long-sleeved and beaded with tiny Swarovski crystals, it was stunning. In her dresser drawer, in a red velvet pouch, were the crystal earrings she'd bought to match.

She went to the mirror and held the dress in front of her. She planned to wear her hair in a simple French twist. It was all very elegant. She couldn't help thinking the word "mature." And in a flash, it was as if twenty-five years evaporated and she was looking at herself as she'd planned another wedding. She'd wanted such different things then. A long dress with a full skirt, strapless and with a small train. A Cinderella dress. The kind all little girls dream of when they're talking about that day to come. There was still a part of her that longed for that fairy tale wedding. Because after she got pregnant in her junior year of college, nothing had turned out as she'd planned. Or dreamed.

But her wedding to Rick was to be a simple affair, a fitting celebration for two practical people who were in their forties and had better ways to spend their money. Rick was right; the wedding would be over before they knew it. Instead, they put the money they would have spent toward upgrades in their new town house: granite counters, a Jacuzzi tub, an expansive deck where they could barbecue, with a view of the eighteenth hole of a new golf course, a lush green oasis with the red desert in the background. She would have preferred to add a front porch, because it was the one thing she'd miss about this old house. But Rick had pointed out how much more use they'd get with the deck. Besides, a porch would look silly on the modern, desert architecture. How could she argue?

She put the dress back in the closet and sat in the rocker next to Rose's crib. The chair was a thrift store find her friend Esther had brought as a gift a few weeks ago. She rocked now, thinking about her postponed wedding. They hadn't talked about a new date, because things seemed to still be in such flux. The few times she'd brought it up, Rick seemed to dance around the subject with the same phrases. He didn't want to "pressure her." It would be better once things "settled down." When the time was right, it would be "perfect." And after all, didn't she want their wedding to be perfect?

With all of the complications from her family, she wondered if there ever actually would be a perfect time. But she didn't push it; she didn't want to cause a rift. They never fought, really. Rick was even-tempered, and she had to trust that these little moments were her own self-doubts unnerving her. They were not one of those couples joined at the hip. After being single for so many years, they'd both agreed that space could be a good thing. So they didn't see each other each and every night. She had her time to dabble in photography. He had his time to pursue golf. She reminded herself that she'd been happy with this arrangement before, and she shouldn't push the panic button now. After all, she wouldn't even have been here if she'd gone on her trip. Their infrequent time together would have been no time at all. He had filled up these weeks she was supposed to be gone, and she had to keep reminding herself that it wasn't his fault. She had to trust and believe in what they had. Because after all these years of being single, she knew that what they had was very special. And she didn't want to spend the rest of her life alone.

Claire heard the door open downstairs. Amy was back with the baby. A moment later she heard her coming up the steps and then Amy was opening the door. She paused a moment, looking at Claire in the rocker, the dress hanging on the closet door.

"Is that your wedding dress?" she whispered.

Claire nodded.

Amy looked at her a long moment, then she lay Rose, who was asleep in her arms, in the crib. She opened the bedroom door to leave, then turned to her. "I'm sorry I ruined all that."

Before Claire could say anything, Amy left, closing the door behind her.

Claire sat there, rocking, listening to Rose's peaceful breathing as she slept.

18

ONCE THEY MADE THE DECISION, THINGS SEEMED
TO happen so fast. it seemed one minute she was having breakfast
with Joe, telling him that maybe it was time to think about their
options. That in an assisted living he could have more physical
therapy and resources at his fingertips that simply couldn't happen
here at home. He'd looked at her, startled. Then she confessed she'd
overheard their kids arguing.

"We don't want to be a burden," she'd said finally.

And now they were moving out of their home.

It didn't take much convincing. They'd tried two home health
aides, and Joe hated having strangers in the house. So did she. Neither one spoke decent English. But more than that, she and Joe
both lived with the dread of another fall, the fear of what an accident could bring. It all came down to what Eugene kept calling
"quality of life," a phrase she didn't really like. There was something
so final about it.

The decision to move to Sunrise Manor had been easy. It was in
Jefferson County, close enough for Claire to visit every day, if she
had the time. If Joe had still been allowed to drive, they'd have been
able to see the baby every day, too, but the doctor had finally put
his foot down after the fall. After that, it seemed Joe just gave up.
If she told him he had to stand on his head, he'd probably listen to
her and try to do it somehow. Her ornery, stubborn husband was
inhabited now by a man who seemed to have a glimmer of fear in

his eyes each morning. What was today going to bring into their lives?

They'd signed their car over to Amy. Joe insisted she needed a safe vehicle for the baby. And they'd reduced their seven-room house to a few dozen boxes. The tiny apartment at the assisted living had just three rooms, and you couldn't bring your own furniture. She'd understood why as they toured one. The rooms were so miniscule they had chairs and tables that would have fit in a dollhouse. Somehow, the tiny furniture and strategically placed mirrors lent a cheerful, homey atmosphere, but Fanny hadn't been fooled. She'd walked through as if in a daze. None of it seemed real. It would be a home where you'd have to leave most of yourself behind.

Claire would be arriving shortly now. Amy was coming, too, with Rose, to help. When she'd called to offer yesterday, Amy said to Fanny "You don't have to do this, Gram. We could figure something out. I can't believe Mom thinks this is a good idea. I'll be free in three or four months, I could come live with you and Grampa. I could help."

Fanny had been stunned. Amy had flitted between standoffish and warm and friendly since coming home; worried about the baby and embarrassed at what she'd done. Fanny knew there was a heart in there, buried underneath the wreckage of that bastard of a father. And that Claire had been the fall guy for too long.

Fanny didn't want to play that game. Claire wasn't the common enemy, as Amy seemed to sometimes think. And Fanny wasn't about to let Amy give up her youth to indulge a selfish old woman.

"This is for the best," she'd told Amy. "Grampa really needs a lot of help now. And unfortunately, it's only going to progress. There's no cure for Parkinson's."

"I know, but maybe we could slow it down." Tears filled Amy's voice.

"You're a good girl, sweet pea. You have a good heart."

It was time to go downstairs now. It was time to leave her bedroom for the final time. She'd decided to do these little good-byes before Claire and Amy came. She didn't want anyone to witness her anguish. But Fanny couldn't bring herself to get off the bed. Was this really happening? Was she going to walk down those stairs, out that door, and never come back to this house that had been her home for forty years?

Annie, where are you? she thought. It always seemed to her that Annie and Mama were still somehow a part of her life, their souls hovering in the shadows of these rooms, watching over her. *I need you*, she begged. *I need you, Annie. Mama. Help me be brave now. I don't want to go. I don't want to leave.*

After they'd died, Fanny believed that they were somehow still there. How could the essence, what the soul was, simply disappear at that last breath? They had to exist, somewhere. She needed them. She wasn't brave like they were. Annie was her big sister, always helping her. Mama always knew just the right thing to say to make her feel better.

She looked at the boxes on the floor by the bedroom door. How did you pick and choose through a lifetime?

On the bed in front of her was the big picture from Cousin Joannie's wedding years ago. The mob of them all, still in Brooklyn. Annie was a bridesmaid, still just a girl really, and at night, sleeping in the same bed, she told Fanny that she couldn't wait for love, a boy, for her life to begin. But her life had ended just before her fortieth birthday. Staring at that young Annie, at herself, at all of those faces, Fanny's throat clogged with the realization that that whole way of life, that little world that revolved around her huge extended family in Brooklyn, was over.

They were all gone. Everyone in that picture. Oh, there might be a cousin or two somewhere. But when the neighborhood got bad and they scattered like seeds in the wind, their close family seemed to unravel over the decades. After a while, the Christmas cards got fewer. Those that came talked of the loss of someone or other. Families weren't like they once were. Not like back then, when she was a girl.

Now her family was small. Her husband, her two children, three grandchildren. And Rose. That was a miracle. Living to see a great-grandchild. She had to focus on the positives in her life. Claire kept telling her that attitude was everything. That sounded more like Rick, and though she tried, maybe she just wasn't one of those people who could bend their moods to adapt. Maybe you couldn't teach an old dog like her new tricks. In the end, it didn't really matter. What was she going to do, ruin Claire's life? Torture Eugene from thousands of miles away? She had to do this.

Finally, she got up from the bed, her bed and Joe's, and stood on trembling legs. Most of all, Joe needed her. And her place was with him. It was her duty.

AT MIDNIGHT, Claire's cell phone rang. She was lying awake, staring at the ceiling. "Hey, it's me. I'm sorry to wake you," Rick said.

"I wasn't sleeping," she said, and then she started to cry.

"Oh, baby, I wanted to be there for you," Rick said softly.

She reached for a tissue and blew her nose.

"But what I accomplished today will go a long way in helping us with our future. I secured the listings on every house and condo that's going to be built. For two years."

"That's great." She turned on the light and sat up. "I know how much that means to you."

"To *us*!" Rick said emphatically. "We just got our future set. Each house that sells is a commission in my pocket, whether I'm here or not. I'm going to hire a few more salespeople, because it's going to be a lot to handle. I'm thinking of making Abbie sales manager."

"I'm sure she'll be thrilled."

"You know I was counting on this, but getting it in writing, well, now it's real. I always said, you gotta dream big to make it big. And now our future is golden."

Claire thought about her parents, and their future. When she'd left them a few hours ago after unpacking each box, keeping her emotions locked in a ball of sadness in her throat, she felt a steel chain of guilt holding her there. She couldn't seem to leave, it was all so…final. After repeating again and again, *Well, I guess I'll go now*, at about ten o'clock, she finally did. They both insisted they were exhausted and were going right to sleep. But she couldn't shake that feeling she'd had all day, like she'd led the lambs to the slaughter. No matter how upbeat she tried to be, there was no injecting even a shred of cheer into that little place.

"Claire, are you there?"

"I'm sorry, Rick. I just…" She paused, searching for words that might convey the depth of her emotions on this day. "Nothing in my life prepared me for moving them today. It was like they were in kindergarten. They did everything I asked, listening, obeying, not a word of…of complaint or anything."

"I'm sorry, babe, I should have been there."

"No, it's okay, I know you're doing everything for us. And I'm sorry I'm so wrapped up in all of this." She sighed and felt a catch in her throat as she went on. "I grew up in that house. They've been there for forty years. Nothing…you know nothing in their lives will ever be the same again." *Or in mine*, she realized. "I'm glad you decided to let an office in Mechanicsburg list it." It wasn't just the distance. Rick thought it best to stay out of it, since Eugene would be handling the details and they hadn't exactly hit it off.

"Do you want me to come over?"

"No, it's okay. I'm fine." She heard the baby begin to cry. "It's late and I'm going to go back in the morning, to try to help make the first real day a little better."

"You're a good woman, Claire. You have a big heart, always putting everyone else first."

"No, I just…" How did she explain that she did what she had to, because it wasn't in her to do otherwise? Duty, responsibility—she simply couldn't turn her back on it. If she was a good woman, she would be one without resentment. Without complaint.

The baby was crying louder now, and Claire got up and went into the hall.

"How about you meet me at the site in the morning and I'll show you around? And then we can have breakfast. I just got the final architect's drawing of our own town house, after those changes we made. That'll cheer you up."

"That sounds great," she said, although she doubted it. She opened the door to the baby's room.

"We'll have a southern exposure, you know. Perfect for a hot tub."

Rose was screaming now and Claire went to her, cradling the phone on her shoulder. The light on the monitor was off. Amy must have forgotten to turn it on.

"Claire, did you hear me? Claire, is that the baby…?"

But Claire couldn't hear Rick over Rose's screams. "I'll call you tomorrow," she shouted into the phone, picking up the baby as Rose arched her back and kept drawing her knees up, as if in pain.

He said something but she couldn't hear him.

"I have to go now." And she hung up.

Claire held her close, kissing her forehead, shushing over and over in her ear. She grabbed the binkie that had fallen out of her mouth, and before she even got it to Rose, her mouth opened, then latched onto it frantically. Claire walked around the room, patting her back as she whimpered and made little sucking sounds on the binkie. The cries slowed and settled into sighs. She sat in the rocker with Rose, looking down at her beautiful face, the pink skin, stroking the long strands of gold hair she'd been certain would fall out after birth. Claire hummed as she rocked, and then began to sing the pigeon song, the one she'd sung to Amy, and that her mother had sung to her. As Rose fell asleep in her arms, she felt her heart swell with love.

RICK WAS LATE. Oh, not that he'd ever admit it, because he always had an excuse. For someone so fastidious about everything else, Claire wondered how it didn't torture him to never be on time. But with Rick it was always a client running late for an appointment and throwing his own schedule off. Or a last minute call from a listing, demanding to know what they needed to do to get the house sold faster. Emergencies always came out of the blue, and he'd warned her from the beginning that no two days were ever alike. It was the nature of the beast, he'd said and laughed. But he loved the freedom. On a beautiful day, he could rearrange things and get nine or eighteen holes in before he went to the office. Everything about him was so easygoing, so upbeat, and Claire longed to have that in her life, especially now. She knew she was a self-torturer by nature. Her latest agony was that the new school year was starting soon and she had not one thing ready.

This morning, before she left to meet him and then head to Sunrise Manor, she'd gone into the baby's room while Amy was out with Rose for an early walk, trying to get her to sleep. She pulled boxes of books and lesson plans out of the closet. It was time to get organized and mentally get herself into the groove of teaching again. She was dreading it, though. Right now, she didn't feel like she had enough emotional energy to manage her parents and her daughter, much less a hundred students a day and all of their needs and dramas walking through her classroom. It made her want to pull a blanket over her head.

"Hey there, beautiful."

She turned and saw Rick walking across the field toward her, his car parked down by the construction trailer. Her own car was parked on the rough dirt road that crossed this field. He gave her a quick kiss on the cheek.

"You're right, the view is just spectacular," she said with a smile, looking at the valley of Lincoln spread out below them. The field they were standing on climbed the side of Lincoln Mountain, a gentle grade that had nurtured a horse farm for generations. Claire used to love driving up the mountain and watching the horses canter across the field, or occasionally race to the far meadow, where the woods began and the land climbed steeply to the top of the rise. She missed the horses and the open land, now a messy maze of dirt roads and backhoes leveling trees and moving rocks. But the artist's rendering for Valley View Estates looked beautiful, too. This project would solidify their future, he'd told her months ago, when they were in Arizona, and she thought they were picking too many upgrades for their new place.

Rick took her hand now and pulled it to his lips. He gave her a little smile. And her antennae went up.

"What?" she asked.

He shrugged, said nothing, holding her hand tightly.

"What's wrong?"

He hesitated before speaking, squeezing her hand. "I did a lot of thinking last night after our phone call. About what a wonderful woman you are and how lucky I am to have you…"

There was a "but" coming, she could hear it.

"But I don't know if I'm the kind of guy who could sign on for this."

She felt her stomach drop.

How could she be surprised? She was, though. He came from a big family. Hadn't he said time and again how families were unpredictable, throwing curveballs when you least expected it?

She took a deep breath. In a calm, reassuring voice she said, "Look, I know things are crazy right now, but in a few months it's going to settle down." It was the tone she used in the classroom when a pop quiz caused panic. Then she would say, *You know this stuff. Just stop and think.* The same words would apply to Rick right now. But she shook her head and said, "It's just bad timing, all of it coming at me at once. We have to be a little patient."

"I know, I know, and that's why I feel so bad even saying this," he said, dropping her hand, rubbing his face as he looked across the field. "You deserve better, you deserve someone who'll help you every step of the way. I don't know if I can move in with a new baby and the daughter struggles and—"

"Wait!" She reached for his arm, pulling him around, forcing him to look at her. "Listen, honey, I understand, of course. But Rose is probably a bit colicky and that'll be gone in a matter of months. And Amy, well she's got some ideas for a job."

He pulled her into his arms with a groan.

"It's still possible, Rick," she whispered in his ear. "All of it. Before you know it they'll all be settled, my parents, Amy, and the baby, and I'll have my early retirement. We can take off next June just like we planned."

He let her go, then stood looking at the cleared land all around them, his hands on his hips. He took a deep breath and said, "Maybe you're right, maybe I've just panicked a little."

"That's understandable," she said with a little laugh, hoping to inject some lightness into the moment. "Who wouldn't?"

He looked into her eyes. "You."

She shrugged. "I'm no saint. And I don't expect you to be. I promise, this'll work out in a few months. You'll see."

"Okay, okay," he said, with a long exhale, in obvious relief. "Why don't we just alter our plans a little. Maybe that's all we need to do. How about if I go and rent something for a few months after my place closes, give your daughter some space with the baby and everything. Give you the time you need to get your folks settled and comfortable without having to worry about me underfoot."

"I think that's a great idea," she said to make him feel better, although it didn't make her feel one bit better. Having him underfoot, in her bed at night, across the table in the morning, that would be comfort and pleasure. But maybe it was asking too much right now.

"And we'll just take it from there, okay?" he said.

She hesitated. He hadn't mentioned rescheduling the wedding. And in that moment she decided not to, either. Maybe it was better to take baby steps. After all, he was still standing beside her, he still loved her. And she had pulled the rug out from under their plans, big-time.

"I think that's perfect," she said.

"Great. I feel so much better." He kissed the top of her head. "And we'll still have fun. Don't forget we've got that swanky golf tournament in a few weeks, the whole weekend away at the Hilton." He squeezed her closer. "A weekend away from the family is probably just what you need."

She squeezed him back. "You're right about that." But needing it and enjoying it were two different things. Hopefully by then her parents would be adjusted and she'd be able to allow herself some pleasure without feeling guilty over them.

19

CLAIRE STOOD IN HER DARKROOM, WITH JUST THE red light on, watching the white photo paper begin to darken as the picture bloomed in the solution. A smile grew on her face as the image came to life. With the rubber-edged tongs, she lifted the photograph from the chemical tray, letting the solution drain from a corner; then she hung it next to the others on the line that ran across the room.

Alone in the darkroom, Claire felt like a little girl as she clapped her hands and kept whispering to herself, "I can't believe it. I did it, I did it!" It was her best work yet. And she hadn't relied on scanners or computers.

When she'd first begun to envision somehow blending the past and present images of the canal, she wasn't sure how she'd accomplish this feat. Because she was a purist. Black-and-white was her medium, her love, and part of her reluctance to use the convenience of a computer or scanner to bring these images together was her lack of experience with the equipment. She'd only been back into photography less than two years. It had been enough to master black-and-white technique, but she didn't have the time, and truly didn't have the desire, to go digital and use a computer like everyone else seemed to be doing. To Claire, black-and-white photography was as artistic as a painting. The results were truly up to the photographer's vision and craft in the darkroom.

She looked at the little clothesline of photographs.

The last ones she'd taken in the past few weeks had involved tracing the canal on the old map John had found in the trunk, like a scavenger hunt. In her car she followed remnants of the canal that wound behind Raynor's feed store and under a little bridge on Main Street, then wrapped itself around the bottom edge of Lincoln Mountain like a lazy snake. When she had to, she got out and followed the trail on foot, shooting the modern remnants of it that might soon be lost to development. But not if it became designated a National Heritage Corridor.

An article on just that had appeared in this week's paper. John had called to tell her to look for it, but she hadn't taken his call. She hadn't, in fact, seen or spoken to him since that night under the stars. She'd listened to his voice on her voice mail, deep, serious, the soft r's and city lilt. And there the story had been, on the front page of the *Newark Star Ledger*.

The Pohatcong River is a congressionally designated Wild and Scenic River. The Pohatcong Canal, built in the early 1800s, was an engineering phenomenon for its era, overcoming large elevation changes by the use of inclined planes... They were quoting James Leeds, a local canal enthusiast who was leading a grassroots effort to get both the canal and river designated a National Heritage Corridor. Claire assumed he was the friend John had mentioned a while back.

Renowned environmental writer John Poole, the article called him. Claire had paused, because to her he'd made himself sound almost like a novice. The article concluded with: *Poole is finishing up a feature article that will appear soon in* New Jersey Monthly *magazine.*

Claire had gasped. She never imagined her photos in such a professional, glossy magazine that was read by hundreds of thousands. He'd been so offhand about it, saying he hadn't even sold the piece yet. And he'd chosen her based on...a few photos hanging in her house? After reading that article, Claire had felt a sudden pressure to give the project her all. It wasn't just the idea of having her work scrutinized by a big-time editor; it was seeing in print how important the canal really was in local historic terms. Helping to have it deemed a National Heritage Corridor would be directly having a hand in history.

She cleaned up and finally turned on the overhead light, exhausted. She was finished. She was planning to mail these photos to John Poole rather than go in person. Those last moments with him had seemed almost intimate. The way he looked at her, those gold eyes so intense; she'd felt certain he was about to kiss her. But then he stopped. And if he hadn't?

She flipped off the light. She wasn't going there; it was ridiculous to even consider. John Poole was not her type. And so what if she might feel a bit awkward to see him; she had to deliver the photos herself. She was too proud of this work; she wanted to see his reaction. Finally, she told herself she'd just make up her mind in the morning. She was too tired right now.

Walking across the yard, she looked up and saw that Amy's light was out. A soft, amber glow shone through Rose's window from the night-light. Claire sat for a minute on top of the picnic table and looked up at the pines circling the yard, like tall sentinels protecting them. In the last week, despite Rose's sleepless nights, something had changed. Amy had been quiet, distant, since their fight. She'd had another session with the psychologist. She helped Claire move her parents. Something seemed to have softened within her since that explosion of emotion. Although her disappointment with Claire was obvious, it was as if the great big ball of anger had deflated somehow. She'd stopped complaining and giving the annoyed looks. It was almost more painful for Claire, because with the veneer of anger gone, Amy seemed like a lost little girl. With a baby girl of her own.

FANNY COULDN'T TAKE all the people. Their new place at Sunrise

Manor was like a revolving door; every time she turned around, someone else was coming through, like a Welcome Wagon that wouldn't end. She liked her privacy.

Joe was polite to everyone and it always amazed her that he was so amiable, almost chatty with so many of them. Like Fred, the widower next door, a man who boasted proudly that he was eighty-five and could still run a few miles each day. Before Fanny could chime in and ask what he was doing here, he admitted that he was having problems with day-to-day things, like paying bills and keeping track of his affairs. He'd never been much of a cook, and here he got "three squares" if he wanted them. And then there was the final admission, spoken softly: he had no family; there was no one to take care of him at all. Joe told him he had Parkinson's and that the disease was progressing, and it was more than their two children could handle on their own.

"We have three grandchildren and a great-grandchild," Fanny boasted.

"You're lucky," Fred said.

Then he and Joe began talking about World War II and Fred's time in Europe. Really Fred talked and Joe listened. And Fanny swore he told the same exact stories the second afternoon he stopped by. She felt herself begin to tremble with annoyance. There were only two places to escape, the bathroom or the bedroom. The bathroom, with its handicap access to the toilet and walk-in shower, was probably bigger than the bedroom, actually, but the only place to sit was on the toilet. So she went into the bedroom and shut the door.

She stood looking at the beds. Twin beds. She hadn't been expecting that because in fact when they'd toured the place, she hadn't noticed. The day they were moving in, when Claire had opened the bedroom door and she'd followed her in with a bag of things to unload, she'd almost cried out. They had never slept in twin beds. They had never slept apart, not one day in their marriage except when Fanny had her babies and then when she'd been hospitalized with her broken hip. And of course earlier that summer, when Joe was in the hospital.

She must have whimpered, because Claire had turned to her, her face stricken with concern.

"Mom, are you okay?"

Fanny nodded. But she wasn't. She turned, emptying the bag of shoes so Claire couldn't see her expression. She'd given up everything—her house, her furniture, so many of her things that just wouldn't fit in this tiny apartment. And now they were taking away her last comfort, sleeping with her husband. It's not as if she was expecting sex. That had sort of evaporated over the past years like a thin fog that when it was gone, you almost didn't notice the exact moment it happened. And of course there was disappointment in that. It was another final milestone, like when your children leave, then your last period happens but you don't realize it's the last until it's long gone, or the day you qualify for Medicare. And now the day you stopped sleeping beside your husband. It made her feel so alone.

She sat on her own single bed and looked around the room now. It was like a hotel room. She was living in a hotel, and this might be her last place on earth. Of course Claire had tried to cozy it up with their pictures and knickknacks, but still. On the dresser sat an enormous vase of flowers from Eugene. Cheerful flowers like daisies and daffodils, nothing depressing like carnations or lilies, which she saw all the time at wakes and made her think of funerals. In the little kitchen, there was a towering fruit basket, also from Eugene. The first few days, he'd called twice a day, and now at least at night he called to see how they're doing. Claire, too, was here every day and then called each night. She constantly wore a worried look.

"We'll go shopping once you're settled," Claire had offered that first day, on her hands and knees, emptying a box. "It'll be fun decorating. We'll make it like one of those shows on television and maybe transform the place. It doesn't take much."

"Will they allow that?" she'd asked.

"Of course, Mom. It's *your home.*"

Fanny didn't dare open her mouth to that one.

They came for their laundry twice a week. She didn't even have to cook, because the dining room served three meals a day. But she drew the line at cleaning, even if it was included. She would clean her own house because no one, she knew, would do as good a job. And at least it would give her something to do. It wouldn't take long, though, to clean the place. What would she do with the rest of her time? How many card games could you play? Or movies could you sit through?

Fanny leaned back and reached for the stack of books next to the bed. Claire had brought her ten paperbacks. She reached for the one on top. But it wasn't one of her romance novels; it was the book on Buddhism that Seth, Joe's physical therapist, had given her. She'd paged through it once, but never read it, and she wondered how it had landed on the pile. She'd tried to return it to him, but he told her to keep it.

"But I'm Catholic," she'd told him, holding the book out to him.

He shook his head. "It's not like most people think, it's not a religion, Mrs. Noble. Buddhism is really a philosophy. A way of living your life that is so much better. It sets you free."

Free. Well obviously that was about as ironic as it could get. Her freedom was over. She put the book back and leaned on her pillow, closing her eyes. She wasn't a napper. Somehow, sleeping in the middle of the day, even at her age, seemed frivolous. But right now she was so awfully tired, why fight it? After all, what else was there to do?

20

THE CALL CAME DURING DONNA LAVERTY'S VISIT.
The social worker stayed for an hour, first just walking through the
house, then sitting with Rose and Amy in the kitchen, while Claire
made herself scarce upstairs. She was sorting through her photos
for the canal, organizing them with notes so that John Poole would
understand it all. She could hear the murmur of their voices and,
if she strained, could probably make out their words. The walls in
her old house were poorly insulated.

Then the phone rang.

"Is this Claire?"

"Yes." The voice sounded familiar but she couldn't place it.

"This is your lucky day!"

She didn't say anything. Could it be a crank call? A new student
already toying with her? School, after all, would be starting in just
a few days.

"Hello? Are you there?" the voice asked.

"Who is this?"

"It's Zoe, from the Cape Cod Arts Center. I'm so excited for
you because this like never happens."

Someone else's bad luck, Zoe went on to tell her, was now
Claire's good fortune. There was a sudden opening in the fall session, but she'd have to leave right away. Could she be there in two
days? Zoe asked.

"Oh" was all she could manage. Claire sat on the edge of the bed, the air leaving her lungs.

"I felt so bad for you when you had to cancel in June, so when Mr. Meyer told me someone dropped out, I told him we had to call you."

"Oh…I don't…So much has changed, Zoe. My life is so complicated."

"I'm sorry," Zoe said in a sad voice. She was very theatrical, but Claire could tell she was sincere.

"I want to thank you, though. For going to bat for me, I mean. I'm sure there are lots of other people who will jump at this chance."

"Sure," Zoe said. "But Mr. Meyer wanted you."

"Me? Why?"

"Well, when I mentioned you, he was like, oh right, the black-and-white nature studies."

"He remembered my portfolio?"

"Yes, that's right. Which is awesome, 'cause he gets hundreds. Anyway, he just said to me, 'Yes, get her. This will take her to another level.'"

Claire stood up and started to walk in circles in the small bedroom as something began to hum inside of her.

"Isn't there any way you can make this work? Wouldn't your family understand?"

"Well…" She was thinking, her mind racing now, the something inside of her pulsating faster, and she realized it was excitement. "I…I'd have to bring my daughter and her baby. The dorm would—"

"No, the dorms are filled already for this session. But you could rent a little house. All the tourists are leaving or already gone now that Labor Day is over. We could find you something, I'm sure. I'll call one of my friends who's in real estate…"

This was crazy, Claire thought. Crazy. What was she thinking? Her father was making progress, but her mother had been on a downhill slide in the short time she'd been at Sunrise Manor. At first the doctor thought she might be slipping into the early stages of Alzheimer's, and Claire knew how much her mother was terrified of that. She'd gone over and sat with her mother as the doctor asked her question after question. It was surreal; after a while Claire felt as if she were looking at a woman she didn't even know.

"What's your name?" he'd asked.

"Filomena."

The doctor looked at Claire. "Mom," she said gently, touching her mother's arm. "Your name is Fanny."

Her mother looked at her coldly. "Would you want to go to school with a name like Filomena?"

"Okay," the doctor resumed, "when were you born?"

Her mother stared out the window, as if she didn't hear him. He repeated the question. "I heard you the first time," she said then. "I was born in 1929."

"But…" Claire knew that her mother was younger than her father. 1929 would make her older by two years.

Claire and the doctor, who kept looking at her mother's chart, exchanged frowns.

"Fanny," he said in a much gentler tone, trying a different approach, "do you know when Thanksgiving is?"

Again her mother stared out the window and Claire felt alarm bells ringing in her head. Her mother turned to the doctor. "Why the hell should I care?" she snapped. "It's not like they let me cook anymore."

In the end the doctor assured her it was nothing more than depression. A common occurrence at her age, after all. He didn't have to say anything further. Claire understood. He wrote a prescription which he guaranteed Claire would have her mother better than new in no time.

Oh, and don't worry about her name or date of birth, he'd also assured her. He saw it all the time, the little secrets and lies people kept for a lifetime, only to let them go finally in the elder years.

"Claire?" Zoe interrupted her thoughts. "Are you still there? Claire?"

"Oh, I'm so sorry, my mind is just...I'm trying to figure how this could possibly work."

It was another chance. Like a carrot dangling in front of her, and if she just took a nibble, it might take her back to the old Claire. Because in the last few months, she'd felt pieces of herself slipping away; the walls of her life seemed to come at her, shrinking her world to her parents, her daughter and granddaughter, and school. On the outside was Rick, photography, and freedom.

"Mom?" she now heard Amy calling her from the bottom of the stairs. "Can you come down now?"

"Be right there," she called back, and then said to Zoe, "Can you give me a couple of hours? Please? I just need to figure a few things out, okay?"

"Sure thing, I'll just tell Mr. Meyer I got your machine and I'm waiting for a call back."

"Oh, you're a doll."

Walking down the stairs, Claire felt as if her heart were beating in her throat. Because the beginning and end of this possibility was in her kitchen right now. If Donna Laverty said no, then it was settled.

"NOT ALL BABIES ARE BEAUTIFUL," Donna said, as she sipped a cup of coffee. "I know that sounds terrible, but it's true. Your little granddaughter, though, is simply gorgeous. That reddish gold hair! Who does she look like?"

Claire shook her head, hoping this wasn't a trick question. Donna always acted like they were long lost best friends from their school days, but Claire got the feeling her demeanor could change on a dime.

"She still hasn't told you who the father is?"

"No." Claire didn't tell her that she hadn't bothered asking in a while. What was the point? There'd been enough to argue about, and now that there was a certain…not peace, but maybe a bit of calm in the house, she didn't want to rock the boat. But the question was on her mind each time she looked at the baby, because Claire was certain Rose must look like her father.

"Anyway, the baby looks like she's thriving and Amy seems better, although it doesn't seem like there's a real job in sight yet."

"Well, I think it all took some getting used to. Now she's trying to find something where she can perhaps work from home. And there aren't lots of options here in Lincoln."

"I know," Donna nodded, putting her cup down. "She seems very reluctant to leave the baby in day care. I guess she saw a few horror stories in that group home she worked in down south. You know, one kid shaken by a sitter and then brain damaged, another one accidentally hit in the head by another kid in day care."

Claire didn't know that.

"She's got a nice background from that, which is good to know. She's up on her CPR and all sorts of training for meds and all. I have to say, dealing with the developmentally disabled in those homes is no picnic, so I give her kudos for that. Cleaning up shit someone decides to paint the walls with would be enough for me to walk out."

"She did that?" Claire asked.

Donna smiled sympathetically. "And worse. Don't worry, Claire. I know there's still tension with you two; I'm not blind. But it'll get better. Don't you remember being young? Weren't there times you thought your mother was your worst enemy?"

Claire looked out the window. "My father hated Liam. And I hated my mother for not standing up for me."

"It's classic. In a way, we're never far removed from who we were in high school, don't you think? I see it all the time. That baggage follows us for years. Have you gone to any of your reunions?" Donna barely waited for Claire to shake her head. "I have to tell you, I went to one just last year and it's always the same. Like everyone, no matter how successful or good-looking, walks in and thirty years disappear and they're still the geek or loser they were back then. I was nervous, too, though. Hardly anyone recognized me."

"Donna, I need to ask you something," Claire said, before Donna continued on her monologue. "I have an opportunity to go to Cape Cod for a few months, to study photography. Obviously, I would take Amy and Rose with me. I want to know if that would be okay. If you would approve it?"

Slowly Donna smiled, a knowing little look on her face. "Are you kidding? I think a change of scenery would be a great catalyst for Amy to think about her future. Getting out of Dodge will give her a fresh perspective. Here she's…well, it's like I was just saying, she's always gonna be the Amy Noble she was in high school."

"Is that how she sees herself?"

Donna shrugged. "Not in those exact words. But Claire, you and I are both old enough to know that sometimes a change of scenery is the best thing a doctor could order." She swallowed the last of her coffee and stood up. "So go. Send me a postcard. I only wish I could go with you. Just make arrangements with the psychologist. She can do phone sessions. And I'll call your cell every few weeks to stay abreast."

It was really that easy? She couldn't help it, Claire hugged her. As she let her out of the house, she felt guilty for second-guessing Donna's intentions all the time. She closed the door and leaned against it. Okay, one down. Now she had to talk to her parents. And Rick. She wouldn't even mention it to Amy until she had all of the rest worked out.

21

CLAIRE DIDN'T KNOW WHAT SHE WOULD FIND WHEN she went looking for her mother down the walking path. When she'd gone to their little apartment, the cleaning people were there. Her father was sitting in a chair outside their unit, waiting for them to finish.

"I thought she wanted to do the cleaning?" she said to her father.

He shrugged. "She decided to just let them."

"What is she doing with herself?"

"She stays in the bedroom a lot. Reading, I guess."

"Where is she now?"

"She went for a walk. There's a little path along the river. It's very pretty."

"How are you doing, Dad?"

"Me? I'm okay. A little better than before. I go to a fitness class with Fred next door."

"But are you..." She was going to say *happy*, but that seemed ridiculous.

"It's not a bad place," he said, not waiting for her to finish. "Go find your mother, she'll be glad to see you. She needs someone to talk to. She's been quiet."

The last thing her mother ever was, was quiet.

Walking down the path toward the river, Claire thought about what Eugene had said on the phone the other night. "I'm worried about Mom. Something's gone out of her voice."

Claire knew what he meant. Whenever she heard her mother talking to him, or about him, there was a happy ring to her voice. He was the special one; the light of her life. But the last few times she'd heard their phone calls, her mother's voice was flat. Resigned. Depressed. Despite whatever the doctor had guaranteed would snap her out of it.

She saw her mother sitting on a bench, staring at the water rushing by, and she wanted to cry. Her mother looked so old, as if she'd aged years in the last few months. Her shoulders were stooped, even sitting, her hair barely combed, a little too long. Her fingers were moving, and at first Claire thought she was crocheting, but she realized that her mother had developed the nervous habit recently of moving her fingers as if she were crocheting when there was nothing in her hands at all.

Her mother looked up, and it took a moment for her eyes to register recognition. She smiled, and to Claire, it was the saddest smile she'd ever seen. She sat and took both of her mother's hands, telling her everything, her excitement, her doubts. Even her guilt.

"Amy's about to finally start looking for a job. If I do this, she won't be able to."

"The job can wait. You have to go," Fanny told her. "There's no question, especially if you can take Amy and Rose."

"It's not that simple. There's my job, too. I start teaching again on Monday. This is my final year."

"So they'll get someone else. What if you were sick? They'd have to work around it."

"And then there's Rick."

"He doesn't know?"

Claire shook her head.

"He loves you. He'll understand."

Claire hesitated, then said, "Maybe your marriage wasn't perfect, Mom, but you've had a good marriage. I'm afraid I've been single for so long that I don't really...I don't know...It's hard for me to see what's right." She paused. "If I'm going to be Rick's wife, should I even be thinking of leaving him now? Shouldn't I stay here? I mean, we've had enough problems lately."

"If he really loves you, he'll want the best for you. Even if it means a little hardship for him." Her mother squeezed her hand. "At least that's how it should be."

She looked at her mother. Sometimes she took it for granted: the unconditional love, the wisdom that came with so many years. Maybe her mother was right.

She had to go and talk to Rick. Now. Time was running short.

"Come on, Mom, I'll walk you back."

Her mother smiled and shook her head. "I think I'll just sit here a little longer."

"Then what are you going to do?"

"Oh, probably take a little nap. So, when will you be leaving?"

"Mom, if I go, it'll be the day after tomorrow. But I'll come back to say good-bye, I promise. And I can come home some weekends to see you."

"Don't be silly, it's what, six, seven hours each way? That's crazy."

"I just..." Claire felt herself begin to choke up.

"Go. It's ten weeks, a little more than two months. In the course of a lifetime, it's nothing, really. We'll be fine."

She stood up. Then she leaned over and hugged her mother.

"I love you, Mom." She couldn't remember the last time she'd said those words.

Then she turned and left.

22

A STORM WAS COMING. IT WAS NEARLY MIDNIGHT and Claire sat on top of the picnic table in her yard, watching the tall pines sway back and forth, looking like they might break in half. A cold front was moving in and already there was a different smell in the air. It happened this way every year, in the first days of September. The world seemed to change suddenly, the sun lower on the horizon, a little nip in the air some mornings, geese flying home at dusk, their haunting calls echoing across the valley—all signs of autumn, the predictability of the seasons. And her life. But this fall might be different, if she had the courage to follow through. She desperately wanted to go. She'd spent two hours this evening finally allowing herself to open the book John Poole had given her. Because before, it would have been too hard, too painful to look at the beautiful photographs and not go.

But now it was possible. Turning the pages of that book of photographs taken by Charles Meyer, losing herself in the scenery, the ocean, the bay, the massive dunes and lighthouses, a thrill of excitement ripped through her. But a big part of her felt she should just let it go, despite what her mother said. Because of her parents. And Rick. And Amy's need for a job.

Earlier, Rick had told her to go. He was being supportive. But part of her felt like he said the things he did because it was what he was supposed to say. When she told him she'd be gone in two days, that she wouldn't be able to go with him next weekend for the exclusive golf tournament, he'd paused, and she could see his mind working as his mouth seemed to search for the right words. Finally, he'd told her it was okay. But his voice didn't sound okay.

What could she expect, really? Once again she'd thrown a monkey wrench into their lives. How would she have reacted if the tables were turned? She knew the answer to that; she'd have been crushed. But he'd held her tight, and that's when she thought she might be wrong. Maybe he was really glad for her. It was as if he couldn't let her go. If he hadn't had a late listing appointment, she knew they'd have wound up in his bed.

And then later, after she'd gotten home, she thought maybe he was relieved she was going. Maybe he wanted a break. Maybe he was still unsure about everything, because when she'd mentioned their wedding again, galvanized by the fervent hug, he changed the subject.

God, why did she torture herself like this? Why couldn't she just trust him and believe what he said? He loved her; he wanted her to have this chance.

So she told Amy, who looked at her like she'd lost her mind.

"Don't get me wrong, I'd love to blow this place. There's nothing for me here. I feel like I'm in a fishbowl," Amy said, standing in the kitchen with her hands on her hips. "But, Mom, I can't believe you're even thinking about leaving Gram and Grampa. So soon? If I go with you, who's gonna go visit them? We're all they've got."

"You don't have a choice. You have to go with me. And Donna approved it."

"You didn't even ask me and you already cleared it with her?"

"If she said no, what was the point?"

"And if I say no?"

Claire took a deep breath and said in a voice that threatened tears, "Don't do this to me, Amy. I'm forty-five years old. When is it ever my turn, huh? When do I ever get a chance?" Her nerves and her emotions seemed to kick into overdrive, and then she did start to cry. "What if I never get another opportunity like this?"

"I'm sorry. I know I've fucked up your life, too. I don't want to trap you here. But I don't want to leave Gram and Grampa. They just seem so pathetic since they moved there."

And then Amy had gone upstairs, leaving Claire feeling more guilty than before.

Thunder rumbled in the distance now. A bird twittered in the pines, a sad, lonely sound in the darkness. She looked up again at the circle of sky above the perimeter of trees. Gray clouds raced across the black night, with stars peeking through every now and then. She had one day to pack up everything. To call the principal and ask for a sabbatical, with a few days' notice. To go back to Sunrise Manor and say good-bye to her parents. And to deliver her photographs to John Poole.

Because she decided it was wrong to just mail them. After completing the final prints, she realized how proud she was of her work. And the responsible, teacher part of her told her it would simply smack of the chicken's way out. Although she'd resented it at first, he'd given her an incredible opportunity. And after paging through the beautiful photography book he'd given her, she felt she had to thank him.

CLAIRE SHOULDN'T HAVE bothered agonizing over whether to mail the photos or go see John Poole in person. He was as aloof and businesslike as he'd been that first night she'd literally run into him in her house.

He was actually walking out the door when she pulled up. He came toward the driveway as she got out of her car. They met halfway, in the grassy clearing that was heavy with the smoky remains of a wood fire, and it felt to her as if that night watching the meteor shower had just happened. And suddenly she felt very uncomfortable.

"I've finished the photos of the canal," she said, handing him the package.

He held it a moment, saying nothing as he looked at it, then at her.

"I'm really happy with them," she continued.

"You weren't at first." There was no smile.

"Not with the job, no. I was overwhelmed by other things. But I'm glad now. I think it's my best work so far."

She waited for him to open the big manila envelope and look at the photos. She was anxious to see his reaction. But he didn't open it; he just held it in his hand.

"You're a good photographer" was all he said.

"Well...I also wanted to thank you for the opportunity." She didn't know what else to say, and then, before she caught herself, she went on, "I forgot to tell you, I'm going to Cape Cod, after all."

"That's...great," he said, seeming stunned. "What happened?"

"Oh, it's a long story. Someone canceled. But listen, I'll let you go, you were obviously leaving when I pulled in."

She turned to walk toward her car. Suddenly, a hand on her arm stopped her. "Claire." He said her name as if it was painful to him.

She turned and he was just inches away, looking at her so intensely.

Then he shook his head. "Nothing. I just wanted to say thanks. And good luck. I have to go, too, my son is waiting for me."

He turned and walked toward his own car. She got in hers, turned around, and pulled out of the driveway. Her knees were trembling.

She wondered if he was getting his son back. Or if it was just a visit. She wondered, too, what he would think of her photographs and, despite her own satisfaction, if they'd be good enough for *New Jersey Monthly*.

But more than anything, she couldn't stop thinking about the way he'd looked at her, his eyes boring into her with a look of wanting. *Stop it*, she told herself. It was good she was leaving town. Because as she drove home along Rockport Road, she allowed the idea that had been suppressed in her mind since the first time she saw him to flare briefly: each time she'd been with John Poole, she felt a physical longing, an instant charge that seemed to defy explanation or reason. Something she hadn't felt since Liam. But if something were to happen between them, it would ruin everything for her. For a moment's satisfaction.

She wasn't stupid. And she wasn't a teenager anymore, too young and naïve to confuse this ache of desire with something real. She'd seen it on the talk shows often enough, when she'd get home from school and turn on the TV with a cup of tea for a while. There'd be a pretty woman crying her heart out over how she'd lost her husband and her children because she'd been seized with a kind of temporary insanity she'd be paying for the rest of her life.

Claire wasn't going there, not this time. She had a wonderful future with Rick; theirs was a real kind of love built on a solid foundation. And she wasn't going to throw it away.

By the time she pulled into her driveway, Claire had told herself it would be best if she never saw John Poole again.

THAT NIGHT, she went to Abbie's to say good-bye. They sat on her deck, drinking hot tea, each of them wearing sweaters.

"I hate how fall just seems to come overnight. It's like as soon as we turn the calendar page to September, Mother Nature thinks, *Oh, that's right, I'm supposed to start dropping things a notch*."

"Yeah, but it'll warm up again. It always does," Claire said.

"I'm going to miss you!" Abbie said, and Claire was surprised to see tears in her eyes. "Who am I going to vent to? Where am I going to run away to?"

"You have my spare key," Claire said. "You know you can go there anytime. It'll be empty for two months." After all the surprises of the last few months, she decided not to rent it out again.

"Oh, you don't know how tempting that is."

"Maybe you should. Maybe it's time to try out a life without him."

Abbie gave a big sigh. "It would be easier to do it now. The money from the job as sales manager at the new development is going to make a big difference in my life. I think I could actually make it on my own financially. Thanks to your wonderful fiancé. God, I love that man."

Claire smiled but said nothing.

"What?"

She put her cup down. "If my life hadn't blown up, I'd be getting married in two weeks, do you realize that?"

Abbie gave her a look. Of course she did. Claire had found out about the bridal shower that should have happened on Sunday in Abbie's yard, because they didn't know whether to have it anyway, or wait until spring. Abbie had finally just asked her, since she figured Claire knew about it anyway. Actually, she hadn't. And the thought of that surprise ruined now had been a bit of a blow.

Abbie reached over and squeezed her hand. "Look, you're not alone. I think we both know that when you're a mother, or a daughter, you're never free."

"I just thought…you know, I had Amy so young, I didn't get to have fun in my twenties, or my thirties. I thought this was my time, finally."

"It is; you're going to Cape Cod after all."

"I know, but I just have this uneasy feeling. Somehow I feel like I'm not doing the right thing. Leaving Rick and my parents."

"Because you're so used to doing everything for everyone else, not you. Rick will get by, don't worry. He'll be busy as hell gearing up for getting this entire subdivision on the market. And when he's not working, he'll be golfing. My God, the man golfs in January when there's a mild day."

"I guess it's more my parents. I went to say good-bye this afternoon. My mother was half-asleep. I'm not sure I like that stuff they put her on, remember? To sort of snap her out of her depression? She just seems like…I don't know, Abbie, like she's disappearing."

"How about your dad?"

"Actually, he's doing better. Not shaking so much. The bathroom issue seems to be under control. And he's using the cane sometimes. I don't know, maybe we made a mistake putting them there, maybe we jumped the gun."

"No, Claire. You and I both know it's only a matter of time with Parkinson's." Abbie's grandfather had had the disease for fifteen years. The final stages, she'd explained to Claire after she'd begged her to tell, were extremely difficult for the family; to watch as the patient lost the ability to swallow and finally the ability to breathe.

"But he could still have a few good years yet, give or take, before it starts to get bad," Claire suggested.

Abbie shrugged. "You know it's a crapshoot."

"I know." She sighed. "It's just that when I left, it was so sad. They looked so lost."

"Honey, they'll be fine. This is about you. Take this time and have a ball. God knows when you'll get another chance like this again. And everyone will be here when you get back."

Claire kept telling herself that all night, as she rolled from side to side, trying to sleep, then sitting up and having to unwrap the top sheet that was twisted around her waist. She had to get some sleep. Tomorrow she'd be driving for up to eight hours if she hit traffic. *Go to sleep, Claire*, she kept telling herself. Shut your mind down for the night! And then worry morphed into excitement.

Tomorrow night she wouldn't be in this bed. Or in this town. Tomorrow night she'd be in Massachusetts in a house on the water, with Amy and Rose. Tomorrow night she'd be sleeping on the edge of Cape Cod Bay.

23

It was early, not quite their breakfast time, when Claire knocked on the door of her parents' tiny apartment at Sunrise Manor. She waited a moment. She could hear the rush of the river through the woods. It was a beautiful place, actually, if there was no other choice.

She had to see them one more time. To assure herself that Abbie was right and they'd be fine. And then she'd drive back home, pick up Amy and the baby, and be on the road by ten.

She knocked again, louder. Finally, she turned the knob and was surprised to find the door unlocked. Stepping inside, she saw her father standing in the middle of the living room, swaying like a leaf in a gentle breeze.

"Claire, help me."

She rushed over to him, slipping an arm around his back, as he slowly rested his own arm over her shoulder for support. They stood a moment, as he regained his balance. She could feel his body trembling with the effort of taking a step. But nothing happened. They were standing so close that she could feel his thigh vibrating against her own leg as it struggled to move. She couldn't remember being this close to her father, ever. He didn't kiss or hug them, not even when they were children. He was simply not a demonstrative man. But now, as she held him, Claire wondered why that was. What was it that held him back from them?

"Just put your foot in front of mine," he said.

She hesitated, then placed the heel of her right foot against the toes of his left foot, as if leading him to take a step.

"No, not like that," he said quickly, as if she should know better. "The other way. Sideways."

She turned her foot, placing it now on the floor in front of her father's foot, as if blocking his. The trembling in his thigh accelerated, and a moment later, he stepped over her foot and began walking without hesitation toward the recliner, where he sat down heavily.

"That's amazing," Claire said.

"A little trick they showed me in therapy. I usually have a little pillow on the floor now that I can step over, it does the same thing."

"So you're walking better?"

"I walked the road yesterday, all the way to the bridge and back."

"With your cane, though, right?"

"Yes, with the cane."

That was huge, Claire knew. To her father, the cane was a blow to his masculine pride. But a fall would be devastating, perhaps permanently debilitating.

"Where's Mom?" she asked, as he said, "What are you doing here so early?"

She sat on the couch, a love seat, really. Everything was small, to create the illusion of normal in the tiny rooms.

"Your mother's sleeping. She sleeps a lot now." He looked confused. "I thought you left already."

Claire said nothing, the lump that had lodged in her throat growing, until she couldn't get a word out.

"I should let her go," her father said then, staring out the window. "She's so unhappy here. It's unfair. There's nothing wrong with her."

"Dad." It came out a sob. Claire tried to control herself so she could speak a coherent sentence, but it was a long moment before she could go on. And without even thinking twice about it, she said, "Dad, I want you to come with me. Both of you."

He turned from the window, looking at her, as if he couldn't have heard right. Still the man who scolded her, who'd smacked her once when she'd talked back. Who'd kept her in line with what he probably thought was a healthy dose of fear, and respect, all those years.

"Now?" he asked.

She nodded. "Yes, now. Let's get Mom up."

He didn't even ask where. And as she followed him slowly toward the bedroom, she noticed his back curling so that his head was forward, in front of his body now, the unmistakable posture of Parkinson's taking root. He was an old man, not a powerful, fearsome father, she realized then; it had never really hit her before. Because in spite of age, in spite of everything, he was still the strongest man she knew, in every way. And she couldn't help thinking about his first words when she walked in the door. That in all her forty-five years, this was the first time her father had ever asked her for help.

In the bedroom, she found her mother still sleeping.

"Mom, wake up."

Her mother's eyes opened. She looked up at her as though from far away.

"Mom, we're leaving. Get up, okay?"

"I'm tired," her mother said, rolling over.

Claire pulled the covers off her mother. "No, Mom. You have to get up. I'm taking you away from here."

Her mother lay on her back, looking at the ceiling. "Are we going home?"

Claire swallowed the lump in her throat. "I'm taking you to the ocean. You love the ocean, don't you, Mom?"

She could hear drawers opening. Claire turned and saw her father taking out piles of clothes and putting them on the bed.

They would follow wherever she took them.

II

Province Land

24

CLAIRE WOKE EARLY AND WALKED OUT THE BACK DOOR
of the house onto the weathered brick patio. Everything was gray,
the fog having arrived with them late the night before. She stepped
off the patio onto the sand, tan and soft, like the beaches in New
Jersey. Her feet sank as soon as she began to walk. She headed
straight for the water's edge, not thirty feet away and just visible
from the patio. Through the heavy mist, she could see the outlines
of boats anchored not far from the shore. The beach was quite narrow, and she wondered if it was high tide.

Instead of shells, the beach was littered with rocks and stones,
smooth and worn and in all colors and sizes. Older homes, mostly
quaint colonials and capes with cedar shingles in the typical, windswept brown or gray, lined the beach. The small boats anchored so
close to shore belonged to these homes, she realized as she stood
there, the early morning air soft and damp on her face. She took a
long breath, savoring the dank, fishy smell of the bay.

Looking through the fog, she noticed a faint brightening where
the horizon would be and realized it must be the sun coming up.
A foghorn bellowed in the distance, its long, deep bassoon seeming
to echo off the mist. She thought to herself that it was as if she'd
stepped into another world from the one she'd left behind in Jefferson County. It was beautiful, in a haunting, ethereal way.

She walked up a few houses through the soft sand toward the
pier, until she could make it out suddenly through the fog, stretch-

ing far into water, lined with boats of all shapes and sizes, their masts swaying with the movement of the tide. Provincetown, she'd read, was still a working fishing village, despite the influx of artists and tourists over the last hundred years. For several centuries, it had been the center of whaling on Cape Cod. Looking behind her, she could barely make out the fuzzy edges of the Pilgrim Monument, a tall granite building that stretched into the sky. Ted, their rental house's owner, had pointed it out to her last night when he'd handed her the keys. It was built to honor the pilgrims, who'd actually landed in Provincetown first, he'd explained, not Plymouth as most believed. It was the tallest building in town, he'd told her, and if she climbed to the top she'd have a view of the entire tip of the cape, what locals called "land's end."

A few morning walkers were coming up the beach, and she turned from the monument. Claire hated heights, so it wasn't likely she'd be going up there. She headed back toward the house. It, too, was a weathered cape with brown cedar siding, a green shingle roof, and green shutters. When they walked inside last night after the long ride, Claire had understood how she'd been able to afford something right on the harbor. An ancient brick fireplace rose in the middle of the living room and went through the second floor and up through the roof. It was the focal point of the downstairs, which was really one very large open room, except for a bedroom that her parents took because the steps to the second floor were steep. It was clean and basic, what Ted had described as "beachy." The wide windows across the back of the house, though, brought something extraordinary. A view of the harbor.

She walked around the side of the house now, where there was an outdoor shower, and up the crushed white clamshell driveway to her car. She grabbed her map from the front seat, intent on getting her bearings and as many errands done today as possible after her morning workshop. Her father had held that map for most of the ride, folding and refolding it as the hours went by. A kind of therapy, she imagined, as Rose had screamed for a spell, or her mother had moaned from her aching hip.

Walking across the red brick patio and in the back door, she turned and took one last look at the beach. Somewhere through the gray mist the sun had come up, and the day was beginning. Last night, she'd been heartbroken because she'd wanted to see the sunset on the harbor, that famous light she'd read about and dreamed of. She needed it after the long, torturous day on the road, and the critical looks of the staff at Sunrise Manor when she stopped at the main building, as her parents waited in the car, to let the administrator know she'd be taking them for a few months. But Claire thought that this itself, this morning, was a gift. The beach held its own haunting beauty right now, a shadow version of itself, with everything in soft relief. A black-and-white study of the fog would be stunning, she decided. She could wait for the light.

They were all sleeping when she went back inside. Quietly she unpacked in her room upstairs. It was the smallest, but that was fine. Her parents were in the downstairs bedroom, and Amy and Rose had the other two small bedrooms on the second floor. The wallpaper in Claire's room was a yellow floral, something she would never have picked, but that she liked. It was old but gave the room a happy feel. The bed was pushed against the wall, to make room to walk around, and beside the double window that faced the bay sat an old cherry dresser. As she put her clothes in the drawers, she kept glancing out the window, hardly able to believe she was really here, on the edge of Cape Cod Bay.

When she finished in her room, she went downstairs to start coffee. She'd stopped at a convenience store last night and picked up a few things, but they'd need to stock up on groceries since the only store within walking distance was a gourmet shop and undoubtedly expensive. It was nearly nine; she was surprised they were all still sleeping, and chalked it up to exhaustion from yesterday's ride. Amazingly, Rose had slept all night, although Amy had given her the last bottle close to midnight, as Claire helped to get their room organized. Her mother, she suspected, would be disoriented. She'd had her eyes closed nearly the entire ride. Last night, Claire found the pills the doctor had given her, as well as an old prescription for sleeping pills, and hid them after Amy whispered that she thought her grandmother was overmedicated. Amy said she'd seen it a lot in the group homes she'd worked in. Claire was surprised at the little things Amy was beginning to reveal. Maybe she'd tell her soon about how little Rose came to be. Right now, though, Claire wasn't going to push any buttons. She had too much to do today.

As she sat down to make a list of what they'd need from the store, she thought of Rick. She missed him already.

FANNY LEFT CLAIRE in her high chair, the tray covered with raisins and Cheerios, her cheeks bulging like a hungry squirrel's. Eugene was sleeping soundly in his playpen. She went into the bathroom, left the door partly open, and then Fanny stripped off her house-dress as she turned on the faucet. A moment later, she relished the feel of the hot water beating hard on her shoulders. She turned then and let the water run over her face for long minutes, her eyes closed. Joe had barely been home the last month or so, as he tried to sell more insurance policies because they needed a new furnace. A week ago Claire had gotten sick, then Eugene, and Fanny hadn't showered in two, maybe three days. Suddenly, the hot water cooled, and then it was cold, and Fanny turned the water off quickly, grabbing a towel. And then she heard the baby crying. She tried to pull her housedress back on but it got caught over her head. The baby was screaming now, and she tore at the dress, frantic.

Fanny woke up tearing at the covers. She opened her eyes with a start. Sitting up, she looked around the strange room, the feeling of panic worsening. The walls were papered in a lilac stripe. The furniture was old, the kind she had as a girl, probably considered antique by now. She turned and saw a window with lace curtains. She had no idea where she was.

Somewhere in the house, there was a baby screaming. She got up as quickly as she could, but she felt groggy and disoriented. She found her robe on a wicker chair by the big window. Looking out as she tied the robe, she saw water and sand and, through a light fog, a long pier in the distance. The baby's cries became shrieks.

Her hip throbbing, she hobbled out into a large room with a huge red brick fireplace in the middle. She followed the noise around the fireplace until she came to an open kitchen. There, to her relief, she found Amy pacing with Rose, who was flailing in her arms.

"Oh, Grandma, I don't know what to do! I can't make her stop. I think she's in pain."

Fanny collapsed in a kitchen chair and held out her arms. "Let me try." Her voice sounded raspy, as if she hadn't spoken in a long time.

Amy placed Rose in her arms, but the baby continued to squirm and cry. Fanny turned her over, laying the baby on her stomach across Fanny's legs. Rose drew her knees up, and Fanny began patting her bottom.

"She's got a bellyache," she told Amy. "Did you try those drops you have for gas?"

"The Mylicon? Yes, it doesn't seem to be doing a thing."

Fanny kept patting Rose's back with the palm of her trembling hand, to break up the gas. But the baby kept thrashing on her lap.

"Is there a good grocery store nearby?" she asked.

"I don't know. There's a gourmet shop a block or two away; we passed it last night."

"Put some water on to boil, then go and see if they have fennel."

An hour later Rose was asleep in the portacrib they'd brought. Fanny sat at the kitchen table, drinking a cup of coffee Amy had made for her, the grogginess lifting as her insides began to settle down.

"Thanks, Gram," Amy said, her voice still shaking. "I just can't take it when she's hurting."

"It's the hardest part," she said with a sympathetic smile. "Nothing in those books can really prepare you for when your children are hurting."

"Do you think she has colic?"

"Well, maybe a touch." She didn't want to frighten Amy. Eugene had colic, on top of his allergies and rashes, and it had been exhausting.

"I just keep thinking if I didn't let them give me that shot to dry up my milk, I might have been able to nurse her. They say that's the best, that babies who are breastfed don't get colic."

"Don't," Fanny said, shaking her head. "You'll make yourself crazy if you second-guess everything. We all want to do the best we can, but being a mother…well, it's the hardest job in the world."

Amy sat down at the table now and put her head in her hands. "Yeah, but most mothers are somewhat prepared. Rose didn't exactly get a bargain with me."

"Amy, you love her. A person would have to be blind not to see that. That's the most important thing. Some parents give things, but they don't have the love they should for the child. You have in your heart the most important thing your daughter needs. The rest will come."

Amy got up then and poured herself a cup of coffee. Fanny looked out the kitchen window, at the unbelievable sight of sand and water.

"You know I had no idea where I was when I woke up. I was dreaming Eugene was crying, but it was Rose. It must have brought on the dream. It was so real."

Amy looked at her with raised eyebrows. "You slept like the

whole way here, Gram. We're on Cape Cod. In Provincetown. You know that, right?"

Fanny nodded, but stared out the window. "Where's your mother?" she asked.

"She just left for her workshop. She wants us to finish the grocery list, okay, Gram?"

The fog was starting to lift, Fanny noticed, and in the distance she saw a blinking green light. Then she noticed Joe out there on the patio, standing and looking out at the water.

"Gram?"

She turned and looked at Amy, who was at the sink with her hands on her hips.

"Those pills are crap, Gram. You don't need them."

She said nothing, her insides crawling with shame. What kind of role model was she for Amy?

CLAIRE COULDN'T REMEMBER the last time she'd ridden a bike to go somewhere, instead of for exercise. It felt very European, especially since the street was so narrow and most of the buildings so old. Ted had told her it was easiest to walk or bike in town, as parking was limited. And there was an old bike he left with the house. Commercial Street was lined with houses and galleries. The town was quiet, with barely any traffic, as if everyone were still asleep, and within minutes Claire felt a surge of contentment.

She was glad to have this time to herself before starting the workshop. Through the breaks in the houses to her left, she could see glimpses of the bay, awash in early silver light, the sun now teasing her with occasional, brief appearances. Their house was at the east end of Commercial Street, what Ted called the gallery district. There were so many on the first few blocks, she couldn't help stopping and admiring the beautiful paintings and photographs, explosions of flowers, sunsets and sunrises over ocean and dune, varying shades of stunning light-filled canvases.

As fishing boats chugged out of the harbor, she noticed an artist setting up an easel on the sidewalk, to capture the scene. She passed another, already at work in an alley, sketching one of the old houses in colorful chalk strokes. A heavenly scent of cinnamon and yeast began to fill the air, and she thought it must be the Portuguese bakery Ted had told her about. They would close for the winter in a few months, and he made her promise to try their malassadas. Always, though, there was the distinct odor of the bay drifting through the air; a murky, earthy smell she inhaled deeply. She couldn't help but smile.

An assortment of characters were walking dogs, riding bikes, or sitting in front of the coffee shops lazily reading the paper. It was warm and humid, and Claire stopped and took off her cardigan and tied it around her waist. As she pedaled slowly, pulling over occasionally to let a car or truck by, she felt like someone in a novel she might have read for her book club. Here she was, embarking on this incredible opportunity, in this new world. There was something so promising about suddenly finding yourself plopped down in a strange land. Here in this new place she could be a different Claire. Here, her untapped potential could begin to flow. And that possibility ignited an excitement within her, a feeling of wonder and self-discovery she hadn't felt since she was a teenager.

In her novels, though, the heroine was usually alone on her adventure. Here Claire was with the entire clan in tow and her fiancé left behind for two and a half months. Was she crazy? She wasn't sure yet. She just knew that when she went that second time to say good-bye to her parents, she just couldn't leave them like that. She'd felt blindsided, suddenly hit with the realization that one day, perhaps in the not too distant future, they would be gone forever. That with all their annoyances and needs, their unconditional love would disappear with them. And her safe harbor would vanish.

She stopped suddenly and stared in the window of a gallery, at a large canvas depicting Commercial Street, where she now stood, in the midst of a nighttime snowstorm, with just the glow of the streetlights and the swirling snowflakes illuminating the scene. It was breathtaking, and she hopped off her bike to go inside. But the sign beside the door said: *Hours—Afternoons, or By Chance.* Claire smiled again. Imagine having such a relaxed life, indulged by whim and artistic mood, that you opened your shop simply when you felt like it? She assumed that gallery owner rarely taxed her brain with multitasking. Not like Claire, who was a master at it.

She turned right in the middle of town, where if she'd turned left, she could have pedaled out onto the long wharf. But she'd glanced at her watch and seen that she was already pressed for time due to her lollygagging, as Abbie would have put it. If she were back home, she would be in the midst of changing classes right now, about to start second period, her ears assaulted by the cacophony of teenage voices, slamming lockers, and the competing ring tones of a dozen cell phones about to be confiscated. But this, Claire thought, as she spotted a sign up ahead and slowed down, this was simply a lovely way to start the day.

The Arts Center was on a quiet side street of town, a quaint array of old gray buildings surrounded by colorful gardens and linked by red gravel paths. Here and there amid the flowers and shrubs, sat sculptures, whimsical chimes, a Zen fountain, and other evidence of the artistic flavor of the place, and undoubtedly the prized work of graduates. Claire parked her bike next to a few others and took a deep breath, a sudden burst of excitement leaping through her middle. This was it. This was what she'd come for. And then she realized that she had no idea which building her workshop was in.

CHARLES MEYER was undoubtedly the most famous photographer on Cape Cod. Originally from the Midwest, he'd fallen in love with the Cape years ago while on assignment. He stood in front of them now in the small room, which needed paint and new windows, as Claire and nine others sat at desks that could have been salvaged from her old Catholic school. She was delighted at Meyer's opening lecture.

"You can't photograph or paint a place authentically," he began, "without knowing its history. How it came to be."

Claire had always believed that. In the moments before she snapped a picture, she often felt that little thrill of knowing that she was providing tangible proof of history. Because within five minutes, five months, or five years, that moment was already in the past.

Charles Meyer now explained that seventy million years ago, Cape Cod lay under a sheet of ice, and the way it looked now was in part due to that glacier's retreat. As it slid back, it scoured the land with massive rocks and debris. As chunks of ice broke off, ponds formed. Claire thought of the many small bodies of water she'd seen off of Route 6 toward the end of their drive yesterday.

"This tip of the cape curves like a fishhook and can be disorienting when you first come. It was created by wind and sea over a span of just ten thousand years," he continued, sitting on the edge of a desk in front of the room.

Later, the Pilgrims were the first Europeans to land there, he explained, coming ashore at the very end of Commercial Street. The land was well forested, and they decided it would be a hospitable place to begin their new life. They lasted a year before discovering they were wrong and moving across Cape Cod Bay to Plymouth, but not before stripping the land of many of those trees.

"Two hundred years later, Thoreau labeled Provincetown *a city of sand*," he said. "Thoreau wrote that *sand is the great enemy here... There was a schoolhouse filled with sand up to the tops of the desks.*

Ironically, we seem to have conquered the sand with blacktop and brick, and now it's the sand we want, that our bare feet crave to feel."

He had a subtle humor and a philosophical air. Claire thought that Charles Meyer was unlike anyone she'd ever met in Jefferson County.

"And what are we now?" he asked. "This tip of the Cape, what is commonly called 'land's end,' is basically a low-lying sandbar covered by massive dunes that grew over the years as a result of that lack of trees. We're a fragile thing. Unlike most land, we don't sit on bedrock, but a shifting bed of sand. And while we've had many storms over the centuries, today, if a major hurricane or nor'easter hit us just right, it could simply wash everything away."

He paused a moment, letting his words sink in. And then he smiled again. "Hopefully, we'll continue to be lucky. Over the last three centuries, Provincetown has gone from whaling capital to fishing village, with a large Portuguese influence. Today, as you know, although the fishermen and many of the Portuguese remain, the tide of energy is changing. Provincetown has become a mecca for artists, and the reason, as you'll see, is simple. It's the light. And the geography I've just explained is an important aspect in reflecting the light. All of this sand, surrounded by Cape Cod Bay and the ocean, provides a unique setting. But it's more than that, I think. There's something almost indefinable, perhaps magical, about the light. We'll see what you think."

He stood up from the desk then and brought his hands together. He was tall and lanky, probably in his sixties, Claire thought. Although his skin was tan and weathered, there was an elegance about him, no doubt due to the longish brown hair that touched his shoulders, flecked with strands of gray beside his temples.

"Like some of you, I was once a black-and-white purist," he went on. "Part of that could probably be my age. But I don't think so. There has long been an attitude that for a photograph to be truly 'artistic,'" and here he made quotes with his fingers the way she often did in class, "it had to be in black and white."

He told them that one of his friends, a very renowned photographer in his own right, refused any electronic manipulation of his photographs. The man didn't even have a camera on his cell phone. "Well, I'm here to tell you that clinging to the purist attitude can also be a side effect of age, or a desire to cling to our comfort zone. But embracing change, while difficult for artists, can also be liberating. Obviously, you wouldn't be sitting in this workshop if you didn't follow that line of thinking."

He began to walk in front of the room now, and Claire felt a little prickle of nerves in her middle.

"When on assignment here a decade ago, I had a paradigm shift. And it happened because of the light. Over the next ten weeks, as you become more familiar with digital photography and the flexibility of enhancing color, shading, and yes, light, I hope you, too, will feel that paradigm shift. That this relatively new method of photography—in historic terms that is—has opened a whole new world to us as visual artists."

Claire sat there and felt her stomach drop to the floor. This wasn't the class she'd signed up for. Somehow Zoe, or Charles Meyer, had made a mistake. It was probably a last minute oversight, and how could it not be, everything had happened so fast.

"But in case there are still some of you who are not convinced, your first assignment is to find a subject, be it a beach, a boat, a bird, I don't care, as long as it's in a natural, outdoor setting. And then I want you to take a photograph in both black and white and color so that we can compare the results."

Claire didn't even have a digital camera. And she really had no interest in studying color photography. She loved her black-and-white work, the journalistic look of it. The subtle shading, the absence of color, created an atmosphere of importance, a more concentrated focus on her subjects. They were not competing with the color.

But this was obviously not a black-and-white workshop.

She felt like she might actually cry as the other students stood and began to leave. She'd done so many crazy, impulsive things to get here. And now it was for nothing.

CLAIRE WAS ANNOYED when her father insisted on coming with her to the grocery store. She needed to get this over with as quickly as possible. She'd thought of asking Amy to go, but she'd been surprised when she returned after her workshop to find Amy sitting on the patio with Fanny, who seemed a little more with it than yesterday. Amy was singing the "Eensy Weensy Spider" to Rose, who intently watched her fingers moving along to the words. Claire's mother yawned, then smiled, and Claire decided it would be better not to interrupt.

Now she was driving toward the Grand Union with her father, a long list in her purse, his cane in the backseat, and thoughts of her assignment needling her. It would be a slow process because she knew he wouldn't use one of those motorized carts most stores had for the handicapped. She headed down Bradford and made a right on Shankpainter, following the directions she'd gotten from Ted last night, after he gave her a two-page list of stores and beaches and other local information. She spotted the sign for the store ahead.

"Don't," her father said, as she turned on her blinker.

"What?"

"Keep going straight."

"But Dad…"

"Claire," her father said in that voice from her childhood that brooked no argument. Then, surprisingly, a bit softer, he said, "I need to see something. It'll only take a few minutes."

Only once in her entire life had Claire talked back to her father.

She was twelve years old, and had been silenced by a slap. She'd been insulted more than hurt, and she'd never done it again. Back then parents, fathers in particular, were so much stricter than today. Claire had wondered over the years, especially with her problem students, if a little bit of fear might engender a little bit of respect in those students. The thought of arguing with her father now was as foreign to her as speaking to him in Chinese. She kept going straight.

Before she knew it, they were back on Route 6, heading in the direction from which they'd come just last night. Five minutes into the drive, she was biting her lip. She kept looking at the clock on the dashboard. She really didn't have time for this. At ten minutes, she was going to just turn around. This was ridiculous.

As they drove, Claire glanced over at the bay to her right, the land curling around it like the end of a fishhook, as it was famously described everywhere, as well as by Charles Meyer that morning. It really was dis-orienting, as she'd discovered on the ride just yesterday, to drive past the bay and then see land in the distance, only to discover it was the town you just drove through.

"Turn here," her father said a moment later.

They were in Truro, the sign said, and they crossed under Route 6, heading left now, to the other side of this peninsula, and toward the ocean. There was nothing but woods on either side of the road as she drove, scrub pines and a few hardwoods that were green and lush. Occasionally they passed a driveway, but she couldn't see a house anywhere.

"Up ahead, make a left onto Highland," her father said.

"Highland?" she asked, turning to him. "Dad, how do you know the street names?"

He didn't answer. He seemed so intent on whatever it was they were looking for. She made the left and drove slowly down a cracked and pitted blacktop road, long ago faded to gray. Up ahead, she saw a rusted chain-link fence crossing the road. She began to slow down, and then the woods gave way and the land and fence stretched as far as she could see. There were big old buildings, long and low, that appeared abandoned. A little shiver ran up her arms, although it was hot out, the fog having ushered in a warm front that felt more like the dog days of summer than September.

There wasn't a person or car in sight. It reminded her of a set from an old sci-fi movie from her childhood, an eerie remnant of some past life, and Claire had an urge to turn around and drive away quickly.

"What on earth is this place?" she asked. "And how did you even know it was here?"

She turned, because her father didn't answer. He was staring straight ahead, his head bobbing now from side to side.

"I spent the worst year of my life here," he said, so softly she almost didn't hear him.

And then he opened his door. Claire jumped out of the car and opened the back door, grabbing his cane. She came around the car, where her father was leaning on his door. She'd never seen him like this before, and worried about the effect on his symptoms.

"Here, Dad, you don't want to fall now."

Her father took the cane, and she saw that his hand shook as he leaned on it heavily. He was trying to walk, but his feet didn't move. She placed her foot in front of his, like a T, and a moment later that foot stepped over hers and he began walking quickly, as if afraid to stop. She followed him as he headed toward the fence.

"I was in the service here in the fifties," he said as he walked. "During the Cold War."

Before she was born, she realized. Or he even knew her mother.

"You wouldn't remember those times. But things were so different then."

She did remember the Cold War, though, in the sixties. She was just a little girl, in kindergarten or first grade, huddled under her desk at St. Mary's school, during air raid drills. The loud sirens terrified her, and she'd tried to make herself as small as possible as her bare knees pressed into the hardwood floors. Years later, in her college History classes, they'd laughed about it, so full of themselves. As if a wooden desk could save them from radiation.

"The fear was real," he said, as if reading her thoughts. "We were afraid of the Russians. That damn bomb we built, that saved the world in the forties, became our worst enemy then."

"Dad, what is this place?"

"It's an air force station. This was where the government put its first radar outpost. Here," and her father lifted a hand and held it out, encompassing everything around them, "here is where we protected the entire east coast."

He began walking along the fence, to the gate. It was unlocked. Her father unlatched it and pushed it open.

"Bring the car," he ordered.

She knew better than to argue.

A moment later, she brought the car beside him and he climbed back in, tossing his cane on the backseat. They drove the worn road, past rows of low, abandoned buildings that must have been barracks. She tried to imagine her father sleeping in one of them, a young man not even eighteen, living his life here. The one thing she did know was that her father had enlisted in the service at sixteen. His childhood had been rough, both of his parents dead by the time he was just ten. He lived with a neighbor for nearly a year, then went into an orphanage before going to live with a foster family. World War II was still going on and times were hard.

At the end of the road she stopped the car and he slowly climbed out again. The blanket of gray that had covered the sky most of the day was beginning to thin finally, and a weak sun shone through. He walked across a grassy field and she followed. The land gave way suddenly, dropping in a sheer cliff to the ocean below, vast and dark blue. Dramatic bluffs ran up and down the beach, like pictures she'd seen of Ireland.

"This is just gorgeous," she said.

"Not really," her father said. "It was an awful place. I lost one of my best friends during that time here."

He didn't speak for a while, and neither did she. She could hear the faint crash of the waves below, the wind off the water, blowing through the high grass around them. Otherwise, silence. Ear-ringing quiet. He simply stood there, staring, and she waited.

She thought of the drive last night, the monotony of Route 6 as it bisected the Cape, and her disappointment that for nearly the first forty minutes of the ride there'd been nothing but trees on either side, no views at all. Then suddenly the speed limit had dropped and they were going through a string of small towns, salt ponds visible in the distance. The roadside was dotted with little shops, motels, lobster shanties, and houses with picket fences and boats in the driveways. When they passed the sign for the Cape Cod National Seashore, the land began to rise and dip, and she remembered from her reading that these were ancient sand dunes they were driving over. And then the towns ended and they passed the sign for Truro, and another for Cape Cod Light.

Suddenly, they came over a large hill, and as they descended, they could see the tip of the Cape, stretching into the distance, the land curving sharply back into itself, as it had been described in her readings. To their right, massive sand dunes, like small mountains, rose and stretched toward the unseen ocean. To Claire, beaches had always been flat. She'd never seen anything like this.

"Wow," Amy had whispered from the backseat. "This is awesome."

"That must be Boston, those lights in the distance," Claire had guessed as they passed another sign, entering Province Lands.

"No, that's Truro," her father had said, breaking his long silence.

"But we just passed Truro," she'd said.

He explained how they were driving around the hook, and although they were continuing forward, they were actually facing the town they'd just passed, across the bay. She thought he knew this because he had the map. Her father had always been fascinated by maps. But now, as they stood in silence, as he relived God knew what memories, Claire knew it wasn't the map. He'd been stationed here. And he'd never said a word to anyone.

"I came to hate sand here," he said, finally. "We could never get rid of it, no matter how much we swept and cleaned. I swore I'd never, ever come back to this place."

Yet here they were.

25

"GRAM, LET'S GO FOR A WALK," AMY SAID. FANNY looked across the kitchen at her. She could tell Amy was restless. Rose was fast asleep in the little bouncy seat on the floor, lulled by its music and vibration. Amy had given her another bottle of the fennel tea mid-morning.

"I'm not really up for a walk, sweet pea."

"Then we'll ride," Amy said, turning back to her.

"You go. I'll just stay here and rest."

"No. I promised my mom I would keep an eye on you."

Fanny looked at her. Amy's return look was challenging.

"She's worried about you, Gram."

Claire had left for her workshop early that morning and said she wasn't sure what time she'd be returning. She looked stressed.

"That's ridiculous."

"Is it really?"

Fanny thought about the pills they'd thrown away. She remembered a time not so long ago when she wouldn't touch such a thing. And then she'd stopped caring. Now it was like she was slowly waking from a dream. But she was still tired, and part of her just wanted to go back to sleep.

"Oh, come on, Gram. Don't you want to see the town? It's so pretty. Let's explore."

She hesitated. Glancing through the kitchen windows, Fanny

could see Joe sitting on the patio overlooking the beach, staring at the water. It was late morning, cloudy, but warm already.

"Grampa will be just fine. He pretty much hasn't moved from that spot since we got here."

It was a lovely spot to sit, to watch the birds and the bay, the boats chugging in and out of the harbor. Since they arrived, Joe hadn't turned on the television once. Mostly he sat outside there. Staring. Remembering, Fanny knew.

Yesterday, when he and Claire had gotten home from the grocery store, he'd gone into their room to lie down, looking exhausted. Claire had to keep putting her foot in front of his to keep him moving, and that's how Fanny knew he was stressed. As she helped Claire put the groceries away, Claire told her where they'd gone.

"Isn't it amazing? You should have seen this place. It was stunning, these dramatic cliffs at the edge of the base, just dropping away, and the ocean, so vast and beautiful. But it was also haunting. It was abandoned a long time ago and it's kind of creepy now. I certainly wouldn't go there alone. He still knew the names of the roads. Imagine, after all these years. And you had no idea he'd been stationed there either?"

No, she hadn't. When they'd met, he'd just told her vaguely that he'd been in New England.

He was right near here, then, as a young man. Before they met. It was where he and Charlie Hoffman obviously became friends. And it was where, she now knew with every nerve in her body, he'd met that woman. Ava. It had to be. He remembered being here, he'd told Claire, as if it were yesterday.

"Come on, Gram. We won't be gone more than an hour. I'll make sure Grampa has everything he needs."

Fanny really didn't care if he had everything he needed. He hadn't said a word to her about where he took Claire yesterday. And she hadn't spoken a word to him since. Not even good night when he got in bed, his hand hitting the mattress over and over, evidence that he was still worked up. She pretended to be asleep. She was sick of thinking about it.

"Gram?"

She looked up. "All right," she said. "Give me a few minutes to change."

THE AFTERNOONS, it seemed, would be different each day, according to Charles Meyer. There would be workshops on some, field excursions for group shoots on others. And then, like today, they would be on their own to produce something for the following morning.

Claire sat on a bench alone, eating her sandwich. The class had scattered after the second morning's session. Everyone seemed eager to get back to work on the black-and-white versus color assignment. Claire threw her sandwich back into the plastic bag, half-eaten. She pulled her cell phone out of her backpack and dialed Rick. No answer. She'd called him last night, but there was no answer then, either. This time she didn't leave a message. Instead she dialed Abbie.

"Hey, give me a call when you have a chance," she said to Abbie's voice mail.

She stood up, pulled her backpack over one shoulder, and walked back into the administration building with a feeling of dread. She'd had no time to get herself a digital camera yesterday. By the time she returned with her father and a carload of groceries, the one and only camera shop in town had already closed. She didn't have the energy to get on Route 6 again and head toward Orleans, which was a bit more built up and had some of the typical chain stores. So here she was on day two, already behind on the first assignment.

Last night she'd gone out the back door of the house after dinner and walked across the old brick patio onto the beach, which was again blanketed in a fine gray mist after a sudden rain. Black and white, she'd thought, really was the perfect medium for this weather. She'd shot an entire roll, feeling alone and cocooned on the beach. The Pilgrim Monument had disappeared once again in the brief fog, and the long pier in the distance, with its fishing boats barely visible, looked ghostly and beautiful. She was planning to develop and print that film today. But that was only half the assignment.

The administration building was old and ramshackle, and now she walked through a large, open area with tiny rooms surrounding it, all of them empty as everyone was apparently out to lunch. But Charles Meyer was there, and she found him in the last room. He was standing over a work table, matting prints.

"Mr. Meyer?"

He looked up. "Yes. Come in."

Deep in her chest, she could feel her heart pounding.

"I'm Claire Noble."

He nodded. "Yes, I know who you are, Ms. Noble." He'd had them introduce themselves at the beginning of their first session. She was amazed he remembered her already.

"I...Well it seems there's been a mistake. This isn't the class I applied for. Back in June, I was supposed to come up for the black-and-white session."

"Yes, I remember. You had some family problems, or something."

She nodded. "That's right. And when Zoe called to tell me about this sudden opening, I assumed it was for the same workshop."

"You're not interested in digital or color photography?"

"I don't really have any experience in it, to be honest. Black and white is my medium. It's what I was really looking forward to focusing on and improving."

"Aaah, you're a purist."

She felt herself blush. "I guess you could say that. And I'm sorry about the mistake. Maybe Zoe did mention it, maybe I was confused..."

"Maybe it isn't a mistake," Charles Meyer said, looking at her with raised eyebrows. "Maybe it's an opportunity."

She didn't say anything for a moment. How did she tell this man, who was an expert, whose work had appeared in some of the finest galleries in the country, that she didn't really have an interest in color photography? Not professionally anyway. That she had her heart set on black and white.

"I don't even have a digital camera," she managed to say.

He smiled. It was the same smile she gave her students when they came up with one excuse after another as to why they couldn't possibly handle an assignment. He turned and opened a cabinet and pulled out a canvas bag.

"Here, a loaner. Give it a few days, and if you don't want to continue, we'll refund your money."

She hesitated, then took the bag. "All right. Thank you."

As she was walking out the door, he called her name.

"Ms. Noble?"

She turned. He stood there with his arms folded, but his smile was kind.

"Good luck."

Walking up the gravel path, she thought again about everything she'd done to get here. Could she really turn back now?

She felt a bit like a petulant child, disappointed when opening a gift, all of her expectations deflated.

Maybe luck was what she needed, after all.

IT REMINDED FANNY of a rickshaw. It was called a pedicab and was similar to a rickshaw, except instead of running, the driver pedaled a bicycle with a high cart for them to sit in just behind him. They'd be driven through town by a young man who introduced himself as Billy. He brought a small stool from the back of the cart and helped Fanny up. Amy climbed in next, with Rose in her arms. They sat beside each other and Amy turned Rose around in her lap so she faced front. The baby's big blue eyes were in constant motion as she sucked on her binkie.

"Isn't this cool?" Amy said, with a gush of excitement.

A moment later they were off.

They rode down Commercial Street, which was one way, past houses and then galleries. As they drew closer to the pier, Billy explained that this was the beginning of the center of town. The street became more lively, with restaurants, sidewalk cafes, and different kinds of shops and boutiques, and Billy commented on things now and then.

"I don't think we're in Kansas anymore, Gram," Amy laughed.

Fanny hadn't seen Amy this relaxed in…she couldn't remember when. Every block or so, Amy giggled, and said, "look at this," or "ohmygod, how about that!" There was the woman in black, with long, frizzy, purple hair, sweeping the sidewalk in front of a gallery. To Fanny she looked like a witch. Amy had just said, "Cool."

In front of a coffee shop called "The Wired Puppy," people sipped their drinks with their dogs at their feet. Fanny was surprised to see people taking their dogs in and out of most shops. She saw women holding hands, like lovers. And handsome men in tight shorts roller skating past them.

In front of the town hall, an old, three-story structure that looked like something from a movie she'd once seen years ago, the pedicab stopped. A throng of people were clogging the street and Fanny could hear singing.

"Come on, Gram, let's go listen."

Fanny didn't want to get down. She knew it was going to jar her hip, which was still sore from the long car ride.

"You go. I'll wait here and hold Rose for you."

"Oh, come on, Gram!"

Amy had already climbed down and was now carrying Rose on her hip. She held out her other hand to help Fanny. Billy also jumped down and held out a hand.

"She's right, Gram," he said in his singsong voice. "You don't want to miss this."

She felt like an old lady as she slowly stood and then perched on the edge of the pedicab. But Billy simply grabbed her under both arms and lifted her like a doll as she squealed in surprise.

They edged through the crowd, and in front of the old building she saw a clear patch of sidewalk around a tall woman, who Fanny guessed must be in her sixties. She had long blond hair that was teased the way women used to wear it years ago. Her orange dress was very short and she had on spiked heels. Statuesque, Fanny thought.

"Look at her legs," she whispered to Amy, as the woman strutted, launching into a torchy version of "The Look of Love," one of her favorites from years ago. "She has some legs. Not an ounce of fat."

"Gram," Amy said and pulled on her arm. "Are you kidding? That's not a woman. That's a man!"

Fanny looked at the sign in front of the woman, who sang into a microphone, a portable speaker perched on one of the benches. She sang and flirted with the crowd, without a shred of self-consciousness. A sign on the sidewalk, beside a basket filled with dollar bills, read: *Miss Lila, 75 years young and living her wildest dream.*

"Amy, you're wrong, look at—"

But Amy was shaking her head. "No, Gram, it's a man."

"Wow," she said. "She…that is he…really is living her wildest dream."

They climbed back into the pedicab, and Billy slowly pedaled on down Commercial Street. Soon the people thinned out again and the stores became fewer. There was a big, brick post office with a parking lot overlooking the water, where Fanny saw ships docked in the distance.

Beautiful old inns and bed and breakfasts now began to line the street, with the occasional shop. A narrow sidewalk ran on the right side of the street, but few people used it. Everyone walked in the street, unconcerned about cars or trucks.

"Isn't it nice to see so many funky stores?" Amy asked. "Not like by us, where they're all the same, everywhere you go."

Billy pulled over then in front of a gorgeous bed and breakfast, with gray clapboard and purple trim, and a wraparound porch filled with people reading and drinking coffee. He turned around, so they could hear him.

"Most of these inns were once the homes of whaling captains. If you look on top of some, you'll see the widow's walks, where the wives would watch for their husbands' ships to return after months, or sometimes even years, at sea."

Between the houses, Fanny caught glimpses of the bay. The boats were bigger here, and Billy explained that this was where the ferries to Boston and the occasional small ship anchored. He began pedaling again, and the street veered away from the water and then, after a few blocks, took a sudden, sharp turn left, taking them back to the water again.

"This is the west end," Billy said. "Probably the quietest part of Commercial Street. Watch for the houses with the wood carvings next to the front door showing a boat on top of a wave. Those houses were actually floated over here a hundred years ago from a settlement on one of the sand spits out in the bay, called Long Point."

"Why did they do that?" Amy asked.

He shook his head. "They couldn't make it out there. It was a hard life back then."

They rode quietly for a while through the residential streets, lined with charming older homes with picket fences, some dripping autumn clematis, its sweet fragrance filling the air. One garden was more vibrant than the next, with tall pink and orange zinnias, purple petunias bursting from pots, and fat mums with buds just waiting for the cooler days of fall to arrive.

"Being near the water, it doesn't get as cold as the mainland," Billy explained. "Flowers last well into autumn."

He slowed down so they could admire the different houses and gardens. Amy nudged her and Fanny turned to see that Rose had fallen asleep. The baby lay across Amy's lap, her little lips partly open, her golden hair curling above her ears. And then she smiled.

"She's dreaming of angels. That's what Mama used to say when they smiled like that in their sleep."

"She is an angel," Amy said. Suddenly her eyes filled with tears.

"What is it?" Fanny asked, touching her cheek.

"I…I just worry about what kind of life I can give her. I want her to have the best."

"We all feel that way about our babies. That's how your mother felt about you, sweet pea. And I felt about her."

"I'm not like her."

"I know things are strained between the two of you, but she really wasn't much different than you are now. Young, scared. Alone." Then she shook her head. "No, not alone. You both have family. You'll never be alone."

"I know. I know what you meant."

Billy stood up then, and they turned, watching him strain as he pedaled up a large hill. Fanny felt bad for him and was ready to say they'd get out and walk for a while, but then they were at the top and he coasted down, not too fast, she was happy to see. He turned to them with a smile, his face flushed.

"At the end, just a few blocks down, there's a view that'll knock your socks off."

He pedaled faster then, and within minutes they reached the

end of Commercial Street. As the pedicab rounded a rotary, with a tree-filled little park in its center, Fanny and Amy gasped together.

The world stretched before them, water and sand as far as the eye could see.

"The moors," Billy announced, hopping off his seat. "Isn't it incredible?"

Marshland and sand flats surrounded them and it appeared the tide was going out, as people walked in the wet sand, stepping over rivulets of the seawater that was quickly draining. A rock jetty stretched into the distance, far out in the water, toward a spit of sand. To their right, massive sand dunes, as high as small mountains, were covered with beach grass and vegetation. A break in the clouds brought a sudden flood of sunlight as they watched and Fanny felt her heart expand.

"Oh, it's just..." She searched for the right word. "It's so immense. And lovely."

"It is," Amy said, standing beside her, gazing from one end of the view to another. "It makes you feel like anything is possible."

"Yes. Yes it does."

They sat there for a while in silence. Then Billy climbed back up and began pedaling again, circling around the rest of the rotary.

"I'll have to take you back on Bradford, because Commercial is one way," he said over his shoulder before making the turn onto Bradford. "If you continued straight, this road would take you through the Province Lands and to the beaches. We have some of the most beautiful beaches in the world."

They were quiet for the rest of the ride. Fanny noticed that Amy had a tiny smile on her face. She didn't seem as tense as usual. It was just two days, but Fanny knew that she, too, was starting to relax a little. The nervousness that seemed to hum in her veins like a current of electricity since their lives had changed so drastically, was easing some. It was a relief. She knew this was nothing but a respite, that in ten weeks she'd be going right back to everything she didn't want to face.

But maybe for just this little while, she could forget about all of that and enjoy this beautiful place.

THE SKY BEGAN TO CLEAR as they ate dinner, and Claire was out the back door and on the beach as soon as she finished. They'd had frozen pizza for dinner, which Claire had gotten at the grocery store yesterday. Amy wasn't much of a cook, and she didn't want to push her mother so soon to help in the kitchen. But she hoped that maybe in a day or two, Fanny would take over that chore. It would be good for her, Claire thought. Her mother hadn't cooked in months and seemed to have lost interest. And she needed to do something.

Ironically, the ancient stove in their kitchen was a treasure, according to her mother.

"My grandmother had one just like it, back in the forties," she told them yesterday. "Chambers stoves were the finest. And this is robin's egg blue, just like Nana's."

"Well, you'll have to show us how it works," Claire had said to coax her. "It looks beyond me."

Her mother had yet to take the bait.

When she'd told her mother about taking her father to the air force station yesterday, she could see the stunned look on her face. It was odd her mother didn't know he'd been stationed here. But her father rarely talked about his past. And never talked about his childhood. She knew those were painful years for him, and it wasn't until she was grown that she could almost understand how it had closed him down emotionally. But she couldn't deal with that now. She had enough on her plate. She'd finally gotten a digital camera, and she'd spent most of the afternoon learning to use it and experimenting with taking shots.

She walked now on the soft sand. What she couldn't see from the house, because most of the beach was in shadow as the sun went below the rooflines of the houses lining it, what made her pause now, was the light. The last moments of sunlight washed over the harbor and the boats anchored close to the water's edge in the high tide. Across the harbor, the black rocks of the jetty glistened as it stretched across from the wharf, blocking the bay, and acting as a breakwater to protect the harbor. A hundred birds or more, she wasn't sure what kind they were from that distance, sat on the rocks as if watching the sunset behind her.

Beyond the jetty, she noticed a narrow strip of sand and a lighthouse and wondered if it was the final curl of land's end, or an island to itself. She'd have to look at her map again later. Farther out, there was land, and the glint of the setting sun on houses, and she reminded herself that that was Truro, and Wellfleet, the towns just before them.

Claire turned and gazed up and down the beach then, awestruck by this evening light across the bay. It was a vivid pinkish white and seemed to illuminate the boats gently bobbing as the tide rushed in. She tried to think of words to describe it, but she couldn't. She sat on the sand, which was cool now through her jeans, in spite of the warm evening. It was truly unlike any lighting she'd seen before. The boats seemed almost lit from within. Yes, that was it, lit by a golden, almost rosy glow. The scene before her was breathtaking, and she remembered reading the word "magical" in the brochure months ago. Yes. It seemed magical. And then she remembered Charles Meyer using that word during yesterday's session. She took a deep breath and smiled. This was what she'd come for.

She picked up the canvas bag, which held both her own camera, loaded with Tri-ex black-and-white film, and the digital camera Charles Meyer had loaned her. She picked up her own camera first, held it up, and looked through the viewfinder, focusing on a little white sailboat about fifty feet away, swaying slightly in the dark water that radiated the setting sun. Through her viewfinder, Claire imagined the print that would result as she clicked. In black and white, the glow of the boat's white body would be lost, the golden sheen of water would appear flat.

She put her camera back in the bag and pulled out the digital. She focused and clicked, already visualizing the results. And in that moment it hit her, what Charles Meyer had tried to convey. That the beauty of this light was its shifting colors, something you could never capture in black and white. Only in a color print would you truly be able to capture the beauty of this light. It would be lost in black and white. She thought about Charles Meyer's words earlier that day in their workshop, as he described his first days here on assignment years ago, and how he'd abandoned black and white after that first week, calling it his paradigm shift.

She kept walking up the beach, toward the long pier, past the boats and houses, the bay curving to her left, the water lapping quietly across the sand. By the time she reached the pier, she'd taken more than forty shots, of various boats, a seagull, a colorful cluster of smooth rocks at the water's edge. She didn't have to stop and change rolls of film.

Sitting on a piece of driftwood, Claire watched the light suddenly disappear, as if someone had waved a wand and it drifted away like smoke. Now as the gray veil of dusk settled, she put the digital camera away and pulled out her own again, quickly shooting a series in black and white. Immediately she took the same shots with the digital, in color.

The thought of printing the same shots in color and black and white, of seeing the results side by side, excited her suddenly. It was an experiment in technique, really, and she couldn't wait to see how they compared. And then she remembered something else Charles Meyer had said: that this wasn't a mistake, but an opportunity.

Maybe it was. Maybe she just had to keep an open mind.

As she walked back to the house to get her things and go back to the Arts Center and print her photographs for the morning, her cell phone rang.

"Hey, babe, sorry I didn't get back to you sooner, I've just been swamped," Rick said.

"That's okay. I've been a bit consumed myself."

He told her they'd broken ground, finally, for their town house in Scottsdale. And…with excitement growing in his voice, he said he'd golfed his best game ever yesterday and was visualizing actually winning the upcoming tournament.

"If you want to be a winner, you've got to think like a winner," he said. He'd been reading up on positive thinking all year, telling her that golf was as much mental as it was physical. "Listen, I hate to cut this short, but I've gotta run. I have an appointment with the new site foreman for the condo development. I just didn't want you to think I was neglecting you."

"I understand. Have you heard anything about the canal?" she asked quickly. "Did it make historic preservation?"

"There was something about it in the paper yesterday. I just caught the headline," he said, "but I don't think so, not yet. I wouldn't get your hopes up, Claire. You can't fight progress, and most of that land is gold."

She hung up disappointed, then thought about John Poole for a moment.

She wondered if he was still in Lincoln.

AMY WOULDN'T go out without her. Not that she'd admit it, but she was staying in the house all the time, as if Fanny, her own grandmother, was a baby that needed watching. How could she not feel guilty? And a little bit annoyed with Claire for doing this to her. Every day Amy wanted to walk somewhere or go explore a beach, and if Fanny said no, she didn't go, but also didn't complain.

If being in Cape Cod was good for anyone, Fanny thought, it was Amy. In the last few days she seemed like a different person.

Now Amy asked her yet again to go out for a walk. It was late morning and like a summer day outside, she insisted, so sunny and warm.

"The exercise will be good for your hip."

She remembered Mama admonishing herself in her last years, forcing herself to walk up and down the street, back and forth, as many times as she could.

Finally, she gave in.

They walked in the opposite direction than the one they'd ridden in the pedicab the other day. With Amy pushing the stroller, they moved slowly past old houses and up the narrow street. On the corner just up their block was the Provincetown Art Museum, and a few doors down was a big white house with a front porch where two white dogs watched them with tails wagging anxiously. English gardens bursting with yellow roses surrounded the green lawn, and Fanny saw a sign advertising the place as *The Copper Fox*. Then she saw Ted, their landlord, coming down the porch steps, and he waved at them. Fanny hadn't realized he lived so close by.

Then they passed the gourmet shop where Amy told her she'd gotten the fennel seed. They stopped for a minute so Amy could adjust the top of the stroller to keep the sun off Rose's face. Fanny was glad for the rest and then smiled, seeing that the baby was already asleep.

"The fresh air always puts them to sleep," she told Amy, as they began walking again. "Sometimes that was the only way I could get Eugene to nap."

"I'm going to do it every day and try to get Rose into a real routine," Amy said. "Besides, I love walking here, it's just so quaint. I almost feel like I'm in a different country."

Fanny looked at her and saw that Amy's face was soft and relaxed. She looked so young, and she was prettier than she'd looked in a long time, with her black hair pulled back into a ponytail. The puffiness had disappeared from her face.

A block later, Amy stopped again, and Fanny presumed it was to let her rest. But Amy was staring up at a sign.

"Hey, isn't this the place the pedicab driver mentioned?" she asked.

Fanny looked up at the sign. *Dominick's on the Harbor*. Billy had told them it was his favorite restaurant and that they had the best Italian food in town.

"Their pasta fagioli is to die for," he'd exclaimed.

Amy didn't have to twist her arm to go inside. They'd been eating nothing but frozen dinners and sandwiches or takeout since they'd gotten there. At that moment the thought of a bowl of hot pasta fagioli seemed like heaven.

It wasn't a fancy place, but the views were incredible. Just off the small bar and reception area, they were seated in a large room surrounded by windows that stretched over the water. Even with the tide out, from their table at a window they could look down through the clear green water and see rocks and sand and the occasional crab slowly crawling across the bottom. Across the harbor, they could see the long, curving beach of Truro way in the distance. And closer in, just beyond the jetty, there was that long peninsula with the square lighthouse.

Rose had woken when they took her out of the stroller, but Amy refused the offer of a high chair. "She's too little for that," she explained to the waiter, who handed them menus. "I'll just hold her on my lap."

As they glanced at the menus, an older man suddenly appeared at their table.

"Good afternoon, ladies," he said with a slight Italian accent, and then, bending to stroke the baby's head, added, "And *bella bambina*."

He introduced himself as Dominick Fortunato, the owner. He

recommended the soup and the day's special, a lobster risotto. "My nephew, he is the finest cook in town," he said with a smile.

He had a way of looking into your eyes, Fanny thought. He wasn't tall, but he was trim, with a full head of salt-and-pepper hair that was more black than gray, and a pencil-thin mustache. He wore gray pants with a yellow dress shirt and reminded her of one of her uncles in Brooklyn from years ago, but she couldn't recall which one.

After they ordered, when he'd left with their menus, Amy whispered, "He's kind of hot for an old guy."

Fanny watched him at another table, kissing the hands of a pair of middle-aged women who giggled with pleasure. "Oh, he's just a silly old man."

"He reminds me of one of those old-time movie stars."

Fanny shrugged.

"Don't you think it's kind of neat, though," Amy said, her fingers stroking the baby's hair. "Everyone here seems, I don't know, just so comfortable with who they are. Or who they want to be."

"Like Miss Lila?" Fanny asked, and couldn't help smiling.

"Yeah. I mean there are some very different people here, no doubt about it. Some of them are a little out there, but no one seems to look twice." Then she chuckled. "I can't believe I'm actually here with my mother and my grandparents."

"We're not dead yet," Fanny teased.

"I know, I didn't mean that. Anyway, what about you, Gram?" Amy said. "What's your wildest dream?"

Fanny thought of Miss Lila. How outlandish she, or rather he, seemed. Yet who was to say what a person could or couldn't dream of? But it was different for her. She couldn't say it. Not out loud. Love? Passionate love at her age? It almost seemed more outlandish than Miss Lila.

Fanny shook her head. "I'm so old, I must have forgotten."

Amy sighed, stroking Rose's hair. "I wish I knew what mine

was. You're supposed to plan your whole life out when your're eighteen, go to college, then start a career. I still don't know what I want
to do with my life. I'm not like my mother. I mean, she's had this
career as a teacher, and now her dream is to be a photographer. But
I don't even care about all that anymore. I just want to be able to
stay home and take care of Rose. I was thinking of starting some
kind of Internet business."

"Could you make enough doing something like that?"

Amy shrugged. "Who knows? Some people are making a bundle."

"What about Rose's father?"

Amy's cheeks grew pink. "I really don't want to talk about that
right now, Gram."

They both turned as the waiter came with their tray of food.
Behind them, Dominick Fortunato followed, carrying an infant
seat. As the waiter set their soup bowls on their table, Dominick
slid another table next to it and put the infant seat on top.

"We keep this in the kitchen for when some of the family visits
with their little ones. I hope you don't mind?"

"That's great. Thanks so much," Amy said, as she stood up and
placed Rose in the seat. The baby turned her head to the side, as
she did when she was about to go to sleep. "Poor baby. She was still
tired."

Fanny smiled up at him in thanks and he turned and gave her a
wink. "Now your daughter can enjoy her lunch properly."

When he was gone, Amy said, "I think he's flirting with you,
Gram."

"Oh, come on, he knows I'm your grandmother. Men like that
are usually more in love with themselves than they could ever be
with anyone else."

"I don't know…," Amy said with a suggestive smile.

They each took a spoonful of soup. And then another. They gave
each other a long, knowing look, but said nothing. Amy poured a

heaping amount of Romano cheese on hers. Fanny barely ate half the bowl. The lobster risotto, which they split, was delicious, however. They were on their last bites when Rose began to fuss, still trying to settle back to sleep. Fanny signaled for the waiter, and as he cleared the plates, he asked, "Isn't the pasta fagioli just the best? It's his mother's own recipe, from Italy."

"Actually, it doesn't compare to my grandmother's," Amy said.

Fanny felt her face flame. So what if it wasn't as good as hers? You didn't insult someone for that. She said, "It was very good, thank you." And she asked him to bring the check.

But Dominick Fortunato returned to the table, not the waiter.

"What's this I hear about the pasta fagioli?"

"It's nothing," Fanny said, as Amy said, "No offense, but my grandmother's is better."

He stood there a moment, and then, looking at Fanny, he said to Amy, "Perhaps your grandmother would like to share her recipe with us?"

Fanny felt herself turn even redder. "What recipe? It's just a pinch of this, a dash of that. We never wrote anything down."

He raised one eyebrow. "Well, then you'll just have to make some for us, won't you?"

Amy's face lit up. "Cool."

That night, Fanny couldn't sleep. Joe's arms and legs jerked as she lay beside him. But she couldn't blame it on that. Or her still festering anger that he never told her he'd been here all those years ago.

She got up and sat in the white wicker chair, staring out the window at a crescent moon rising above the dark bay. As they walked home from lunch, Fanny had finally learned the real reason for Amy's change in demeanor.

"Gram, I have to tell you something," Amy said, stopping suddenly and turning to her. "I'm gonna explode if I don't tell someone."

"What is it?" Fanny asked, smiling herself, because Amy's excitement was so obvious.

"Well, I wasn't going to say anything until I had all the details, but…my father is coming!" she said. "Here. To see me, and Rose."

Fanny's own smile froze.

"Can you believe it?"

She couldn't actually believe it. The last time she'd seen Liam Walker was more than twenty years ago. The bastard.

"That's wonderful, sweet pea," she'd said, as they started walking again.

She sat there for a long time that night, until the crescent moon was above the lighthouse, lighting it up like a Christmas ornament. Fanny knew that Claire wouldn't be too happy about Liam coming. Not one bit. But Amy had made her promise she wouldn't say a word.

26

BEFORE CLAIRE KNEW IT, THE FIRST WEEK OF WORK-shops was over. On Saturday morning, she woke early and left the house while everyone was still sleeping. She'd been hearing about the moors, both from Charles Meyer and then, surprisingly, her mother and Amy. It sounded like the perfect place to take pictures of the day's first light. So far, she'd been shooting mostly in the afternoons and evenings, still awed by the last moments of light that spread like a blush across the beach for a little while, then disappeared. As she drove down Commercial Street now, it was still dark, the colorful shops and cafes quiet and closed up, the narrow street peopled only by a few early joggers and dog walkers.

Already Claire loved it here. Not just the town and its vast array of people, from artists and writers to street musicians and dark-haired fishermen or construction workers, but even the ordinary residents, walking to and from their daily errands. Although Lincoln itself was a small town, it was different. This was a walking town—or biking, which she already preferred—and there was always a sense of living differently somehow, as you pedaled through meandering alleys and byways, or your bare feet sank in the soft sand at the bay's edge. Later, she promised herself, she would take a few hours off and stroll down Commercial Street for fun, not purpose, with Amy and Rose, and perhaps even her parents.

She was finding it hard to concentrate on her work at times. Even now, in the midst of enjoying this slow drive, the windows down, the smell of the bay coming at her on the cool, damp morning air, she felt with it a trickle of guilt, flooding through her a little more with each breath. She knew she'd made it clear how things would be when they got here. That she wouldn't be around much; she'd have no time to cook. And Amy would have to step up to the plate. Not that anyone was complaining. But it was hard. Claire was so used to being in control.

Although things still seemed to be strained between her parents, her mother was becoming her old self again, for which Claire was grateful. She had Amy to thank for that. At dinner the other night, Amy had told them about their lunch at Dominick's restaurant up the street.

"I think the old guy has the hots for Gram," she said. "He wants her to make him her pasta fagioli."

Claire had seen her father blink rapidly across the table, and then go back to eating.

"Maybe you could make some for us, too, Mom," she said. "And just think, it would be like making it on your grandmother's stove."

Her mother looked over at the big blue stove and shrugged. It was old, but polished to a shine. Just waiting.

"I'd love to watch," Amy had piped in. "I could even write it down as you make it. You're always saying no one ever wrote any of your family's recipes down."

Even little Rose was not so fussy, her colic seeming to disappear finally. Claire missed her time with Rose. She hadn't given her a bottle since they'd arrived, settling for quick kisses on her sweet-smelling forehead as she slept when Claire got in at night. One more thing to feel guilty about.

And then there was Rick. Turning as Commercial Street wound to the west end, Claire felt the particular tentacles of that guilt pull hard. He was probably up by now, getting ready to leave for the big golf tournament this weekend, the one he'd been so excited about taking her to. Now he was going alone. On the phone last night they hadn't talked long. It was after ten when she finished her printing and called him on her walk back to the house. He opened his end of the conversation by saying he needed a good night's sleep. When she apologized again for not being there, he told her to forget worrying about it, it was no big deal. In fact, maybe it was better that way, because he'd probably play better without her there. *Oh, that's comforting*, she'd thought, and, as if reading her mind, he quickly added, "You know I wouldn't be able to keep my hands off you and sex before a big sporting event is supposed to sap your gusto."

She'd heard that before, of course, but it did little to ease the feeling that her fiancé didn't seem to mind so much anymore that she wasn't with him.

She came to the end of Commercial Street, facing a rotary, which appeared to be a tiny park, grassy and tree-covered. Next to a concrete bench was a sign: *Pilgrim's First Landing Park*. As she turned right, rounding past the trees and coming to the other side of the rotary, her mouth fell open, and she heard her own gasp. Even in the easing darkness she could see a vast tableau of marsh, sand, and water stretching to the horizon.

She parked the car and grabbed her new digital camera. Then she sat on a bench and waited, as the darkness slowly lifted, revealing a still gray landscape, all of it in shades of sepia as the last of night played itself out. She still wasn't quite sure about what she was doing with the workshop. Her first day of photos, the black and whites of the beach as she walked were beautiful, somber and gauzy with the fog, tangible proof, she thought, of her "purist" belief. Then it was time to work on the color shots she'd taken.

The surprise was that they didn't print the color photographs in a darkroom, as with black and white. "You can take your work to the store here in town and they'll send it out for you, but then you're at the mercy of the color lab," Charles Meyer explained as he had them group around a computer and giant printer. "We'll be printing our own work on this pigment-based inkjet."

He held up a stunning picture of a rose. Claire thought at first it was a painting. The rose was in soft focus, the deep crimson petals brighter than they could possibly be in real life.

"With black and white, a lot of the work of getting a good print is in the darkroom, burning and dodging to enhance what you want to stand out. The real difference with digital printing on this inkjet, as you'll see, is color saturation. With film, you could never get roses this red. With digital, what you do with the color is up to your imagination, much like a painter."

She'd raised her hand then. "It seems the digital prints are a bit softer in focus. Is it possible to sharpen the subject?"

"You're right about that. With digital you're not going to have the razor-sharp clarity of what we know as a standard thirty-five-millimeter print," Charles Meyer admitted, "but not all images need to be sharp. Think of a baby's face, a woman's skin, and this flower. Your artistic intent is really about communicating a feeling or emotion. Sharpening can be done in Photoshop, but we'll save that for another time. You may get used to this effect and come to prefer it. I think it has that 'artistic' quality you like, Ms. Noble."

For the next few days, Claire had played with the process, and after a while, as she became familiar with the computer program and the printer, it began to be fun. The first photograph she tried was of a white dory anchored in front of their house, which had seemed so luminous that evening as she shot it again and again. Her first print looked flat, with none of the radiant light she'd experienced coming through. As she increased the saturation of color, adding more gold, then pink, and even white, suddenly the picture came to life. And there it was, just as she'd seen it on the beach. The evening light was captured and the boat seemed to glow with it, as if lit from within. She'd smiled, amazed at how with a few punches of the keyboard, she'd created a gorgeous, lifelike print.

She began to see that Charles Meyer was no doubt right. That with this technique, the vision you had for a print as you looked through your viewfinder and then clicked the shot, that vision that sometimes eluded you no matter how many shots you tried to capture it, was suddenly more possible. Not that she was turning her back completely on black and white, she told herself.

Lost in thought, she suddenly looked up and saw a ribbon of fuschia light slowly blooming far in the distance, where the sea met the horizon. The windswept moors surrounded her, much of them still in shadow as the dawn broke, but she could see that the tide was out. Two lighthouses sat in the distance, one almost straight out at the end of the jetty, blinking red, another farther to the left, blinking green. She couldn't tell if they were on the same peninsula of sand or two separate ones. Or if the farther one was the one across the harbor from their house. She'd have to check her map again later.

It was a wild and romantic place. The quickly rising light of the sun was already reflecting off the sand and the water. She noticed a few painters, who must have arrived when she was daydreaming, standing at the beginning of the long rock breakwater that led to the peninsula of sand. Claire grabbed her camera and got up from the bench, heading toward the jetty as well, eager to capture the first moments of this new day as it unveiled itself before her.

For the next hour, as the sun rose over the ocean, as the world shifted in color and shade, she carefully picked her way across the wet rocks, standing, squatting, moving constantly to catch as many different angles as she could. In the quiet, she worked along with the other artists, each of them, she knew, hoping to capture something special.

When she finished, she was exhausted. She would have kept shooting, but hunger began to gnaw at her stomach. Stepping gingerly from rock to rock, she came back to the jetty's beginning. When she reached the sidewalk, she turned toward her car and then stopped suddenly. There, sitting on a bench and watching her with a half smile, was John Poole.

FANNY WOKE EARLY. Through the lace curtains she saw that the sky was brightening. She lay there a few moments, listening to Joe's soft snores. Despite her anger with him, when she'd gotten into bed last night, her body had slid against him, huddling into his back. And then, before she even knew it, her arm was across him, curled around his chest. He didn't even wake. Always, he slept like the dead. She opened her hand, her palm against his heart, and felt its steady, reassuring rhythm. After almost fifty years, this was how she needed to fall asleep.

Last night, when he came into the room for his pills and she was putting her robe on, she'd said to him, as if it were no big deal, "What's all this business about an air station near here? Why didn't you tell me?"

"It's nothing," he said, dismissing it with a wave of his hand.

She wondered now if their life together would end and she would still not really know this man. Never had he opened his heart to her.

She got up and shuffled across the room and still he slept. She pulled on her robe and quietly went into the kitchen. Through the wide windows the beach stretched quiet and still to the dark water, which sparkled with the early sunlight. Far across the bay the lighthouse blinked rhythmically. She turned away to fix the coffee. She had a lot to do today. As she puttered in the kitchen, the idea that had seized her the other day came back to her again. Maybe cooking could somehow be the answer for Amy.

When they'd taken the Tupperware bowl of pasta fagioli over to Dominick's, Fanny had been nervous. And embarrassed.

"This is crazy," she said, as Amy opened the door to the restaurant.

She knew the soup was good, it wasn't that. Dominick Fortunato was a gentleman, of the old school. He would say he liked it even if he didn't. It was just ten o'clock and the restaurant had been quiet. But there were noises in the kitchen and a moment later its swinging door opened as they stood there, unsure what to do. Dominick Fortunato came out, saw them, and a smile lit up his face. Amy held out the bowl. But Dominick Fortunato walked straight to Fanny. Instead of taking the bowl from Amy's hands, he took one of Fanny's hands, pulled it slowly to his lips, and closed his eyes, kissing her fingers with a slow inhale of breath that sent a ticklish shiver up her arm.

"Ah, *bellas*, I don't even know your names," he said, letting her hand go.

"Filomena," she said and saw Amy's eyes widen, as she hadn't used that name since she was a girl. "This is my granddaughter, Amy. And her little one, Rose."

She knew from the way he tasted the soup, slowly, rolling the broth around his tongue, his cheeks softening, the pleasure obvious in his eyes, that he was more than appreciative. With a nod of his head, he took them into the dining room, away from the kitchen, and admitted, yes, it was far better than theirs. But...he couldn't change theirs. Not now. Not when everyone already loved it. His first rule of business had always been, don't change what works. The real problem, though, he said in a low voice, shaking his head dramatically, was his cook, who happened to be his nephew, Vito. "He's a lazy mensch," he said and then chuckled, "but family, so what can I do?"

But, he went on, that didn't mean he wasn't interested in some new recipes. There were lots of restaurants in town, getting fancier each year. Each one had its own specialty. Gimmicks. His was simple: real, authentic homemade Italian dishes. And his repertoire, he admitted, was getting a little stale.

"My nephew, Vito, he comes up with these crazy dishes. He makes them up." He wrinkled his nose and looked like he might spit, and Fanny heard Amy start to giggle. "They stink."

And then he asked if they'd be willing to share a few more recipes.

It seemed ridiculous, Fanny thought, as they walked out of the restaurant. A ploy, really.

As the door closed, Amy gave her a sly smile. "Gram, you're a flirt."

Fanny shrugged and gave a little laugh. No, she wasn't a flirt. She was simply an old woman who knew how to flatter a man when it was necessary. Because as they stood there in the restaurant, as she watched Amy looking around with interest, that's when the idea began to take hold of her. Amy liked cooking. They'd spent hours in the kitchen over the previous few days making the soup, and she'd seemed to really enjoy it. They laughed and cooked and Amy wrote everything down, and then tried it herself, so she'd be able to cook healthy for Rose.

In a few months, they'd all be going back to reality. So maybe she could help Amy do something with cooking. She knew how to play Dominick Fortunato's game.

HE STOOD UP as she walked toward him, and Claire felt an awkward little squeeze in her stomach.

"Is this another of your coincidences?" she asked when they were face-to-face.

John Poole's half smile grew and his face lit up with amusement. "No, I knew at some point you'd be here to take photos. Especially at dawn."

"So you were looking for me," she said.

Then he had the grace to look a little embarrassed as he shoved his hands in the pockets of his jeans. "I was."

"Why?"

Facing her, the sun was right in his eyes and he squinted, but he was bathed in early sunlight and Claire couldn't help thinking how handsome he looked, his hazel eyes flecked with gold.

"Two reasons," he said. "First, I want to apologize. The last time I saw you, I wasn't in the best frame of mind. You brought me your finished work and I could have taken a few moments, at least, and looked at it."

She thought about that morning, standing in his driveway as she handed him the envelope with her photographs of the canal, her hands shaking. Almost glad he'd been rude. Because the current that had been running between them since that night they'd watched the Perseids was making her uncomfortable. She was engaged, after all. In love with another man. She knew better than to get caught up in a shallow attraction that could go nowhere.

"It's no big deal," she said, finally. "I think I was relieved you didn't look at them."

"Why? The photographs were top notch."

She shrugged.

"Don't you believe that?"

"I thought they were good, but sometimes it's hard for me to be objective." It was true. In fact, since she'd started the workshop, surrounded by others who were clearly so talented, she'd begun to doubt her own skills. Their work was edgy, modern. Her photographs, to her at least, were starting to seem boring and almost old-fashioned.

John turned and unzipped the backpack that was sitting on the bench. "This is the other reason I was looking for you," he said, and handed her a folder.

She opened it. Inside were galley pages from *New Jersey Monthly*.

"Reclaiming a 19th-Century Treasure" by John Poole. Underneath his name she saw her own: Photographs by Claire Noble.

"This is just a proof, obviously. The piece will appear in November. They loved your work."

"They did it so quickly," she said, staring at the pages, as a thrill raced through her and she couldn't help smiling.

"They were just waiting for your pictures, but I didn't want to rush you. The art director said they were worth waiting for. So maybe you should trust your instincts next time."

She looked up at him. "Why didn't you tell me the article was for *New Jersey Monthly*? I mean, you knew all along, I read it in the local paper, the piece they ran on the canal?"

He cocked his head. "I guess I was going with my gut on that one. I thought it might intimidate you. And I didn't want you to feel pressured."

"I'm a big girl, John. I think I could have handled it."

He stared at her. "You're right. I'm sorry."

They stood another moment, an awkward silence growing.

"How's the workshop going?"

"Fine. It's not quite what I expected, but I'm adapting. And what about you? You're here to finish your article on the fishing industry?"

"I am, yes."

"You must be glad to be back with your son." She often thought that accounted for his sudden mood shifts when they'd worked together on the canal piece. He'd seemed distracted at times, even worried other times. Not that he'd talked about it.

"I am glad to be back." He smiled, but it held no humor. "But Ryan's not with me."

"Why not?"

He took a deep breath and stared out toward the breakwater. "It's a long story."

Obviously he didn't want to talk about it. "Are you staying here on the Cape?"

"My grandfather had an old fishing shack in Wellfleet. It's still in the family, although it's a bit rough. But that'll be fine. It's just a place to hang my hat. I'll be working long hours."

"Well, John, I wish you luck with it."

Finally, he turned and looked at her again. "Listen, Claire..."

There was a long silence. And the way he was looking at her..."I really have to run, John," she said, before he said anything else. "It's getting late."

She could see the redness climb his face. "Sure. Sorry, I just wanted to—"

"Thanks for taking the time to show me the piece," she said, turning toward her car. "I hope it does some good."

She turned and got in her car without looking back. As she pulled away, she saw him in her rearview mirror standing there alone, the moors surrounding him.

As she drove up Bradford Street, she pulled into a convenience store parking lot suddenly and got a cup of coffee. Then she sat in the car and called Rick on her cell. Once again the call went straight to his voice mail. He was no doubt on the golf course already, three holes into the tournament. "Good luck," she said. "I love you."

27

Fanny wasn't a fool. She told herself she was cooking, and carrying on about it, for Amy. And that was true, but she was also doing it for herself. How many hours could she sit in her room? Stew about Joe? During the first few days, she'd sat on the wicker chair with her door closed. On the dresser was her stack of books that Claire had obviously taken from the assisted living. She'd picked up one romance, and then another, tossing them onto the bed to put in the garbage later. Because she was done with that nonsense. And there, lumped in the middle of the pile was the book from Seth, *Buddhism for You.*

She wasn't really sure what to make of it as she'd paged through the beginning. The first chapter was called "The Human Condition." She skimmed the paragraphs. She read that "dissatisfaction is the first truth of existence." Well, she could have told Buddha that nugget. But she sat and thought about it for a while, watching a ship cross the harbor and then round the jetty into Cape Cod Bay, trying to distract herself. Dissatisfaction was something she'd been carrying, it seemed, all her life. From her girlhood, when she'd had to wait on her brothers, at Mama's insistence, simply because they were boys, to her desire to go to college and study accounting, because she was good at math. *And what good will that be when you're home with your babies?* Daddy had asked. The money for college went instead to her brothers, neither of whom finished.

The same paragraph went on to say that suffering, and the

ability to stop it, lay within you. That, too, was pretty obvious to Fanny, especially when it came to how she felt about Joe. How many times had she put up the mental stop sign, like she'd read long ago in one of her women's magazines. Sometimes it worked. But right now, here, it was much harder. There was definitely something bothering him. At home she couldn't get him to go out the door; now he took three or four little walks a day. Not that she wasn't guilty about holding things back, too. She wished she could tell Claire that Liam was coming, but she knew it would be devastating to Amy if she broke that confidence. Amy was really starting to open up to her, especially when they worked in the kitchen.

Amy had gone to the Grand Union to get what they'd need for the pasta puttanesca they were making for Dominick Fortunato. While she was gone, Fanny gave Rose a bottle and sang her the pigeon song. The baby was so tired she fell asleep with a few ounces left. Fanny put her in the crib on her back, as Amy instructed her.

When Amy returned with two big bags, Fanny emptied them as Amy rooted under the sink, finally finding a huge clam pot that would have to do. Fanny put Amy to work chopping the garlic, lots of it, as she opened the cans of tomatoes and capers.

"Oh, Gram," Amy said suddenly. "Look at that."

Fanny looked up, past the big kitchen table and through the wall of windows. The setting sun flooded the beach and the dark bay with a breathtaking golden light. "It's..." She hesitated, a little soaring feeling in her chest. *Beautiful* seemed inadequate.

"Beyond gorgeous," Amy piped in. "I can see why people are crazy about the lighting here. It really is different."

"Your mother seems to think so. She's been working very hard taking pictures. She seems a bit frustrated, though, don't you think?"

Amy put her knife down and dumped the garlic into the clam pot. "That's probably because this isn't the course she was supposed to take."

"What do you mean? She didn't say anything to me."

Amy shrugged.

"Maybe she didn't want to worry me," Fanny said. She didn't like that, her own daughter keeping things so as not to worry her. Did they think she was fragile? She dried the oregano and began tearing the leaves from the stems.

"Why didn't your mother ever write her recipes down? Or you, either?" Amy asked.

"I don't know, I think we didn't realize how important it was. We figured they'd just keep getting cooked, one generation after another. But everything started changing when your mother was growing up, it seemed. Women started having real careers. They didn't have time to cook; how could they when they were at a job all day?"

"Do you think that's a bad thing?"

Fanny began to mince the anchovies. "No, not a bad thing. It's good women have choices now. Not like when I was young. But…I think it's still important to try to hold onto some things." She looked up and saw the colors shift on the beach, the golden light now a pale pink, as the sun slid behind the houses. "Food is part of our history. There was a time a meal wasn't an afterthought, but had meaning, symbolism."

"Like the fish supper on Christmas Eve?"

"Yes, each of the seven fishes stood for something." She paused and shook her head. "I'm guilty, too, of taking it for granted. I could have written all of Mama's recipes down, but I didn't. This is our little bit of heritage, Amy, and we should hold onto it. Or Rose won't know a thing about our past."

"So is this exactly the way your mother made her pasta puttanesca, and her mother, all the way back to Italy?"

Fanny shrugged. "Who knows? These recipes have been handed down for generations. But everyone had their own little way of doing things. This probably isn't Mama's recipe exactly, either. I might have added a little something over the years I can't remember. I always liked more salt. But it's close enough."

They were quiet for a while, the only sound in the kitchen the rhythmic chopping.

"When I worked in the group homes down south, we used to make some crazy meals," Amy said then. "We'd let the residents help cook each night and they always wanted to put some wacky ingredients in, like raisins in the tuna salad or barbecue sauce over the spaghetti. It was usually revolting, but every once in a while something would surprise you."

Fanny scraped the anchovies into the clam pot and turned to begin breaking up the tomatoes with a spoon. "You haven't really talked about what you did all that time you were away."

"I know."

Fanny saw Amy look out the window again. The last of the sunlight had gone, the sky and bay now a solid gray. In the distance, she could see the lighthouse winking its green light every few seconds.

"I really didn't plan to stay in North Carolina, but I ran out of money," Amy went on. "My aunt Bonnie helped me get the job. It was decent pay, plus benefits. And, I don't know, maybe because of growing up with Missy—you know, Abbie's daughter who has Down's—I just felt good working there. It was the only job I ever had that I felt like I was doing something worthwhile. And I didn't suck at it."

"Why did you go to your aunt Bonnie's?"

Amy picked up the knife and began chopping the onions. A moment later she said, "I was trying to find my father."

"Well, obviously you did."

Amy stepped away from the counter and grabbed a paper towel, wiping her eyes. "These onions are really strong." Then she looked at Fanny, her eyes shining. "No, I didn't see him then. But I will soon," she said and suddenly her face lit up. "And maybe here, I don't know, maybe we can get it right. I feel like something's been missing my whole life. And I want him to see Rose. He seems excited about that."

Fanny stood there, remembering the lie she'd overheard Amy telling Liam on the telephone a few months ago: *She looks like you.* She wondered what else Amy had lied about to get Liam to come here.

The pasta puttanesca turned out perfect. How could it not? She'd watched Mama make it every week for her entire life it seemed. An inexpensive, nutritious meal that took them through the tough years of the war.

Amy put the big clam pot into the refrigerator. "This was fun, Gram. I forgot how much I used to like cooking with you when I was little. I always felt so cozy and safe in your kitchen."

They'd been at it for three hours and Fanny was exhausted. But she said, "I really enjoyed it, too, sweet pea."

"Tomorrow morning we'll take some over to Dominick Fortunato and knock *his* socks off."

When Amy went to bed, Fanny sat in the living room, paging through a magazine. Joe had gone to bed a while ago, but for once Fanny wasn't thinking about him and Ava. It was late, but Claire was still at the Arts Center, working on her prints. Fanny's heart went out to Claire, struggling to nurture this love of photography and agonizing over her distance from Rick. A choice Fanny had never had to make. With all of the choices that had come to women of Claire's generation, and Amy's, it seemed that what had come with it was more uncertainty. Rick was a nice guy who could give Claire the security she never had. How many men like him came along for a forty-five-year-old woman? But Fanny felt that Claire was right to do this, to take this time to improve her craft. She'd worked so hard her whole life. She'd raised a daughter all by herself. And she was so passionate about her photography. Fanny wished she'd found something like that years ago. Maybe her life would have been different. Maybe it wouldn't have mattered so much that her husband really loved someone else. She would have had something of her own. Because really, her job, her passion, had always been her family.

And then she heard the crunch of the shell driveway, as Claire parked her bike. Her thoughts shifted to Amy once again. And Liam. Poor Claire, she was certainly getting more than she bargained for up here, and she had no idea what was coming.

28

CHARLES MEYER HAD AN APPOINTMENT AND LET THE class go before eleven, so Claire decided to go home for lunch and spend a little time with the family after her morning workshop. She found a note from Amy on the counter: *Took Gram and Rose for a walk to Dominick's.* That was thoughtful, something the old Amy wouldn't have bothered to do. They must be dropping off the pasta puttanesca, she realized. She fixed herself another cup of coffee and popped a bowl they'd left in the refrigerator into the microwave, glancing out the kitchen window to see if her father was up yet. There was no sign of him, and she assumed he was still sleeping.

All her life, her father had been an early riser, even on his days off. Before he left for work, he would often spend an hour or two in the old detached garage behind their house, tinkering with the car. Or down in the basement, battling a leaky pipe or checking the water level on the old steam boiler. They never had much money, and she assumed that was why her father had become so handy.

When she lived home with Amy for that time after college, she'd often find her own car, a cheap used Dodge Dart, in the garage, her father changing the oil or checking the fan belt. With good care, he insisted, that car could get her 200,000 miles.

He wasn't a reader, and back then he rarely ever watched television. After dinner, while she and Eugene did their homework, he'd glance through the newspaper, close his eyes for ten minutes on his recliner, and then head out for his evening appointments to sell insurance. He was a hard worker and a good provider, her mother always said, when she or Eugene would complain that he was too strict.

He never talked much, either, and shared nothing about his youth, not like her mother did, or his time in the service. When she was young, Claire had never thought much of it. He was her father. He was simply there. But for years now, she'd been wondering how you could share a life with someone and not really know that person. Not their innermost thoughts, their intimate fears and dreams. How so much of that shared life was important, and yet so much on the surface. She had a desire to know her father more deeply. But in truth, she didn't really know how to make that happen. He simply didn't like to talk.

Since she'd brought them all to the Cape, he'd been sleeping late—near nine some mornings. But this was really late, even for him. She knocked on her father's door, but there was no answer. Quietly opening the door, she saw the bed empty. She hurried to the porch, but there was no sign of him walking up and down the block out front, either. She went out back and saw that the patio was deserted and so was the beach. Then from the kitchen she grabbed her tote bag with her cell phone and left. As she stepped off the patio, she looked down and saw footprints in the sand, a man's shoe, and then another blurred print, that looked as if the foot had been dragged. She followed the footprints toward the water, where they stopped just before the tide line, littered with rocks and smooth stones.

She began walking up the beach toward the pier, her pulse quickening. The little boats moored close to the beach were now in water, swaying gently with the incoming tide. She couldn't imagine where her father might have gone. She looked out, across the water toward the lighthouse on the long spit of sand that cut into the bay. Since they'd come here, her father had spent hours on the patio, just staring across the water. In the direction of that lighthouse.

Alarm bells went off in her head at the same moment she turned, before she even saw the empty stretch of beach where a small yellow motorboat was always anchored next door. It was gone.

Turning, she ran toward the house just two down from theirs, a tall, weathered white colonial with an upstairs balcony and an enclosed porch overlooking the beach. She knocked on the porch door. A young boy about fourteen or fifteen answered.

"I'm looking for my father, he's an elderly man, and sometimes walks with a cane."

"I know him," the boy said, nodding. "He borrowed our boat."

Claire felt her mouth fall open in horror.

The boy then pulled something out of his pocket. "He gave me this, but I told him he didn't have to. It's an old boat and we hardly ever use it."

The boy handed her a twenty-dollar bill.

"No, it's all right, keep it. But my father…he's not well. How long ago did he take the boat?"

"Not long, maybe a half hour, forty minutes."

Claire looked across the water, a cold sweat breaking out on her skin, despite the warm morning.

"He made it across," the boy said, as if reading her mind. "I saw him. It doesn't take long, maybe just ten minutes."

"He's sick," Claire said. "He might decide to come back across and not be able to move." Claire turned and looked up and down the beach. "Listen, I don't really know anyone here, but do you think we might be able to borrow one of these other boats? Could you help me?"

Ten minutes later they were motoring across the harbor, past dories and then sailboats anchored farther out in the water. To their right, the pier seemed quiet, the lobstermen already long gone to check their traps. The boy, Sean, was polite and apologetic to Claire as she sat in the front of the boat, the soft wind in her face, staring ahead at the peninsula of sand growing closer each minute. Long

Point, the boy had called it. Claire wondered what on earth had made her father go there. She thought about when he'd taken her to the abandoned air force station in Truro last week, just after they'd arrived. How emotional he'd seemed. Almost haunted.

Her mother had asked her the other day if he'd mentioned it anymore, but he hadn't. Then she told her about finding the brochure for the Arts Center Claire had given them months ago with his tiny scrawl, which she now realized spelled Truro. Obviously something was going on with him.

She saw the yellow motorboat then, near the tip of the long peninsula of sand that she now knew was called Long Point. It was empty, and there was no sign of anyone nearby. A line of dunes ran down the center, covered with tall green grasses swaying in the breeze. The boy motored in as far as he could, before turning off the engine, and Claire took off her shoes, rolled up her jeans, then stepped out of the boat and waded through the cold water, a shiver running up her calves. Sean had agreed to wait for her in the boat, in case her father came back while she was gone.

There was no one visible, although the boy had told Claire that people often came out here to fish on the ocean side because it was so quiet. Long Point was about a quarter mile wide, a lengthy distance through soft sand for someone who had trouble walking on solid ground. She didn't think her father had walked across to the ocean. She went over to where the yellow boat bobbed with the rising tide and again saw the footsteps in the sand. She followed them in the direction of the lighthouse. It was hot as she headed in toward the dunes, and she pulled off her light cardigan and stuffed it into her tote bag. She pulled out her cell phone and checked it. No service.

The path up to the lighthouse was sloped, the sand caving under her bare feet, and although Claire climbed without a problem, it was taxing and she couldn't imagine her father making it this far. She prayed he was okay.

When she reached the top of the rise, she stopped, stunned. Before her rose a weathered wooden cross, with an old tattered flag tied to it, flapping in the wind. It wasn't visible from below, and she wondered if it was some kind of war monument, or a tribute to someone's loved one who'd died there. Rising in the middle of nothing, the silence around it almost ear-ringing, she thought it was a powerful sight. Then she looked around.

About twenty feet from the cross, her father sat at the base of the lighthouse in the sand. His face was ashen, and even from a distance she could see his left arm hitting the sand over and over, his cane lying at his side.

"Dad," she said softly.

But he didn't hear her.

THERE ARE MOMENTS in life when everything shifts. When something happens in the present that colors everything in the past. It had happened to Claire just once before, with Liam. Looking back now, she felt like a fool for being surprised. Everyone else, it seemed, had predicted it.

The week before they were to be married, and he was supposed to legally adopt Amy and give her his name, she finally saw him for who he truly was—not the illusion she'd carried with her for years, the sensitive, troubled boy who'd captured her heart. After that week, everything in her past had changed. Everything she'd done over the years, from defying her parents to turning her back on the life she'd carefully put together, when he first left her after she became pregnant—everything that she'd done out of love and her desire to be with him—was suddenly tainted. He'd left her again, and Amy, without a backward glance.

And now here was another of those moments, but one that she didn't think anyone could have ever predicted. With her father.

Sitting at the base of the lighthouse in a ray of morning sunlight, he seemed to be someone else. Not her father at all. He hadn't heard her. She was in awe at finding her father sitting in this strange place, in the shadow of the cross, with the tattered flag snapping in the breeze. Then, he looked up at her, straight into her eyes, his own filled with something she was all too familiar with from those long ago days: regret.

Quickly she walked toward him. Kneeling in the sand beside him, she waited a moment, and then she couldn't help herself, she took his hands, raw from scraping across the coarse sand over and over, and held them steady.

"Oh, Dad, what are you doing here?"

"Claire…the life…I've lived," her father began, in a voice that trembled as badly as his hands, "is not…the life I thought I would have." After a long pause, he added, "There was a girl."

His words halting with the effort, he told her about a Portuguese girl he'd met when stationed there years ago, in North Truro. Her name was Ava. She was from a local fishing family. He was young, not even eighteen, and homesick. She was looking for a way out of her life. She was supposed to marry a local boy, from another Portuguese fishing family.

"When my workday was over at the base, I would hitch a ride into town to the shop, where she'd be getting off work. We'd take a small boat over here to Long Point, where we could be alone. Because she'd get into trouble if anyone saw us together."

He paused for a long time. "I was stupid. I did wrong by her."

Claire felt her breath catch. It was an old-fashioned phrase, but she didn't need graphic words to understand what he was saying.

"Dad, you were so young."

"But I was going to marry her, even though I knew by then I didn't love her. And I don't think she loved me. Not really."

Claire was speechless, afraid to interrupt his words that flowed in a halting rhythm, not because he didn't remember. But because it was so difficult to say.

"I took leave and went home and asked my foster father for money, to marry her. He was…extremely disappointed in me." He turned and looked out toward the ocean side of the sand, where a flock of gulls were circling. "By the time I got back here she was gone. Her mother told me there was never really a baby. That Ava had lied."

And then he looked right into Claire's eyes. "I was…so… relieved." He shook his head, his own disappointment in himself all over his face. "Six months later I was discharged and I never came back. Eventually I met your mother. You children came, I worked long hours. And the next thing you know decades have gone by and it all doesn't even seem quite real. There's an occasional flicker in your memory, but…All these years, I always wondered if that was the truth. If they didn't just marry her off to that Portuguese boy." Again he shook his head, then closed his eyes. He looked so tired. "I should have stayed to find out."

"When you first told us that you might be coming to this workshop here, well…I started to wonder again. You would be right here, where she lived. Where another child might be now. And then when Rose came…it became an obsession. Like God was taunting me for what I did. I was gutless." He paused for a long time, his breathing the only sound in the quiet. In her hand, his hand jerked as she tried to hold it still. "Would I die without ever knowing the truth? I look at Rose every day and think of what I might have done to a child."

"Does Mom know any of this?" Claire asked.

He shook his head. "And I don't want her to know. I've been enough of a disappointment to her as a husband."

"I don't think that's true, Dad."

"It's always been there. In her eyes."

"Dad, you've been a good husband. And a good father. Men have let me down all my life. I know we haven't been…well, close in a lot of ways, but you were always there for me. You never disappointed me." She waited a moment. If he never told her mother, that didn't necessarily mean she didn't know anything. Her mother was witchy that way, intuitive. That would explain a lot about her behavior toward him lately.

"I think you should tell her."

"No. What good would it do?"

"I don't know. I just think it's the right thing."

"Not yet. I just want to find her. Or them. And if I have to, make up for any wrongs I did."

"Do you really think…" But she couldn't finish the sentence. The thought that her father could have another child, a middle-aged man or woman actually, older than her and Eugene… well, that was surreal.

On the boat ride back, Claire's eyes kept going to her father in the boat ahead of her with Sean, chugging across the harbor slowly as she followed. He was bent over, and his whole upper body twitched as if to some distant music that only he could hear. The stress of this morning, of what he'd revealed, was taking its toll on him. It had taken them nearly an hour to get back to the boat. His feet refused to move; the sand reflected heat back up at them and they both began to sweat. Finally, Sean arrived, and with one of them on each side, they managed to get her father back to the boat. As they labored through the sand, she tried to imagine him, so young and handsome—she'd always thought so in his pictures— coming here with a beautiful Portuguese girl. She thought about the secrets he'd harbored for nearly a lifetime. And how you never really knew another person. Not really.

Look at her with Liam, how she'd bent the truth to suit her own purposes in the end. How no one knew what had happened that final week because after a while, when she thought she was over it and could finally tell her mother, or her daughter, she simply didn't. Too much time had passed.

As shocked as she was by his revelations, how could she possibly judge her father? He'd been young and scared, much like she'd been herself. And their secrets had become buried in the busyness of the ensuing years. Until now.

29

F ANNY STOOD IN THE KITCHEN OF DOMINICK'S RES-
taurant, her eyes resting on the stainless steel monster of a stove
with twelve burners, and knew she was a dying breed. Women
like her, who married and took care of their husbands and homes
and never worked again, were going to die out soon. All wives
and mothers worked now, even if they didn't have to. It seemed
unthinkable for a woman today to do what she had done. But in
this efficient marvel of a room, with side windows that actually
looked out over Provincetown Harbor—well, if she'd been born a
decade or two later, this is where she might have found a different
part of herself. And for a moment she felt the pang of something
lost; something more that she could have grasped onto in life.

The ingredients were all chopped and measured and laid out on
a long stainless steel table, pretty and colorful like Easter baskets.
Imagine, someone did all the preparing, and someone would do
all the washing up. All she would have to do was cook. It was like
a fantasy, and for a moment she dipped her toe in it, imagining
herself as the center of this little universe. The one they referred to
when they said, "My compliments to the chef." But this was for
Amy, she reminded herself. For her, it was just too late.

When, after they'd dropped off a taste the other day, Mr. Fortunato came to the house asking for the recipe for Mama's pasta
puttanesca, Fanny had told him it was a family secret. However,

her granddaughter could come and make it in his kitchen one day if he'd like to offer it as a special. It was a dare, really.

Amy had flashed her a look that could kill, but as her mouth opened to protest, Mr. Fortunato agreed enthusiastically. And here they were.

It was a quick dish to make. After all, the puttanesca, or "whore's sauce," supposedly originated as a meal the prostitutes made in the short breaks they had during the day, between customers. Legend had it they would set a bowl of the sauce in an open window to lure the hungry men. But Mama's secret, and Fanny agreed, was to make it the day before, and to use black olives, not calamata olives. Then you let it sit overnight in the refrigerator, the flavors deepening and infusing the chopped tomatoes with a luscious blend of garlic, capers, briny black olives, anchovies, and extra virgin oil. You could make a feast just mopping up a plate of it with soft, crusty bread. However, Dominick wanted to offer the special today, so here they were.

They brought her a chair so she could sit and watch. Dominick Fortunato carried in the infant seat again for Rose. Amy went to work, as Fanny had instructed her and they'd practiced, but Fanny could see the nerves in her trembling hands as they watched. Her hair was pulled back tight in a low ponytail and her cheeks were pink, her mouth pinched. The flame was a little too high and the olive oil began to smoke, browning the minced garlic too quickly, and they nearly had to start over. But Fanny jumped up, pulling the heavy pot off the burner, and stirred quickly, before the bottom scorched.

Within moments, the heavenly aroma of sizzling garlic and olive oil filled the kitchen. And must have wakened Rose, who suddenly let out a piercing wail. Fanny could see that Amy became distracted, and she tried to quiet the baby with a bottle, and then the binkie, but Rose kept shaking her head from side to side, refusing everything. Fanny rocked and shushed her, but she didn't stop.

As soon as the sauce was finished, and it took less than ten minutes even when you weren't rushing, Amy grabbed Rose and carried her outside, too upset to linger for the results. So she didn't get to see Dominick's face light up, or his nephew Vito's when he came in to begin prepping for the lunch shift. Fanny was good at reading people's faces and bodies. Vito had the soft face and doughy body of someone who wasn't overly ambitious. Instead of feeling threatened, as Fanny had feared, he smiled and then said with a laugh: "*Delicioso!* You're the answer to my prayers! Maybe now my uncle will get off my back."

And Dominick Fortunato, instead of being insulted, cuffed him gently on the cheek.

"This bum would rather go fishing with his friends than spend more time in the kitchen," he joked.

Fanny saw the easy love between the two men, and her opinion of Dominick Fortunato moved up a notch.

"If you think that's good, wait until tomorrow," she told them. "The sauce gets better with age, so if there's any left, you could serve it tomorrow, too."

He insisted on walking her back to the house when they stepped outside and saw the stroller gone, Amy nowhere in sight. She said no. She didn't want him to get ideas. And really, she wasn't sure if it was proper. Little red flags were beginning to pop up in her head. She wasn't used to such attention. But he kept insisting.

She thought of coming home the other morning to find Claire and a young boy helping Joe out of that yellow boat. He'd stood in the ankle-deep water, and it looked as if they were dragging him across the beach. Then Claire saw her, and a stricken look crossed her face. Fanny realized then that they hadn't wanted her to witness this, that she would have been kept in the dark if she and Amy hadn't arrived home that morning when they did.

Ava. Fanny was certain it was all about her again. And now Joe was sick and had been ordered to rest for a week.

She turned to Dominick now with a smile. He could walk her a block or two, but then she'd let him go back to work. They strolled slowly and talked about the town. He'd come here twenty years ago, he told her, after his wife, Lena, died and he couldn't figure out what to do with his life. They had just one daughter, and she'd already moved far away with her husband, who was a pilot. Oh, she came to visit often with her free flights. But she was a career girl and didn't seem to want children.

"So I found myself alone and I said to myself, 'What, are you crazy? Why are you staying in a place where there's no one for you?' My wife's parents, they had lived across the street, but they had died just the year before, both of them. And my sister Carmella was begging me to move up here. So I did. And the next thing you know, I'm buying a restaurant." He turned and gave her a smile. "It's a beautiful place."

Fanny couldn't agree more. Her hip still hurt here, but not as much. Or maybe that was the walking, because she was doing more of it. Or the fact that when they walked, there was so much beauty all around, how could you think of your little aches and pains?

Or was it that she was starting to see things a little differently. Was it that light they all talked about? Or could it possibly be the book on Buddhism she now found herself reading more and more? She was trying to live in each and every moment.

A block from her house, they stopped, and once again he took her hand and put it to his lips. "You are an interesting woman, Filomena," he said. "I thank you for the puttanesca. I think it will be a hit."

"You're welcome," she said, pulling her hand back as quickly as she could without appearing rude. "It was nothing."

His look deepened. "No, it was something."

Fanny felt a slow rise of warmth crawl up her neck and her cheeks. She'd never mentioned a husband. He'd never asked. She turned and walked as fast as she could before he could say another word.

LATE SUNDAY NIGHT Claire stood in the darkroom at the Arts Center, staring at the black-and-white photographs drying on the line. But the one picture she couldn't stop thinking of was the one she hadn't even taken: her father at Long Point, old and weathered like that flag tied to the wooden cross, a lifetime of memories creased into his face. Haunted by an indiscretion more than fifty years old. The sins of a young man, a man far removed from the responsible, stern father she'd known all her life.

Why was it so hard to let go of the past? she wondered.

When they'd brought him into the house, after they managed to get him out of the boat, he was shivering badly, his clothes soaked with cold seawater, his Parkinson's tremors out of control. They took him right into the bathroom. Claire had never seen her father naked before, but he barely uttered a word of protest as she and her mother stripped him and then put him in the walk-in shower, already filled with steam. There was a small seat attached to the tile wall, and Claire blessed Ted for renovating the bathroom at some point.

While he sat there in silence, staring at the floor as the hot water beat on him, her mother told her to leave. That she could handle the rest. Claire wasn't so sure, but she closed the bathroom door and hovered out in the hall. Five minutes later, the water stopped and she heard the shower door open. Before she could decide whether to call in and offer help, she heard her mother's voice, loud and angry as it reverberated off the tile walls.

"I want to know what happened. Why did you do a crazy thing like that? What's over there?"

There was a long silence.

"Joe," her mother said, "I'd rather have the bitter truth than a lie." That was one of Mama's favorite sayings.

Again, nothing from her father. Claire felt guilty, lurking in the hall and listening. But she couldn't tear herself away. Her mother had every right to be upset, but her heart flooded with pity for her father.

"I know about her," she heard her mother say. "Ava."

Claire eyebrows shot up. But really, how could she be surprised? Her mother wasn't stupid.

"Do you still love her?"

Claire gasped out loud, then quickly covered her mouth with a hand.

"Love her?" Even his voice quivered, and Claire thought how old he sounded, although it was still laced with annoyance. "Don't be ridiculous."

"Do you love me?"

"Jesus Christ, Fanny. How can you even ask me that?"

"Because," her mother said, "in fifty years I don't recall you ever actually saying those words."

"I didn't think I had to."

And then the bathroom door opened and Claire fled back into the kitchen while her mother got him dry clothes. She, too, couldn't ever remember her father saying he loved her mother. Or, for that matter, her mother saying those words to him. But they had never been a demonstrative family. Not like her friend Robin's, where her father kissed them each night, and her mother sent them off each day with a hug and a "love ya!" No, Claire never doubted her parents loved her, but it was a quiet, stern kind of love. The thought of kissing her parents or saying those words out loud would make her squirm with discomfort, even now.

She cleaned out the trays and wiped down the sink, waiting for the prints to dry. There was something so powerful in her father's gaze that morning. It was almost as if you could look back across the forgotten, busy years to the moment he'd been on that very same spit of sand, with Ava. When in a moment of loneliness, and longing, he'd let go of himself. And he was still paying the price.

Her mother wanted the truth, and it was painful that Claire couldn't share that with her. But what was the truth, really? Until they found this woman, or her family, it was all just a "what if?" Unclipping the prints from the line now and slipping them into an envelope, she thought about the last words her father had uttered to her, just before Sean had come up the dune path: "Will you help me find her?" Of course she'd agreed. How could she say no?

Ava wasn't in the phone book, her father told her, obviously having already looked. But he remembered where her family lived. Their search would have to wait, though, because her father was sick with a bad cold now, and the doctor in the urgent care where she had to take him, all the way in Orleans, had told her that he was to stay put until he was better. They didn't want to risk pneumonia, not at his age. He'd waited this long, she told him in the car on the ride back, what would another week be? He must have been feeling sick, because he didn't argue. Now it was hard for Claire to actually imagine. Next week they would go back to Truro and hopefully locate Ava. And she would find out if she had a half brother or sister. If her father indeed had another child.

Her cell phone rang just then and she dug in her tote bag, noting how late it was and hoping nothing was wrong at the house.

"Hey, Babe," Rick said, and she could hear the smile in his voice. "You are now talking to the first place winner of the prestigious North Jersey Invitational Golf Tournament."

"You won?"

"Hey, don't sound so shocked," he said with mock disappointment.

He was exuberant. And then he told her he was starting to think about competing on a more serious level. He was going to try and play in the regionals. If he won, and that was a big if, he could possibly qualify for the U.S. Open, which had a certain number of amateur slots.

"Can you imagine that, Claire?" he said, his voice full of excitement. "And you know what? I think I could do it."

"Oh, Rick, that's wonderful."

"I wouldn't be the first to start in my forties. Let's face it, not everyone's a Tiger Woods out there, able to do nothing but play golf since they could walk. Some of us have to wait for our dreams..." And then he took a deep breath. "Anyway, we'll see. I don't want to jump the gun here."

"I'm so happy for you."

"Well, it gets better. I golfed with Seymour, the builder, and then sat with him and his daughter, Sammy. She's actually the site foreman for our project. And they're interested in looking at more land. They see Jefferson County as an untapped market, a part of New Jersey that's pristine and overlooked. I told them I couldn't agree more. That's exactly why I originally bought the business, remember me telling you that, Claire?"

"I do. And it sounds like things couldn't be going any better," she said. And she wasn't there. "Listen, remember I mentioned you coming up for your birthday? We haven't really talked about it, but I saw that there's a nice golf course not too far from town. So we can celebrate and you can put another notch on your golf bag."

There was a pause. "You know what? That sounds like a plan."

"That's great."

"Well, listen, I'll let you go. I just got in and I've got an early day tomorrow. I'm meeting Sammy on-site to start going over the floor plans and extras. I'll call you in a few days and we'll nail down the details for my birthday visit. Good night, babe."

Riding her bike through the dark streets of town, it was quiet, but Claire could hear music playing softly somewhere, drifting to her on the cool night air. Rick had never once asked about her, about the workshop, her family, Rose. Was she managing? Was she lonely? Did she miss him? It certainly didn't sound like he missed her. And she wondered about this Sammy, although she knew she was being ridiculous. Rick had never given her any reason to be jealous or mistrust him.

The music grew louder, and as she approached a big house set back from the street, she saw a canopy strung with lights, a table filled with candles, and people singing softly as they drank wine. A wave of loneliness washed over her. Just for that moment, she wished she could walk into that yard and be part of that scene. That simple life.

For a moment she thought of that night under the stars with John Poole in August. How much she'd enjoyed herself. And then she told herself to stop. She was being silly. If Rick seemed self-absorbed, wasn't she guilty of the same thing? Wasn't she buried in her workshop right now? So what if Rick didn't ask about her; he was obviously floating on a cloud of victory.

But part of her kept thinking something between them had shifted since the summer. When he came up for his birthday, she had to somehow make it right. Maybe she needed to remember that marriage wasn't about indulging your own dreams, but sharing those dreams. Sharing her life with a man wasn't something she had a lot of practice with. And wasn't she the one who put hundreds of miles between them for ten weeks, at a time when things were tenuous? So she had no one to blame but herself.

Maybe coming here had been the wrong thing to do, after all.

FANNY SAT IN THE SHOWER, the water beating on her aching shoulders and back. How quickly you get used to some things, she thought. This big walk-in shower was similar to the one in their little apartment at Sunrise Manor. It was much easier for her and Joe to get in and out of than their old tub, and she'd gotten used to that quickly. But the apartment, no. She would never get used to it. It would never feel like her home.

She wished she never had to go back to it.

She toweled off, blotting her damp hair, then pulled her nightgown over her head. She opened her jar of cold cream and went to smooth it onto her face, but her hand stopped midair. She stared at herself in the mirror. Sometimes it shocked her, how old she looked. Her short gray hair stuck up in damp tufts, like a wild halo above her head. The skin above her eyes drooped, the hooded lids falling closer and closer to her lashes, so that her eyes were getting smaller by the year. Once, her big almond-shaped eyes had been her best feature. If the drooping kept up, she'd be squinting in a year or two. The fan of deep wrinkles that spread across her cheeks did nothing to enhance them either. Age spots blotched her crepey skin, and tiny lines furrowed above her top lip. No matter how she might try to doll herself up, or tell herself she still felt twenty-five inside, there was no denying it. She was old.

She wondered how Annie would have looked if she had lived to be old. She and Annie had the same soft brown eyes, the same high cheekbones. Everyone could tell they were sisters. To the world they were Annie and Fanny. But to Mama and Daddy they were always Antoinetta and Filomena. How nice it would have been to grow old together. When Annie died, a hole had opened in Fanny's heart, one that never filled up again.

She thought back to when everything in her life changed. That first phone call from Annie she'd never forget. *I think there's something wrong with me.* And Fanny telling her that was silly, she was a mother with young kids, of course she felt run down. Two years later, a week before she died, they finally got the answer to the mystery of what in fact was wrong with Annie. Systemic lupus, the doctor told them. They'd never heard of it. Ironically, it didn't seem all that rare today. And it was treatable now. But then, it was still new. And for Annie, treatment came too late.

A few months after she died, Annie's husband, Phil, moved to Georgia with their three kids, trying to make a fresh start. Leaving no forwarding address or phone number. Mama and Daddy were simply shattered, their only link to Annie taken from them. When Daddy died suddenly a year later, Fanny knew it wasn't an enlarged heart but a broken heart that took him. Annie's children weren't at the funeral. How could they be? Fanny had no way to reach them to even tell them that their grandfather had died.

Phil was like Liam, coldhearted. Both of them leaving a train of broken hearts in their wake. But now Liam was coming back, and Fanny had to keep that secret. She was plagued with guilt over it, even though she was quite sure Claire was keeping her own secret about Ava. Claire felt bad about it; it was all there in her eyes. Fanny didn't like any of this. It wasn't right, family keeping things from each other. If Annie had been there, Fanny could have unburdened herself of all of this. They'd told each other everything. Annie was the only person she'd ever told about Ava.

Back then, Annie kept encouraging her to talk to Joe about it, to find out the truth. But Fanny wouldn't. She knew it was her stubborn pride. She didn't have Annie's soft and easy way with people. Never once when she was sick did she get angry with Phil or his mother.

Fanny suspected it was guilt that drove Phil away from the family. Because for a long time, he didn't really believe Annie was sick. And then there was his mother, how she interfered in their lives. How nothing Annie ever did was good enough for her son. But Annie always made excuses for her. Annie was so good. Fanny always wished she could be as free with her forgiveness as her sister, but it just wasn't in her. She'd never forgive Phil for what he did to them. How different everything might have been if Annie had met someone else. But he was Annie's first and only boyfriend.

Fanny only had two boyfriends before Joe. First there was the good-looking, well-dressed older man. With his cashmere coat and well-manicured nails, he seemed like a movie star. When she found out on their third date that he was an undertaker, she told Annie, who wrinkled up her nose. "He's not for you," she insisted. Fanny never went out with him again. And so there'd been Ernie the plumber, who was suspicious from the start, but such a nice guy. He had to be home early every night because his day started at five a.m. But after a month, Annie asked their brother, Michael, to follow him. He was married, of course. She should have trusted her instincts from the beginning.

Then there was a long dry spell. She watched the world around her pairing up, marrying, making children, and she wanted it, too. Just when she was about to give up, Joe came into her life, quiet, but good, responsible. Handsome as hell. When he asked her age, she lied. Because she already knew he was four years younger, from what Anthony had told them. And she was nearly an old maid. So she lied, and Mama and Annie went along with it.

She wondered what Joe thought when he looked at her now. Did he even see her? Or did he see the girl she was when they'd first met? Sometimes, when a certain look crossed his face, or he'd turn suddenly, it was as if she were seeing the man she'd met all those years ago. As much as he'd aged, he was still handsome. There was still so much of the man she'd fallen in love with that November afternoon.

Rubbing extra cream under her eyes, Fanny wondered what Dominick Fortunato saw when he looked at her. He would have to be blind not to see the folds in her skin, the blotches, the sag of her neck. But when he looked at her, she felt as if he wasn't seeing any of that, but searching for the real her. The part of her he was trying to find inside of her. The part of her that no one had touched in a long, long time.

What if he wasn't just a silly old man who was in love with himself? What if he was really a lonely old man who was looking for something more in life for whatever time was left? Like her.

30

DESPITE EVERYTHING SHE'D TOLD HERSELF ABOUT staying away from him, Claire found herself climbing into John Poole's old car after her morning workshop. Part of her felt like a fool for agreeing to this. The other part was excited. She was going on an adventure. She was going to see whales.

He'd called her cell phone a few days ago and told her he had a release he forgot to have her sign for the photos of the canal, and that the magazine needed it right away. Reluctantly, she'd told him to come to the house. But when he got there, she discovered she'd already signed the release back in Lincoln, just as she'd thought.

"Sorry about the ruse. I didn't think you'd agree to listen to me unless you had to," he'd said, as they stood on the front porch. "You seemed in a hurry to get away from me last time."

Embarrassed, she'd said nothing. She knew there'd been several missed calls from him, but he hadn't left a message, so she didn't bother calling back. But she felt bad. He'd given her an incredible opportunity with the photo assignment of the canal, and she should have been grateful for it. It would be an impressive piece in a portfolio or on a resume, something it would have taken her years to achieve on her own. And she'd been acting like an idiot, perhaps misconstruing his moodiness for feelings toward her.

"Okay, I'm listening," she'd said, finally, as she watched her father walking up the driveway toward John's car, a dusty old yellow Land Rover that had seen better days.

"The piece I'm working on here is really important to me. Probably more than anything else I've ever done, and…I'd really like it if you'd do the photographs for me again."

Surprised, she'd looked at him. His face was serious. There was no amused smile.

"John, besides the fact that I'm up to my eyeballs with this workshop, I've got my family here. I barely have time to breathe. I couldn't possibly take on anything else right now."

"You might be passing up a once-in-a-lifetime opportunity, Claire," he said in a challenging tone.

"Look, I'm sure there are dozens of photographers in this town who would be happy to work with you. And who'd probably have the time to do it—"

Now he smiled, shaking his head. "But I want you."

She felt her heart trip in her chest, at the way he said it. The way he was looking at her. "I can't."

"*New England Life* can get stock photos; they'd be fine with that. But I want something as up-to-the-minute as possible."

She'd stood there, shaking her head.

"Claire, you did an unbelievable job with the canal photos."

"Because I cared, it was right in my own backyard. I'm not really interested in fish…"

"Oh, come on, Claire, this isn't just fish," he interrupted. "It's a much bigger story than that, but most people have no clue what their sushi really costs as far as the environment goes."

"Well, I don't eat sushi, John, just to set the record straight."

He stood there, running a hand through his hair. "I'm sorry. I don't know why, but I always seem to say or do the wrong thing around you. Can't we just be friends? All you have to do is come out with me on the boat one time. It'll take two, maybe three hours. Then decide."

"Why? Why are you so intent on me doing this?"

"Because, it's not really about the fish, Claire. It's really about the whales."

That had done it. Her mother and Amy had been going on about the whales since the other day, when they'd seen a spout in the harbor, just in front of the breakwater. Claire had gone outside every moment she could after her workshop, hoping to spot the whale, but with no luck.

And now she was in John's old yellow Land Rover, driving toward the pier. "This is quite a vehicle," she said, as they bounced down Commercial Street.

"Your father seemed to like it," he said in a teasing tone.

It was the kind of beat-up truck she saw on the Discovery channel, driving through the African bush. "My father loves old cars of any kind."

"This was actually my grandfather's. It's more than fifty years old."

"I guess that explains why you didn't have it in New Jersey."

He laughed and turned to her. "It's not exactly luxury highway driving."

He turned into the large lot at the pier and parked; then they walked all the way down the wharf. He introduced her to the Coastal Studies crew, who were waiting for them. First, Moby, a wiry gray-haired man wearing a Red Sox hat, who was captain of this boat, but also an old friend.

"Yeah, he was just a young tyke when I first met him," Moby said, with that thick Cape Cod accent. "Nothin' but a little pain in the ass back then."

She watched as John blushed, but she could see he respected Moby, who must have been fifteen years older or so. And then he turned to the woman who was just stepping off the boat.

"And this is Libby," he said. Claire judged Libby to be somewhere in her thirties. She was a tall, lanky woman dressed all in khaki, the wind and sun etched into the fine lines of her otherwise youthful face. She held out a hand, and as soon as Claire shook it, they turned and all headed quickly onto the boat.

The Coastal Studies boat was much smaller than the touristy whale-watching boats, which could hold a hundred people or so. Above the cabin, there were seats on the roof, and above that, perched atop a high pole, was yet another seat.

Claire hadn't been on many boats in her life, and as she stepped onto the deck, the boat swaying beneath her, she steadied herself, worried for a moment that she might get seasick. When they'd gotten out of the car, John had taken her hands, and before she could protest, again assuming the wrong thing, he slipped two snug rubber bracelets onto her wrists, maneuvering them to hit the acupressure points to avoid seasickness. Now she was grateful for them.

It was another warm day for late September as they chugged out of the harbor with no wake, the angled autumn sun to their right. Claire felt that tug of excitement again as they passed a few fishing boats on their way back to the wharf. As the boat rounded the breakwater and then the sandy edge of Long Point, Claire watched the lighthouse. Sure enough, as they came to the ocean side, she saw just the top of the cross, a corner of the flag lifting and falling with the gentle breeze.

"We're lucky," John said, coming to stand beside her after a conversation with Libby. "Sometimes it can be freezing going out this time of year. The wind'll pick up soon, though."

Sure enough, as they finished rounding Long Point and headed out into the ocean, a stiff breeze came at them head-on. Claire pulled on her jacket and put a hat and gloves on, too. The damp ocean air felt twenty degrees colder, and with the wind cutting through her, Claire found herself huddling next to the cabin for warmth.

Libby came over and stood with them. She pulled up a pair of binoculars dangling from her neck and scanned the horizon, talking as she looked. She told Claire she'd always loved wildlife and had a degree in Marine Science. Coming from the Midwest, the ocean was like an exotic otherworld to her. Like going to Mars, she joked.

"We're all thrilled about the article John is working on for *New England Life*, although we'd hoped we were gonna hit the big time," she said with mock disappointment, elbowing John in the rib.

"Yeah, yeah, Nurse Ratched," John joked back, leaning toward Claire as he tried to avoid what Claire could see was more of an affectionate jab. She wondered if Libby had a thing for him. "At least I tried. *National Geographic* turned me down, as you well know."

And then Libby turned to Claire, serious again. "We need people to realize what's going on here. Hopefully this piece of John's will lead to bigger and better exposure."

Libby told her they were on their way to track a pregnant right whale. The right whale, she explained, was one of the rarest mammals on earth and the rarest large whale on the planet. They were called the "right" whale, Claire learned, because back in the days of whaling, they were the easiest of all the whales to catch, and so were the "right" one to go after. Hence, their rapid decline.

There were no more than 350 left, and most were now on their migratory route back south, from northern Canadian waters to the birthing grounds off Georgia and Florida, where they would spend the winter.

"It's a long, slow, dangerous journey each spring and fall," Libby said. "Losing even just one female could tip the population toward extinction."

"Why is it so dangerous?" Claire asked.

"In a nutshell, because of fishing. The ocean is loaded with fishing gear: huge nets from factory ships, right down to the lines of sport fishermen that can go for thousands of feet. And then there are the lobster pots. You name it, it's like running an obstacle course swimming up and down the coast. When a whale gets caught in a net, or entangled in a line, it's horrible. They can drown, or die a slow death from infection. We started our disentanglement program years ago, and since then we've saved eighty-nine whales. But what would be better is to prevent entanglements in the first place. It's an education process."

"The fishermen think that by protecting the whales, we're hurting their catch," John said. "And that's just shortsighted, because that's not the case. With just some modifications, everyone could be happy."

"And it's not just the whales, the seals get caught, too," Libby said. "But that really burns up the fishermen, protecting the seals. Because they think the seals are eating up all the fish out here and that's why their sources are drying up, so to speak."

John shook his head. "Again, they're not dealing with reality. It's the factory ships that are taking the fish in droves, not the seals."

"Anyway, we're probably overloading you with information," Libby said. "Why don't you just enjoy the ride. If we get lucky, you might see a humpback or fin whale on our way."

When Libby left them to confer with Moby, they huddled again on the bench against the wall of the cabin, where they were more protected from the wind. Claire was still able to see the ocean through the railing.

"It's not just the entanglements," John said. "Getting struck by ships is another big hazard, but I'm not going to get into that. We've gotta take baby steps here. One change at a time."

"Can't they just swim out of the way when a ship comes near?"

He shook his head. "They're slow, especially when they're feeding. And the ships are going fast. From 2002 to 2006, seventeen right whales were struck and killed by ships, and six were adult females."

"Wow," Claire said, gazing out at the endless seawater surrounding them. "I had no idea."

He smiled. "How could you? Where you live, inland, it's not

part of your life. But here, well, the fishing industry is a major occupation for a lot of average people who live week to week on what they catch. Trying to tell them to change their nets, or their lobster pots, the way they've been doing things for years, doesn't go over so big."

They were quiet for a while as the boat traveled farther out to sea, the land of Cape Cod long gone behind them, nothing in sight as far as she could see, not even another boat. Claire had never been this far out into the ocean. It was like another world. She thought about the universe below them, quietly existing except for interference by man. And how most of the world went about their busy lives with no idea of how they were affecting these other living creatures.

LIBBY CAME OUT OF THE CABIN a while later and explained to Claire that the area they were heading toward was part of a series of track lines across Cape Cod Bay. The Coastal Studies aerial survey team searched regularly and recorded any marine mammals they saw along these lines. If they spotted a right whale, the pilot circled the plane so the researchers could photograph the whale for individual identification and to record its position and behavior.

"It's tough to get a good picture from that high. On the boat here, we can get closer, and then we compare what we see with the aerial survey team. The whale's ID becomes part of the database we have on the North Atlantic right whale. We have a system to pass this info to mariners, so they can hopefully avoid hitting them. It's another big problem, boats colliding with whales."

"Yes, John was telling me."

"Our pictures aren't always so great, either, especially if the whale isn't fully surfacing. Having you here, taking professional photos, well, that'll be a big help."

"I hope so."

Libby pointed ahead and Claire saw buoy markers dotting the water.

"We have stations set up where we can monitor the zooplankton; that's what the right whale eats. If the zooplankton is dense enough, it gives us a good idea that it's a place a right whale might come to feed and stay awhile. And it gives us a chance to study their eating habits and get a little closer. They're the toughest whales to identify, because they don't typically surface a lot. Just up ahead is where our plane spotted the pregnant female."

They spent the next hour slowly sailing from buoy to buoy with no sightings at all. Finally, Libby said they had to turn around. Claire was disappointed, and could see by his face that John was, too.

They headed back toward land, the boat cruising at a steady clip, and then suddenly the engine slowed. Libby came down the ladder from the perch above the cabin.

"You might want to come to the other side of the boat. We've got some nice humpback activity," Libby said.

As they got up and walked across the boat, the engine went quiet and the stiff breeze died. Standing at the railing on the other side of the boat, Claire gasped. Floating on the surface of the water, not thirty feet away, was the biggest mammal she'd ever seen, far larger even than their boat.

While Claire unzipped her camera bag, the whale lay still, as if resting on the ocean's surface. A big eye seemed to stare right at her.

"Look," John said, pointing excitedly straight down over the rail. A much smaller mammal was coming out from under the boat. "It's a calf."

Claire's hand froze as she watched the small whale swim toward the mother and then nestle onto its side.

"She's nursing," Libby said.

The calf stayed there feeding, the mother just lying still. Claire felt her heart expand. She couldn't move, could not even speak, it was so touching.

"You should take a picture, this may not last," Libby said, coming up behind her.

Claire reached again for her camera, almost unwilling to let her eyes off the mother and young whale. Pulling the viewfinder to her eye, she zoomed in on the mother's face and clicked. Then she zoomed in on the baby, wondering if the results would be good enough, since the calf was about ten feet down in the clear green water.

She zoomed out, trying to get a shot of the entire body of the humpback, but they were too close.

"Could we back up a bit?" she asked. "I mean, without disturbing them?"

"We can try. Humpbacks are the friendliest whales," Libby said, and motioned to Moby through the cabin window. "They like to tag along after boats, which the whale watchers love. Unfortunately, the whalers loved it, too, because it also made them easy prey."

The engine came on gently, and the boat began to circle back behind them.

"Fortunately, they've made a nice comeback," Libby went on. "As you can see, they're pretty playful, so they're much easier to identify than the right whales. They each have distinct white markings on their tails, or flukes."

The boat stopped suddenly. Claire focused her camera and began clicking again and again. Suddenly, the calf dove down and underneath the giant body of its mother, and disappeared. Within moments, the mother whale swam away, too. Libby went back into the cabin and Claire turned to John.

"You know, you don't really think about whales being mammals, but of course I knew that. It's just that watching the calf nurse, you realize how much that mother-child relationship is similar to ours," she said.

"I know what you mean," he said.

"What about the father? Does he help with feeding and rearing?"

John shook his head. "No. Unfortunately, like a lot of other mammals, the father just impregnates the female."

She almost made a sly comment, but her words caught in her throat as she watched a whale suddenly shoot straight up out of the water no more than fifty feet away, and then crash down onto the ocean's surface on its side with a tremendous splash.

"That's her," Libby called out from the cabin. "She's breaching, being playful, or teaching her calf."

Three more times she breached, propelling herself out of the water and high into the air like a rocket. Claire imagined the energy it must take to launch her huge body like that, and the fun of the crash. Again, she felt a wave of emotion flood her chest.

"It's unbelievable," she said.

"Like a celebration of simply being alive," John added.

She smiled, and they both turned as the humpback swam to the surface now, headfirst, then arched and dove into the water, like Claire had seen dolphins do, flipping its tail flukes high above the water, and finally disappearing.

"She's diving deep now, probably leaving us," John said.

Claire sighed. "This was incredible."

"If we get lucky enough to see the right whale, that'll be even more incredible."

"It was still amazing," she said. "Thanks for taking me."

John smiled. "I'm not such a bad guy, Claire."

31

It was hard to believe three weeks had gone by. Claire was busier than ever, but found herself drawn more and more to the whales. The print of the mother humpback, that huge eye staring back from the photograph, mesmerized her. Below the surface, through the clear green water, you could indeed make out the outline of the calf nursing. Claire had played with the photo for days on the pigment inkjet printer and was finally happy with the results, and planned to turn it in for her assignment tomorrow. The image would have been lost in black and white.

Riding back home now on her bike, she thought how much had changed in these three weeks. Her mother, who'd slipped into a depression in the assisted living, was now like a woman transformed, out the door walking each day, or cooking inside, and not complaining about one thing. Her father had revealed a former life no one had known about before. And Amy had finally opened up to her about Liam.

When she'd returned late from the whale excursion with John Poole that day, she'd found her parents at the table. Her mother told her that Amy had missed dinner and had been up in her room for hours. She felt that something was wrong, although Amy just claimed to be tired.

Claire had gone up and found Amy sitting on a chair in the corner of the room, staring out the window, with Rose on her lap. As she walked in, Rose looked up, a rattle in her hand that she'd managed to get into her mouth. She smiled around the rattle, her joy at seeing Claire lighting up her eyes. Claire's heart swelled; Rose really loved her. Then she looked at Amy and her own smile froze.

"Honey, what's wrong?" she asked, walking across the room.

"Nothing." Her voice sounded worn out, as if she'd been sitting there crying for a long time.

Claire sat on the bed beside them. Rose was excited now, still smiling at her, waving the rattle in the air. Amy just stared out the window.

"We haven't really talked in a while," Claire said. "I'm sorry I've been so busy."

Amy said nothing.

"Things seem to be going well with Rose. And Grandma tells me that you've both been cooking up a storm, and sharing some recipes with that restaurant. That's wonderful."

Rose managed to get the rattle back into her mouth and bit down on it hard. Claire wondered if she was teething already, although four months seemed a little young.

"Would you like me to take the baby for a while? Give you a break?"

Amy shook her head. "I'm not tired."

"Then what is it?"

And then Amy turned and looked at her, the misery apparent in her eyes.

"My father was supposed to come this week. To see me. And Rose."

Liam? Coming to Cape Cod? Claire bit the words back that nearly escaped her lips.

"You don't have to worry," Amy went on. "He's not coming. But I knew you would have said, *Don't get your hopes up, Amy*, and I just didn't want to hear it. That's why I asked Grandma not to tell you."

Her mother had known? And hadn't said a word? And here she'd been feeling guilty over not telling her mother about Ava.

"I really believed him this time," Amy said softly. "I hate him. I wish he wasn't my father."

"Oh, honey."

"He didn't even have the fucking guts to tell me himself. He left a message on my cell."

"I'm so sorry."

"Why does he feel nothing for me? I mean, there's no excuse not to come here; he can't get into trouble here, right? He's either lazy as shit or he really doesn't give a damn about me. I just thought that maybe he'd want to see Rose. His only grandchild."

Amy leaned down and kissed the top of the baby's head, then lay her cheek next to Rose's. The baby dropped the rattle and reached back, grabbing a strand of Amy's hair, pulling it again and again. It must have hurt, but Amy said nothing.

"It wasn't until I had Rose that I really realized he can't possibly love me. I mean, I love her so much it hurts. I would do anything to make her happy, to give her the best life possible. To protect her." She paused for a long moment. "He doesn't feel any of that for me. That's pretty obvious."

Claire leaned forward, putting her arms around both of them, her daughter and granddaughter.

"He's just a self-absorbed, thoughtless man. Once I thought otherwise. I was young and desperately in love with him. But he was never the man I thought he was. And when I had you, I felt just like you do about Rose. I wanted to give you the best life possible. He just wanted different things. He couldn't stay in any place for long, and he was always chasing his next dream."

"He says he's about to go bankrupt."

Claire sighed. How many times had she heard that line? After the bar he bought with two friends failed. After he'd gone to California to start a winery. Then there were the properties in Florida;

easy flips, or so he'd thought. There was always money for his next great scheme, but never anything to send to his daughter. Not that she'd ever told Amy any of it, because she knew that would have done nothing but hurt Amy even more.

"Maybe I was better off not having him in my life after all. He's not exactly what you'd call father material. He's like a bum in one of those awful Lifetime movies Grandma likes to watch." She looked down at the baby.

Claire brushed the hair off of Amy's face. "Time is a funny thing, Amy. When you get to be my age, you do a lot of looking back. Seeing so clearly the mistakes you've made. And wondering how things would have turned out if you'd been smarter." She ran a finger down Amy's cheek, remembering how much Amy had loved that as a child. Sometimes Claire would stroke her cheeks until she fell asleep. At that moment, her heart was breaking for Amy. "I also see that if I did things differently, if I'd been smarter, I would never have had you. And I wouldn't trade anything for that. He did one good thing in his life. He gave me you."

Amy looked up at her and managed a little smile through her tears.

"Thanks," she said softly. And then after a long pause, "You've been a good mother to me. I see that now."

How long had she waited to hear those words? But at that moment, they were bittersweet, not just because of Amy's pain, but because Claire needed to tell her the rest of the story, while Amy was being so open and honest with her.

"Maybe fathers are overrated," Amy had said then. "Maybe a good mother is enough."

Turning onto Bangs Street now, Claire wondered if her decision to hold back then was the right one. Amy was in pain, and she hadn't wanted to add to it. So she'd said nothing.

She also said nothing because no matter how Liam's bad behavior had played into her daughter's way of justifying her own actions, Claire thought that Rose needed a father, too.

But again, Claire wondered if Amy even knew who Rose's father was.

As she came down Commercial Street and slowed her bike to turn into their crushed white shell driveway, Claire saw her father sitting on the front porch, waiting for her.

Waiting to go find Ava.

FANNY FELT HERSELF GETTING STRONGER. She walked every day now, never tiring of the view of the bay between the houses as she made her way up and down Commercial Street. At first she did it to get away from Joe, and from her anger, because the house was small, and now that he was better, he'd once again claimed the patio overlooking the water. No, she was walking now because she enjoyed it. It was her alone time with her thoughts. And she was controlling her thoughts better now, thanks to the little book Seth had given her.

Often she'd stop at the Episcopal church, a bay-front wooden structure that was quaint and rustic. She'd walk through the gravel parking lot and sit on a bench that overlooked the beach. It was there she saw the seals for the first time. At first she'd thought they were buoys bobbing in the dark water, their round, brown heads peeking through the surface. Then one catapulted itself onto a small, wooden dock out in the water, and lay there in the sun, its shiny nose and whiskers glistening. Soon there were three of them, and Fanny couldn't help smiling. There was always something surprising turning up on these walks. Yesterday it was Dominick Fortunato.

She'd left the house early yesterday, before Joe had even gotten up. It was barely eight-thirty, and a fine mist drifted from the water and the gardens as she made her way up the street. The air was warm and soft, damp and sweet with the smells of the fall flowers that seemed to love this climate. As she walked by Dominick's, she heard a hello and turned to see Dominick with a watering can by his side, waving her over. He stood in the midst of the small herb garden at the side of the restaurant.

They chatted for a moment and he pointed out the different plants, a spiky bush of rosemary, bright green parsley, fresh garlic, oregano, cilantro, and fennel, Mama's favorite. But when he pointed to the basil, Fanny couldn't help herself, she bent and picked a leaf, then tore it and lifted it to her nose. Ahh, it never failed, the sweet fragrance of fresh basil always brought her back to Daddy's garden in Brooklyn. She closed her eyes, seeing Daddy in his old corduroys and a worn button-down shirt, smudges of soil on his knees, smiling and holding out a clump of basil for her to take in to Mama. But first he always brought it to his nose and sniffed, then smiled. "Heaven," he would say.

Dominick smiled when she opened her eyes. "My favorite, too," he said, taking her hand and pulling it toward him, then inhaling the scent of the basil. When she got home, she didn't wash her hand for hours, not wanting to lose the aroma that filled her with such happiness and longing.

She sat now looking at the water awhile longer, waiting to see if the seals would show up again. One thing she had to admit: since that ridiculous boat ride he'd taken last week, scaring them all to death, Joe had made a turnaround. Whatever was pushing him forward, whatever he needed to accomplish with this Ava, he seemed more determined and, after resting a few days, more energetic than he'd been in months. Will was a potent thing, Fanny knew. People could will themselves to live or die sometimes. Annie had hung on long after the doctors had given up, and they'd attributed it to her strong will to survive. Fanny knew that Annie wouldn't have fought so hard, suffered so long, if it hadn't been for her young children. What mother could bear to leave when her job was unfinished?

Will was also propelling Amy, Fanny knew. She'd heard her crying last night in her room. A year ago, Amy's life was so different, filled with nothing but the minor cares of a young woman trying to decide what to do with her life. Now the stakes had been raised. She had a baby to care for, a life to figure out. And there was a determination in her each morning as she gave Rose her bottle, and then her cereal, planning the rest of the day. She, too, liked to go for long walks, but Fanny didn't want to slow her down by joining her. It was good for her to explore on her own, think about her options. Before they knew it, they'd all be heading back to Jefferson County.

Or maybe not all of them.

Fanny loved it here. She felt free. The thought of going back to that assisted living was as appetizing as the thought of going to prison. There was nothing wrong with her. As for Joe, well, maybe that wasn't her problem anymore. He seemed to have found a renewed zest for living for someone else.

He'd left with Claire a little while ago, supposedly to go back to the doctor in Orleans. But Claire could barely look at her. It didn't take a genius to figure out where she was really taking him.

SHE COULDN'T SLEEP. It was nearly midnight when Claire slipped out the back door and walked onto the beach. The moon was just coming up across the water, bathing the bay and the little boats docked close to the shore in a soft white glow. In the distance she could see Long Point, the spit of sand lit up with moonlight and the reflection of the lighthouse. She sighed, and sat down on the cool, soft sand, wrapping her cardigan around her. Things were getting more and more difficult with her parents.

Her cell phone vibrated in her pocket and she grabbed it quickly, longing to talk to Rick. But it was Abbie.

"Are you in the darkroom, slaving away?"

"No, I'm out on the beach. I can't sleep."

"I miss you!" Abbie said.

"I miss you, too." Claire knew she was lucky to have Abbie, a best friend you could tell anything to; a soul mate.

"How's it going?" Abbie asked.

"Oh, where to start," she said, and sighed. "Amy's had her heart broken by her father, again. John Poole managed to lure me into another project, photographing endangered whales, which I don't really have time for. But I have to admit, I'm totally enthralled. Rick hardly calls, he's so busy, and I know that's my own fault, for abandoning him. Oh, and best of all, are you ready for this? My father may have a love child."

"What!"

And then Claire told her about Ava, because she had to tell someone.

"Holy shit!" Abbie whispered.

"I feel guilty even telling you about it. Like I'm betraying him."

"You know my lips are sealed. Oh, Claire, how does your mother feel about all of this?"

"That's the big question. She doesn't say much because she doesn't really know the story—that there might be a child, at least a grown-up son or daughter. And he refuses to talk to her about it; he's so ashamed. He asked me not to tell her either."

"You're kidding. Can you really do that?"

"Oh, Abbie. I don't really have a choice. You know my father, the man doesn't talk. For him to tell me this, something so personal, well, just blew me away. If I tell her..." Claire shook her head. "But my mother's not happy about it. She's annoyed with me. She told me point-blank that she knows all this running around is about Ava, and she thinks he's being secretive because this woman was the love of his life. I did tell her that she was wrong about that. So why are we going on these secret missions? she wants to know. She can get so dramatic. 'You have to ask Dad,' I tell her, all the while feeling guilty and rationalizing what I'm doing by telling myself that she has kept things from me. She knew that Liam was coming and didn't tell me because Amy asked her not to."

"Oh, honey." Abbie let out a low whistle. "You can't be mad at her about Liam, though."

"I'm not. I understand," she said. "Anyway, so today I took my father to try to find Ava."

And then she told Abbie about their trip that afternoon back to Truro.

They couldn't find Ava's house. There was a winery on a hill, where Claire's father thought it should be. Claire realized it was another ancient sand dune, overlooking the Province Lands in the distance, part of that beautiful stretch of dunes and small ponds that went from the eastern side of Truro all the way to the tip of the Cape, east of Provincetown, where Route 6 ended. They'd sat there for a long time as he looked out the window of the car. He looked confused, sad.

"I'd only actually been to her house twice," he'd admitted.

"Dad, it was over fifty years ago. Maybe this isn't it."

But he insisted it was. Ava's father was a fisherman, but he'd also grown grapes.

"The people who owned the winery never heard of Ava or her family," she went on telling Abbie. "The neighboring houses sat far apart; several had swing sets, and were obviously now occupied by young families. Time had moved on and so, apparently, had Ava's family."

"Did you try the post office?" Abbie asked.

They had. They'd driven through the tiny village of Truro and asked at the post office, with no luck. There were no longer any Oliveras in their rolls. On the way back to Provincetown, she'd once more tried to convince her father to tell her mother the truth, but he'd said nothing. During the long silence, she wondered what he was thinking, knowing how her own mind jumped and clattered with the noise of her insecurities, her decisions, everything in her life. His mind had to have been teeming at that moment, but his face was like stone, as it usually was when he was quiet.

She and Eugene used to just think he was a hard-ass, a stern disciplinarian devoid of human emotions. But Claire knew better now. She'd hated him for forbidding her to see Liam years ago, and then blamed him when things didn't work out between them in the end. Liam had even thrown that in her face. *This will make your parents happy*, he'd said to taunt her.

It had struck her in that moment yesterday that her father might consider himself no better than Liam in his own mind. Fathering a child and leaving it for someone else to raise. He'd watched Amy grow up with one parent, and now Rose. Maybe he thought himself no better than those other men who simply turned their back on their responsibilities. But he wasn't like that, she knew. He'd worked hard, fed and clothed and housed them. She and Eugene had had security and two parents. And despite a lack of affection or emotion, as an adult she realized that they were loved, in a quiet, different, nonverbal way, by this man. He was a father to them both.

"Claire, this is like an episode of *Days of Our Lives*," Abbie said now, interrupting her thoughts. "What did you tell your mother when you left today?"

"We told her we were going back to the doctor. Not that she believed it for a minute, but he doesn't want to hurt her. He says he's put her through enough already."

"Wow. Are you managing to get any work done?"

Claire chuckled. "Actually I am. I don't have a minute to myself, except for times like this. But I feel myself getting better. I was intimidated at first. Some of the other people are young and really good, and they've been doing this digital stuff for years. Probably some of them have never even used film."

"Makes you feel old, huh?"

"You bet. But then I think maybe I've got something over on them, too. I don't think I'll ever stop using film. I love the magic in the darkroom, you know? But digital is definitely helping me with the whale photographs."

She told Abbie about her whale excursion with John Poole and sighting the humpbacks.

"Abbie, it was like nothing I've experienced before. I never expected to be so moved. They're such beautiful creatures and they're getting damaged out there. I hope my pictures can make a difference."

"And would John Poole be part of that reason? I only met him that one time, when I showed him the house he rented on Rock-port Road, but God, that man's a hunk."

"Abbie! How can you even ask that? Rick's coming up for his birthday in a few weeks. He's much handsomer than John."

"Yeah, but John's kind of got that bad boy air about him."

"Exactly. And I had my fill of that with Liam. Anyway," she said, "tell me about this Sammy, the site foreman, or woman, I should say."

"Young, pretty in that athletic tennis star sort of way. Wears diamonds and blue jeans and really knows her stuff in construction…"

"I think golf is her game," Claire piped in.

"Oh, I get it. Listen, don't do that to yourself. Your guy is behaving himself. He barely has time to breathe with us launching this subdivision."

"You're right. And enough about me, how are you doing?"

"Well, sweetie, I think I may actually have you beat in the family drama department. Missy came home yesterday and announced that she wants to have sex!"

"Oh, Abbie."

They had talked often about Missy's longing for a normal life. She was twenty-four now, but had the mind of a seven-year-old.

Since she'd gotten a job at ShopRite, rounding up the shopping carts, she was more exposed to the real world; a world Abbie wasn't part of. And Missy was such an innocent that Abbie worried constantly.

"There's a boy like her who also works with the carts, and they've taken a liking to each other. Daniel. He's all she talks about. And he lives in a group home. So now Missy wants to move out and into a group home."

This, Claire knew, was Abbie's biggest fear: Missy living on her own, although she'd be supervised.

"Daniel seems to be a sweet boy, but Claire, he told me the other day, when Missy was in the bathroom, that he wants to marry her." And then Abbie started to cry. "I go for such long stretches just accepting things and then…I don't know, all of a sudden I get angry with God again. Why did He have to do this to her? Why couldn't she have been given a normal life? And then other times I think I'm so lucky. She's innocent and lovable, like they were when they're little and they bring you such joy. That childlike beauty you want to hold onto forever. But she's not a child. She's an adult."

"You should talk to Esther," Claire advised. As the high school nurse, Esther was like the local shaman who knew everyone's secrets and knew how to deal with the worst parenting issues.

"I did. Esther says to let her go. That it's inevitable."

"And how does Tom feel about all this?"

She could hear Abbie take a deep breath. "I haven't told him."

Abbie and Tom had been arguing about Missy for years, since she'd become an adolescent.

"How's he doing?"

"The same. He'll go three days without drinking and we'll be fine, and then the fourth day it all goes to hell. I get so frustrated I just want to beat my head against a wall. But you've heard it all before."

"If Missy goes into a group home, you'll be free to do what you want."

"I know. Listen, speaking of the devil, he's coming upstairs, so I'm gonna run. I'll keep you posted."

Claire stood up and brushed the sand from her jeans. The moon was higher now, illuminating the pier in the distance and lighting up the entire beach. She turned to go to bed, suddenly exhausted.

It seemed as if everyone was keeping secrets, even Abbie. But where was it really getting them? And was it that way in every family? Maybe they'd all spent their lives in pursuit of something that would never really exist: a perfect family. Was there ever such a thing? Claire wondered. Like the ones that she dreamed about when she was a kid and hated her father?

And that she was sure Amy had spent her life longing for, as well.

32

Most of the dune shacks on Race Point Beach had been built during World War II to guard the coast. Abandoned after that, a number of them were claimed by locals, and others eventually taken over by the National Park Service. Because of the remoteness and the wild beauty of the location, they became havens for artists, writers, and photographers over the decades. Tennessee Williams and Norman Mailer stayed in one at different times; renowned photographer Joel Meyerowitz spent time in another.

Situated on high dunes overlooking the ocean, the dwellings were notoriously primitive. There was no electricity, no bathrooms, and only a few had running water. Here you would be cut off from civilization. Here, Charles Meyer explained, you could concentrate on the surrounding beauty without distraction and create, hopefully, outstanding work. He called it a unique, once-in-a-lifetime opportunity.

It might be exciting and adventurous, but to Claire it also sounded a bit scary, alone in the middle of nowhere. She imagined trying to sleep at night, the roar of the ocean and the wind playing tricks on her imagination. And having to go outside in the dark to use the outhouse, wondering what might be lurking in the shadows. But, along with the rest of her classmates, she climbed into one of the two huge Suburbans driven by guides for Art's Dune Tours.

That morning, Charles Meyer had told them this was not mandatory, and it probably wasn't for everyone. But if they liked what they saw today on the tour, and if they decided they were game to try it, they could spend three days in a shack alone. Those three days would be at the end of the session. They would be able to focus on their final projects, a portfolio to exhibit at the Provincetown Art Museum, without distractions from the outside world.

Claire wouldn't mind some alone time. It was hard living in the crowded house on Commercial Street, the only place to escape the tension building between her parents being her bedroom. Or heading out the door on a photo shoot. Even Amy was difficult to be around again, despite their new moments of closeness. Amy was off in another world at times, her look far away. Something was eating away at her and Claire had a feeling it was more than just Liam. The lighthearted hours of cooking in the kitchen had come to an end, as well.

The Suburbans drove out of town and into the Province Lands National Park, following the blacktop road past Race Point Beach, the ocean beach just around the curve from Herring Cove and Cape Cod Bay. The vehicle made a slow right turn onto a sand road. It was like driving on snow, soft and slippery in spots, the car's back end swerving and righting as they drove on. It was truly another world, Claire thought, as they headed deeper into the dunes, nothing but sand and occasional green patches of grass surrounding them. Through the windshield, she saw a steep hill, a dune big enough to be called a small mountain, and then realized the road was taking them there. Within minutes, Ed, their driver, switched to low gear and they were suddenly climbing and fishtailing, angled so steeply that Claire felt a lurch in the pit of her stomach. And then they were at the top and sliding down the other side. She was reminded of the roller coasters of her youth, before she was afraid of heights and abandoned crazy rides like this. A few of her workshop buddies hooted in the back, hoping for more thrills, but Claire silently prayed that that was the worst of it.

It was hard to imagine that anyone could survive all the way out here for long periods of time. Their guide explained that people who stayed in the shacks for a duration had standing appointments to be driven in and out. Or they could leave a note at the gate where the road began. Art's also dropped off supplies occasionally.

"Up ahead is our first dwelling," Ed said, as the car slowed down.

It was what Rick would have called a "teardown," a box of a structure covered with cracked old cedar shingles, some missing, and a flat roof. A clothesline ran between two poles, and Claire saw a barbecue pit and some old beach chairs on the side of the house, overlooking the ocean.

It was impossible to look at the shack and not think of the town house they were building in Arizona. The package of selections arrived yesterday, and when Claire opened it, she was overwhelmed by the decisions she had to make. The color of the siding, the shutters, the interior walls. The kitchen cabinets and countertops. She sat there trying to envision what things would look like when she was having a hard time actually imagining herself living there, suddenly, in the middle of the Arizona desert. As alien to her as this dune shack in the middle of this desert of sand. She tried to drum up the initial surge of excitement she'd felt as she and Rick had toured the models last winter, the sun shining brightly through soaring windows, a view of the red rocks in the distance, the mild weather a heady contrast to the foot of snow and bleak gray skies they'd left behind in New Jersey.

The package of selections was still sitting in the corner of her bedroom, and she'd promised Rick she would make her decisions by tonight. The builder was waiting.

About a quarter mile down the road, they slowed for another dune shack, this one larger, that had obviously been added on to haphazardly. It was painted bright green with orange trim, and on the side of the house Claire saw a large tank and a shower head. The driver explained that the tank collected rainwater, but the showers were cold.

Claire asked if they'd get to go inside one of the shacks, but the answer was no, unfortunately.

"There are artists in each of them and we don't like to disturb them. Everyone here respects each other's privacy."

No two were alike and each was rustic and distinct. One actually had a chair on the roof, which Claire imagined caught incredible views of the ocean below, or the night sky. There were some that simply could not be seen, perched as they were on the edge of the sand before it dropped away to the ocean, and hidden by dunes. When they reached the last one and turned west, away from the ocean, Claire could not imagine herself actually doing this. But then the car stopped and they all got out.

The silence was incredible. There was no sound at all except the ripple of the wind in her ears. One of the other students giggled. And then they all followed a footpath through the sand toward the ocean. It was tough walking, the sand soft and deep. Claire was out of breath, her calves aching, when she heard someone shout back, "Wait until you see this!"

A moment later, she was there, and she took a quick step backward. They must have been fifty feet above the beach, the dunes dropping suddenly. She had a moment's vertigo until she looked out over the vast expanse of dark blue ocean toward the horizon, where it met the cobalt blue sky. You could actually see the curve of the earth here. She felt small, insignificant, in the face of such endless beauty. She thought of the whales, the world of mammals and fish living below the ocean's surface, quiet and hidden now. Easy prey. And she realized how little most people ever knew of such places; taking from the ocean, taking from the land. And she thought of John Poole, devoting his life to protecting things. Keeping the world as it should be.

"If you decide to stay," their guide said, "you'll see seals and dolphins and maybe even whales from the beach."

But you probably wouldn't see another human being, Claire thought. Still, when in her life would she ever be able to experience something like this again? Alone for three days in a world of dunes and ocean and wild-life. It was an artist's dream.

THEY HADN'T FOUGHT A LOT over the years. It wasn't their way. Maybe it would have been better if they had. To scream and shout and set your anger free. But how did you fight with someone who wouldn't fight back? Who simply clammed up and refused to talk?

Or walked out the door?

As Joe had just done.

Fanny sat down on the couch in the living room, thankful that Amy was out with the baby. She felt like smashing a window. Again, she'd tried to find out from Joe what was going on. For the second time, he had returned from one of his drives with Claire looking defeated. Oh, Claire came in with a few grocery bags dangling from her hands, as if they'd really just been out running errands. But Fanny knew from the lurching of Joe's shoulders, his head bobbing from side to side, that he was stressed. He'd stalled in the middle of the living room until Claire went and got him started again, putting her foot in front of his, so he had to step over it. Fanny could have done it, but she'd chosen not to.

She picked up her purse now and her sweater, and walked out the front door. Two could play his game. He'd headed right, so she walked to her left, toward the pier.

For the past few days she'd been reading the book again, *Buddhism for You*. When she felt the roar of anger begin to ring in her head, she would go into her room, shut her door, and open the book randomly. Inevitably something she read began to soothe her, but she didn't want to be soothed today. She wanted to wallow in her anger.

She walked slowly. She had no choice. Her hip might have been feeling better, but she still had the legs and the joints of a woman just a stone's throw from eighty. A block later she stopped a moment to let her breathing settle down. She didn't want to have a heart attack in the middle of Commercial Street, for God's sake. For a moment she looked at the beautiful flowers in front of the Copper Fox, which she'd learned was where Ted lived, his two white dogs now wagging their tails at her. Walking slowly again, she told herself that those two dogs had probably had more adventure on that front porch than she'd had in the last fifty years.

She'd lived in the same house, the same town, with Joe, for more than forty years. Before that, on the same block in Brooklyn since she'd been born. She was baptized Catholic at just nineteen days old, to rid her infant soul of its stain of original sin. What kind of a religion branded an infant with guilt before it had even begun to coo? And yet she'd asked Amy a few times about christening Rose. Because deep inside her was that little sliver of doubt: what if those pompous priests and nuns were right? So she'd clung to the same beliefs, the same way of thinking, for her entire seventy-eight years. And now, walking up this sunny street in a little fishing village far from her old existence, she began to realize what she'd missed.

A whole world that had gone on about her, and she'd not once ventured into it. She'd led such a sheltered life.

Oh, she'd had what her religion had deemed was enough. A marriage. Children. What she'd always wanted, really. But she'd missed so much!

She was four blocks from the house, where the little shops clustered close to the street and a tiny sidewalk wound across from the bay side. Exhausted suddenly, she saw an empty bench and went for it, sitting hard with a deep sigh. What was she doing to herself?

Making herself crazy, Mama would have said, as she'd said when Fanny was a girl. "Filomena, why can't you be more like Antoinetta?" If Annie were still alive, she'd be telling her to bide her time, that things would work out. And what good was it to hold grudges, when you knew eventually you'd make up anyway?

Across the street, through the gap between a shop and a restaurant, she saw the harbor, shimmering in the late morning sun. Beyond it, the black jetty stretched across the water from the pier, protecting the harbor. A boat chugged through the water, under the cloudless blue sky, like a picture.

"Sorry to keep you waiting."

She turned. A tall, thin man was smiling down at her.

"What?" she asked.

"You're waiting for a chair massage, right?"

She looked at the contraption beside her that he began fiddling with and saw the sign then: *Chair massages, $10.*

"Just hop on over and put your face right in here," he went on, draping a piece of fabric over a hole at the top. "And kiss your aches goodbye."

Fanny sat there a moment, unsure what to do. He reminded her of Billy, their pedicab driver, a bit effeminate, with that singsong way of talking. And sweet.

"Oh what the hell?" she laughed, then stood up.

Fanny had never had a massage in her entire life. When his fingers sank into her shoulders, she let out a moan, without even realizing it, and her eyes closed.

"You are very tight, sweetheart. And this is one big knot."

He pressed on a spot in her shoulder then, and she let out another moan, this one not in pleasure. But as he continued to press, it was as if the little lump of tension melted away. As he rubbed her back, her upper arms, then kneaded her neck and scalp, Fanny wondered if she'd died and gone to heaven.

"I think you really need this, my dear," the man said.

And then Fanny realized that no one other than Joe had ever touched her in such a way. His hands were all over her bra straps, not too far from the sides of her breasts when they veered under her arms. And here she was, right on the sidewalk in front of this shop, letting herself be practically groped by this man, no matter if he liked other men better.

"Wait," she said, sitting up, pulling her head out of the hole where it rested, what he'd called the cradle.

"You've got two more minutes, relax." His palm came down on the top of her head and gently squeezed, again and again.

So she did.

His name was Manuel. When it was over, he brought her inside for a cup of green tea. The spa had paintings all around the little room, like a gallery, and there was a big bay window and a window seat covered with cushions. She sat there as he brought her the cup, setting it down on the little table.

"And here's your angel card," he said, handing her a little card with a picture on it. It was a drawing of a cherub.

She sat looking at it.

"Turn it over."

She did, and on the other side was just one word.

Change.

CLAIRE MADE IT A POINT NOW to spend at least a little time each day with Amy. In her daughter, Claire recognized so much of her own angst and insecurity as a young woman suddenly facing the most challenging time of her life. Knowing that every step you took, every decision you made, would affect your daughter's future. And that one day, that daughter might turn around and call you on it. Accuse you of not caring enough, not being smart enough. Guilt and motherhood, she'd decided long ago, were synonymous. She and Abbie had often joked that as soon as the fertilized egg attached to the uterine wall, a chemical was released that activated the guilt gene.

It was guilt, in fact, that had made her take the time late in this day, when she should have been at the Arts Center, to shoot some pictures of Amy and Rose.

They were at Herring Cove, the bay beach that lay on the curve of land's end, before it rounded to the ocean side at Race Point. There was little wind, and the sky was softening to pink as the sun began to sink. The bay water was calm, and there were only a few other people there. Claire felt a rush of love as she looked through the viewfinder at her girls. Rose wore little blue jeans, a pink sweatshirt, and tiny sneakers. Amy, too, was in jeans, and a navy sweater, her long black hair falling past her shoulders. Rose was pink and golden, and Amy had alabaster skin and dark hair, so that it was hard to believe they were mother and daughter. Claire's bloodline.

As a History teacher, she couldn't help but think that way. In centuries past, two girls would have brought disappointment. But not to Claire. It was hard for her to believe as she watched the two of them, so beautiful as they sat on the sand, Rose's gray eyes following her and cooing out loud with excitement, that four months ago Rose had not existed. And that Amy was far removed from her life.

In November they would be back in Lincoln, and by the end of the year, hopefully Amy would be free to start her own life. And Claire would finally be free to pursue hers with Rick. She realized now how precious their remaining weeks here were.

And then yesterday, when Elaine, one of her classmates, had shown her the photos she'd taken of her own children, Claire had realized that she was acting like the shoemaker whose children had holes in their shoes. So caught up was she in her projects and assignments, the beautiful scenery, that she rarely took pictures of her family. She wanted to capture Amy and Rose here, in this special place, in this magical light. Because it was here that Amy had finally begun to change.

After about thirty shots, Amy called out, "Mom, that's enough. Come sit with us."

Claire went over and sat. The sand felt cool through the blanket, although the air was still mild. Claire thought this quiet, still time of late afternoon was her favorite time to be on the beach. She held her arms out and Rose smiled, crinkling her nose with excitement and shaking her legs in that way Claire loved. She pulled the baby to her, burying her face in the golden hair that now covered Rose's ears.

"Oh, my little honeybunch!" she whispered, as Rose began devouring her chin with her gums. "I think you're teething already. You are so adorable."

"She is, isn't she?" Amy asked. Claire looked at her.

"Of course she is. She's beautiful, Amy. Don't you think so?"

Amy shrugged. "I do. But I guess all mothers think that, don't they?"

"Sure. But isn't there beauty in everyone? If you look hard enough?"

"Even me?"

"Oh, Amy, how can you ask that?"

Amy paused. "Why didn't you ever get married again? I mean when I was young?"

Claire blinked, taken aback by the sudden turn in conversation.

"You didn't date very many men. You're so pretty, I'm sure there could've been more."

Claire sat Rose on her lap and looked at Amy. "I didn't want to have a revolving door of men in our house."

"Jerry was a nice guy. So was Matt."

"I just…Well, to tell you the truth, I didn't think any of them were good enough to be a father to you."

"I realize now how you always put me first. I didn't always. It was just too easy to blame you."

"I know that," Claire said softly.

Amy didn't say anything for a while and Claire waited.

"I called Rose's father."

Claire's eyebrows went up.

"His name is Jared. He's five years older than me. He was a grad student at UNC in Asheville when I first met him, right after I moved in with Bonnie."

Amy stopped and Claire didn't dare interrupt.

"He didn't know about the baby. I broke up with him before I even realized I was…"

"Did you…," and Claire hesitated, not wanting to seem accusatory.

"Love him?" Amy asked, finishing the sentence for her. Her face softened into a smile. "I did. I really did; he was so nice, a real Southern gentleman, you know what I mean? But I knew he'd end it eventually. He was older and smarter, and I just felt like a dumb, fat girl who—"

"Amy, stop," Claire said, reaching for her arm.

"Anyway, I broke it off before he could."

They sat there for long minutes, the only sound the soft lapping of the bay and Rose's gurgling noises.

"But I realized the other night that I wasn't being fair to Rose," Amy said. "I can't make her suffer because of my insecurities. She deserves a father. And just because mine was such a fuck, doesn't mean Jared will be."

"How did he react when you told him?"

"He was stunned." Amy bit her lip and her eyes welled with tears. "He wanted to know how I could do something so awful. To keep this from him."

"Why did you, honey?"

"Because." And now the tears streamed freely down her checks.

"I was afraid he might try to take her from me. And he'd probably win."

Claire put her arms around Amy, with Rose between them. The baby began to squeal with delight, grabbing a piece of Amy's hair and tugging hard.

Amy pulled away, gently pulling her hair from the baby's grasp and giving her a finger to tug instead.

"I may not be the best mother material, but no one will ever love her like I do."

Claire couldn't say a word; her heart was breaking.

33

THERE WAS A CERTAIN AMOUNT OF SPITE TO WHAT she was doing; Fanny knew that. she'd have had to be a fool not to. But she wasn't dwelling on it. No, she was simply taking a walk, and then having lunch with a friend who wanted to show his gratitude.

And who knew? She might not even make it, might be done in by her hip, because Dominick Fortunato lived in an apartment above the restaurant. Fanny wasn't sure how her hip was going to cooperate when it faced the flight of steps after the walk. Hopefully the staircase wasn't steep, and perhaps there was a landing where she could catch her breath. She imagined Dominick would have no trouble at all with it.

Was she crazy to do this? An old woman who was maybe about to make a fool out of herself? Well, what did it matter? She'd lived her entire married life with a man who'd never stopped thinking about someone else. If she wanted to look at it fairly, hadn't she been robbed of the kind of life she'd expected all those years ago?

She read women's magazines. Plenty of women sought comfort or satisfaction or even just plain old companionship elsewhere. It didn't make them bad women. Was she going to die without taking this last chance because she was afraid someone might think badly of her?

It was just lunch, she told herself, as she approached the restaurant. She was probably making more out of this than it really was.

She'd done Dominick a great favor, he'd told her. The two recipes were hits. And now he wanted to cook for her. Just a simple lunch, that was all.

Joe was gone for the day, at his new job. What a joke. He sat in a chair in a parking lot, three blocks from their house, taking dollars from people who couldn't find a spot in town and didn't want to walk too far. When she'd come home from seeing Manuel the other day, after allowing herself another chair massage, Joe was telling Claire that he would be gone for six hours each day now. That he'd been admiring an old El Camino parked up the street in the lot and gotten to talking to the owner, whose son had gone back to school and who needed someone to man the lot; otherwise everyone tried to park there for free. Claire thought it was great.

"That's awesome, Grampa," Amy had said. "You'll probably get to see some really cool cars."

He'd left with a spring in his step this morning. Amy was off on her late morning walk, which had become her routine. Rose was now on a good schedule because of these walks, which lulled her into long naps twice a day. And Amy was slimming down. The baby weight was already gone, and Amy was now working on the pounds she'd gained since high school. She wanted to be healthy for Rose. It was also good for her to look in a mirror and be happy with herself. Because in the end, that was all you had: yourself.

But Fanny suspected that part of it was because Rose's father was coming soon to see her.

Dominick turned from the herb garden when he heard her approach, and his face lit up with a smile. *He's really happy to see me*, she thought.

The steps weren't too bad, since there were two landings as they curved through the old building. She insisted he go first, and he walked slowly, talking and turning often, which slowed their ascent. On the landings, he offered her his hand. It was a thoughtful way to ease her embarrassment over her hip, and she appreciated his kindness.

A small table was set in front of the wall of windows that overlooked the bay. It wasn't a big apartment, he explained, but it was cozy, and not too much for him to keep tidy by himself. Fanny looked around and saw not a speck of dust, or even a fingerprint on a mirror or glass.

It was odd for her to sit and wait for him to bring the food. All her life, she'd waited on men. Italian men in particular were used to that, trained early on by their mothers that they were the kings of the house. Joe wasn't Italian, but her ways had already been ingrained when they'd met. And back then, well, men went out to work. It didn't matter that a woman might have twice as much to do in the course of a day. It was still her job to put a meal on the table, and then to clean it up.

Dominick had prepared a simple meal. First, fresh tomatoes and mozzarella drizzled in olive oil, with fresh basil scattered like confetti over the dish.

As they ate, they talked about their families. Wasn't it that way always with older people? Fanny thought.

Dominick told her about his childhood in Vermont, in a small town where being Italian was an oddity; not like her old neighborhood in Brooklyn that was full of Italians, as well as Irish and Jewish people, barely a generation or two off the boat.

"My father died when I was a boy. Within a month, my mother turned our living room into a restaurant. Maybe they didn't like that we were different, but they sure loved our food. She called it Casa Bianca."

As soon as he got home from school each day, his mother put him and his sister to work in the kitchen. Then they'd wait tables while she prepared the meals. Their living room could fit no more than twenty, but it was always packed. After a while, the place became a local institution, although there was no sign. He quit high school to help his mother full-time, and stayed on until his early twenties, when she died.

"I always regretted selling the place, but I wasn't much of a cook, not without Mama in the kitchen. When I came here ten years ago, and saw this restaurant for sale, I couldn't help myself. But so many of our recipes were lost over the years, too." Then he added with a laugh, "How is it we always go back to our youth, it seems?"

Fanny smiled. "I know what you mean." Didn't she spend so much time herself lost in the past, wondering about the dreams that had never happened somehow?

"From day one, every chef I hired had the same issue. Wanted to do those hoity-toity recipes and change my ways. I couldn't stand it. Mama would have had a fit. So I wound up with Vito. My nephew, he has that thing where they can't concentrate for long. ADD or something like it. My sister, Cecilia, she worried and worried. Vito failed out of college. He was more interested in having fun than working. And she shipped him off to me one summer. He's a good and simple cook. Here, work is hard, but also like a party. They go out, a lot of them, to the bars down the street after we close. But it's not just that. In my kitchen, we have fun, because what good is life if you can't have fun?"

Fanny couldn't help but smile. "You have a point there."

"So, when the summer was over and she wanted him to go back to a different college, he was desperate and begged me to let him stay." Dominick lifted a hand and waved a finger. "I laid down the law to Vito. And he works, hard some days, not so hard others. But he's a good boy." And then he gave a little smile, but it was sad. "And, he's all I've got. My daughter, she's far away with a big job, married to a pilot, so they travel for free. I gave up on grandchildren long ago. Well, I told you all that before, didn't I?"

"That's all right," she said, "I sometimes forget, too."

"It's the age, what can we do? But you're lucky, you know, not just a granddaughter, but a great-granddaughter."

"I also have two grandsons. They live in California with my son and his wife. I don't see much of them, though. I miss my son."

He shook his head and looked out the window. "Aaah, yes, the world, it's so different from when we were young, isn't it? When it was all about family."

He got up and went for a small platter of lemon chicken, as she thought of her entire family in that little neighborhood in Brooklyn. Her own grandmother living with Mama and Daddy in her last years. It was that way with so many of the families back then. Today they called it "extended families"; it was another hot topic in her women's magazines. They also called Claire's the "sandwich generation." She started to laugh, explaining it to Dominick as he spooned the chicken on her plate. She was now one slice of bread; Amy and Rose the other.

"I guess that would make my daughter, Claire, the bologna," she said dryly, as Dominick roared with laughter.

Again, she had not once mentioned a husband. Again, he had not once asked.

"You're a fascinating woman, Filomena," he said then, his deep brown eyes locked on her own. He reminded her in that moment of Omar Sharif in *Doctor Zhivago*. You could get lost in those eyes as Zhivago looked at Lara with such love, such longing. Dominick was looking at her like that right now.

Her heart began to beat faster.

"You know, it's been more than ten years since my Lena passed away and…well, I've met many women here in my restaurant. But you're different."

Now her heart was galloping in her chest and it was difficult to take a complete breath. This lovely, handsome man was making her feel excited. And scared. And then it was as if a little bell went off in her head, a tinging sound, reverberating all through her, warning her that she was stepping onto dangerous ground.

She stood up.

"No, don't, you've barely touched your chicken. And I have a nice dessert." And then he jumped up, shaking his head. "I'm sorry, forgive me, I do not mean to make you uncomfortable. I just like to talk to you."

He went to get dessert, before she could argue. The chicken was tough, too lemony, and she thought, no wonder he loved her recipes. He brought back a plate of pignoli cookies and a pot of demitasse, with the tiny cups and spoons, which she hadn't had in... God, she couldn't remember how long. Fanny decided it would be smart to change the subject.

"What you did for your nephew was kind."

He waved a hand. "It was nothing. He's my blood."

"I want to do something for my granddaughter. She hasn't had it so easy. No father in her life, my daughter raised her alone, and now she has the baby and no real career. And she wants to take care of the baby herself, not put her in day care."

"That's admirable."

She didn't mention that now the baby's father would be showing up; that she was worried sick for Amy.

"Well, the dishes we've brought over for you to try, she really made them. I just gave her the recipes. She likes to cook. And I was thinking..."

Before she could finish, he reached over and took her hand again. "Filly, you don't have to ask." He squeezed her hand and smiled. "I taught Vito myself, in the kitchen downstairs. Although most of what he cooks is his mother's recipes and his own crazy concoctions. But we get by. Now, if you'd be willing to share some more of those recipes," and here he gave her a very flirtatious smile, "maybe she could prepare them in our own kitchen, just like with the pasta puttanesca."

"I think that's a wonderful idea."

"And with a little experience here, who knows? A lot of my kitchen help is from Jamaica, and I've been short-staffed this year anyway because of visa problems. The college kids have all gone back to school. This could be perfect."

Afterward, he offered to walk her home, but this time she was adamant in her refusal. She had only been gone an hour and a half, but in case anyone was back, she didn't think it was a good idea. They stood there in front of the restaurant, then he quickly leaned forward, and before she knew it, he brushed her cheek with his lips. He smelled wonderful, of spicy cologne and soap, and his lips were soft. She turned away quickly, in case he had anything else in mind. But she caught his look, that longing, Omar Sharif look. She must have seen that movie a dozen times.

She walked slowly. Yes, her hip was aching a bit, but she didn't mind. As she walked, she thought over every moment of the lunch. When she arrived back, the house was still empty. She sat at the kitchen table and stared out across the bay. My God, she'd just done something unthinkable. Yet she'd had a wonderful time. If her mother were alive, she would smack her right now. But Annie, Annie might have understood.

Was this the second chance she'd always hoped for?

Maybe it was. And maybe it was her last.

34

THE STRING OF WARM, GOLDEN DAYS CONTINUED, the kind of autumn weather Claire wished could last forever. Taking one last look in the mirror, she thought, *Not bad for a grandma*. She was wearing a long peasant skirt with a yellow V-neck top that accentuated her brown eyes. Her dark hair was swept up with a clip, because she knew Rick loved her long neck.

She heard voices then and looked at the clock. Was he early? She opened her door, and immediately the smell of the birthday feast hit her, homemade spinach ravioli with a marinara sauce that Amy and her mother had worked on for two days. Mingled into the aroma was the sweet scent of dark chocolate. They'd outdone themselves with a triple-layer German chocolate cake, Rick's favorite. Her mother was doing it in part for Amy, she knew. Rose's father coming soon was all they could think about. And now Amy had a little job at the restaurant up the street, which she was nervous about; cooking for Rick was a welcome distraction.

They were all in the living room to greet him, and Claire watched as he gave her mother a quick kiss on the cheek, shook her father's hand, then nodded toward Amy and the baby. To her credit, Amy leaned forward then and gave him a brief hug. Then he saw her. She waited for his face to light up, but all she saw was nervousness.

"Hey, babe," he said, coming toward her.

She walked right into his arms and held him tight. She was off balance, too. They'd been treading on unsettled ground for months now. Her family retreated to the kitchen, and she stepped back and took his hand.

"I've missed you," she said.

"Oh, Claire," he said and pulled her into another embrace. "Can we take a walk or something?" He nodded toward the kitchen, just the other side of the massive brick fireplace, the only thing separating them from her family. She felt the same way. She wanted privacy to talk, and to be alone with him.

"I've got a better idea," she said, grabbing her car keys. "It's actually a surprise for later, but what the heck?"

The bed and breakfast was on the west end of Commercial Street, and as they drove through town, she pointed out the wharf, a few galleries, including Charles Meyer's, and the Portuguese bakery, which she'd come to love. Then she pulled in front of The Red Inn, a picturesque two-story red building overlooking the western end of the harbor, a favorite of artists and photographers. Rick looked at her, puzzled.

"Happy birthday," she said. "I booked us a room for the night, so we could be alone."

"Oh, Claire," he said, clearly astonished. "That was really sweet of you."

They got out of the car and walked through an arbor covered with sweet autumn clematis. The cottage gardens surrounding the inn were colorful and wild, linked by aged brick walkways and surrounded by white picket fences. Claire had fallen in love with the place the first time she saw it. She'd spent an afternoon here, photographing one exquisite flower after another.

Because the inn was on the western edge of town, its view was expansive, sweeping across the bay on the left and straight out and to the ocean on the right. They stood for a moment on a terrace above the sandy beach where guests sat with their wineglasses, admiring the view.

"Isn't it just breathtaking?" Claire said. "Just look at that light."

The colors, Claire thought as they stood there, were simply bolder here. The sky bluer, the dune grasses greener, even the flowers were brighter purples, oranges, pinks. It was as if the air bent the light and infused everything with life and beauty.

"It really is beautiful," Rick said, and took her hand and squeezed it. "I can't wait to explore tomorrow."

Then she led Rick by the hand indoors and up a flight of stairs. Claire took a key from her pocket and opened the second door on the right.

She stepped inside the room, pale blue with lace curtains and a cherry four-poster bed swagged in more lace, where she imagined them cocooned for the night. Three tall windows looked out at the water. When she'd first seen it, it occurred to her that she might have picked a place like this for their honeymoon, it was so pretty. Maybe they could come back here in the spring. Springtime on the Cape would be even more beautiful, she imagined. And once they were settled in Arizona, they would be far from the ocean.

Rick walked in and stood beside her, taking it in.

"Happy birthday, honey," she whispered and leaned toward him and brushed his lips. "I'm glad you're here."

He pulled her into him, held her tight, then squeezed even harder so that she let out a little yelp.

"Sorry," he said, letting her go.

"No, I'm glad you missed me."

"I did miss you." He sat on the edge of the bed and looked at her. "I was hoping to have you all to myself, since we've only got about thirty-six hours."

"I know. I'm sorry. They've just been cooking up a storm here. Amy's actually been working a little bit for a restaurant near the house, and she's quite good. And my mother, well…"

She stopped herself. She didn't want to say that when her mother was cooking, at least she wasn't throwing dagger looks at her father. That cooking seemed to be the glue holding them all together in that little house, and they were all in a bit of a panic over Rose's father coming.

"Well, let's just get dinner over with, and we'll have the whole night here to ourselves."

She went and sat on his lap, burying her face in his neck.

"You smell so good," she giggled, breathing in the designer cologne that had a musky, sexy scent. "I've even missed the way you smell."

His hands ran up her back, then slipped inside the yellow sweater.

She pulled her head back and looked into his eyes. How could she have doubted him? Have doubted this?

He unhooked her bra, and a shiver of longing shot through her.

And then his watch beeped. His new watch beeped every hour, his way of ensuring he'd never be late again.

"Shit," he said. "It's six o'clock."

"How could that be?" She stood up. "I guess we dawdled too long. Anyway, they were cooking for six."

"All right. Let's go and eat fast," he whispered, running a finger along her breast as she hooked her bra. "And let's get dessert to go."

As she took a last glance at the room, she thought about her mother and Amy, so excited over this meal. "No, we'll stay for dessert. We'll be patient. We've got the whole night ahead of us."

"Well, thanks for the surprise. I wasn't looking forward to spending the night with the whole family."

But when they got back to the house, another surprise was waiting for them. First Claire saw her parents sitting together on the couch, something they hadn't done in weeks. Then she turned and looked in the kitchen, where Amy stood by the stove with a stricken look on her face. Beside her was a tall young man, holding Rose. His cheeks were pink, and his eyes glistened as he looked at the baby, who stared right back at him.

JARED, IT SEEMED, had wanted to surprise Amy. He told Claire later that evening, after an awkward dinner, that he was afraid she might bolt if she knew exactly when he'd be showing up. After all, she'd done it to him before.

He seemed like a nice guy, Claire thought, as he went with Amy into the bedroom to put Rose to sleep. But his anger was palpable. He kept looking at Rose, and then at Amy, and Claire could almost hear his thoughts. Accusing thoughts.

Amy had barely spoken a word. To Claire, she seemed terrified.

Rick, of course, had no idea at first what was going on. And after dessert, he looked at her expectantly.

"Let's take a little walk on the beach," she suggested, as her mother and Amy began to clear the table. Jared and her father sat there in silence.

A moment later they were out the door.

"Listen, I've got to stay for a little longer. I need to talk to Amy. I can see how upset she is."

"She should be glad the father's in the picture now. He can help her financially."

"It's not that simple. She's afraid he'll want custody of Rose."

Rick took her hand and squeezed it. "Honey, maybe that would be for the best."

She couldn't even answer at first.

"Listen. It will free Amy up to make a life for herself. And if he can do better for the baby?" He pulled her hand to his lips, brushing her fingers softly. "And then there's us. Maybe it'll be better for us."

She shook her head. The thought of Rose disappearing from their lives, of Amy losing her, was unthinkable. "No. I won't let that happen."

"Come on, Claire," he said. "If he's the better parent, then I don't think you're going to be able to stop it." He took her face and held it, looking right into her eyes. "This is where you make your mistakes, Claire. Learn from the past. Think with your head, not your—"

"Heart. I know," she said, and pulled away. "Do you remember how to get back to The Red Inn? You just go straight down Commercial for a—"

"I remember. And don't get mad, I'm just trying to keep you focused."

"I'm not mad."

After a quick good-bye, he was gone. Claire stood on the sidewalk out front and thought, no, she wasn't mad. She was afraid. Afraid for Amy, afraid of losing Rose. And she knew in that moment she'd do anything to keep that from happening.

Rick couldn't understand that. He hadn't spent enough time with Rose, or her family. And it was time for that to change.

35

Breakfast was delivered to their room in a small basket, covered by a red checked napkin. Claire put the basket on the little table by the window and looked out at the beach. Rick was probably out walking. She'd awakened to find him gone.

He'd been fast asleep last night when she got in. She'd simply crawled in next to him and wrapped an arm around him, then lain awake for a long time. She wondered if he was disappointed she hadn't come back earlier, so that they could make love. She assumed they would in the morning. But she woke to find the bed empty and the bathroom steamed up, so he'd even showered. And she'd slept through it all, exhausted from the long night before.

Once the baby had gone to sleep, Jared did, too, in Amy's room. Amy took the twin bed in Rose's room, and Claire helped her mother clean up the kitchen, a big job due to all the dishes they'd made earlier. Then she knocked softly and tiptoed into the baby's room.

Amy was sitting up in bed, hugging a pillow to her chest, her face raw from crying. "He hates me," she whispered to Claire, as she sat on the bed.

It was nearly midnight and Claire was anxious to leave, wondering if Rick was even still awake. He was a dedicated early riser due to his golf schedule before work.

"And I can't even blame him," Amy went on. "What I did was awful."

Claire pulled Amy into a long hug. "Honey, it was wrong, but it's in the past. You have to let that go."

"I'm twenty-four years old, without a degree. Whatever job I manage to get, it won't be much money, maybe not even enough to pay for day care, which I don't really want to do anyway."

There was no comfort in hearing her own warnings from years ago coming out of her daughter's mouth. She'd only ever wanted a secure future for Amy, and now Amy was finally realizing she was right.

"The bottom line is, I don't think Rose and I can make it on our own. And if there's a custody fight, I'll lose."

"Listen, I told you before, you can stay with me. I'll help you in whatever way I can. We won't lose Rose."

Amy sat in silence for a while, exhausted.

"Mom, that really means a lot to me. But what about Rick? I mean, do you really think he'll go for that? Living with us? He's never even held Rose, and she's four months old."

"Rick is a good guy. We'll make it work."

But as she'd driven over to The Red Inn, Claire had wondered if she could in fact make it work. She was almost glad he was asleep when she slipped into the room, too exhausted to get into it that night.

Claire got up now, showered and dressed, nibbled on a muffin, and went downstairs to look for Rick. He was nowhere in sight. She decided to drive back to the house and talk to Jared. If Rick was on one of his long treks, he might not be back for a while. She told herself he wasn't here for that long, either. If he wanted to explore, she couldn't get upset about that. This might be the best time to talk to Jared, without further interrupting her weekend with Rick. Jared, apparently, was only there until tomorrow night. He couldn't get any time off, so he'd flown up just for the weekend. She needed to convince him that Amy was fully capable of taking care of Rose.

Her parents must have been in their room, because when she walked in, she found only Jared and the baby in the kitchen. Rose was in her little seat on the table, biting on a teething ring. Her eyes lit up when she saw Claire.

"Amy's in the shower," Jared told her.

"Good. I wanted to talk to you alone, if you don't mind."

He nodded.

"I know you have every right to be angry with my daughter. What she did was wrong. But she's had…That is, her father—"

"I know all about him," Jared interrupted. "She told me after she moved in. And that's what pisses me, I'm sorry, that's what makes me so mad. That she'd put me in the same category as him." He stood up and ran a hand through his hair. "She knows me. I am not like him."

Claire had had no idea they'd actually lived together. She remained silent, deciding it was better to let him blow off steam.

"I haven't even told my parents about the baby yet. I don't want to get them all upset and emotional if…" He paused and just stared at Rose. His eyes slowly filled with tears. "It's hard to really believe. I look at her and I…I have a daughter."

"Amy loves her, Jared. She's a good mother. I wasn't sure in the beginning how this was going to go, but she's grown up. Rose is her first priority, over everything else."

He swiped his eyes quickly and turned and looked at her.

"A baby wasn't exactly in my plans, either. But neither was a serious relationship. And then I met Amy. I really cared for her, and one day, I just find her gone. A little note saying it wasn't going to last anyway."

"I've watched my daughter beat herself up her entire life, Jared, because she felt her father didn't love her. So how can she be worthy of anyone's love, right? That's how she thinks. She told me she thought that…"

"What? That I would dump her, too?"

Rose began to fuss in her seat and Claire picked her up. She smelled of Baby Magic lotion and powder, the sweet baby smell Claire loved. She held her close, and Rose's mouth searched her face for something to sink her gums into, settling for her chin. Claire let her gnaw a few times, then pulled her away, and she began to cry.

"She's teething," she said.

"She looks like my mother," Jared said. "Maybe that'll help her get over the shock when I tell them."

Claire felt her heart sink. His family, of course, would want to see Rose. And then what?

"And I have no intention of being a Liam with my daughter," he added.

WHEN SHE PULLED UP to The Red Inn, she saw Rick sitting in his car in the parking lot, on his cell phone. He turned at the sound of her tires crunching on gravel. She walked over as he got out of his car.

"Hey, sorry about last night," she said. "Amy was pretty upset."

And then she noticed his overnight bag on the backseat of the car.

"Are you leaving?"

He looked away uncomfortably.

"Rick, you were gone when I got up. And you didn't come back. I just ran over to—"

"Claire," he said, taking her hands. "Stop. Don't do this to yourself."

She felt panic rising up in her chest like bile.

"Listen, when I got here yesterday," he said, "I honestly wasn't sure about what I was doing here. This has been building for a long time. But I saw you and you looked so beautiful. And then you brought me here and I saw all the trouble—"

"I'm sorry things didn't turn out the way…"

But he was shaking his head. "Don't you see? There's always going to be something. I'm sorry. I don't know how to say this, except to just say it."

"This is about my family again?"

"Claire, I do love you. That's never been in question. But when you marry someone, you don't just get the person. You get the whole package."

She leaned against the car and felt the breath leave her lungs.

"You guys are really close, and they're always going to be a part of your life. And that's a beautiful thing. But I know myself. I don't want to be tied down, you know that. I thought things were going to be different for you. Your life seemed to be pretty settled when we met. But it's not, is it? If we get married, you're going to be torn in two because you're not the type to turn your back on them. Even if they're asking too much of you."

"I can't believe you're doing this."

"Come on, Claire. I see how you love that baby. Could you imagine not being around her for months on end? And are you really going to leave your parents in a nursing home and come gallivanting all over the country with me? You'd be miserable. And we'd start to fall apart, little by little."

She stood there, shaking her head. Seeing her dreams, her future, evaporate like the mist over the morning bay. She hadn't even told him about offering Amy and Rose a home, for however long they needed it.

"I think you're being unfair. I think I can have both."

"Maybe I am being unfair. Maybe I'm selfish, but I know who I am. I see my brothers and nieces and nephews a few times a year, and that's enough for me. We didn't grow up like you did. We all have our own lives; we haven't been intertwined like your family. But I don't want to be saddled with the kind of responsibilities that'll inevitably come down the road for us. I've worked hard since

I was fifteen years old. I'm pushing fifty; my dad died at fifty-four. I know I'm in better shape, but who knows? And I'm finally gonna have the money to do what I want."

There was no more "we." What about her dreams? He was at the center of them all. Was she going to spend the rest of her life alone, filling the empty evenings and weekends babysitting for Rose or visiting her parents? What if Amy moved far away again? Inevitably, there would come a day her parents wouldn't be here anymore. Where would she be then? All alone.

"I think—" she began.

"Don't," Rick interrupted. "I'm not asking you to make a choice. I'm making it for you."

She looked at him, her eyes filling with tears. "What about our new town house in Arizona? I finished choosing all the colors and other selections."

"We'll figure something out," he said and then gave her a brief hug. "Claire, hopefully one day you'll thank me."

The new house, the new life, all of it over in a matter of minutes.

"I don't think so," she said. She turned and walked back to her car.

36

In the middle of the next week, Claire sat in her workshop, barely able to concentrate on Charles Meyer's words. She'd had a hard time concentrating on anything since Rick left early Saturday. How did she go back to her old life now? There would never be another Rick, she was sure of that. She'd waited so many years, convinced she'd never find anyone again, until he appeared. She knew she had a better chance of winning the lottery. That was a common fact these days.

Even worse, she was out of a job come June, and on her own financially. She'd resigned her teaching position because she was supposed to be married by now and, after the school year, they would have been moving to Arizona. The love, the security, the fun—it was all gone now.

She looked up as Charles Meyer displayed some of their assigned photographs on an easel, going over the good qualities and the bad; she was happy to see that none of them were hers. Jared had gone back to North Carolina on Sunday night. And on Monday morning, right at nine o'clock, Claire had called Donna, the social worker, which she knew would make her late for her workshop by at least a half hour, because Donna was such a talker. But she wanted to do damage control before the damage actually hit.

Their next update wasn't for another week, but she told Donna she felt she just had to check in and let her know how great things were going. She raved about how well Amy and Rose were doing. Donna asked what Amy's plans were once the six months were up, which would be at the end of the year. And then Claire said the words without even thinking. *I've asked her to stay on with me.* Donna seemed very pleased by that.

"That's great. You know, families today are every kind of scenario imaginable," she'd said to Claire. "In my job, I've seen fathers who've gotten custody move back in with their parents. And even stepchildren who stay with the stepparent after a divorce, rather than the real parent. Whatever works, and is in the best interest of the child, is what's important."

Hopefully, if it came down to it, a court would see that it was in Rose's best interest to stay with a mother and grandmother who loved her dearly and had a stable home. Finding a job for Amy would be their top priority once they got home. But once again guilt reached out to jab Claire in the gut. Because if she hadn't come here to Provincetown, not only would she not have just lost Rick, but Amy could have started looking for a job, any job, right away.

Claire would have to think about finding another teaching job for herself, too, unless she tried to get full-time photography work. She'd have the one magazine credit, thanks to John Poole, and the workshop now, and of course, the fund-raising photos for the schools, as well as some passport photos and family portraits. A mishmash of experience, really, that might get her nothing more than a position taking pictures of babies at the mall in Morris County. But if the whale photographs were good enough, maybe *New England Life* would use them.

"…and the whole point of what you're doing is to find the feeling in that moment and then go after it with your camera." Charles Meyer's words intruded on her thoughts.

Claire looked up and forced herself to pay attention. My God, she was like one of her daydreaming students. How often had she been teaching only to see the eyes staring out the window, the soft face, and know that a student was somewhere else entirely. She'd often reprimand them with a silent, but annoyed look. But if Charles noticed that her mind was absent, his expression didn't acknowledge it.

He displayed a series of photos called *Provincetown Porch* from one of the Cape's famous photographers. Each one captured the same white porch overlooking the bay at a different time of day, and each portrayed a distinctive mood.

Their assignment now was a series of the same subject, with different lighting and varying angles, like the porch series. Hopefully she'd be able to get started this afternoon. Her father wanted her to take him back to Truro again, but she would tell him she couldn't. They had to understand that she needed every moment each day if she wanted to do quality work for these assignments. Thank God for the job he'd gotten. So what if he just sat at the front of a parking lot collecting five-dollar bills for half a day of parking? It was better than nothing. And the times she'd ridden by on her bike, he always seemed to be talking to someone about his or her car. It was perfect, and it kept him out of range of her mother's searching looks.

On her way home today, she thought she'd stop and talk to him. Tell him that maybe it wasn't meant to be, finding Ava. Maybe they should let it go. What good would come of it now? If there was, in fact, a child, she didn't think her mother could get past it.

As everyone around her began to gather their things, Claire looked up and realized she'd done it again—lost herself in her problems and missed the last minutes of the lecture.

FRIDAY WAS AMY'S FIRST DAY working at Dominick's, and Fanny could see how nervous she was. Fanny kept insisting that she would be fine taking care of Rose by herself, but Amy didn't seem so sure.

She left at ten-thirty that morning, leaving the phone number for the restaurant written on a piece of paper that also held her cell number, as well as detailed instructions on the front and back of what to do with Rose in case any of a hundred things might go wrong. As if Fanny had never cared for a baby. As if she hadn't been helping with Rose for weeks now.

But she didn't argue, because she just wanted Amy to do well today. She was going to assist Vito with the lunches, and on Monday, she'd bring in Mama's recipe for osso buco. They would need to find a good butcher in town to get the veal shanks. Just thinking of it made Fanny's mouth water. Like the puttanesca, it was peasant food, really. Mama would make a big pot of it that would be gone in a day because her brothers loved it so much. But she and Amy had begun watching some of the cooking shows at night, and yesterday's peasant foods had somehow become today's sought-after dishes. Tonight, they would start to work on the recipe.

This wouldn't just help Amy; this would help Claire, too. When Rick had not come back on Saturday, Claire acted like it was no big deal; that he had urgent business that came up. But Fanny saw the flat look in her eyes. She stared all the time, lost in thought. It didn't take a genius to figure out what had happened. He hadn't seen his fiancée in weeks and he walks into her entire family, and then Jared showed up, too. They'd never gotten particularly close to Rick, but he'd always been polite to them. He was certainly good-looking and stable, and he had a solid future ahead of him. Maybe how he felt about them didn't really matter. It was Claire who deserved better. Fanny wanted to leave this world knowing that her daughter had security, someone to take care of her, and if that was old-fashioned, then so be it. Claire had lived alone for way too long. If Amy had a career, and could make a life on her own, that would unsaddle Claire from that responsibility.

Life was so hard, she thought, as she warmed a bottle to give Rose for her nap. When Amy left with that scared smile, Fanny had thought: *That could be me*. Because all these weeks, watching Claire and Amy, she had seen herself years ago. The whole idea of reincarnation, as in her Buddhism book, began to make sense. Her blood was beating in Amy's veins, taking this chance she never had. And wasn't reincarnation about coming back all over again, this time to get it right?

She picked up Rose from her little chair, which Amy had put on the table. The baby squirmed because she was tired and getting fussy. She was also getting heavy. In a year, Fanny wasn't so sure she'd still be able to pick her up, or hold her for long. But she wasn't going to worry ahead. Sitting on the couch, with the baby in her arms drinking her bottle, she kept leaning back and forth, as if she were rocking her, and Rose's eyes slowly began to close as she drank.

Last night Eugene had called her, to see how things were going. Fine, she told him, the same as she did at the assisted living. How could she dump more problems on him when he had his hands full at home, with Barbara and the boys, and such a demanding job? One of the tubes had come out of little Evan's ears and they had to put it back in again. Which meant another surgery. Evan was like Eugene as a child, an exhausting and endless battle with rashes and sinus problems, and Fanny asked if he wouldn't outgrow it, like Eugene did with the allergies. But no, Barbara had done all the research and this was the best solution, he explained in a weary voice.

They talked for ten minutes and then he told her that there was finally someone seriously interested in her house. It still hadn't sold and he was trying to reassure her, she knew. For a moment, she thought about telling him not to do it. To keep that house, just in case. But that would throw her children in a tizzy. That wasn't in the plans. "Take care of yourself," she'd told Eugene as they hung up, wishing she could see him again, just for a little while.

Rose was fast asleep, her pink rosebud lips parted, a little dribble of milk slipping from the corner of her mouth. Fanny leaned over and kissed her forehead, inhaling her sweet baby smell. Such joy they were. And such work. And later, a bit of heartache. But worth it. She couldn't ever have imagined a life without children. She stood and carried the baby to her portacrib, and was just adjusting the light blanket when Claire came racing in the door.

"What's wrong?" Fanny whispered, startled, yet afraid of waking Rose.

But Claire just looked at her, then Rose, and said, "Nothing."

They didn't trust her. Amy must have pleaded with Claire to leave her workshop early and check up on her. But Fanny didn't get angry. How could she? Maybe she was a little annoyed with Claire, but she also felt sorry for her, at everyone's beck and call.

She picked up her purse and her sweater, instead.

"I'm glad you're back. I think I'll go for a little walk. It helps to keep my hip moving."

And out the door she went.

She walked slowly up the street, just as she'd done last week. When she saw the empty bench in front of the spa, she sat down and waited. Sure enough, Manuel came out a few minutes later and smiled, before leading her to the chair. It wasn't really the massage she came for, although once again, it was like heaven and she moaned in pleasure as he kneaded her old muscles and that stubborn knot in her shoulder.

No, it was for the cup of green tea and the conversation afterward. Because except for Dominick, Manuel was the only person who talked to her like an equal.

Today, when he handed her the angel card, she turned it over quickly.

"Opportunity," she said aloud.

"That's my favorite one," Manuel said. "Did I tell you last time how I ended up here?"

With the sun shining into the room, Fanny sat in the little window seat, picked up her cup of green tea, and listened to Manuel's story.

How he had had a business and a house, an entire life, in California. But then he came to Provincetown one day ten years ago with a friend, and felt something shift inside of him. Was there any place more beautiful than this? he asked. And he'd decided to stay, leaving everything in his old life behind.

37

SUDDENLY EVERYONE WAS TALKING ABOUT THE whales; two had been spotted in the harbor. The first time Claire saw the sleek black arc of a body come up out of the water, her heart seized with the thrill. At Dominick's, Amy told them, people were clamoring for window seats, where the whales could easily be seen. Even at low tide, they seemed impossibly close, well inside the rock breakwater. Claire had called John Poole on her cell as she'd stood on the beach in front of her house, and he'd come right away. But by the time they borrowed the neighbor Sean's boat, the whales were gone. John had been hoping to get close enough to get some impressive photos.

As she waited for him, Claire had tried zooming in with her camera, but the results were disappointing; the dark bodies in the dark water were just too far away from her, although she could tell from the white underside of the tails that they were humpbacks. Libby had called those white spots "fingerprints" when they were on the boat previously, and explained that they helped to identify individuals.

When she finally joined them that day, Libby had also said that the two whales in the harbor were "ding-dongs," whales that were the equivalent of a human ten-year-old in age, and just as headstrong and impulsive. Although exciting for spectators who could watch from land, these whales could get themselves into trouble, she explained. They should be on their way south by now, but just like errant adolescents they were ignoring the grown-ups and doing their own thing, out having fun.

After Libby left, Claire's mother invited John to stay for supper, and she was surprised when he accepted. As they sat eating one of her mother and Amy's experiments, thin chicken breasts in a lemon garlic sauce, her father asked more about the old yellow Land Rover and how John had come to own it. John then explained that he'd inherited it along with his grandfather's place in Wellfleet.

The original fishing shack, he told them, was long gone. It had actually been built by his great-grandfather over a hundred years ago, on the shore of the Herring River, which was a great place to fish back then. In an effort to rid the area of mosquitoes, and to claim some marsh for land, which was becoming valuable, a dike had been built to keep the tides from flooding the marsh as they were supposed to do.

"And that was the beginning of the end," John explained, as her family sat listening at the table. "The river, you see, was part of the lifeblood of that whole wetland system here, and it was one of the most productive in New England. But they just didn't understand back then how wetlands are vital. Over time, eleven hundred acres of salt marsh have shrunk to seven acres. Can you imagine that? In places you can barely even find the river anymore. The little fishing shack is now surrounded by acres of nothing but junk, invasive plants, thickets of shrubs and forests."

"Is that why you got into environmental writing?" Claire's father asked.

John nodded. "Yeah, actually, it is. From the time I was a little boy and would go for weekends with my grandfather, he would tell me stories of what it was like when he was a lad. And I watched it just get worse and worse. When I was in college, he kind of commandeered me to write a few letters to the powers that be, and then the local papers, and then the Boston papers. So I just kind of fell into it. But I'm glad, to tell you the truth."

"So are they going to do anything about it?" Amy asked.

"It took a lot of years, but things are starting to happen," he said.

"That must be a good feeling for you," Amy said.

John smiled and nodded again. "Yeah, it is. The fish depend on those salt marshes, as well, for some part of their life cycle. As we all know, the ocean's becoming depleted of lots of different kinds of fish, and probably more to come. So it's good for that, too."

After dinner, when John left, her father said, "He's an interesting man."

That was three days ago. This morning he'd called her and asked if she could come right away. A boater had spotted a right whale, and it appeared to be in trouble.

Now Claire huddled in the cabin of the Coastal Studies boat and watched John and Libby talking on deck. The weather had turned that morning, the golden days of autumn suddenly gone. By afternoon, the winds had picked up. When she'd stepped on the boat a little while ago, she thought she was sufficiently bundled up, but it was still too cold and blustery on deck as the boat raced toward coordinates from the tracking plane. There was no teasing, no glib talk between John and Libby as they headed farther out to sea. Moby's face was grim as was Nelson's, another Coastal Studies team member who'd come to help. Claire got the feeling this wasn't going to be easy.

As they followed the grid markings of the tracking plane, John came in and told her that the plane had to turn back finally, because of the weather. He and Libby joined her in the cabin. The boat rose and fell with the swells, and Claire prayed her stomach wouldn't turn on her. She watched the horizon as Libby had instructed. Thirty minutes after leaving the dock in Provincetown, the boat finally began to slow down. Libby flew out the cabin door with her binoculars, John right behind her. Claire got her camera ready and followed a moment later.

Claire went to the railing and looked over it down into the water.

"Is this one of the ding-dongs we saw in the harbor?"

"No, this is a right whale," John said. "You can tell by the white patches on the body. They're calosites and they form patterns; it's where the skin thickens from whale lice."

"Whale lice?"

"Not the same as people lice. They're a type of crustacean. That's how they're identified."

"Like the humpbacks are identified by white patches on their flukes?"

"Yeah, that's right. The patterns are different on each right whale, usually on the head or around the mouth, or even over the eyes. The tough part is that the right whale is kind of shy compared to the others, especially the humpback. They don't often bring their heads above the surface, which makes them harder to identify."

Just then Libby came over, handing her binoculars to Claire. "She's logging," she said. "That's when they lie like that on the surface not moving at all."

"Like a log," Claire said, relieved. "I thought maybe it was dead."

"No, she's fine, in fact we have a match," she said. "When they log like that it's easier to check their patterns and identify them. I'd like you to meet EGNO 1503. She's an adult female, and the last time she was recorded here was almost two years ago, with a new calf."

As the boat bobbed in the sea, Claire scanned the giant body with the binoculars. It was black and shiny, its head larger than the hump-back's, more than a quarter of its body. Also, there was no dorsal fin, as John had mentioned. The white patches, the calosities, covered a large portion of the head.

"So this is good. She's not in trouble, after all," Claire said as she handed Libby back the binoculars and went for her camera.

"Oh, this is a good sighting," Libby said. "But this isn't the whale we were tracking. I'm going to radio in and check their coordinates again while you take some pictures."

Claire shot photo after photo for a good ten minutes, simply watching the whale float at the surface. There wasn't much she could do about changing angles, because the whale simply didn't move. It was sleeping, she assumed, or just resting. And she saw how difficult this job of photographing them really was. Then the boat took off again.

"A boater spotted the other whale and radioed in a few minutes ago," Libby said. "She's a few miles from the last plane spot."

A light rain began to fall, and the cold cut through Claire. She went inside the cabin once again, careful to keep her equipment from getting wet. There was nothing pleasant about this trip, not like the last one a few weeks ago, when it was still sunny and mild. The boat began to slow down and the cabin door opened.

"We found her," John said, and she picked up her equipment and went back out on deck.

The rain was steadier now, and Claire decided to leave her camera in the cabin for the moment and head for the rail where John and Libby stood. She recognized it as a right whale immediately from the white patches, the calosites. As before, it lay at the surface, its smooth, dark bulk not moving at all. But its head was covered with a net, as if it had tried to swim through one and couldn't shake it free. Tendrils of rope swirled around the whale's head, like strands of hair floating in the water.

"A net, damn it," Libby said to both Claire and John. "Unfortunately, that's our pregnant female, Joy."

"What do you think?" John asked.

"We'll do as much as we can. If the weather was better, we could get in the dinghy—"

"We're using the dinghy," Moby said, as he came out of the cabin.

As they gathered their equipment, John fetched a big umbrella, which he held as Claire got her camera ready.

Claire began shooting, the net reminding her of the plastic netting wrapped around produce. The white lines of the net formed an intricate pattern across Joy's head. Claire couldn't imagine how horrifying it must feel to the whale. The image blurred, and she pulled the camera away to wipe her eyes.

"This is just awful," she said to John, who held the umbrella and looked at her grimly.

"I know. Most of them drown."

They lowered the small rubber raft over the side of the boat. Libby helped Moby and Nelson as they climbed in, then handed them the gear. Slowly they began inching closer to the whale.

"We don't want to spook her, or she'll just dive and take off," Libby said. "Even if we can just get a telemetry buoy on her, we'll be able to keep track of her."

It was hard to tell how long she'd been netted, but Libby said it probably wasn't too long because there was no obvious sign of infection yet, which often happened as nets and fishing line cut into the whale's blubber.

"How can you tell she's pregnant?" Claire asked.

"It's not easy, but it's late in the season, so we can tell from size if we see them often enough. Joy here has been spotted several times since summer, so it's obvious from her growing size. If all goes well, she'll make it back to the birthing grounds and have her calf in January."

"I hope so," Claire said.

The dinghy rose and fell with the rough water, but a few minutes later it was by the whale's side. It seemed crazy to be so close to the creature, which dwarfed the men and boat. Then Claire watched in horror and awe as Moby leaned way out of the dinghy, a long knife extending from his hand. As the little vessel rose and fell, he began to cut through some of the netting. Nelson held onto the back of Moby, steadying him and keeping him from falling out, as Libby shot the buoy into Joy's blubber. They had only been at it a few minutes when the whale suddenly moved and a second later dove, creating a wake that sent the dinghy rocking dangerously. Claire had gotten all of it, perhaps a hundred shots in a matter of ten minutes.

"She panicked," John said.

"They'll be able to keep track of her now, though," Claire said, a lump of disappointment in her throat.

"But they may not be able to get that close to her again."

She walked toward the cabin, her fingers numb with cold. Then she turned and focused quickly, taking several shots of John Poole as he stood at the railing, notebook in hand, his mouth set. The look on his face was fierce. He wrote furiously in his notebook, the pages rustling as he held them with his other hand against the wind. Claire remembered what he'd said the last time they were out here: *We could be looking at the last of a dying breed.*

THEY DROVE TO HIS PLACE in silence, as the wipers swished and the late afternoon sky darkened ominously. She couldn't go home yet. His mood was somber, as was hers. They left Provincetown and drove on Route 6 through the otherworldly Province Lands, then through Truro, and Claire saw the winery on the hill where Ava might have lived. Then it was gone, and there was a long stretch of woods on either side of the road.

For a few moments, her mind drifted from the sad events of the last few hours to the sad events going on at her house. Her mother still wouldn't budge in her silent treatment toward her father, and Claire couldn't really blame her. The charade had gone on long enough; her mother had every right to know what was going on. But her father was just as stubborn. The two of them had so much pride. Why couldn't they just talk to each other?

When she'd suggested to her father that perhaps it was time to let it go, he'd met the statement with a long silence, which was not so unusual. Claire still had a difficult time talking to her father on such a personal level; it was something she wasn't sure she'd ever get used to. But Claire was beginning to realize that his long silences were simply the product of hard thinking. Finally, he shook his head no. He would not give up the search.

"I made a lot of mistakes," he'd said eventually. "The first was not going back to find out the truth all those years ago. I've never forgiven myself for being so gutless, so irresponsible. And the second was not telling your mother back then. She deserved the truth, but I was afraid. I'd never had a real home. She had such a wonderful family, and I wanted what she had, all of it. If I told her, maybe her brothers and father…"

"But Dad, isn't that all the more reason to tell her now?" She'd prodded him in a gentle tone. "Doesn't she deserve the truth?"

His head was bobbing badly and his hand waved as if he were conducting an orchestra, as he sat on the beach chair in the half-empty parking lot. She realized he was shaking his head no, but she hadn't even been able to tell.

"Not until I know what the truth is."

Claire heard John put his blinker on and realized they'd come to Wellfleet, a small, quaint village not much bigger than Truro. She lost track of the back roads, but after a while, they were on a dirt road that was surrounded by brush, fading with the cold autumn air to shades of parchment and gold.

The fishing shack was sparsely furnished. It reminded Claire of the dune shacks she'd seen from afar. It was a basic three-room cottage; one large room that served as living room and kitchen, a tiny bedroom, and a bathroom that was little more than a closet. Everything was old—the cabinets, the sink, the spare furniture—but it was all clean and tidy. John told her that the original structure had been destroyed by a nor'easter in the forties, and that his grandfather had built this one back then.

John brewed coffee and then poured a generous shot of whiskey in each cup.

"Sorry I don't have whipped cream, to make it a real Irish coffee. How about a little honey and lemon?"

"That's fine."

On an old chrome-and-formica kitchen table, she saw a picture of a young man.

"Ryan sent me that. It's his class picture for sophomore year."

"He's a good-looking boy," she said. He looked like John, but his coloring was much fairer.

"He's a good kid."

"What happened? Why isn't he with you?"

"He was supposed to come back with me and continue school up here, but I knew he didn't want to. He didn't know how to tell me." He shrugged. "So I did it for him."

"How did you do that?"

He turned and looked at her. "I told him that this piece was going to keep me on the Cape for a few months and that he should stay with her for now."

"That must have been hard for you."

"It was. But he feels this need to be with his mother, like she's still fragile, and I get that. It makes me proud of him, but he's still a kid, you know. I don't want him to have to be the grown-up all the time."

"That takes amazing maturity," she said. "I've had kids in class like that. They're usually the ones who do well in life."

"Anyway, I could've stayed. I was offered a piece on horseshoe crabs, which would've kept me in Cape May, but I would've been hanging around, trying to be near my son. I think my ex-wife was sick of me dropping by all the time. So I made a deal with her and agreed to leave. She can have him for the school term, and I'll get him for the whole summer next year."

She was surprised he was telling her all this. Except for the night they watched the meteor shower, he'd never talked this much.

"To be honest, I've wanted to write this article for a long time. And if he was with me, I'd be going back and forth to Boston, which would have been tough. Maybe it all worked out for the best. I'd rather be here than in New Jersey, no offense."

She took a sip of the coffee. It was hot and the whiskey burned going down, but it felt good. She was finally starting to warm up.

"How about you? How are things going with your daughter?"

She looked out the window. It was nearly dark, but she could still see the dune grasses being battered by the wind.

"My mother did an amazing thing. Somehow she got my daughter hooked up with this restaurant up the street from us. Amy's been going in and making a lunch special a few days a week. At night, they stay up late, perfecting my mother's old family recipes. Although half the night seems to be spent with my mother trying to remember them. They never wrote any of them down."

He smiled. "Well, that was the oral tradition. For generations, stories and recipes and folklore just got handed down. No one seemed to realize, I guess, that it was all going to come to an end."

She pondered that for a moment. "I never really thought of it that way, but that's a good point."

"It's good they're writing them down now; otherwise, once your mother's gone, the recipes will be, too." He took a sip of his coffee and then looked at her. "You're lucky, you know. You have a wonderful family."

She laughed a little. "Oh there are moments when I wonder…"

"Take it from me. My parents both died young, and I had no siblings. It was just me and my grandparents, and they've been gone a long time now, too. Ryan's really all I've got."

"That must make it even harder to let him live with your ex."

He shrugged. "It's what he needs to do…"

A sudden explosion outside interrupted him midsentence.

"What was that?" she asked.

"Sounded like thunder," he said.

He got up and went to the window. Claire saw the sky flicker a moment later, and then the house shuddered from another crashing roar.

"There's a warm front moving in and it's hitting the cold air. Let's go out and watch. You'll see it for miles because there's nothing to obstruct the sky here."

Claire felt as if she'd just warmed up, but she put her coat and things back on.

John zipped up his own coat and then refilled their cups.

"This'll keep us warm."

There was a small overhang and they stood under it, protected from the wind. The rain hadn't started yet, but the lightning bolted across the sky in zigzags, an endless show, and it reminded Claire of pictures she'd seen of the blitzkrieg during World War II.

"This is the most amazing lightning I've ever seen."

"It always seems more dramatic here. I don't know if it's all the water surrounding us, or that the Cape juts far out into the ocean."

A bolt shot from a cloud and seemed to hit the ground nearby. The thunder roared endlessly now.

"Is this safe?" she asked, suddenly remembering reading once that when thunder came right on top of the lightning, it was dangerously close.

She felt soft fingers on her face and turned. He took her cup and set it on a windowsill.

"I would never put you in danger, Claire, don't you know that?"

The sky lit up again and so did his face. She watched as he leaned toward her. Then he pulled her to him so quickly she didn't have time to stop him. A moment later, his lips were on hers.

38

ONCE AGAIN, FANNY FOUND HERSELF DOING SOME-thing unthinkable. As she rode down Commercial Street in the pedicab with Billy, she again asked herself how she could be thinking or feeling the things that were going through her mind. It was as if the old Fanny had been left behind in that assisted living; perhaps she'd floated down that river she used to sit beside and simply disappeared. Because up here a new Fanny seemed to be emerging.

She had a hunger now, for whatever years were left. To see and do. To learn. Was it that book on Buddhism, or her talks with Manuel? Or just the realization that she didn't have to bend her life to suit anyone anymore but herself?

She wondered now how she could possibly go back to New Jersey. How she could resign herself to those tiny rooms, that false sense of living. That waiting room for the final breath.

The pedicab rode past the pier. Now she could hear Miss Lila's voice floating up the street on the cool autumn air.

Then they were passing Land's End Marine, where Joe sat on a folding beach chair. Fanny watched him for a moment, talking to someone, taking money, and then they were past. He had a view of the harbor there, and in the distance Fanny could see the lighthouse where he'd foolishly gone that day. What did he think about as he sat there? It was ironic that at home, she'd wished he would find something to get him away from the television, to get him involved in life again. And it had finally happened here.

Everything was changing, though, not just her. Last night Claire told them that she was going to spend three days in the dune shacks. She was still struggling with her final project, a portfolio of work that would be exhibited at the Provincetown Art Museum. She kept asking if they'd be all right if she did that, and Amy kept telling her yes, they would be fine. But Claire's eyes kept straying to her and Joe. Finally she said of course they would manage, and Joe nodded. So Claire was going.

Claire wasn't the only one with opportunities, and tough choices, now.

Fanny wished there was someone she could talk to, because she was starting to wonder if she was crazy for even thinking what she was thinking. Maybe she needed to slow herself down.

She had managed to avoid Dominick Fortunato since their lunch. Until she made some decisions, she thought that might be best, although she longed to see him. She kept thinking of those soft brown eyes when she walked away. He was a man who wasn't afraid to express himself.

The pedicab slowed and parked in front of the little Buddhist temple. It was an old house, really, with a room added on in the back, Manuel told her. It wasn't until Manuel had mentioned it that she remembered passing it that first week, when Billy had driven them through town.

Billy helped her down and told her he'd be back in a little while.

She thought she would be nervous as she walked up to the front door, wondering if she should knock or just walk in like at her church back home. She was a little nervous, but more than that, she was curious. She had been glued to the same track of her life since her birth all those years ago. But there were other ways to go; other ways to live.

She wondered if her own church would condemn her to hell for doing this. But she knocked on the front door anyway.

THERE WERE EIGHT OF THEM and they sat in a big circle, in a room that was probably once a family room. It had a brick fireplace and a wall of windows overlooking a deck and a beautiful garden, but nothing else, except for a carpet on the floor.

She couldn't sit on the floor, not with her hip. The rest of them sat in a lotus position, which was like an Indian style. They had a chair for anyone who couldn't manage that for an hour. An hour! She'd nearly left, imagining herself sitting in a room full of people, no one talking for sixty minutes.

There was a young man whose girlfriend had brought him for his birthday surprise. During the quiet hour, he breathed loudly, and a middle-aged woman swallowed constantly. Someone else's stomach rumbled with gas. Fanny was self-conscious of all those bodily noises at first. She had on her watch, and for the first ten minutes, the seconds seemed to crawl. The swallowing, the breathing, the gurgling were endless, and annoying. People seemed almost to be sleeping with their eyes half-shut while Fanny just watched them, her own eyes wide open. What the hell had possessed her to come here?

She thought about everything, her thoughts colliding between Joe and that woman, Claire and Rick, Rose's father, and even her grandson, Evan, and his endless ear infections after his surgery. And then there was Eugene, who always seemed so overwhelmed when they spoke. When her thoughts drifted to Dominick Fortunato, she forced them to stop.

The room was utterly still now. She sat there, listening to the silence, and her breath began to slow. The others were there in the room with her, but really not there, almost as if she was in a trance. Fanny stared at the floor, as they were, and felt her heart beating deep within her chest. Her eyes began to close. She felt as if she was on the verge of something.

And then a chime tinkled, startling her. The entire hour had gone by. And then they began to chant: "*Chon-ji yong-ki as-shim-jong...*"

It seemed silly, all of these people who did not understand this language, singing it. But then she remembered the Latin masses of her youth, memorizing each word of the liturgy by the time she was ten. Knowing the meaning of none of it, but trying to lose herself in its mystery. And failing, again and again.

Fanny noticed the pamphlet at her feet and picked it up. There was one on the floor beside each of them, but she hadn't noticed. The purpose of this prayer they were chanting was to "balance our mind, heart, and body; to gain wisdom from life..."

After that first meditation session, she felt like a failure, and didn't plan to go back. But they were all so nice. Afterward they all walked barefooted into the kitchen. The Korean girl who presided over the meditation was so sweet. She served them bamboo tea and crispy rice chips. Fanny just sipped her tea and listened to the others, who were so enthusiastic. The middle-aged woman had been coming every day since her divorce. Another man, probably in his sixties, used to own the house, and apparently came back frequently. The young man who came with his girlfriend was celebrating his thirtieth birthday, and he'd had no idea where she was taking him. Fanny was the oldest one there, and they thought it was "awesome" and "inspiring" that she was open to something new.

She went back the next day, and then the next, and it wasn't until that third time Fanny went to the temple that she got it; that she found that place inside herself that she'd read about.

For a few moments during that third visit, she experienced a brief stretch of silence in her mind. It was startling. Peaceful. A welcome place that seemed almost familiar. She could just be, and not think.

It was like she had found herself, finally, after all this time.

EARLY IN THE MORNING, Claire arrived at the Arts Center before her workshop and went to the matting room to spend some time working alone. She was starting to panic. She looked at her photographs laid out on the huge table and shook her head. What she saw was a mish-mash of images. There was nothing she could put into sequence, no theme emerging. She simply had a pile of pictures that were not resulting in a portfolio that could be displayed. Her final project was going to be a failure.

And whose fault was that? She had allowed herself to be distracted by everyone, and everything. The whales, her parents, her daughter and Rose, even John Poole. At the thought of him, she felt a slow blush crawl up her face. Instantly, she put on the brakes. She wasn't going there. Not now. She needed to focus.

The stack of photographs of the Cape were the smallest of all, so even a series featuring different aspects of the light would be impossible. She simply didn't have enough material. Her only hope was to use her stay in the dune shack to bring it all together somehow, although it was expected that the portfolio would be mostly complete by then, and that the free time would be used for tweaking and enhancing.

She still had mixed thoughts about staying in the dune shack. She was dreading it, and looking forward to it. When was the last time she'd been completely alone? When Amy had left home, and before she'd met Rick, there was that long stretch of almost a year, with an ear-ringing loneliness that threatened to swallow her at times. Night after night in her old house in Lincoln, the TV on downstairs, her little clock radio playing upstairs, the noise of those voices somehow cheering her with their false sense of company. But she'd been alone.

As she gathered the photos, her cell phone rang. When Claire saw Rick's office number, her heart skipped. But it wasn't Rick.

"Why didn't you tell me?" It was Abbie, obviously working at the office.

"Is he there?"

"He's upstairs, and yes he told me, because he's been walking around with a hangdog face every time I see him. What the hell happened?"

"He didn't tell you that part?"

"Just that you both agreed things weren't working out."

"I didn't agree." Then she told Abbie the whole story. "I just didn't want to talk about it. It didn't seem real, and I think I was in a bit of shock. My whole future down the tubes. Besides, I figured you had enough on your plate right now."

"How are you doing?"

"Holding it together. I mean, I asked for this. I abandoned him for ten weeks, and his birthday visit turned into a fiasco with Rose's father showing up and throwing my daughter and mother into a panic. And me, too."

"The baby's father? Oh Lord."

"Yeah, oh Lord."

Neither one spoke for a long moment. "I can't turn my back on Amy now. And I never even told Rick that, but I'm sure he guessed."

Abbie let out a long breath. "Well, he's stressed, I can tell you that. He's upstairs in his office with Seymour and Sammy right now, hoping to sell them a farm he just listed. Normally he'd be pumped, but he looked like he was going for a root canal instead."

"Well that makes me feel a little better. You know we should have been married by now."

"I know, sweetie. But quit blaming yourself. He's a good guy. I think he'll come around."

"I don't think so. This has been coming since June, since Amy came back."

She didn't say a word to Abbie about John Poole. But just the memory of those arms around her, his intense kisses, sent a shiver through her middle.

It would have been so easy to give in to her feelings that night. There was no doubt she was attracted to him. But she was smarter now, and knew in her gut that despite this attraction, nothing good could come of it. She was vulnerable after losing Rick; she wasn't about to get caught up in something with John.

On the ride home, she'd told him it would be better if he stayed away from her. There was too much chemistry there, and she was adult enough to admit it, not that she told him that. Even without Rick in her life, and just thinking those words now sent her stomach lurching, she knew better than to get involved. It would be nothing but a rebound romance.

"Hello? Earth to Claire?"

"Oh, I'm sorry, Abbie. My mind just seems to take off on its own lately."

"That's understandable. I was asking about the baby's father. Who is he? Did you like him?

Claire told Abbie everything. "He seems very nice, and responsible. I wasn't sure Amy actually knew who the father was, which sounds awful now. But she lived with him and he apparently really cared for her. Now he's just really hurt and angry. And he obviously intends to be a part of Rose's life."

"Not like the bastard."

"No, not like Liam."

Abbie sighed. "Jesus, sweetie, you sure do have your hands full. And I almost forgot, what about your dad? Have you found the mystery woman yet?"

"No, I've about given up."

She told Abbie about all of the places they'd tried, and how everything seemed to be a dead end. Once again they batted around ideas for a while, and then Abbie suggested trying the local Catholic church in Truro.

"That's a great idea," she said, realizing she should have thought of it herself. The Portuguese community was staunchly religious. A baby would have been christened and there would be a record of that. Or if Ava had married or died there'd be in the parish a record of that, as well.

"Thanks Abbie. For always listening."

"Me, too, sweetie. I can't wait until you come home."

"Just one last thing," Claire said, before they hung up. "This Sammy, the builder's daughter. You don't think she had anything to do with Rick's decision?"

There was a long pause. "I'll be honest, I think she's got the hots for him. I mean the guy's handsome, doing well financially, and he's not married. But he doesn't seem to be interested, if you ask me."

"Or maybe he's just being careful not to show it around you."

39

THE NEXT DAY, CLAIRE TOOK HER FATHER BACK TO Truro.

She sat with him in the tiny rectory next to the small Catholic church, waiting for the priest, who was late. The housekeeper, an old woman, explained that he'd gone to give last rites to a sick parishioner. They sat listening to the sound of pots and dishes clattering in the kitchen.

Claire felt certain they would find something here, but the priest, too, turned out to be a dead end. Father Renaldo, who was Hispanic and spoke with a thick accent, couldn't have been more than thirty. He searched the records in his office and told them that there was a record of Ava's parents' deaths, but no record of a marriage for her. Or a christening for a child. Of course he was too young to have heard of any of them.

They were standing to leave, her father having a difficult time getting his legs to move and nearly falling, when the housekeeper stepped into the room, her demeanor hesitant, apologizing to them in broken English as her hands clutched her apron.

"Excuse me, please. I don't mean to be personal, but I…well, I couldn't help but hear you," she said in a voice raspy with age. "I knew Ava. We went to school together."

Claire stared at her wide-eyed, and her father sat down hard in the chair it had just taken him moments to get up from. The old woman came farther into the room, and Father Renaldo put a hand on her shoulder, encouraging her to go on. She told them that Ava had left Truro when she was a young woman, but that she'd heard she'd come back to the Cape a few years ago, and was living somewhere in Hyannis, in a nursing home.

"Does she have children?" Claire asked.

The woman shrugged. "I wouldn't know. The last time we saw each other we were so young." Her face softened at the memory. "A lifetime ago."

"Thank you," Claire said. "I'm so glad you were here. We've been trying to find her for weeks."

"You're very welcome," she said, looking at Claire's father for a long moment and then turning and leaving the room.

As they drove back to Provincetown, her father stared out the window.

"We're lucky she was there," she said, hoping to cheer him up. But still he said nothing. "We'll find her, Dad."

His face was ashen and he looked so sad.

"Hyannis is less than an hour away. We'll find her there."

"That was my biggest fear," he said, his voice trembling. "That she'd died. But she's alive. Thank God."

And in that moment, Claire began to wonder. Was it possible that he still had feelings for this woman? That he hadn't told her everything? That it wasn't just learning the truth about a child, but really finding this woman after all these years, and opening the door again to a fifty-year love affair?

ALL IT TOOK was a few phone calls. Once they found out where Ava was, the exact nursing home in Hyannis, there was no stopping her father. He even told the man who owned the parking lot where he worked that he wouldn't be in that day. He'd been going there six days a week since he'd gotten the job. For Claire, though, the timing couldn't have been worse. She was leaving to stay in the dune shack in a few days.

Ava didn't know they were coming. Her father had insisted on that. The young girl at the reception desk assumed they were relatives here for a surprise visit and went along with them. Perhaps her father was afraid, after all these years, that after finally finding her, Ava might slip from his fingers again before he learned the truth. They waited for her in one of the front parlors of the nursing home, in side-by-side wing chairs, her father surprisingly still, just his head bobbing slightly. Claire couldn't imagine what restraint that must take, and wondered again at what he was feeling inside as he waited to see his lover from fifty years ago.

She was pushing a walker when she came through the open doorway, a nurse by her side. She was taller than Claire had imagined, with a thick head of still-dark curls, laced with silver, and dark eyes. She wore a long red skirt and a white cardigan and was surprisingly pretty. Ava stopped suddenly as her eyes landed on Joe, shifted to Claire, and then back to her father. She stared at him with a frown. Then her eyes widened slightly and as her lips parted, her eyes suddenly lit up with joy.

"Oh, Joseph!" she cried, in a surprisingly girlish voice that still held a slight accent. Her eyes filled with tears and the nurse suddenly took hold of her arm. "You've come back!"

Her father stood up slowly, staring at the woman, his right arm now waving in the air, his head wobbling harder, his face hard as stone. But his own eyes glistened. Claire felt a threat of tears suddenly lodge in her throat.

"Claire, wait in the car," he said.

She hesitated. She wanted to shout, "No!" She'd waited too long for this, and felt she should have been allowed to stay.

"Claire."

What if he stalled and couldn't move? Or worse, what if he had an accident? But she turned and left the front parlor, as Ava sat in a chair and the nurse also left. The two of them would be alone.

Out in the hallway she hesitated, then convinced herself that she had to stay close by in case he needed her. God forgive her, while nurses and orderlies bustled through the main hallway, Claire found a chair and slid it toward the open doorway to the small parlor, one of many off the hallway that allowed visits in some sort of home-like privacy. It wasn't so difficult to overhear them. Their aging ears were overcompensated for by their loud voices, Ava's ringing with joy and emotion, her father's trembling badly, sounding so very old.

"You look well," she said, again with a girlish laugh. "So much the same, Joseph."

There was a long silence, and Claire wished she could peek in and make sure her father was all right.

"I knew you would come back, one day. I knew it," Ava said, breaking the silence.

"I had to," her father said.

"I know," Ava said, in a softer voice. "Oh, Joseph, I have waited so long."

"I…I had to find out the truth, Ava."

"I never stopped thinking of you. Or…or loving you, Joseph."

Another long silence and Claire sat quietly, hoping no one who passed would stop and ask what she was doing.

"About the baby. I need to know the truth about that," her father said. "Was there really a child?"

Her intake of breath was so sharp that Claire could hear it through the open doorway, fifteen feet away.

"How could you ask that now?" The friendly girlish tone was gone. "After all these years."

"I need to know. Before I die."

"Do you doubt it was the truth? Isn't that why you ran away?" she asked accusingly.

"I didn't run away."

"You left to get money from your foster father, I remember that. I also remember I never saw you again."

This was getting ugly. Claire stood up, but couldn't bring herself to go in. She worried about the stress of this on her father now. Her father had been beating himself up about what he'd done for fifty years. Now the woman he'd left behind was doing it for him.

"I did come back, Ava. But when I went to your house, your mother told me you'd gone away. And that there was never a baby."

"Huh!" Ava spit. "She told you lies."

"Then there was—"

"How dare you!" Ava cried out, interrupting him. "Nurse!"

Claire hadn't seen her waiting down the hall, so intent was she on her own mission.

"Then you're saying there is a—"

"I'm saying I never married. That I waited for you and you never came back. After all those visits to Long Point..."

The nurse was approaching the doorway where Claire stood frozen. Claire looked away, out a window, as if she'd just been waiting there nonchalantly. But even the nurse heard Ava's final words.

"Yes, Joseph, there was a child. My child. But not yours, because you never came back!"

And then the nurse went into the parlor and Claire followed. Her father was on the edge of the wing chair, his right shoulder jerking up and down, his right leg keeping rhythm with it. It was a miracle he hadn't fallen off. His right hand slapped his thigh over and over, enough perhaps to cause a bruise.

"Come now, Ava, come, we must watch your pressure," the nurse said, helping her up. "You know what the doctor said."

Ava was trembling, too, her rage all too apparent on her swollen, red face. Claire hoped she didn't have a stroke or heart attack on the spot. But they were out the door a moment later.

"Come on, Dad," she said softly. "Let's go home."

But to her shock and horror, as she put out her hand for him so that she could help him up, her father began to sob.

40

⌒

T HEY WERE GONE FOR HOURS. JOE HAD TAKEN A LONG
time getting ready, and when Fanny had asked Claire if they'd
located the woman, Claire at least had the good grace to nod
silently. He came out of the room carefully dressed and wearing
the cashmere cardigan Eugene had given him.

So, today would be the day.

She felt a bitter lump lodge in her chest. Tears sat just beneath
the surface as she busied herself with Rose. There were just a few
times in her life she'd felt such crushing hurt, the kind that squeezed
your heart like a rag. One was on her wedding day, when she'd first
heard the name Ava mentioned.

Now she waited for Amy to come home so she, too, could
leave.

Rose, fussy and refusing to nap, kept her busy. She bounced
her, sang to her, gave her a Zwieback to gnaw on, and by the time
Amy came home from the restaurant, in the middle of the afternoon, Fanny was pacing inside because it was too chilly and blustery out today for a walk with the stroller. Rose lay on a blanket by
then, with a colorful toy that sat on the floor and dangled farm animals above her. As "Old MacDonald" played over and over, Rose
reached for the little pigs and cows and cooed along in her sweet
little baby voice, content finally.

Amy gave her a kiss, then collapsed on the sofa.

"How did it go, sweet pea?"

"Oh my God, that Vito is some party boy. This is the third time I've gone in and he had a raging hangover."

"I'm sure his uncle wasn't too happy about that."

"He's such a nice man, Mr. Fortunato. He never gets angry with him. Oh, and he asked about you again."

Fanny hesitated. "So what did you make today?" she asked, avoiding the question in Amy's voice.

Amy got up and lay on the floor next to Rose. The baby turned from the animals and reached for a strand of Amy's hair, trying to put it in her mouth and babbling with delight. Fanny realized that Rose's disposition changed the moment Amy entered the room.

"I tried to make the spinach ravioli, but it fell apart."

"Oh, it's not easy. It took me years to get that right."

"No. We did it for Rick's birthday, remember? It just wasn't my day, Gram. My mind was elsewhere."

"Rose is just fine, Amy. You don't have to worry when you leave her."

"It's not that." She rolled onto her back and stared at the ceiling. "It's Jared."

"What?"

"He's been calling me every day. Torturing me. He wants to take Rose to see his parents."

"But I thought you were going to take her there."

"I was stalling him. So now he's saying he'll just take her himself, that he has every right."

Fanny sat down on the sofa and sighed. "Amy, is it possible the boy still has feelings for you?"

Amy shook her head. "No. He hates me."

"And what about you? Do you have feelings for him?"

Amy said nothing, still staring at the ceiling. The baby babbled away, dropping the hair now and going back to the toy overhead. Fanny saw a tear slip down the side of Amy's face.

"Do you?"

"What does it matter?" she asked miserably. "He'll never trust me again."

"He might."

Amy said nothing.

"When does he want to take her?"

"Right away." Amy sat up and looked at her. "But I told him he couldn't because I'm still nursing her."

A bold-faced lie.

Rose began to fuss again, and Amy jumped up to make a bottle. As she sat on the couch, feeding her, the baby making little grunting sounds as she drank heartily, Fanny began to straighten up.

"Amy, you have to stop lying. It won't get you anywhere. People tell lies and then the next thing they know the lies are coming back years later to haunt them."

"I know, I know," she said, with a tinge of annoyance in her voice, not looking up from the baby. "Listen, I think once Rose is asleep I'm going to take a little nap, too, okay?"

"Sure. I've got some things to do anyway," Fanny said as she got up and went to get her coat and purse.

"But it's awful out, Gram. You should wait until it clears up."

"It's beautiful here no matter how bad the weather is. How will we ever be able to leave?"

"Gram, wait. Where are you going?"

Fanny hesitated a moment, as she buttoned up her coat. "Just to get a few things at the store up the street, and maybe walk a little and get my hip moving."

She heard Amy call her name once again, but she closed the front door, walked down the porch steps, and stood on the crushed shell driveway. Fanny knew she could go left, to either Manuel's or the little Buddhist temple. Or she could go right, to Dominick Fortunato's. The wind seemed to have ceased and the air was filled with the dank smell of the bay. In the distance, a ship's horn bellowed, the low bass haunting and sad. Fanny knew that all of the disappointments of the last forty-eight years had led her to this moment. What happened next was her choice alone. And this moment could change everything, if she turned right.

She buttoned her top button, and as she began to walk, the sun peeked from between the clouds, illuminating the wet street. The sky was clearing, and suddenly Fanny's mood lifted.

CLAIRE HAD JUST MANAGED to get her father to stand when Ava's nurse came back into the room. She was afraid the woman was going to chastise her for upsetting Ava, because she looked extremely upset.

But she came over and took her father's hand and spoke to him slowly and deliberately.

"I couldn't let you leave like this," she said, and her father sat down hard in the chair, as if his legs had gone out from under him.

And then, as Claire watched in shock, the nurse told them that Ava had had several small strokes.

"She has no children," the nurse went on. "I can tell you that for sure."

"But everything she said, that she remembered, it was all true," Claire's father said.

The nurse shrugged. "Her early memories seem to be intact. That's often the way with these things. But there was no child."

"How do you know?" Claire asked. "Maybe she put it up for adoption."

The nurse shook her head. "No. She lied." And then the nurse hesitated before continuing. "She's a bitter woman. I'm sorry to say that, because she's old and failing, but unfortunately it's true. She never did marry, that was accurate. But there was a man she lived with, and after he died, she had her first stroke, and that's when she came here. She didn't seem to remember him at all."

And then the nurse squeezed her father's hand. "Trust me,

Joseph. From what I can gather from the few visitors she's had, Ava wasn't the most pleasant, or honest, person. God forgive me for saying that."

And then she left them. Her father sat there, and Claire went and asked the girl at the reception desk for a glass of water. She had to hold it for him, because his hands trembled so badly it was spilling all over his pants.

"It's over, Dad."

Her father said nothing; he simply closed his eyes and sighed.

When they were nearly in Provincetown, after forty minutes of driving without either one of them talking, Claire turned to her father.

"Please, Dad, now you've got to tell Mom what's been going on."

He said nothing, staring out the windshield.

"This hasn't been fair to her."

"I know," he said softly.

When they got back to the house and Claire managed to get him inside, it was nearly dark. Amy was feeding Rose her cereal and fruit at the kitchen table. She turned at the sound of the door.

"Thank God you're back," she said. "I've been calling your cell for over an hour."

"Oh, I turned it off and forgot to turn it back on."

"Gram went out a long time ago, supposedly to go to the store, and she still hasn't come back. And Abbie called. Rick was rushed to the hospital."

THE TEMPLE WAS CLOSED, but the door was never locked. Fanny sat in the meditation room, willing her breath to return to normal, her face to stop burning. Her blood pressure could be dangerously high right now. It was dark, but tiny lights in the ceiling illuminated the room in a soft glow, like candlelight.

She took a deep breath and imagined she was drawing a river of air into her lungs, then slowly let it out. Again and again, until she felt her pulse slow down.

But her monkey mind kept chattering away.

She was a fool. An absolute fool.

Because she'd let herself believe that she'd finally found the love she'd been searching for all her life. She'd been floating on a cloud of anticipation for days, knowing that the day would come and she would go to him. Yet she was held back by guilt. Only today, that yoke of guilt had been broken. Joe had gone to see Ava. So why shouldn't she go to Dominick?

The tension had built just like in her novels, until she felt she was in a fever of anticipation as she walked slowly toward the restaurant, imagining him cupping her face, looking longingly into her eyes as he searched for her very soul. And then brushing her lips tenderly before crushing her in a wild embrace.

Oh, she'd imagined it all.

He was surprised to see her. And she was embarrassed at first. But then he let her in and she could sense a moment of unease. He poured them each an anisette, and Fanny sat and slowly savored the hot sweet drink as it warmed her insides. They talked about the crazy weather, a nor'easter brewing somewhere in Canada, but nothing about Vito or Amy. Nothing about their families.

When she shivered a moment, which he mistakenly assumed was from the raw weather, not her nerves, he brought her a small blanket and wrapped it around her shoulders. Then he sat beside her and stroked her face with a soft finger before lifting her chin. And she knew it was here, the moment she'd waited for, and her heart galloped in her chest.

"Oh, Filly," he said softly, "I have dreamed of this."

Then he took off his glasses and leaned toward her, his lips pursed, his eyes closing. And she froze. Her eyes widened and then his lips were on hers and she sat there like a statue. His arm circled her back but she couldn't move. From the moment he removed his glasses, he looked so different. Like a stranger. And she felt the romance evaporate.

He pulled away. "What is it?"

She stared at him but couldn't say a word. How did she tell him? His eyes without the glasses were no longer like Omar Sharif's. They were small and hard; the eyes of a stranger.

"I have to go," she said, jumping up, the blanket sliding off her shoulders onto the floor.

It was probably the fastest she'd walked in the past twenty years.

Once she was outside, the late afternoon air had hit her like a cold slap. She couldn't go back to the house; she couldn't face Amy. And Claire was undoubtedly back with Joe by now. She didn't even trust herself to talk. She was burning with shame. She'd walked a few blocks, then gone into the Provincetown Art Museum and sat for a while, catching her breath. She asked the woman who worked there to call her a cab, a regular cab, because she didn't want to see Billy. She didn't even want to share this with Manuel, who would have something wise to say about it all. She just wanted to hide.

In the temple now, her breath slowed finally, and she realized she'd been saying an Act of Contrition over and over as her thoughts collided. She nearly laughed out loud at the ridiculousness of it, saying her Catholic prayer for forgiveness while she sat in the silence of a Buddhist temple.

She heard the door open behind her and assumed it was the nice young Korean girl who led the meditation sessions, who must be wondering what she was doing there. But then she heard footsteps.

"Mom?"

She looked and saw Claire walking toward her.

She turned away, looking out the sliding doors to the Zen garden below. A peaceful setting that gave her no peace at this moment. How did Claire find her?

"Mom, what's going on?" Claire asked as she sat beside her.

Fanny sighed. Where did she begin? Why would she burden her daughter with her own disappointments in life, when Claire certainly had her own?

"I'm sorry about Rick," she said.

"Mom, I'm not here to talk about—"

"Claire, you deserve so much. The kind of life he can give you. And we've ruined it for you. I thought by going into the assisted living it would help your situation, but—"

"Are you saying you agreed to go there because of Rick?"

Fanny shrugged. "Do you think I want you to spend the rest of your life alone?"

"I know, Mom, I know how you feel. I don't want Amy to be alone either. But I can't believe that's why you moved there."

Again Fanny shrugged. "We could have managed at home. After his medications were adjusted, your father was doing much better. And the physical therapy helped, too. But it doesn't matter anymore."

"Why, Mom? Why doesn't it matter anymore?"

She stared at the Zen garden, the little waterfall gurgling peacefully, the neatly trimmed shrubs arranged artfully around gray gravel paths. Neat, tidy, serene. She thought about all of her morning walks, sitting by the bay and watching the seals nap on the dock in the morning sun.

"Maybe I don't have to go back there. Maybe I can just stay here. In fact, Amy and Rose could stay here with me. She can continue working at the restaurant, and I'm sure we can find a little place to rent. Your father will be well taken care of at the assisted living. And you can marry Rick and have your own life."

Claire let out a long breath. "That's quite a plan. I guess you've been thinking this all through."

Fanny shook her head. "No, it actually all came to me as I was sitting here. And it makes sense, don't you think?"

"Mom, what about Dad? Can you really leave him?"

She looked at Claire, a flicker of anger flaring in her chest again. "The man kept something from me for our entire marriage. He was in love with another woman, and since we've been here, he's spent every moment obsessed with finding her."

"Oh, Mom, if you only knew the truth…"

"Well, he certainly won't tell me. And you won't, either."

"Mom, I wish I could. But Dad has never confided in me. No, let's get it right; he's never really talked to me about anything personal in my entire life. If I tell you, he'll never talk to me again. I don't want him to die one day and me feel as if I don't even know him."

"Try being married to him."

She was surprised to hear Claire laugh. "Mom, I know, it can't have been easy. You deserve a medal. But I think sometimes we don't realize when we set these things in motion. Sometimes it's out of fear, or shame, but the next thing you know, years go by, and the secret just seems to disappear. Or occasionally rear its ugly head, and you think you want to bury it even deeper."

"Is this about him? Because it sounds like it might be about you."

For a moment Claire sat there, and Fanny could see her thinking hard. Then she shook her head. "I was just speaking in generalities. But I'm really worried about you, Mom. And Dad. I decided not to go to the dune shack. It's just bad timing. And I haven't even come up with a portfolio theme."

"Wait a minute," she said. "This is what you came up here for."

"No, I'm not leaving you and Dad. Or Amy. I can see she's worried sick about Jared taking Rose."

"I can watch out for Amy while you're gone. It's just a few days. This is what you need to do, Claire."

"I…"

But before she could say another word, Fanny took her hand

and squeezed it hard. "Claire, don't do something here that you'll regret. We only get so many chances in life."

Claire smiled. "You won't do anything impulsive while I'm gone?"

Now Fanny felt her own face flood with red shame. How much did Claire know? She fought back the tears that pinched her eyes. She was a foolish old woman.

Claire stood up then and waited for her. She could have told Claire now before they left the temple. About the disappointments with love during her life. About nearly doing something stupid with Dominick Fortunato. But Fanny knew this was one secret she'd never share. Even with Annie, if she were there. Because she understood shame better than ever. No matter how desperately she'd longed for love, or how angry she was, going to Dominick today was simply wrong.

41

$\mathscr{C}\mathscr{O}$

I T WAS LATE IN THE DAY AND THE SUN WAS BEGINNING its quick descent, the sky blooming with pinks and purples. The beach before her once again glowed, like her living room at home when she'd light all her candles. It was a warm yellow light that changed the look of the room, and instantly changed her mood.

And here, sitting on the sand after her first full day alone at the dune shack, the light on the beach seemed to do the same thing. Or was it the fact that everything in her life had just changed again in the last twenty-four hours?

She'd nearly given up her chance to stay in a dune shack. How could she possibly leave for three days when everything in her life seemed to be in turmoil? Late the night before, she'd stood in her bedroom, sorting through the clothes she'd planned to bring. Wondering if she was crazy for still considering it. She couldn't come up with a portfolio. She could barely think, her mind was so cluttered with the problems surrounding her with her family, and the loss of Rick. But now she knew it had all been worth it.

It had taken hours for her to let it all go today, the stress over her parents, the worry over Jared taking Rose, the anguish in Amy's eyes, to finally find a sense of peace she'd been seeking here. A brief respite from her life, and her family, to allow her mind to wander, her eyes to see, and to look for inspiration. It was the reason she'd wanted to do this all those months ago, after all.

Staring at the endless ocean surrounding her, Claire wondered what it was about water that caused her to feel so content. In spite of everything going on, it never failed. She might walk out the back door of their rental house, or bike down to the moors, or simply glimpse the bay through the houses, and it would wash over her. Contentment. Possibility.

Was it the water? Or being someplace new? Amy had said a while ago that she felt like a different person here. Claire had seen changes in both her parents. She realized that she felt the same way. Or was it because her life was back on track again?

Rick hadn't had a heart attack, as he'd first feared. Before she went looking for her mother yesterday, she'd quickly called Abbie, who told her about his chest pains at the construction site. Abbie told her that his first words when she arrived at the ER were for her to call Claire.

Claire knew he must have been terrified. She remembered him telling her how he watched his father keel over and disappear from their lives at fifty-four. Here one minute, gone the next. It was why he took such good care of himself, at the gym three times a week, walking instead of using a golf cart. His father, too, was fit and handsome and the picture of health. Just like Rick.

When she finally got to speak with him on the phone, he told her the whole story, his voice thin and tired. He'd had chest pains, and when the ambulance took him to the hospital they were assuming it was a heart attack. Luckily, it wasn't. But his cholesterol, they found, was dangerously high, as were his triglycerides. And there was one small blockage, which they'd immediately taken care of.

When the angioplasty was over, they told him he'd have to be careful. He had a dangerous family history, and his numbers indicated it was genetic. Apparently it was enough of a scare to cause him to question everything in his life.

"I've been a shit to you," he said to her. "My brothers are right, you're the best thing that's ever happened to me."

Claire closed her eyes, unable to believe what she was hearing.

"I honestly thought this was it, you know. But while I was lying there, waiting, all I could think about was you, Claire. How I wanted you near me. And that you would always be there for me, no matter what, if I hadn't pushed you away."

She sat in a chair in her bedroom, looking at the open suitcase, wondering if she should go back to Lincoln. "So you're saying…"

"Yeah, babe," he said with a small laugh, laced with relief, "I'm saying let's get married. As soon as you're finished up there and get back, we'll make arrangements, maybe do it over Christmas. Then let's get our asses to Arizona come June, and start living that life we dreamed about. Nothing else matters, just you and me."

"But what about—"

"Just let me take care of everything. I've been lying here for hours, with nothing to do but think. And I've figured it all out."

Her parents could go back to their little house in Lincoln, he suggested. It wasn't sold, after all. And Amy could live there with Rose. She could help take care of them, and they could help her with Rose. And if her father started to get bad, they'd get a home health aide in to give them breaks. It was ideal, and he made it sound so simple. He would make sure she came home every three or four months to see them. And of course they were welcome to come out to Scottsdale.

"It isn't a permanent solution, but it could get everybody through the next year or so. Get Amy on her feet, keep your folks out of the assisted living, which you admitted your mom loathed."

Her mind had been reeling, part of her wondering if it was really happening.

"Claire, what do you think?"

"It's…a great idea, actually. After seeing how well my parents are doing up here, you're right, I don't think there's any way I could take them back there and not be riddled with guilt."

She didn't tell him that she feared her mother had no intention of returning with them. Maybe this was a way to get her back to Jefferson County.

Before they hung up, she asked him if he wanted her to come home.

"No, that's okay. I'll be back home tomorrow and golfing again in just a week."

"Are you sure?"

"Finish what you started up there, Claire. I'll be waiting for you."

Before dusk settled, she went back into the dune shack and lit candles, then scrambled some eggs on the tiny propane stove and sat eating them with a cup of tea. She expected to be afraid once it got dark. She thought she would be creeped out by the thought of being so alone in the midst of thousands of acres of nothing but dunes and sea. But she smiled, because she felt surprisingly content.

She walked for a long way through the soft sand, more than fifty feet above the beach below, looking for a way down. For a moment she thought of sitting on her butt and trying to slide down, like riding a sled on sand. But the pitch was steep, and far below there might be rocks or shells that she couldn't see. So she kept going. About a hundred yards from her own dune shack, she saw a dip between the dune grasses and there was a path. Going down wouldn't be so bad, but she imagined coming up would be difficult.

She made her way slowly down, going sideways, so that if she lost her balance or the sand gave suddenly, she could catch herself, rather than pitching forward. Out of breath, with her legs aching, she made it to the bottom and found herself on a stretch of beach that was breathtaking. There was not a person to be seen, not a footprint in the sand, and all around her the ocean rolled and shimmered in the morning sunlight. Behind her, the high wall of dunes stretched as far down the beach as she could see. It was a different feeling here from the beaches back in New Jersey; more remote, with a sense of being farther north, in a place that was unto itself. Again she remembered seeing pictures of sheer cliffs on the coast of Ireland in that old movie *Ryan's Daughter*, a favorite of hers years ago, windswept and isolated, romantic and forbidden. She looked north. If she headed that way, she might run into people wandering down from Race Point Beach. She didn't want that. While she was here, she wanted to do it right; be completely alone for these days, an experiment in survival of sorts.

So she turned southward and began to walk. It was late morning and surprisingly mild for the end of October. She realized that the wall of dunes created a buffer from the wind sweeping across the Cape from the bay side, so that except for a light breeze off the water, the air was still.

A feeling of elation swept through her as she walked, and after a few moments, she unlaced her sneakers and pulled them off with her socks, then rolled her jeans mid-calf. The sand was warm, and she burrowed her toes into its silky softness and smiled. Then she picked up her camera bag and kept going, filled with anticipation. What would she see that she could photograph?

Once she took the pressure off herself, she was finally able to relax and really enjoy this. She told herself that if nothing else, she'd spend this time taking more pictures. And focus on what she had managed to accomplish during these weeks. So what if she was lacking a final project? No one else, she was certain, had come with so many distractions. And hadn't that been the point of the workshop? To work to the point of obsession and reach a new level of craft? She wasn't going to beat herself up anymore.

Her eyes swept from the sand to the water as she kept moving, alert for shells, rocks, birds, or any kind of wildlife or formation that could provide an interesting picture. The waves were surprisingly big, much bigger than she remembered from other walks on the ocean beaches. She thought of the nor'easter she'd heard of, much farther north, in the maritime provinces of Canada, and wondered if it could affect the tides here.

Just then she saw something in the waves, a log rolling or floating, big and brown. She wondered if it could be a piece of a telephone pole dredged from the bottom, because that's what it looked like from a distance. She walked closer to the water's edge, then saw it surface again. She laughed aloud. It had whiskers, big brown eyes, and a smooth round head. She watched it ride the next wave, the way she and Amy used to, although it did not come all the way in. The seal spotted her, stared at her for a long moment, then dove beneath a wave and disappeared. She stood there for about five minutes waiting for it to resurface, but it was long gone.

A few hundred yards up, she saw red spots in the sand and followed them toward the massive dunes, where just at its bottom she saw the remains of a seal pup. She'd heard about the coyotes who preyed on the baby seals, and a shiver ran through her at the thought of encountering one. But she'd been assured that it was much the same as the bears back in Jefferson County; they'd be much more frightened of her, and would steer clear.

She walked quickly away from the carnage, her eyes scanning the ocean a bit farther out, wondering if there were any whales nearby. By now, they all should have been well on their way south, as they were each fall by this time, although there was speculation in the local papers that week that either the mild weather or the still-abundant zooplankton could have contributed to their lingering in the area much longer than they usually did.

She thought about Joy, the pregnant right whale, swimming through those seas with her head enshrouded in that net. It would be difficult for her to eat, Libby had told her on the ride back that day. Claire wondered if they'd encountered her again, if they were able to help her. If so, John hadn't called her. When Claire asked about her name, Libby told her that right whales usually weren't named, like the humpbacks were. They were given numbers. But from the first time they'd seen her seven years ago, Moby had developed a soft spot for her.

"She breached every time we saw her," Libby said with a soft smile. "Right whales don't usually breach, not like the humpbacks. Moby started calling her Joy. Because she seemed so full of it. And also for his great-great-grandfather, who was a whaler from Nantucket. His last name was Joy."

Then Libby told her that Moby had committed his life to saving the whales, to make up for all the ones his ancestors had taken.

She stood now searching the endless sea, but it seemed empty of spouts or flukes. Claire kept walking, saying a little prayer for Joy and her baby, hoping they would make it south to the birthing grounds. After another half hour of walking, she decided to turn around. But then she saw something up ahead in the sand that she couldn't make out.

She picked up her pace and began to perspire, so she pulled off her sweatshirt and tied it around her waist. When she got back, she told herself, she might just lie in the warm sand at the base of the dunes and take a nap. What heaven that would be. It had been a long, long time since she'd had a chance to just wander and be like this. To do whatever she wanted to.

Her heart began to beat faster as she got closer, and then, not twenty feet away, she stopped, realizing what it was. The remains of an old ship. The curved, wooden rib bones of the vessel sprouted from the sand, its middle buried. And then she saw the small plaque. It was the remains of an old schooner, presumed to have sunk early in the 1900s and most likely built in the 1800s. It had washed ashore during a nor'easter a few years ago.

Claire knelt and studied the hand-hewn beams, fingered the wooden pegs that held it together. It was absolutely amazing to her. Then she walked around and into it, sitting in the middle, on the gully of sand at its center, where the wood was buried. She imagined the men who'd sat in this vessel, sailing the ocean, their families waiting at home. The lives, the stories, and the pictures these pieces of wood had witnessed.

It was an incredible piece of living history. She felt a spark of excitement light within her. As much as she loved vistas, and the incredible photographs she'd taken of the magical lighting here, nothing moved her as much as history, and possibly capturing a piece of it in a print.

She opened her camera bag and went to work.

AMY TOOK ROSE to have dinner with one of the other girls who worked at the restaurant, a waitress who was also a single mother. That left Fanny and Joe alone. She made a pathetic dinner of hot dogs and baked beans, and they ate in silence. She knew he was in pain; yesterday he'd taken a fall. But he wouldn't complain, and she wouldn't ask.

As she washed the dishes, he went out on the patio and sat there with an afghan over his lap. And she felt as if Annie was there, just like she'd always been, telling her the right thing to do. *Don't be so stubborn, Fanny. Just ask him.*

So she dried her hands, pulled on her sweater, and went out the back door. She sat in a chair, watching the colors shift as the sun set behind their house. Beside her, Joe sat quietly, his hand sliding back and forth across his lap. Occasionally he cleared his throat, something he'd begun to do a lot lately. She knew it might be part of the Parkinson's, and that difficulty in swallowing would be part of his life down the road. It was the only sound either of them made.

She stood up then, and slid her chair over, turning it around to face him. And then she sat down, directly in the path of his view of the water. Startled, now he had to look at her.

"This is stupid," she said.

His head rocked from side to side. It seemed it never stopped anymore.

"How much longer are we going to dance around this, Joe?"

She couldn't tell if the wobbling was getting faster or if he was shaking his head no.

"Talk to me, Joe. I'd rather have the bitter truth than a sweet lie."

And then he did something that surprised her. And scared her. This man who rarely showed emotion, or affection, leaned forward and took her hand.

"Fanny, I...I spent my whole life torturing myself. For nothing," he said. "It's over. And I should have found that out long ago."

He was silent again. Was that it? Was that all he'd say?

"Do you want to know about torturing, Joe?" She pulled her hand away and stood up. "Do you know the first time I heard about her? On our wedding day. When Charlie Hoffman was teasing you about the one that got away."

Joe shook his head. "God damn that Charlie Hoffman. He was an ass."

"Do you know how that hurt? Because it's not as if you ever made me feel like I was the one." She could barely catch her breath as the anger exploded from her. "All these years, Joe. All these years that woman has hung over our marriage. You acted like a man haunted by her."

"Sit down, Fanny."

Her heart was pounding. Damn it, she was not going to cry. He leaned forward and grabbed her hand again.

"Sit," he said again, pulling her down into her chair. "That woman was nothing to me."

As she tried to catch her breath, as she kept telling herself she was going to have a stroke if she didn't control herself, he told her everything. He said the words she'd waited her whole life to hear:

that he'd never loved Ava. He'd simply been a lonely young man, and she was a girl looking for a way out of her life. Fanny felt a flicker of jealousy when he said the words out loud: that they'd made love, and that he was then going to marry her. But when he talked about his relief, when her mother told him there'd never been a baby, he couldn't look at her anymore. He looked down, his shame obvious.

"I didn't want Ava," he said. "I never did."

And then a fresh blaze of anger fired up in the pit of her stomach, because of the waste of all those years that he'd ruined for her. The fever of her jealousy coming and going throughout their married life. For nothing. He'd kept this from her their entire lives; this secret that he could have had another child.

She stood up and walked across the patio. Then she turned.

"I'm your wife," she spat at him. "You should have told me."

Still he couldn't meet her eyes.

42

On her last night, Claire sat in an old chair behind the dune shack and watched the sky. She was surrounded by nothing but sand, dune grasses, and far down below, the ocean, which she couldn't see from where she sat. The beautiful, sunny weather she'd had since first arriving was gone. It felt more like a moonscape than anything earthly, and now, alone in this desolate place, she watched it darken and change. A little unnerved, she sat outside, deciding to face it head-on.

In less than two weeks, she'd be heading home. She kept thinking about everything that would happen then. She would marry Rick, after all. They would move to Arizona come June. She would leave her parents behind, and Abbie. And now Amy and Rose. None of it seemed quite real.

Here she was, not far from fifty, and she still felt unsure about so much. Years ago, she'd imagined that at some point she would find someone, marry, maybe even have another child. But it hadn't happened. That dream had evaporated by the time Amy was in high school. And once Amy left home, the lonely nights, the long weekends alone began to add up, broken by occasional visits with her parents or a movie with Abbie or Esther.

All of that changed the night she'd reluctantly gone to the Booster Club dance at the American Legion with Abbie and Tom and some other couples; the fifth wheel once again. But she'd met Rick. He brought her home in his vintage Corvette, with the top down, although it was nearly winter, and the heat was blasting. She thought she probably laughed more that night than she had in the previous year. She liked the feeling of inclusion, being part of a couple with other couples. Looking at each other across a crowded room and knowing there would be a "later." It wasn't perfect; he wasn't perfect. But she was old enough to know that neither was she. She knew, though, that what they were building would make up for those things that might be lacking. After all, who had a perfect marriage? She had only to look around her to know that reality was very different from the fairy tales of her childhood. There would be compromise, and occasionally settling for something that might not be to your liking. But a shared life, someone to wrap your arms around each night and look at over a cup of coffee and the morning paper, to face the troubles of the world with—that was real.

For a moment, John Poole's face popped into her head. The hungry look in his eyes as he devoured her with kisses, murmuring her name again and again that night at his fishing shack in Wellfleet. That was the stuff of her mother's romance novels; she was smart enough to know that, too. John was brooding and complicated, and she wasn't sure why she'd found herself attracted to him. Just before she'd left for the dune shack, he'd come to her house and apologized for that night. Knowing that she was engaged, he explained, what he did wasn't fair to her. Or to her fiancé.

"I don't always think things through, Claire," he said with that crooked smile. "Probably my biggest downfall."

At that moment, she didn't tell him she wasn't technically engaged the night he'd done that. Nor did she explain why she'd kissed him back, and had nearly lost herself in the moment when his hands began to roam her body and a fierce need for him took over her senses. But only for a few moments.

Instead, she asked about the shiner on his right eye, a nasty purple bruise that was already yellowing.

"Bar fight with a local," he said and shrugged.

Once again, he looked like the handsome, sexy bad boy she knew most women swooned for. Like Liam, years ago. But she knew from experience that lust would wane. Mutual respect and security, those were the building blocks of a lasting relationship. This time she was thinking with her head, as Rick had cautioned her, and not her heart.

THE WEATHER WAS deteriorating rapidly and the wind whistled and groaned through the many cracks and crevices in the shack. She was glad to be busy that night. Claire knew if she let her imagination run wild, her nerves would probably get the best of her, so she'd lit every candle, even the extra ones she'd brought. Then she'd laid out her photographs all over the old wooden table in the kitchen.

She kept going back to her favorites. Amy and Rose sitting on the beach at Herring Cove, washed in the golden Cape Cod light that she still had trouble grasping. The handful of pictures she'd taken of John Poole, writing on the deck of the Coastal Studies boat. There was something about those pictures, the fierce look, the intensity of him at work. And then, of course, the whales. The beauty of the mother and calf playing, nursing, living their simple existence. And then the netted right whale, Joy, with her baby inside of her. She'd enlarged that print again and again, until the final version showed just a portion of the whale's head, looking like an abstract, the dark flesh of the whale striated with the lines of netting and in the midst the round eye, just staring at you. She wondered at that moment where Joy was. If it was at all possible for her to disentangle herself. Claire knew that would take a miracle. Was she even still alive?

She sighed and poured herself a glass of wine, the only luxury she allowed herself here. Then she sat in a wooden kitchen chair and looked through the pictures in the digital camera. There were more than 150 images she'd shot since she arrived in the dune shack. The last ones, taken yesterday, were, ironically, of herself.

After her trek back from the schooner, and then the long climb up the sand cliff to get back to the dune shack, she'd been exhausted. She threw an old blanket out on the sand in the yard, lay down, and fell fast asleep. When she awoke, she wasn't sure if she'd been asleep for minutes or hours. Her head was groggy and her body still thick in the throes of deep slumber. She had that drugged feeling you get when you're wakened in the middle of a dream; there was a surreal sense to everything around her. For a split second, she couldn't quite remember where she was, or even who she was. For that instant, there was a spontaneous disconnect with her life as Claire, and she was simply a woman surrounded by sand and dunes.

She sat up, spotted the camera bag beside her, and the world began to come back to her. And then she did a strange thing. She set the self-timer and took a series of pictures of herself, as if she were a subject she didn't know at all; one she was studying and trying to capture in a print. Who was this woman? And what did she really want?

Now she stared at each miniature image of herself completely unself-concious. It was near the end of the series that she saw the resemblance to Amy that she'd never seen before. Because of her coloring, she'd always thought that Amy looked like Liam. But there in the picture was Amy's hesitant smile. In another she saw her mother's eyes in her own face. Her mother was really no different than she was, just at a different stage. The last stage. And Claire would be there next. Then one day Amy. And then Rose. Claire saw in herself a woman who wasn't much different from the young girls in the hallways of the high school where she taught, struggling to find her place, her way in the world.

There was something to it all, some thread of commonality in her favorite photos that she could taste but not name, like a word that's on the tip of your tongue. It wasn't until she clicked back to the images of the schooner and then turned to the right whale on the table that it finally crystallized in her mind. She smiled, and then actually laughed out loud. It had been there all along, and it was perfect. She couldn't have planned it better if she'd tried.

She had her theme, and her portfolio, right in front of her. And it was better than she could have ever imagined.

EARLY THE NEXT MORNING, she woke to howling winds. She stepped outside and braced herself against strong gusts as she managed to walk to the edge of the cliff. Far below her, the ocean was dark and roiling, spitting white peaks like a churning brew. She knew this couldn't be good. But on her way back to the shack, she saw the Suburban from Art's slowly making its way down the sand road. She walked on toward the road, and Ed, the driver who'd taken them in, rolled his window down and informed her that the nor'easter wasn't far off and he'd come to take everyone a little earlier than planned back to town.

Ed and two other workshop participants were in the midst of a conversation when Claire threw her things in the back and climbed in. Slowly, they drove on to the next dune shack and waited for that person to gather his gear and join them. She wondered how her family was doing, and suddenly felt relieved to be going back. It wouldn't be fair to leave Amy with all the responsibility when a storm was coming. Despite the alone time and the wonderful solitude, she felt a sudden longing to hold Rose. And she missed her parents.

Just then her ears pricked up as she heard Ed's two-way radio crackle on and a voice on the other end mentioning a whale in Truro. It was difficult to hear, as she was in the third row of seats, and the wind howled noisily, buffeting the car occasionally.

When she heard the radio call end, Claire asked Ed what had happened.

"Someone out for their morning walk stumbled on a beached whale a little while ago. Must've washed in from the storm," he said.

"Where is it?" someone else asked before Claire even got the words out.

She wondered if it was one of the "ding-dongs," the foolish, young whales Libby had described.

"At Cold Storage Beach. Not far from here, actually."

She asked the driver if he could possibly stop there before they headed back into town. He hesitated, and as everyone chimed in, he gave up. And so they went.

When they came out from the sand, they were on Route 6, halfway to Truro. Five minutes later, they were turning off the highway toward the bay and Claire felt her stomach begin to tremble. She had to see this, but she was also dreading it. They drove down a country road lined with small ponds, a cranberry bog, and old houses that sat far apart. The trees had turned and the color faded, so that the bright orange and golds of a few weeks ago were now beiges and browns. The road curved sharply to the left as the ocean came into view on their right far below, and Claire wondered how she'd never come to this stunning beach. It was a curving slice of sand, with Provincetown in the distance to the right, and Truro and Well-fleet arcing to the left, as her eyes followed the curl of land way into the distance. It was the first place she'd come since arriving here nearly two months ago where she felt oriented. And the beach was breathtaking.

They all looked out the windows, but there was no sign of a whale.

As they drove down the hill and pulled over, Claire saw the yellow Land Rover parked in the distance. She'd known, somehow, that he'd be there.

They climbed out of the car, and she zipped up her hooded sweatshirt, but the wind here wasn't as fierce as at the ocean. The group of them, along with Ed, headed across the road and onto the sand, but Claire turned suddenly and ran back for her camera bag. A few minutes later, as she descended to the beach by herself, she looked to the left, at a row of houses, high above the beach, with tall flights of wooden steps leading to them. When she turned right, there was a similar line of houses, set on lower dunes, and in the distance, she could make out something. She walked fast and caught up with the group. Claire felt a swell of emotion rise up in her chest at the thought of what was down the beach. She thought of how moved she'd been by each of the whales she'd seen from the Coastal Studies boat. She couldn't imagine how awful this might be, a whale stranded on this beach. But she kept walking.

It wasn't long before she could make out a huge dark shape on the sand ahead, and a few people scurrying around. Then she began to run, holding her bag by her side so it didn't bounce. She passed her classmates, but didn't bother to pause. She was perhaps fifty yards away when she began to slow down and walk, her breath coming in spurts. Sudden tears filled her eyes and she held a sob in her throat. He didn't see her; he never looked up. The giant dark body of the whale lay at the water's edge, the tide out and its huge, netted head lying on dry sand, its wide tail partially submerged in the surf. Kneeling by its face was John Poole, tenderly stroking it, the same way she stroked Rose when trying to comfort her. He murmured softly as his fingers patted the whale's head, the huge eye seeming to stare right at him. Murmuring something she couldn't hear. The net had gouged its way into the thick blubber, and the skin around it was raw and infected, even she could see that. She had seen this net before, in her photographs.

Slowly she walked over. He still didn't look up. She couldn't believe she was this close, within just a few feet of the massive whale, its body rising high above her just like the cliff walls of the sand dunes.

"Is there any hope?" she asked.

He looked up at her for a long moment. His eyes were full of sadness. Then he shook his head.

"All we can do is make her as comfortable as possible," he said softly, as his hand continued to stroke up and down her face.

"Is this…?"

He nodded. "It's Joy."

She couldn't help it, she reached out and touched his own face with her fingers, tenderly stroking his cheek. She saw him clench his jaw.

"Oh, John, is there anything I can do?"

He said nothing for a long moment. Then he turned to her. "Take pictures," he said, his voice suddenly harsh. "Lots of them. People need to see this."

WHEN SHE FINISHED SHOOTING, Claire noticed a crowd gathering. Then she saw Libby and Moby, along with a few others. Their faces were grim. They'd been out on the boat at sea, working on a calf entanglement, and so it had taken them a while to get there.

They began wetting the whale with buckets of seawater, then covering her with wet blankets. It was a tedious process, and others from the crowd began to help. Claire began shooting again.

Libby came over as she was taking pictures and waited for her to take a break. The sky was nearly dark, although it wasn't even five yet.

"I know this isn't pretty, but your pictures might do more good than we could ever accomplish."

"That's what John said." She zipped her camera back in her case. "What will happen to her?"

"If she wasn't so sick, we'd try to get her back into the water.

That's no easy feat, but we've done it before." Libby hesitated, then sighed. "She won't make it, though. The net is practically embedded in the blubber, and she's infected. And you can see, she's lost weight. She can't feed. We'll just keep her as comfortable as we can until she dies. Then we'll study her."

"All this because of that net?" Claire asked.

Libby nodded. "It's a shame, because sometimes we see a whale months or even years after it's entangled, and we can still help. But she really didn't stand a chance. And as I told you before, losing one female right whale could be devastating for the population."

"How long?" Claire asked.

Libby shrugged. "God knows."

"What about...?" she began and stopped. Her throat ached with unshed grief. "Is there any way to save the baby?"

Libby's eyes filled with tears. "It's just too soon. It wouldn't be able to survive."

So they would both die.

Claire walked up the dark beach alone, her heart as heavy as a stone. The joy and relief she'd felt coming from the dune shack and knowing she could show her work in the Provincetown Art Museum had evaporated. Suddenly the pictures of Joy in her camera mattered more than anything else.

43

It was the middle of the afternoon when she finally returned home. it had been three days since she'd seen her family. Neither one of her parents were there, and Claire held a moment of hope that they'd somehow reconciled. She found Amy upstairs on her bed, with her laptop opened. Rose was napping across the hall.

They were three rough days for Amy, she soon learned. Her father began to have stalling episodes again. On his way to the parking lot to work that first day she was gone, he fell on the sidewalk. Amy took him back to the doctor in Hyannis while her mother watched the baby. He was bruised, but not badly hurt, Amy told her.

"Why didn't you call me?" she asked. "Is that why you're crying?"

"It's no big deal, I handled it. They called his doctor back home and they changed his meds a bit, and he seems fine now. He's back at the parking lot, sitting there since this morning."

"What about the storm…?"

"Mom, you know there's no arguing with him. So I walked him there and made sure he was settled. In fact, I should go back and get him now, it's almost—"

"No, I'll get him. I want to talk to him," Claire said. "And where's Grandma?"

"Out walking, I guess. She doesn't always say."

"What do you mean?"

Amy shook her head. "I don't know. She just seems…not herself. Grampa, too. She's mad at him, that's for sure."

"Sorry I left you such a mess," Claire sighed. "Thanks for taking over for me. I mean it. I'm really glad I got to experience a few days in the dune shack."

"Was it scary?"

"No, it wasn't. It was actually kind of liberating."

"Really?"

"Yeah, really. I've never been that alone before, and I was okay with it. I thought I'd be afraid, but I wasn't." Then she couldn't help smiling. "And I finally came up with a portfolio idea for the final project."

Amy's eyebrows shot up. "So you're going to display at the museum, after all?"

She nodded, then realized she'd been dominating the conversation. "Anyway, enough about me. What about you, honey? You're obviously upset. Is it about Jared?"

"We've been instant messaging all morning." She closed her laptop and leaned back against a pillow. "I told him I'll take Rose down to see his family as soon as we get back. It's only fair. I did lie before and tell him I was nursing, because I didn't want him to take her without me. But then I told him that wasn't true. I don't want to lie anymore, you know? I feel like a loser when I do. And Jared thanked me. He said he just wanted me to be up front with him now, so hopefully we won't have to get lawyers involved."

"Is that why you were so upset? He was going to get a lawyer?"

"Yeah. He's talking to one, but he doesn't want to go that route. And neither do I, so I agreed to get the birth certificate amended."

"I'm glad." Claire sat on the edge of the bed. "Do you still have feelings for Jared?"

Amy stared at her feet, then began chipping the polish off her toes. She nodded, and Claire saw the tears spill down her cheeks. "He really is a good guy. Not like Liam at all."

"Honey, there's something I need to tell you. Something I should have told you a long time ago."

Amy looked up and wiped her face with her sleeve. "About you and Liam?"

She nodded. "I thought a lot about truth when I was alone in the dune shack. And I haven't really been truthful with you, or even my parents, about something." She paused. "You always asked me what really happened. What really went wrong. I just didn't want to tell you because, honestly, I thought it would hurt you more. I kept telling myself I was just trying to protect you. I think, though, maybe I was just too ashamed to admit the truth."

"I don't understand."

Claire took a deep breath. "Your father and I were never married."

Amy blinked. "What? I thought…"

She shook her head. "No, it's what I wanted everyone to think. That I left him. That I came back to Jefferson County because I realized it wasn't going to work. The truth is…" She paused, then got up and walked over to the window, knowing that what she was about to confess would no doubt infuriate her daughter, and make her look like a hypocrite.

"The truth is, he left me. He was a selfish man who was incapable of commitment, or responsibility." Then she turned back to Amy. "When you were two, he came back and told me he was sorry, that he'd made a mistake taking off after I got pregnant. He said he wanted to marry me."

"I remember him coming. I was really little. And then we left Grandma's and moved away with him," Amy said softly.

"That's right. I took you and went to be with him in New York. We found a place together, he got a job tending bar, and I was going to try for a teaching job there. When we got married, I was going to change my name, and yours. Because when you were born, he'd already left me, so I denied him that. I didn't think he deserved you."

Amy watched her, waiting.

"The week before our little wedding, he told me about this job in California. He was going to go out there first, get settled. He never could stay in any one place very long. Anyway, he said we'd get married out there, but I didn't hear from him for months. I started running out of money, and things got pretty desperate. It was hard for me to face them, but we had to go back to Grandma's for a while. I put everything in storage, but I screwed up and didn't pay for a few months because I kept thinking we'd be getting it out soon. And we lost it all."

"My monkey…I remember crying like crazy for that thing," Amy said.

"I know. I was beside myself. I hated everyone back then; Liam, my parents, the world."

"It was the only thing he ever gave me."

"I tried so hard to get it—"

"But all this time," Amy interrupted now, looking straight at her, "you let everyone think you'd been married?"

She nodded. "Things were so different back then, I knew I'd embarrassed my parents. Twice he'd shamed me. Shamed them, really. I just couldn't let them know. No one really had to know the truth. I just told them we'd gotten married and quickly ended it. Truthfully, they were just so happy to see you again. They hadn't seen you in six months."

"Wow, you must have been devastated," Amy said.

Claire shrugged. "I was and I wasn't, not really. I think I finally grew up and saw what my parents had known all along about your father. But I was heartbroken for you. When you're fifteen and fall in love, it's so easy to make mistakes, yet you have no idea the repercussions that will come down the road. If I had known the hurt I would cause you…"

"Why did you tell me that it was you who made him leave?"

"I lied partly to salvage some of my pride. But mostly because I thought it would be easier on you. I thought I could love you enough to make up for that hurt if you blamed me. But if you thought your father didn't love you? I had no idea how I could make up for that."

Amy leaned back against the headboard. "I can't even imagine how awful that must have been for you. What a bastard."

"I'm sorry, honey," she said. "I've held that in for so many years. I guess I thought you'd hate me for what I did."

"Hate you? Oh, Mom. I feel so bad for what you went through. I can see how you'd do that. I would do that for Rose. I'd do anything if I thought it would hurt her less in the long run." Amy sighed. "Mom, I'm so sorry. How many times did I blame you? Treat you horribly? Because I thought…" Amy paused, pressed her lips together tightly, then shook her head. "I was so wrong. You had nothing to do with him not visiting me. He just didn't care enough."

She sat on the bed again and took Amy's hand.

"Why did you tell me all this now?" Amy asked.

"I don't know. It just felt like the right time. And I want a clean slate. I've been hiding behind this secret for more than twenty years, and I'm tired of it. And because you deserve the truth. Jared isn't like your dad, honey. He's a good guy, I can see that."

"I know." Amy said. "He's seeing someone else. She was there when I called him."

"The two of you are going to be bound by Rose for the rest of your lives. You need to be friends, at least."

Amy nodded. "I know. But listen, I'm really glad Rick came to his senses. You really deserve this, Mom. And now you will be married."

Claire leaned over and hugged her daughter.

"I thought you'd hate me," she said, holding her tight. "I was so afraid, all this time."

"Oh, Mom. You've been such a great mother to me." And then she pulled away. "I'm sorry about that day, when I left town. You were right, I let Tish smoke pot in the house because I knew you'd flip out. I was so freakin' scared, I was having panic attacks, I felt like my life was sliding down the tubes. I had to get out of Lincoln but I felt like I was paralyzed. I thought I was mad at you, but I think I was really just angry with myself. And Liam."

"Well, maybe leaving was what you really needed to do. You've changed, grown up."

"And I have Rose."

And hopefully, Claire thought, Jared would let her keep her.

CLAIRE WALKED the three blocks to the parking lot. How could it be November already? In some ways, the past ten weeks felt like ten months, and in others, it felt like they had gone by in the blink of an eye. The days were getting shorter, and at times you could feel the promise of winter nipping the air. It was four o'clock in the afternoon, and already the sky was darkening. The usually placid harbor, with its soft lapping even at high tide, had tiny frothing whitecaps. The sound of the small waves could be heard a block away.

As it whipped across the parking lot, the wind cut through her jacket, and she zipped it up higher and pulled on her hood. She saw her father sitting there at the mouth of the driveway, his cane beside him, as still and peaceful-looking as if it were a summer day. Waiting for cars that would not be coming today.

At various times in her life she'd imagined having a real talk with her father. Finally breaking through his barrier of silence and reaching that part of him he never shared with the world. She really didn't want it to be in a parking lot, but he was alone now, and this might be her last chance.

It wasn't until she was a few yards away that he looked up and saw her. She noticed that the lot was empty, but it didn't matter to her father. He'd found himself a purpose again. When a rare or old car pulled in, he had the pleasure of conversing for long minutes with another car lover. The money wasn't much, but he came home each day and put his tips into a jar in the kitchen, calling it Rose's college fund. Amy was touched, but she hadn't said a word, watching the coins and bills pile up each day. How would he fill his time once they returned to New Jersey?

"Hi, Dad," she said, standing there, looking down at him. This wasn't any way to start the conversation. She glanced over, but there wasn't another beach chair near the shops. So she knelt on the cold ground, her knees instantly complaining, and then settled into sitting, her knees drawn up to her chest, a shiver of cold already running up her backside.

"What are you doing?" he asked with a frown.

"Dad, no one's coming. There's a storm on its way."

"Not until tomorrow, I heard."

He waited for her to get up and leave, but she didn't. She looked out at the bay, the square white lighthouse on Long Point still visible in the dampening air. A constant reminder, she hadn't realized. Each day he must stare at it from here.

"Dad, we need to talk."

How did she say this? *I don't want you to die, to disappear from my life, without me really knowing you?* Was he any different, really, from most of the other men of his generation? Except for Robin's father, who'd been so open and affectionate and teasing when they were kids.

"Dad, you've always been quiet. I know that's just your way."

She paused, embarrassed.

"Dad, I think you might be losing Mom."

He looked out at the water. "I know that."

"I think she wants to stay here, when we go home."

Now he looked at her. Maybe it was from not seeing him for three days, but he suddenly looked so much thinner, frailer. His head bobbled constantly as his hand shuffled across his thigh. She wondered if it did that when he slept. If there was any way to really rest when your body never stopped moving.

"She hates that place," he said suddenly.

"It's more than that, Dad. You need to really talk to her."

"We talked. I told her everything."

"I don't think she feels loved."

"That's ridiculous," he said, with a tinge of anger in his voice.

"Maybe not to her."

He looked at her sternly. "Enough, Claire."

And after that, Claire knew she wasn't going to say the rest. That she loved him; that she didn't want him to die without her knowing him, really knowing him. That if he could just open up... But it was too uncomfortable; for him more than her. She could see that now.

But there was something else she needed to say. Now that she'd told Amy, she wanted to be free of that burden.

"Dad, I just want to say I'm sorry. All those years ago, you were right about Liam. And I was a fool. I hated you for it. But after I had Amy..."

"Don't worry yourself about that. It was a long time ago."

"But it wasn't..."

"Claire, enough, I said."

He didn't want to hear her secret, and he didn't want to talk about his. She was prepared to say more, to tell him everything. But she realized now that she didn't have to. It didn't matter; it wouldn't change anything anymore. He loved her and she loved him. Not that she could remember either of them ever saying it out loud to the other.

She stood up and looked out across the harbor again. The peninsula of sand had disappeared, along with the blinking eye of the lighthouse. Just then the foghorn bellowed.

"I love you, Dad," she said softly.

He nodded, not looking away from the water. "I know."

"Please come home soon," she said, and turned to leave.

FANNY SAT ON THE TOP FLOOR of the library staring out the big glass window at the town and the entire harbor spread out below her. The little shops and restaurants were quiet today, and there weren't many people walking. Across the way she could see a corner of the gravel parking lot where Joe was sitting, although she couldn't see him. Beyond the dark water, the rock breakwater stretched across the harbor, protecting the wharf and the boats from rough seas. Beyond that, the peninsula of sand that began with Wood End Light snaked across the bay and ended at Long Point, where that square white lighthouse blinked green, over and over, like a beating heart. A little while ago, she could even see the curving stretch of land to Truro, and then Wellfleet, in the distance. But that had disappeared as the air grew heavy with moisture and the nor'easter moved closer. The library probably had the best view in town, Fanny thought. And this was her first time seeing it. If she'd only known, she would have come here sooner.

If she'd only known...

If she'd only known so many things, so much of her life might have been different.

She watched the sky for what seemed like hours, as it changed from a pale gray to the dark, menacing color of steel. Lamenting over wasted years. Blaming Joe, and herself.

Occasionally she opened her book, the one on Buddhism, seeking some answer, such as how did she go on from here? How did she make peace with the years she'd squandered?

But how could she have known? The truth about her husband and that woman was nothing she'd ever imagined. She'd spent years thinking one way, wrapping her mind around a nugget of information until it was smooth and hard like a stone that embedded itself in her heart. For nothing. For nothing! Now she was expected to just pull it out, like a sharp, bloody splinter, and toss it away. But there was still the wound. After all those years, how could that wound possibly heal?

She'd been obsessed with *a lie!* One that Charlie Hoffman had planted in her head just moments after she recited her wedding vows, blushing with happiness and longing to touch her new husband. That day was supposed to be the happiest of her life, but the joy had been stolen from her with Charlie's words. She'd been tormented by the words of a woman she'd never even seen, who came to her over the years in unbidden moments. *He wants me,* that faceless Ava would say. *He never wanted you.* But it was all her own invention. She'd taken Charlie's words, a teasing statement, and made them real. And it wasn't the truth at all. Her husband hadn't been haunted by Ava, as Fanny had long thought. He'd been haunted by his own shame; a shame she could only imagine. This man who prided himself on being a good provider, who never missed an opportunity to drum into Claire and Eugene the importance of responsibility. But wasn't the shame really Ava's? She had lured him; she had lied. And he had done the right thing. He borrowed the money and he'd gone back for her. There was no reason, really, for his shame.

Fanny wished she could say the same for herself. If only she'd opened her mouth, that very first day! It's what Annie would have done. She would have set it right from the beginning, not nursed her hurt for years, building up a mountain of indignation in the process. But Annie didn't have that awful pride that Mama had always warned Fanny would get in her way.

From now on, every time she looked at Joe, she knew she

wouldn't be able to stop thinking about how she'd ruined all those times. She might have been so happy! But it was too late.

She knew what she needed to do.

And then suddenly she spotted Claire, coming up the street, crossing the parking lot. It had been quiet without her the past few days. But Amy had taken over and Fanny saw how much her granddaughter had changed since she came home last June. Dependable, thoughtful. Amy loved it here, too. Together they could make a life here and help each other. It wasn't so crazy. But she'd have to wait a little longer to ask Amy. Claire had just a few days left to work, and then, hopefully, she'd be displaying her photos at the Art Museum. It was the chance of a lifetime, she'd said, when she first heard about it. And Fanny wasn't going to ruin that for her.

She would bide her time.

44

CLAIRE WOKE AT FIVE AND PLANNED TO GO RIGHT to the arts center. But she found herself on Route 6 and then turning off in Truro, toward the bay. She'd gone to bed early but couldn't sleep, her mind cluttered with images of Joy, their dying whale, and thoughts of the unborn baby whale. She alternated between crying and praying for them. At some point she'd fallen asleep, but then woke exhausted.

The winds had picked up overnight and it began to rain, a vicious, lashing downpour that cut through her the moment she got out of her car. She should be in the darkroom right now. She should be working on her portfolio for the exhibit, if she hoped to make it in time. It would take hours to accomplish what was ahead of her. But she needed to come out here one more time, she told herself.

By the time she walked up the beach, she was shivering. She found the Coastal Studies team still keeping vigil. John was nowhere in sight, and Libby told her she'd ordered him home to take a hot shower and grab some dry clothes. It was going to be a long couple of days. The rain and the dark skies made it all seem even sadder, as Joy lay there, unmoving, pelted by large drops. Claire reminded herself that she was a creature of water, and maybe the rain was comforting. But that sad eye just kept looking at them, the other eye buried in the sand.

She thought of taking more pictures, but it was raining too

hard. She was shivering so much, she doubted she could hold the camera steady. Moby brought tarps and more rain gear, and it became difficult to speak over the wind and the crashing waves, which were breaking higher and higher on the beach. The whale's head and part of her upper body were lying in the shallows now, and Claire watched Moby put on a pair of waders and make his way out to her side. Claire wished a storm surge would carry her back out into the ocean, to allow her to end her life in the comfort of her home, but she knew that wasn't going to happen. She wondered now what the whale was thinking; if she knew she was dying, and her baby, too.

"Claire?"

She turned and found Libby beside her.

"Do you want to take a break?"

They went and sat in the Coastal Studies four-wheel, which was on the beach a few hundred yards away, with the heater on.

"How do you do this?" Claire asked her. "It's so awful."

"I've seen it more times than I care to think of," Libby said. "And it's always a difficult thing to witness. It's even worse for someone like you, or John, who comes for a brief spell, gets caught up in the lives of a whale or two, and then watches tragedy happen. Sadly enough, though, it's a perfect end for his article."

"Because it will move people to get involved?"

"Hopefully."

"How did John get involved?"

"Oh, he and Moby have been friends for years."

"Yes, I remember him saying that."

Libby nodded. "Moby lives in Provincetown, in one of the old whaling captain's houses that have been in his family for generations. His great-great-grandfather was a whaler in the last century. So he's pretty much dedicated his life to saving as many of them as he could. I guess his father and John's grandfather were friends. Probably the first big environmentalists in the area years ago."

"I thought Moby was crazy that day we were out and he hung on the edge of the dinghy, trying to cut the net."

Libby smiled. "Yeah, we do get a little crazy out there sometimes. I think that's what life-and-death situations do to you."

"Thanks again for letting me be a part of this. I'll never forget this experience."

"Well, you'll have to come back in the spring. See the ones who make it, and the calves. That's the other part of doing this. There's nothing so beautiful as that."

"Oh, I'll be back in the thick of teaching come spring, but I'll try."

A group of fishermen walked past, carrying thermoses and blankets. Libby leaned forward and then smiled.

"Well, I wish John were here to see this," she said.

"It's touching how people want to help."

"Oh, this is more than helping. This is a bit of redemption. The ring-leader there, the one in the red jacket, he's the one who gave John that shiner."

"What do you mean? I thought he got it in a bar fight."

Libby chuckled. "Yeah, it was that. The Old Tap Room, where the fishermen hang out. I told him he was crazy to go there, but John's a stubborn coot. He sat there listening to all the complaining about the seals and how they're eating all the fish, and that's why there's not enough fish for them. John tried to set them straight."

"And?"

"Let's just say they weren't interested in being educated."

Claire shook her head.

"It wasn't his fault. He meant well."

"He just seems to attract trouble."

"Well, that's part of the job for him. People don't want to hear about things that are inconvenient, and a lot of what we do, and what he writes about, requires change. People usually don't want to change."

"Do you care for him?" Claire asked, immediately sorry she had. "No, that's none of my business."

Libby held up a hand. "Hey, I love the guy, but not like that." And then Libby looked at her. "Do you?"

Claire felt her face redden. "Oh, no, we just worked together. I'm actually engaged to someone else."

Libby's eyebrows lifted. "Really?"

"Yes, why?"

"Oh nothing. Listen, I gotta get back out there. You warmed up?"

"Actually, I'm going to head back to town. I'm going to be buried in work for my final project. Would you tell John I said good-bye?"

Libby gave her a long look, and then said, "Sure."

CLAIRE KNEW she worked best under pressure, and now that she was focused, she didn't want to break her concentration. Once she started going through the photos she'd shot at the dune shack, her excitement returned. It took her the rest of that day, and part of that night, to go through, print, and then whittle that batch down to the chosen few.

She went home, slept a little, and returned the next day to continue. Around her, her classmates were putting the final mats on their prints, and then were off to the Art Museum to begin arranging their displays. She ran home for supper, glad that they were all hunkered in. Her father was watching the local weather. It seemed the brunt of the storm would hit that night, although it wasn't expected to be bad. Her mother and Amy kept asking how far she'd gotten, and she told them she'd probably be gone all night if she expected to have her work done and displayed for tomorrow evening's public showing. They sent her back with sandwiches and a thermos of coffee.

Now she worked on the photos she'd taken before the dune shack, choosing the ones that would best showcase her theme. If she got this right, she would be thrilled, because it wouldn't be just pretty pictures; her work would hopefully have a powerful emotional impact on the viewer. As she sorted and printed, her thoughts once again turned to Joy, lying on Cold Storage Beach. And John Poole, kneeling beside her. Outside, darkness shrouded the town as the wind howled. She couldn't imagine how awful it would be to wait on that black beach in the midst of a storm.

She went to her printing tray and saw that the last photograph she'd taken of the whale was finished. It was a distance shot, Joy's long body stretched out on the sand at the water's edge, rising high above the tiny figure kneeling by her side. Libby said the dying process could go on for days. As she pulled the print from the tray and hung it to dry, she kept looking at it, saying a prayer whenever she did. She worked that way all night, printing, drying, enhancing the black and whites, and then leaving the darkroom and working on the digital color prints on the inkjet printer. All the while she could hear the storm outside. All the while she thought of them on that beach.

It was nearly morning when she stretched her aching arms and shoulders, then left the building and went outside. The sky was still dark, but there was a brightening on the horizon, beyond the rooftops toward the bay. Trees that just yesterday were clinging to their precious leaves were nearly bare now, the storm's wind having scoured them clean. All in all, though, it looked as if it hadn't been too bad. Amy had promised to call if there were any problems at home, and since there hadn't been a peep from them, Claire decided to go right to the matting room next.

She got coffee and some pretzels from a vending machine in the main building. That would have to suffice for breakfast. Then she began cutting mats and playing with the framing of each picture. She wanted it simple; the pictures were powerful enough, she hoped, to speak for themselves. She couldn't remember the last time she'd survived on such little sleep for days; probably when Rose was born. She was surprised she wasn't falling asleep on her feet when she looked at the clock on the wall and saw that it was after ten. She called the house, and Amy told her everything was fine and not to worry about them.

"But guess what, Mom?"

"What, honey?" She could hear the excitement in Amy's voice.

"Rose got her first tooth. It just popped through. On the bottom in the middle."

"Wow, that's young. You were seven months when you got yours."

"Jared said he got his really young, before five months."

"So you talked to him again?"

There was a pause. "He wants to know everything about her. The least little detail. It's kind of sweet."

"That is sweet."

"You know, it made me think, I'll never know when my father got his first tooth. Or if he had the chicken pox. Or anything about him that might be part of Rose," Amy said softly. "Or even me."

Claire sighed. It would always come to this for Amy. No matter how good everything else in her life was going, there would always be the wondering about her father.

"It's his loss," Amy said then, more firmly. "It's Liam's loss. Not mine. Or Rose's."

"You're right."

"Anyway, get back to work and we'll be there at six. We're all really excited for you, Mom."

It took her two hours to mat the twenty photographs. Then she drove over to the Provincetown Art Museum to arrange the display on her assigned wall. The place was empty. She couldn't help stopping and looking at everyone else's work, already displayed. She caught her breath at some of the photos; they were simply stunning. She felt the first flicker of uneasiness since she'd come up with her idea while in the dune shack; there was nothing like it here. She had no idea what Charles Meyer would think of it. The rest of them had finished up yesterday, lucky enough to have some last minute input from him. Claire was doing this on her own, and she hoped he'd approve of her somewhat unorthodox approach.

She played with the sequence of her prints for another few hours. Moving just one print changed the feeling of the exhibit. The more she worked, the more she tried to shoo the doubts away. Here was the culmination of her two loves, photography and history. Here was the best work she'd ever produced.

Her arms trembled with exhaustion when she hung the last print. She looked at her watch. How could it be three o'clock? Their show was at six. One last time, she walked along the wall, her eyes going from photograph to photograph. And once again, she stopped at Joy and stared.

Then she turned and left. She should go home right now. She'd barely have time to shower and nap, and be ready to return at five to meet with her workshop buddies and have Charles Meyer formally critique their work before the public arrived. Walking to her car, she realized that if she skipped the nap, she might be able to go back to Cold Storage Beach one more time. She had to. She'd stay just a few minutes, and she'd say good-bye to John in person.

FANNY WAS STUNNED when she opened the front door to find Rick standing there, with a big bouquet of flowers. "Hey there, Mrs. Noble. I'm here to surprise Claire," he said, coming in and then stooping and giving her an awkward little peck on the cheek. Then he looked around. "Is she here?"

"No, she's not back yet. She spent most of the night in the darkroom, printing her pictures for the exhibit." Fanny asked him to sit down, certain Claire would be very surprised to see him. "I'm sure she'll be back any minute."

Rick looked at his watch. Fanny decided to distract him. He seemed impatient.

"Are you feeling better?" she asked. "Claire told me you had a bit of a health scare."

He smiled warmly. "Scare is an understatement. I thought it was my heart. My father died young, and the family history isn't so great. I had a moment there where I thought it was curtains."

"You poor thing."

"Well, it makes you realize really quick what your priorities should be. And that's not such a bad thing." And then Fanny was surprised to see him blush. "I was being a fool with Claire. I'm sorry about that, Mrs. Noble. Claire is such a good person, and so beautiful. I can't believe I almost let her go."

"She is a good woman. Sometimes too good. She nearly didn't come here, because of us, and that would have been a shame. She's a very gifted photographer. Did she show you the piece from *New Jersey Monthly*? It just came out."

"No, actually, I haven't seen it yet. But you're right, sometimes she's almost too good, she's always putting herself last. In fact, there's something she's been having a hard time dealing with..." He paused.

Fanny waited, sensing something big coming.

"We're going to be moving to Arizona next year, after the school term is over."

"Arizona? What are you talking about? I thought you were moving into her place."

He nodded. "I am, but that's just until she finishes the school year. We'll sell that house in the spring, hopefully close it in June, and then move. Our town house should be done in May, so it's perfect timing."

"Your town house?"

"It's on a brand-new golf course. With views of the desert, warm weather. Claire just fell in love with it. She's excited about starting a photography career out there."

"She is? She never said a word to me." Her tone was sharp, and she saw Rick's face change.

"She was waiting for the right time. That's what she kept telling me, although I think she was just afraid you'd be upset. But I kept telling her you'd be overjoyed for her. She's worked so hard all her life, she deserves this."

Fanny sat there, feeling as if someone had sucked the air out of her lungs.

Then the clock in the kitchen chimed. A moment later, Rick stood up. "I think I'll try her cell again." He dialed, then closed his phone. "She still doesn't answer."

"The service up here is sketchy at best."

"Well, I'm going to go check into the B and B. If she comes back, let her know I'm here, would you? If not, then I'll just go to the Arts Center and find her. She probably got sidetracked. She does that."

And with that, he took the flowers and left.

Fanny sat down again. So, Claire was planning to move to Arizona. Clear across the country, next June. And she still hadn't said a word about it. Fanny felt her heart squeeze at the thought of Claire being so far away. Like Eugene. She'd probably see her once a year or so. But did it really matter? Hadn't everything begun to change from the moment they got here? As much as Fanny hated the idea of having her daughter so far away, maybe it was for the best. Maybe it was one more sign that her thinking was right, and her plan not so crazy after all.

WHEN CLAIRE PULLED DOWN the road curving toward Cold Storage Beach, she saw just a few cars there. She parked and pulled on her coat, zipped it up. The sky was clearing finally, the last gray clouds of the nor'easter breaking up, a weak November sun peeking through.

As she walked down the road and onto the sand, she came face-to-face with Libby and her crew, as they were putting gear into the Coastal Studies 4x4.

Claire looked at her expectantly and Libby just shook her head. "It's over."

"Oh…I'm so sorry."

"Me, too," Libby said.

"Is—"

But she didn't even get the words out of her mouth. "He's still there. The last one."

"He's torturing himself."

Libby shrugged. "He's just seeing it through, finishing up some last notes."

She walked onto the beach and turned right. A cold breeze came off the water, despite the sun, and the smell of the bay was strong. She picked up her pace; she needed to hurry to make it back to shower and change.

As she came closer, she saw that John was sitting on the sand beside the whale carcass, staring out across the water, his leather notebook on his lap, his pen in his hand, as if he were thinking about his next words to be written. She could see that his jacket was wet, as was his hair.

"John?"

He looked up.

"Hey," he said, with a sad smile.

She could see that he was shivering. "You should leave now."

"I know." He stood up.

They both turned and looked up at the giant body, towering above them. Claire bit her lip, but she still felt the tears come. The blubber had turned white where the netting had dug into her.

Ironically, they'd finally managed to cut most of it away. But still, the net had killed her bit by bit. Infection or starvation, or maybe a combination of both. And had taken her baby, too. A sob escaped Claire.

"Come on," John said gently, taking her arm and turning her around.

He slipped his notebook into his backpack and zipped it as they started walking.

"What are you doing here? Isn't your show today?"

"Yes, it is. But I needed to come back." She paused, her voice cracking as she searched for the right words. "I don't know, I just had to see her, one more time."

"I understand."

"What will happen now?"

"They'll do a necropsy, an autopsy. Study her, see what they can learn that might help in future endeavors."

They walked in silence for a few moments. Claire couldn't imagine how they would move Joy's body. She didn't ask.

"I got my copy of *New Jersey Monthly* a few days ago. It was just incredible," she said.

"You did fine work, Claire."

"So did you. You're a wonderful writer."

When they reached the path to the road, they both turned and stood there for a moment. Joy's huge dark body lay in the distance, alone, a sad and dismal sight. Claire felt her throat clog once again. Then, without a word, they turned again and walked across the road. They came to his yellow Land Rover first.

"I'll be heading back to Boston tomorrow, so I guess this is goodbye."

She stood there a moment, unable to speak.

"And you'll be leaving soon, too, right?"

She nodded. "In a few days."

"Good luck with your show today." He smiled, that crooked,

devastating smile, his eyes filled with grief. "I'm glad we met, Claire. You're very gifted, and your photographs show a real sensitivity. A heart." And then he shrugged, as if he'd gone too far. "Anyway, I'm glad I tortured you to help me. Send me these last photos when you can."

"They're powerful. Gut-wrenching, really. I only printed a few," she said, gesturing toward the beach. "I just wasn't ready."

"That's okay. Maybe in a few weeks." Then he put a hand on the car door. "Take care of yourself, Claire. And your family."

"Good-bye, John."

She began walking toward her car. A minute later, she stopped.

Turning, she could see him beside the open car door, tossing his things inside. As she began walking back toward him, he unzipped his jacket, his back to her, then pulled his wet shirt over his head. By the time she was just inches behind him, he was naked from the waist up, his skin pink from the cold. Without even thinking, she lifted a hand and ran her fingers down his arm, and then up again, over the soft hairs and across the hard bulge of muscle, as her other hand came up, so she stroked both his arms as he stood there, motionless, his eyes closed.

How could she have known that everything would change with one touch? Suddenly, she couldn't help herself. She leaned into him, her face on his shoulder, her breasts pressing into his back, her arms wrapping around his chest. And then he turned and looked into her eyes, his own filled with pain and longing. He pulled her to him, crushing her against his chest with a moan, and she felt as if she were melting into him.

"Oh, Claire," he whispered as he buried his face in her neck and she felt his own need.

He pulled back, cupping her face in his hands, and with that half smile he shook his head, as if he couldn't believe this. "Claire." He said her name as if it were a prayer.

And then she heard her name again, louder this time, and she froze.

"*Claire!*"

She pulled away from John and turned.

Rick was standing not twenty feet away, looking stunned.

45

After Rick left, Fanny pulled on her coat and a kerchief and walked down Commercial Street, breathing in the damp, cold air that smelled like the bay. She'd seen worse storms in Brooklyn as a young girl. Except for the piles of seaweed and rocks and some of the boats scattered higher up across the sand than they normally were at low tide, you'd never have known there'd been a nor'easter.

She walked up to the little wooden church and sat for a while, hoping to see if the seals had survived the storm. But the little dock was gone. Here, where the houses were closer to the water, she could see that some of the patios must have been under some water. Then she looked farther up the beach and heard herself gasp. The dining room of Dominick's, which jutted out over the water, was missing a wall. She could see right inside.

She stood, ready to walk up there. Her hip had begun to ache last night like it hadn't since she'd broken it. The pressure from the storm, she assumed, or too much activity each day. Or perhaps her arthritis had finally taken its toll and it was time to have the hip replaced. She dreaded the thought.

Slowly she made her way up Commercial Street and finally found herself in front of the restaurant. She crossed the parking lot to its back edge, where it overlooked the bay. The entire right side wall was gone. Inside, she saw the tables and chairs all over the floor, tufts of seaweed and kelp littering the beautiful hardwood.

And then she looked farther into the room and saw that Dominick Fortunato was standing there. Staring right at her.

He looked distraught, and for a moment she thought how easy it would be to walk inside, to pick up the fantasy. To comfort him and ease his obvious distress. Because after a while, she would get used to him without his glasses. You could get used to almost anything; she knew that now. Look at the little rental house up the street. They'd been there for just a few months, but already it felt like home. This place at the edge of Cape Cod, curling around the ocean and into the bay, felt like a place she'd been waiting to find all of her life.

But she turned without even a wave. Just a tiny smile. And as she passed the herb garden, she saw that the rosemary had turned yellow and the basil was withered and going to seed. Still, she stopped and bent over, tearing a handful of leaves and crushing them in her hand.

As she walked back, she inhaled the spicy aroma of the torn basil. And for that moment, Mama and Daddy, and even Annie seemed to be walking beside her.

THEY LEFT HER CAR at Cold Storage Beach. Rick said they could get it later. He'd been looking for her for hours and seemed very frustrated, and she felt bad for him. He'd gone to the Arts Center and someone there finally told him she'd gone to the Provincetown Art Museum. But it was locked. And when he finally found someone there, they had no idea where she was. Then he called the house again and Amy mentioned perhaps she'd gone back to the see the whale.

And he'd found her in John Poole's arms.

What had she been thinking?

With that first touch, all reason went out the window. How could she, a rational woman who knew what she wanted, who reasoned with her head, how could she not have seen this coming? But in that moment she didn't care. It didn't matter.

Before they pulled away, Rick turned to her. "Do you want to tell me what that was all about?"

Her heart was pounding and her eyes filled with tears, as she explained about the dead whale and their shared grief. That seemed to appease him. She could see his frustration and annoyance evaporate. Then he touched her cheek.

"Hey, sorry, babe."

She shook her head. "It's okay. It's just hard to stay objective when you get so involved in something like that."

"Well, I think maybe you should focus on projects that are a bit more cheerful."

"I don't think…," she began, and then decided to let it go.

Rick was determined she wouldn't be late, and drove too fast. Or was it anger? But Claire had a hard time focusing. Now Rick was talking about Christmas.

"Everything's arranged. I got the priest, and he's willing to do it on Christmas Eve, which wasn't easy. And I even booked our honeymoon," he said, turning to her with an excited smile. "A cruise to the islands."

"That's wonderful," she said. But she thought of Amy, home for Christmas for the first time in two years. And Rose's first Christmas. She would miss that.

"Hey," Rick said, and she turned to him. He gave her a kind smile. "I know you're bummed about the whale, but there's nothing you can do. Try to forget about it. Just think, you've worked your ass off for this day. Your big showing. You should enjoy it."

"I know. You're right."

"Close your eyes, you must be exhausted."

And she did, for a few minutes.

When she opened them, they were driving through the Province Lands. She couldn't help but think of the first day they came here, two and a half months ago. Amy in awe in the backseat. She herself was disoriented. Her parents were like shells of their former selves. How much had changed here. It was going to be hard to leave.

Rick turned off of Route 6, toward the bay and Commercial Street.

"Please take me straight to the Art Museum," she said.

"You don't want to shower and change?"

She shook her head. "I don't have time. I'll freshen up in the ladies' room. I want to catch Charles Meyer before the public shows up."

A few minutes later, Rick pulled over.

"Since we have a few minutes, there's something else I'd like to tell you," Rick said, turning to her. "I think it'll make you feel better."

"I really need to get inside if I want to—"

"Babe, relax," he said, "I'm only trying to help."

"What do you mean?"

"I spent some time with your mother when I got here. And we talked about you, and I found myself telling her about Scottsdale."

"You what?" she said, her voice filled with alarm.

"She was fine with it, Claire," he said, holding his hands up as if fending off her annoyance. "I'm just trying to make things easier for you. Your mother gets that."

"You had no right—"

"Come on, Claire, I had every right. I'm going to be your husband. We're moving there in June."

"What did she say?"

"She said she wants only the best for you," he said, reaching into the backseat and grabbing a big bouquet of flowers. "Here, these are for you. Congratulations."

She looked at the gorgeous bouquet. Yellow roses and white

lilies. Her favorites. He leaned over and kissed her, then he looked at his watch.

"See you in twenty minutes."

She got out and went into the museum, her clothes damp and disheveled, her hair a mess from the wind, holding the bouquet in her hands. Her classmates were gathered around a table of refreshments, already drinking wine and smiling; relieved, she could tell, that their work had already been judged.

"Hey, Claire, have a drink!" one of them called out.

"Later, thanks," she said, as she hurried toward the ladies' room across the main gallery; then on her way she peeked into the alcove where just a few hours ago she'd finished arranging her photographs.

"Well there you are, Ms. Noble," she heard.

She turned to find Charles Meyer standing across the alcove, arms folded, studying her prints.

CLAIRE KNEW that most of her classmates had high hopes of career moves based on their showings, and hers were no different. After these ten weeks, after tasting this different kind of life, she wanted to continue to pursue her art. She fairly burned with anticipation of what she could do now.

She stood just a few feet from Charles Meyer and watched as he read the plaque she'd made: *Endangered Species: Photographs by Claire Noble.* He read it again, his head cocked to the side, as if unsure of what he saw. Then his eyes went from photograph to photograph as he moved slowly along the wall. They were in both color and black and white. She'd tried to use one medium, but there were some pictures she simply preferred in color, and others she thought much more expressive in black and white.

There was a photo of Amy and her mother working in the kitchen, frozen in a moment of cooking, her mother's glasses steamed, Amy stirring a pot with a look of puzzlement. And then the two of them standing on either side of her mother's bed, covered with ravioli drying on a pure white sheet. That one in black and white was like a moment out of time. It could have been her mother and grandmother, she realized. And then, a picture of her father, an old man patiently sitting in a chair in a parking lot, with the harbor in the background; his life, his dignity, etched in the lines of his face.

There was the print of the schooner, its ribs half-buried in the sand. Then there were the photographs of the whales, the humpback and its calf nursing, then both of them breaching, followed by the netted whale, Joy, in the ocean, and then dying on Cold Storage Beach with a man kneeling beside her. The close-up of John as he tried to comfort her was probably the most stirring of the group, she thought, the agony of loss all over his face.

"This is quite an interesting assortment of photographs," Charles Meyer said now, standing by her side.

"I know it's not quite what you had in mind. And I know it's very different from the landscapes and vistas. But I'm a history teacher—something happened as I took these photographs. I saw this common thread running through man and animal. Each of us losing pieces of the past. Things that our children, and perhaps their children, will never see."

His eyes roamed the photographs again, and stopped on the scenes of Amy and her mother with a questioning look.

"There are recipes and ways of cooking that have been lost over generations," she explained, as he stepped closer to it. "Just like mammals have been rendered extinct. We need to value those things, things as simple as cooking, and hold onto them. Even working with film. I can almost see film disappearing like eight-tracks or vinyl albums, and that would be sad, because I don't think you get the real effect of black and white with digital."

He nodded. "You're right."

Now he was looking at the last photo, of Amy holding Rose that day on Herring Cove Beach, the two of them washed in that magical last light of day. The hope of the future.

"Your daughter?" he asked.

"And my granddaughter," she said, feeling a bit embarrassed. "It's funny, but I came up here looking for that light. And I realize I didn't really capture much of it in my photographs. My intention was—"

But Charles Meyer put a hand on her arm, stopping her.

"Whatever it was you were looking for up here, Ms. Noble, it's there. Your work is exceptional, both the black and white and the color. As for the light...well, it isn't really just that beautiful light we're so known for here, it's more a metaphor for how you see things. And I think you've captured the light, probably more than you realize at this moment."

She smiled as a wave of pure pleasure washed over her.

"Something changed for me up here," she said. "I see lots of things differently now. I love it here. In fact, my whole family does. We really hate to leave."

"Well then, maybe you should come back," he said with that challenging smile of his.

And then he walked toward the front entry and opened the doors.

AT THE STROKE OF SIX, people began to walk through the glass doors and into the first gallery room. Claire stood before her work, waiting for Rick and her family, nervous again. They had no idea that she'd used pictures of them for this project. She hoped they didn't mind, especially her father, who was such a private person.

Amy found her first, with Rose in a carrier slung across her front. When they hugged, the baby between them, Rose grabbed

Claire's hair and she laughed out loud, suddenly filled with joy. This was her moment, and they were all here for her.

And then her parents were in front of her and she gave them each a kiss on the cheek.

"Oh, Mom, these are unbelievable," she heard Amy say and turned to see her studying the prints.

She watched as her father began looking at them, his eyes slowing, traveling from one to another. He stopped when he reached the photograph of himself and stared, while Claire waited. Then he moved on to the others. Finally he turned to her.

"It's very good, Claire," he said, nodding, or bobbing, she wasn't sure which. That alone was high praise coming from her father.

Then she saw her mother dabbing her eyes, her mouth twisted as she tried not to cry. "You work is so beautiful, Claire. I'm so proud of you, so glad you had this chance."

She hugged her mother, elated.

"Mom, there's Rick," Amy said.

She turned and saw him just inside the doorway, in a throng of people. He must have changed, because he looked like a Ralph Lauren ad in a navy blazer with an open neck white shirt and his hair brushed neatly. She wished now she'd had her mother bring her a change of clothes. He saw her and waved, smiling, and Claire smiled back, then froze. Just behind Rick she saw another man, looking right at her, with a look of determination.

Claire felt her heart jump in her throat. But there was nothing she could do, because a moment later Rick was beside her, pulling her into a hug.

"Hey, congratulations," Rick said, letting her go. Then he glanced at her photos.

"Claire, I'd like a moment with you, if I could?"

They all turned to John, who stood there now looking decidedly uncomfortable.

"I...I thought you were leaving," she stammered, as her parents looked at each other, and Amy looked at Rick.

"I was," he said, thrusting his hands in his pockets. He, too, had changed, into worn blue jeans and a green windbreaker and he looked like he hadn't slept in days. Which she knew he hadn't.

"Look, John," Claire began, but then Rick stepped between them.

"Hey, buddy, I'm Rick, Claire's fiancé," Rick said, with an edge to his tone.

"I'd like to talk to Claire," John said quietly.

"John, please, go," Claire said.

"Not until I say what I came to say." And then he took a deep breath and stepped closer to her. "Claire. Everything I've ever believed in my life, I've fought for. Except you. Somehow, I kept backing away. But I can't anymore."

"Now wait a minute," Rick said.

"I'm not going to just walk away and let you go," John continued.

Then Rick put a hand on John's arm, pulling him away from her. "Hey, who do you—"

"Rick, don't," she said, taking his arm.

"Who is this?" he asked her, turning to her.

"This is John Poole. I forgot you two never met in Lincoln."

Rick's eyebrows shot up. "Oh, right, the canal guy."

"Please, Rick..."

But John pulled his arm from Rick's grasp and held his hands up, as if surrendering. "It's okay, Claire. I've been called worse by the likes of him before."

Rick grabbed John him by the collar.

"Stop it!" Claire cried, stepping between them.

Her father sat suddenly on a bench and her mother watched with wide eyes. Amy's mouth was open, and Rose simply babbled at the spectacle. Luckily, hers was the only display in the small alcove, and the noise in the surrounding galleries was loud enough so that barely anyone else glanced at them.

She looked at the two of them out of breath, and they both looked at her, waiting. And in that moment, she saw two men. Two different futures.

"I want you both to leave," she said.

46

It was that soft, still time in the early evening, like a pause just before nightfall. and it was warm, incredibly warm for November. Indian Summer. The calm after the storm, Fanny thought. Although what she was about to say could cause a bigger storm than they'd already seen, she imagined.

She sat in a beach chair with Joe beside her, watching her daughter, granddaughter, and great-granddaughter as they played. The picnic supper was Joe's idea. Fanny was stunned when he'd come into the kitchen that morning, as she and Amy were deciding on what to make for Claire's celebratory dinner. Claire had told them that Charles Meyer had called her work the most original of the show. He was writing her a wonderful letter of recommendation that would hopefully help her to pursue some kind of job in photography. Then Joe announced that the weather was mild enough, and he was taking them on a picnic. He asked them to make something suitable.

Now Fanny looked at her husband. In just a few days, they would be going home. It was time to tell him she wasn't going back. Not that she still harbored any illusions about Dominick Fortunato. She realized now that she'd been caught up in a fantasy with him and had lost her senses for a while. Just last week, walking Rose down Commercial Street, she'd watched a policeman pull over a convertible filled with middle-aged women, some of them sitting up on the back, as if they were in a parade.

The policeman chastised them, saying "Now, would you do something like this at home?"

They looked mortified, their moment of glee deflated. Fanny realized then that the same thing had happened to her.

Claire walked past them, up toward the dunes with her camera, capturing her last images of Cape Cod. So many dreams came to life here, and some ended. Last night, Claire had told Fanny as her voice cracked with tears, that she didn't want them to go back to the assisted living home. And that she had hoped to take them back to their own house; she'd called Eugene to take it off the market. But he was traveling, and Barbara had apparently forgotten to give him the message, so another family would be starting their lives there soon.

But maybe that was just another fantasy, Fanny realized. She could see how upset Claire had been with Eugene. But neither she nor Joe would condemn him. "Maybe it's for the best," she said. "We were in a rut there anyway."

"Well," Claire had said, "I thought you could stay with me for a while, until we figure things out. I know Amy would like that. And so would Rose."

So she didn't have to go back to the assisted living after all. Claire hadn't mentioned Arizona, or Rick. Neither had she.

Lives came and went. One day, she and Joe would be part of the past. Rose was just beginning her journey. Amy was hopefully on the way to settling hers. Fanny hoped Jared would be part of her future, not just Rose's father. And Claire? She deserved everything. She'd worked so hard all her life, but more than that, she was always there for whoever needed her. Above all, Fanny wanted her to have someone not just to love her. To cherish her. She had a feeling John Poole already did. But Claire wasn't sure of him; Fanny could see that. She'd been scarred once, badly.

And then there was her. Whatever days were left, Fanny knew now she wanted them to matter. She wanted to be happy. And if that was too much to ask for, she'd settle for contentment. She wanted to leave the past behind, start a new life, even at her age. But how did she make that happen when the regret of her mistakes stared her in the face every time she looked at her husband? Now she turned to Joe. It was time to tell him.

She was startled to see that he was looking at her. His face was serious, set, as if he'd been looking at her for a long time. Staring at her. And then he reached into his jacket pocket, his hand shaking badly, fumbling. A moment later he took out a small box and handed it to her. She held it, the gray velvet smooth in her hand.

"Happy anniversary," he said.

"What? Our anniversary isn't until April."

At first she thought his head was bobbing, but she realized he was shaking it.

"No, not that anniversary. Today is the anniversary of the first day I met you. When your brother brought me home for dinner."

"What?" But she couldn't continue. She took the small box and opened it. Inside was a silver filigreed heart on a fine chain. She looked up at him. "How did you remember?"

"What do you mean? I never forgot."

But she had. And now on a mild November evening in Cape Cod she was suddenly back in her mother's dining room, on a blustery November day in Brooklyn. Watching a handsome man come in the door with her brother. Taking his coat, silently admiring the wide shoulders, the clear blue eyes. And then her mother in the kitchen giggling and whispering that he looked like Montgomery Clift. She'd forgotten, but he hadn't.

"It's not much, Fanny," he said. "We've never had much; I always wished I could give you more." And then he looked at the girls on the beach, and Claire. "But we've got what really matters."

She sat there, holding the necklace.

"Put it on," he said, nodding at it in her hand.

"There's something I have to tell you," she said, putting the necklace back in the little box. "I'm not—"

"I know," he interrupted. "You don't have to tell me anything."

"What do you mean, you know? Know what?"

He hesitated and his hand began to wave across his leg. "I know about your friend. I went to see him."

She nearly fainted. She turned away, looking at the water. She couldn't face him. "You...you..."

"Yes. I told Mr. Fortunato that my wife was a good woman, and he shouldn't be trying to take advantage of her because she's trying to help our granddaughter. I told him you're the kind of woman who might not see that he was putting her in a compromising position, because she only ever sees the good in people."

Fanny felt her body flood with shame. She wanted to crawl under the beach chair, hide her face in the sand. "What did he say?" she whispered.

"He told me I was a lucky man." Joe chuckled. "I told him I already knew that."

She couldn't speak. He didn't either for a long time. She held the box in her hand, staring at the waves, feeling the nip of night descend in the air, and wrapping the blanket tightly around her legs.

"I'm not leaving here without you, Fanny."

She thought of the angel card she'd gotten yesterday from Manuel. *Forgiveness.*

It could be so easy, if it weren't for her pride. She'd finished the Buddhism book, and she knew one thing for certain now. This was a moment, and now it was gone. And then there would be a next one, and a next. Her life was made up of a certain number of moments, and then it would end. If she chose to only live in this moment, and not worry ahead, or dwell in regret, maybe she could change future moments from what they might have been. Or probably would have been. The angel card, she told herself, could have been a gift from Annie.

And then, from the corner of her eye, she saw him reach over and hold out his hand, trembling as he held it there, waiting. Without looking at him, she put the box on her lap and held out her hand, her fingers open. He clasped it, folding his hand around hers as he slipped his fingers through hers. She could feel his hand trembling. She held it tightly, willing the shaking to stop.

Fanny turned and opened her mouth, but the words didn't come. Joe was staring after Amy and Rose, who'd gotten up and were walking toward the water. Then he turned to her again, and smiled.

It was that moment in the late afternoon where there's a sudden shift in light, and everything changes. There are yellows, whites, pinks, and later the silver gray of twilight. But now, looking at Joe in the golden Cape Cod light, Fanny felt her breath catch and then her heart begin to thaw. He was old and frail, but he was still handsome and strong, in his own way. He was still a man.

"I was wrong, Fanny, to keep things from you. I see that now. I'm sorry."

She couldn't speak. She just squeezed his hand tightly.

They sat there as the sun began to sink behind them, and Joe never let go of her hand. Through his warm fingers she felt the certainty of his love, and her heart flooded with love for him, and pity. How he must have suffered because of that woman. He'd been nothing but a boy, a lonely boy with no family, and she'd tried to trap him. The lie she'd concocted all those years ago had driven a wedge into their lives.

Fanny had to smile as it occurred to her that her life had, in fact, been like one of her romance novels. Something had kept her and Joe apart all these years, just like the lovers in all of those books. And now that something was gone.

She squeezed his hand and he turned and looked at her. Then he winked.

And Fanny wondered if starting over might be the most romantic thing she could ever ask for.

CLAIRE WAS PACKING UP THE CAR, trying to fit the last of their things in her trunk. Somehow, they'd accumulated more than they came with, and she was shipping home a few boxes, as well. The weather was still mild again, no doubt the last days of Indian summer. Thanksgiving was in a few weeks, so Claire knew the mild, sunny days wouldn't last.

"Need help?"

She turned and saw John coming up the driveway.

"No, I've just about got it all."

"When are you leaving?"

"After lunch. Rose will be ready for her nap by then, so we'll be able to drive for a long stretch without stopping." She stood there with her hands on her hips. "I thought you left."

"So you have a little time?" he asked, instead of answering her question.

"Well, not really. I still have to—"

"There's something you've got to see before you leave."

"What's that?"

"It's not far. We can walk. And we'll be back in thirty minutes."

"John, I—"

"Claire, please."

She hesitated. "All right." She went and opened the door and yelled in that she'd be back in a half hour. Her mother, she could see, was cleaning out the refrigerator. Amy was giving Rose a bath in the kitchen sink.

They walked down Commercial Street, which was quieter than Claire could remember seeing it. Most of the shops had signs or notes that said they'd be opening in spring, or May 1. One restaurant, she'd heard, made their entire year's earnings in just a ten-week summer span. As lively and fun as the town had seemed, Claire believed this could be her favorite time here. Zoe had told her that the silence over the winter was enough to make your ears ring. Claire wanted to tell her to relish it. She was about to go back to the cacophony of a thousand teenagers housed in one building for eight hours a day.

She looked over at John, walking silently beside her. He turned to her and smiled. It was the smile, she realized, that transformed him from a rugged-looking man to a devastatingly handsome one. Slightly crooked, always with a hint of amusement in his eyes.

At the wharf, they turned right, toward Bradford. Five minutes later, they were climbing up a steep street, and to her dismay, Claire found herself in the parking lot of the Pilgrim Monument.

"I don't do heights," she said, turning to him.

"Look, the view is incredible, but I'm not standing here asking you to do this to overcome your fear of heights. There's something you have to see at the top. And it's not like the lighthouses. The steps aren't see-through. You won't get vertigo."

She hesitated.

"I promise," he said, and then took her hand and began to lead her toward the door.

They climbed one flight, then two. Claire got that strange, slippery feeling in her chest. "People who don't mind heights don't get this," she said.

He stopped on the next landing and looked at her. "I get it, but I'm asking you to trust me."

"Why should I?"

He looked hurt for a moment. "I told you before. I would never do anything to hurt you, Claire."

She turned and began walking in front of him, up the next flight, holding tightly onto the railing. She already anticipated coming out at the top, the harbor and the town spread out below, the dizzy, knee-weakening sense of the world falling away, and tumbling down with it. Her fingers clutched the wall, not that there was anything to hold onto. And then she stepped out onto the platform.

There was water all around her, dark blue, shimmering, and she could see the curving hook of Cape Cod curling around and back into itself. Then she felt him take her hand off the wall and hold it tightly.

"I love you. I think if you'll stop being afraid, you could love me."

"I know that."

"I didn't bring you up here for the view," he said. "Look up."

She looked up and saw a large nest in a corner of the building way above them. A big black bird, fierce-looking with yellow eyes, sat there.

"It's a peregrine falcon," he said.

Suddenly another bird swooped past.

"That's the father bird. He won't come with us here."

"I get the feeling he'd like us to leave," she said, feeling breathless, looking up almost more difficult than looking down.

They ducked into the doorway and she watched as the bird flew in, and then hovered above the nest, as a small beak opened to the sky, and he dropped something in.

"Is it unusual for them to nest in a place like this?"

"No, they like high places; they're protected then. But this is the first time they've nested here, and the building is nearly a hundred years old."

The father bird flew off and Claire heard a raucous protest from the nest.

"Claire, I think you and I are meant to be together," he said.

She turned from the nest, and he was looking at her intensely.

"The real reason I wanted to show you this is because there

are exceptions in nature. Unlike the whales, the male falcons don't leave." Then he smiled that crooked smile that she loved. "They don't disappear, no matter how bad the weather gets, or how many squawking mouths there are to feed."

He took her hand and raised it to his lips. "They mate for life."

47

It was mid-afternoon when they reached Jefferson County, but the november sun was already low on the horizon. The trees were bare and the mountains barren, and to her left, Claire had a clear view of the Pohatcong River, swollen and fast from the nor'easter that had blown through here, as well, clearing the trees and dumping several inches of rain on northern New Jersey.

Her father sat beside her and she saw that he, too, was watching the river. Behind her, Rose babbled in her car seat, squealing each time Amy covered her face and said, "Peek-a-boo."

Then Claire leaned over, so that she could catch her mother's eye in the rearview mirror, on the other side of the car seat. Ten weeks ago, when they'd been in those exact same seats, driving up to Cape Cod, her mother had barely seemed alive. Now she was like a new person.

Something had changed the night of the picnic on the beach.

As they sat around the blanket eating fried chicken, Amy had announced that she had something to share with them. "I think I finally found what I'm meant to do; what I want to do. I love to cook." Her face was lit with something Claire couldn't recall seeing since she was little. Pure happiness. "And I want us to write a cookbook, Gram. I kind of got the idea from Mom's exhibit. It would be all the old recipes. Can you imagine? I mean if we don't do this, they'll be lost forever. We can call them 'Heirloom Recipes' or even 'Endangered Dishes.' And maybe we can make some money."

Her mother hadn't said a word. Claire knew Amy was sincere, because then she said she was investigating culinary schools and hoped to go part-time in the evenings, so she could work from home during the day. But Claire also knew part of this had been a way to get her mother to go back to New Jersey.

After they'd finished eating, Claire climbed the high dunes, with the sand and the ocean spread out below her, glowing in the late afternoon light. Beauty was everywhere, even in the most mundane moments.

She took pictures of Amy and Rose as they played on the blanket. Then she turned the camera on her parents as they sat beside each other on beach chairs, facing the water. She zoomed and clicked, and at that moment she saw her father hold out a hand, and after a long pause, her mother took it. They had not let go of each other the rest of the night. Claire had said a prayer of thanks.

They were old, imperfect, and theirs was not a storybook marriage. But even with their imperfect love, they were a rarity, a relic from another era. They'd lasted nearly fifty years together.

Her father, too, seemed different once he'd confessed his secret to her mother. They looked directly at each other now; they touched occasionally. That her father had kept such a secret from them all for nearly fifty years was something Claire never could have imagined when they left ten weeks ago. Or that her mother could possibly think of leaving him. Back then Claire didn't even know who Rose's father was, or if Amy knew. And she'd thought Rick was the answer to all her dreams.

The doubts had been there all along, but it was always so easy for her practical side to fight them. When she went to The Red Inn just after her exhibit at the museum, his face had softened with hope as she walked into the room. She saw in that moment that he truly loved her, as much as he could love anyone. But in a marriage, she'd realized, Rick's needs and Rick's wants would always come first. In the end, she wasn't willing to give up her family, and the independence she'd built her entire life, for security. For a fun future. He looked so hurt as she told him it couldn't work.

"Claire, you can't be serious," he said, sitting on the edge of the bed, his arms folded in anger. "What can that guy give you—"

"This isn't about him," she said. "This is about me. I know marriage is compromise, and shared dreams, but to tell you the truth, I see things clearly now. I realize that I've never been quite comfortable with any of this. Our future was like a fantasy to me, not real. Not for me anyway. I don't want to leave my family. They mean the world to me. And I don't think I'd be happy after a while just having fun. It's just not me."

She kissed him on the cheek, wished him the best, and left him sitting there, hurt and stunned. She had no doubt that Sammy or someone else in Lincoln would snap him up in a heartbeat. Or someone in Scottsdale. Luckily she hadn't put any money into the town house yet; the final deposit was to have been from the sale of her house next year. But Rick coldly assured her it wouldn't be a problem. The place would probably be worth 20 percent more than what they paid by the time they closed. Maybe he'd flip it, he said, looking for a reaction out of her. But she felt nothing. The desert was beautiful, the town house magnificent. But it just wasn't her.

She realized she'd fallen for John that night under the stars, when she first began to see the man behind the brusque demeanor. He was a diamond in the rough, but he had a tenderness that brought tears to her eyes. She chose John because she wanted him, not because she needed him. Yes, he was intense, sometimes moody, and she knew it wouldn't always be easy. But this time she knew her choice was right. This time she was thinking with her heart.

The river took a sharp bend to the left, and the blacktop followed. This river that had once defined her life. She had gone far up that river, beyond its reach, and tasted a different world. A different kind of life. All of them had been touched by the magical light of Cape Cod.

For now they were going back, behind the bend of the river, to her old life.

But just for a little while.

EPILOGUE

They say that no one who hears the whales at Hatches Harbor leaves unmoved. They trumpet loudly, the sound similar to an elephant's or a swan's, and if they're close enough, you can hear a whoosh of breath as they surface.

Claire stood at the water's edge on an April morning, her camera ready, marveling at the number of whales.

"These waters were once almost silent," John said, wrapping his arms around her from behind. "And each year the songs are different. They come up with a whole new set of sounds and melodies."

"Tell me more," Claire said softly.

"On a boat, with the right equipment, you'd be able to hear the males singing loudly in the water. Their lower notes can travel hundreds of miles through the ocean. The songs are really just a pattern of rumbles, roars, and squeals, and they can last from five to thirty minutes. What's neat is that all of the males are singing the exact same song."

"And why are they singing?"

"Oh, it's thought that they're looking for love."

"You don't say…"

She turned and gave him a long kiss. "I'm starving. Let's eat."

John took her by the hand and they sat on the blanket spread on the soft sand. Then he poured them coffee from a thermos and opened a bag of sandwiches.

"Your mother sent enough food for an army," he laughed.

"Well, that's my mother for you," she said, as she sipped the hot coffee.

Back at the rental house on Commercial Street, her mother and Amy were busy getting Easter dinner ready. The ravioli were no doubt drying on a white sheet, and her father had brought all the makings for Brandy Alexanders, something he hadn't made in years.

Jared had come to see Rose, and even Eugene and Barbara had flown in for the holiday with their wild boys, who raced around the house giggling as the baby crawled after them, squealing with delight. It was loud and crowded, and Claire could see that Barbara's nerves were on edge. She was glad she and John could escape for a little while.

But nothing could dampen her parents' joy at having all of them together.

ACKNOWLEDGMENTS

I can never thank my sister, Jacky Abromitis, and her partner, Kathy Ulise, enough for their generous hospitality at their beautiful place, the Copper Fox, in Provincetown, where I've spent so much time researching and writing. Also, for all of my sister's technical advice and patience with computer issues. She deserves a medal!

And to the rest of the Copper Fox "Porch Crew," for unforgettable happy hours and making me feel like one of the locals: Joe Rustin, Paul Fanizzi, John Gagliardi, Peter Gaffney, Betsy Bowles, Pat Meny, Ted Jones, Peter Petas, Lauren Crockett, Jan Thomas, Sacha Richter, and Bob and Claire Woodwards.

My sincere thanks to the following, who gave of their time and knowledge: Peter Ryan, for sharing the stories of his mother's restaurant, Casa Bianca; Judy Jalbert of Iona Digital Media, one of Provincetown's best photographers; Madrone, and Blu Day Spa, for soothing sore shoulders and reminding me to breathe; Fanizzi's Restaurant by the Sea, for providing the inspiration for Dominick's; the one and only Art's Dune Tours; and the kind staff at the *Won*-Buddhism Meditation Temple in Chapel Hill.

To my friends, family, and supporters who have made the last few years a reality, especially: Kimberly Sine of the Carolina Club; Karen McFadden and Steven Maixner, consummate hosts; Debora Messina, Helene and Tom Timbrook, Janet Bejarano, Liz Cornett, and others who would take pages to mention!

And much gratitude to the Provincetown Center for Coastal Studies, especially Lisa Sette and Chip Lund, whose work with whales, seals, and other marine life is an inspiration and gift to all of us. With ever shrinking funding and big hearts, the Coastal Studies team relies on the generosity of others who want to protect the ocean and its inhabitants. Contributions can be sent to them at: 115 Bradford Street, Provincetown, Massachusetts, 02657, or www.coastalstudies.org.

ABOUT THE AUTHOR

In 2007 Maryann McFadden "won the literary lottery" according to writing blogs, when her previously self-published novel, *The Richest Season*, sold at auction to Hyperion Books. *The Richest Season* became a Target Breakout Novel and was awarded an Indie Next Pick by The American Booksellers Association. Her next 2 novels, *So Happy Together* (Rereleased as *Cape Cod Light*) and *The Book Lover*, are also Indie Next Picks. Her 4th novel, *The Cemetery Keeper's Wife*, is a historical novel set in her NJ hometown. *The Richest Season* was also rereleased in 2018. Her novels have been translated into multiple languages.

Maryann is a speaker and writing coach, and loves to chat with book clubs. Her unusual publishing journey has inspired many aspiring authors. Maryann lives in Northwest New Jersey. You can reach her at maryann@maryannmcfadden.com or her website: maryannmcfadden.com.

CAPE COD LIGHT

READING GROUP GUIDE

1. Just as Claire reaches for own dreams, her family demands halt her in her tracks. Do you think Claire's response to her family is in her best interest? Could she have acted differently? Why did she do what she did?

2. Claire and Amy have been estranged for nearly two years when Amy suddenly returns. Why did this happen? Who is at fault?

3. On her wedding day, Fanny overhears that her husband was in love with another woman. For years it tainted her happiness. Why didn't Fanny simply ask Joe about the girl in his past?

4. Why was Claire so drawn to John Poole? How would you compare him to her fiancée, Rick?

5. Why do you think Fanny became infatuated with Dominick? How did their relationship affect her? Was this something that you think was out of character for her?

6. What issues does Amy grapple with as an adult child of divorce who has never really had a father? How would you describe her journey as a new mother with Rose?

7. Claire takes photos of endangered species. What are some of them? Do you think the extended family can fall into that category? Why?

8. In the end Claire reveals to Amy she was never married to her father. Why did she lead everyone to believe for all those years that she'd been married?

9. Why did the right whale, more than any other whale, become endangered? Why were they so focused on Joy?

10. How did being on Cape Cod change the way Claire began to see things? And her family?